Colorblind

Mia Sanders

It is time for parents to teach young people early on that in diversity there is beauty and there is strength.

Maya Angelou

Colorblind is an enlightening story about race and dating; openness and intolerance. The book is a measure of just how far we still have to go when it comes to the issue of race in America. Although I was a little disappointed with the ending, Colorblind is a book worth reading. I highly recommend it.

Melissa Brown Levine
for Independent Professional Book Reviewers
www.bookreviewers.org
www.melissabrownlevine.com

Colorblind is a work of fiction. Names, characters, places and incidents either are the product of the authors imagination or are used fictitiously. Any resemblance to actual persons, living or dead, events, or locales, is entirely coincidental.

2013 Write Story Press

ISBN: 978-0615923895

Cover design: Ann Proyous

DEDICATIONS

First and foremost, I'd like to thank God. You are my Creator, Stronghold and Source of strength. Without You, I am nothing.

To my parents and sister: I love you three so much! Thank you for your unconditional love & support.

A very special thanks to Formatting Experts, for patiently answering my endless questions and preparing the manuscript for print.

Tina Bergin Photography: I appreciate your patience and understanding as you listened to me whine & complain about getting my picture taken. Thanks so much!

Ann Proyous, you are awesome! The cover is absolutely perfect.

Chris Lindman, I had so much fun tossing around ideas for scenes and characters with you. And I'll never forget how you always encouraged me with my writing. I admire your creativity and imagination!

Bruce, thank you for your support & advice.

Mimi, you're my biggest fan!

Penny, Joanna, Maria, my extended family: I love you all! I wish I could dedicate fifty-five pages to thank everyone!

PART I: SAM

CHAPTER 1

Patience glanced at the clock. She was positive time really *could* stand still. Looking out her living room window, she felt both nervous and excited. Sam was picking her up at seven for their date. Anxiously brushing a stray curl from her forehead, her green eyes focused intently on the driveway. She could have sworn a dark blue truck was parked there. However, after blinking a couple of times, she discovered it was only an illusion. The mind was so powerful, able to make one see things that weren't really there. Sighing heavily, she headed toward the kitchen for a drink of water, her mouth suddenly dry.

There she discovered her dog standing on her new dining room table.

"Rory, get down now!" she yelled, her voice echoing throughout the otherwise quiet house. He jumped off expertly, bounding toward his beloved owner while sliding on the slick floor. Unfortunately, he didn't care that she'd mopped it ten minutes before. He happily licked her cheek as she knelt to pat him. Patience was sure she was just rewarding his bad behavior.

"You're rotten," she told him, laughing despite herself. "I thought Labs were supposed to be obedient."

As she stood up to refill his water bowl, the phone rang. It was her best friend, Jana.

"Hey, what's up?"

"Oh my gosh! Are you nervous? Has he called to say he's on his way? What are you wearing?"

Jana was known for being hyper, sort of like Rory.

"I am *extremely* nervous. No, he hasn't called. I'm wearing my jeans and the new top we bought at the mall last week."

"Good choice," her friend approved. "The blue top looks great against your skin color."

Patience had received many compliments on her caramel skin tone.

"Thanks. He's supposed to be here by seven."

"You only have to wait twenty more minutes."

Patience began twirling the phone cord around her finger. "But you forget that I've had to wait all day for this evening to get here. The minutes have crept by, let me tell you. I even cleaned the kitchen and bathrooms to pass the time."

"You'll be fine! He seems really sweet. I bet the two of you will get along perfectly."

Jana was such a good person, always there to encourage and lift her up. Actually, she had her friend to thank for making this night possible. Had it not been for her, she and Sam would not have met. As Jana tried to distract her with a play by play of the horrible experience she'd had at work the day before, Patience let her mind drift to the day she and Sam had met.

When she'd gone shopping for swimsuits with Jana, who had somehow brainwashed her into going, it had taken most of the morning and early afternoon for her friend to find the perfect one. Convinced she'd die of either hunger or boredom, Patience began complaining that she was exhausted. She figured it was more mental than physical, knowing how much she loathed shopping. Feeling sorry for her friend, Jana had finally suggested they take a break at three o'clock. Five minutes later, the girls were in Bunch a' Books, their favorite bookstore.

While giggling in the humor aisle, they noticed a tall, blond guy browsing through the mystery section. Walking slowly in their direction, he stopped and picked up a book, an intense look in his blue eyes. He appeared to be deep in concentration. Both girls were struck by his boy next door good looks.

Nudging Patience with her elbow, her friend whispered,

"I'm not usually attracted to white guys, but he's hot!"

"Shush. He'll hear you."

"Good."

They both laughed. Patience chose a particular book and began reading the inside flap.

"He keeps looking at you."

She glanced over at him. Blushing, he quickly turned away.

"Okay, don't look now, but he's staring at you again."

Jana gave her a little push.

"Why don't you go start a conversation with him?"

"I absolutely will not! No way!"

"Come on, you've made the first move before. Just do it."

"I'm not feeling brave today."

"Okay, okay. I'm going to go look at the magazines. I'll be right back."

Patience moved to a different aisle after that. She wanted to find a good romance to buy. After finding a book by one of her favorite authors, she was walking up to the checkout counter when, to her dismay, she saw Jana walking toward her with the blond guy at her side.

"Patience, this is Sam."

She wished the floor would have opened up and swallowed her, she was so embarrassed. The two shook hands, and what felt like electricity shot all the way up her arm.

"It's nice to meet you."

He smiled at her, displaying perfectly straight, white teeth.

"I just invited him to eat lunch with us," Jana said, looking like the cat that had swallowed the canary.

"Oh??" Patience could feel her face turn red.

"Yeah, isn't that great? Remember when you were saying how hungry you were before we came in here?" She winked.

"Um, can you come with me to pay for this book? We'll be right back."

She grabbed Jana's arm, practically yanking it out of the socket.

"What in the world did you *say* to him?" She was mortified.

"I just walked up to him and asked if I could help him find anything. When he asked if I worked here I said 'No, but we're in here so much, we know where everything is.' He told me he was just browsing, and we started talking. He asked me what your name was, so I told him a little bit about you. Then I invited him to lunch."

She shook her head in disbelief. After she paid for the book, the three of them went to the food court. They had a blast getting to know each other. By the end of lunch, the attraction between Sam and Patience was hard to ignore. They exchanged phone numbers, and he called her that same night. They talked for almost four hours. He called her every day after that. He was so shy that it took him two weeks to ask her out on a date, but he finally did.

* * *

Jana was still talking when the doorbell rang. Rory barked, bounding for the front door excitedly.

"He's here. I'll talk to you later."

Jana squealed with delight.

"Okay. I know you've got to go, but be sure to call me as soon as you get in."

"All right." Patience started to hang up.

"I am so serious. Because sometimes you say you'll call but you don't. Then I have to wait for *hours* till we can talk."

"I promise I'll call you."

Rory was hysterical by the time she reached the door. She flung it open dramatically. Sam stood there, looking handsome in a wholesome way. She'd have bet money he was raised in Iowa or Kansas. His blue eyes seemed to sparkle when he smiled.

"Hi," he said shyly.

"Hi."

Rory ran out to him, nearly knocking the poor guy over.

She invited him in, trying her hardest to put the rowdy animal in a headlock.

"It's okay," said Sam. "I love dogs." He started rubbing Rory under his chin, which calmed him down.

"Whew. That's good to hear. He usually runs my new guests off by being too, ahem, forceful."

She ran to the restroom to check her makeup. Looking in the mirror, she was pleased with her appearance, except for the out-of-control hair she'd fought with for years. Although most of her friends envied the free flowing curls that were the color of honey, she'd always longed for straight hair. Squinting in the mirror, she reached up to smooth the flyaway strands that framed her face, but to no avail. She was grateful that at least her skin was blemish free for the moment, while her new eyeliner made her eyes look bigger.

Patience returned to the foyer where Sam was teaching Rory to roll over. The dog just sat there with a blank expression on his face. Laughing, she shook her head and gathered her purse, and the two left for their date.

"What kind of music do you listen to?" Sam was quick to make small talk as he rummaged through his CD collection in his truck.

"Well, I love alternative. But when relaxing, I prefer classical or R&B."

"*You* like alternative?" he asked, glancing at her with a curious expression.

"Sure. What kind do you like?"

"Alternative. That's cool we listen to the same type of music. It's just that you surprised me. I figured you would like hip hop or rap."

"Why?"

"I don't know. I just assumed ... well ... I mean ..." he stammered.

"No, I don't know what you mean."

Silence.

"I thought African-Americans preferred soul music," he confessed finally.

She turned in her seat to look at him, folding her arms across her chest.

"That's pretty weird. And it's a stereotype."

She sighed. "Just because my skin is brown does *not* mean I only like music sung by brown skinned people, or that I only watch movies with minorities."

"I know, I know. I'm sorry," he stammered, his face turning red. "I'm so embarrassed."

She laughed again. "You should be!"

Patience changed the subject, mentioning a great Mexican restaurant, Mild or Hot. She preferred going there because the atmosphere was upbeat and lively. There was always so much excitement: parents trying to get control of their rowdy children, a couple having some sort of argument, or a server picking up a tray of food he dropped. Once, she'd witnessed a man choking on a piece of hamburger meat. His teenage daughter had saved his life.

"The people there are always so friendly. And the food is unbeatable. Yes, let's go there," he agreed.

The two chatted nonstop on the way to the restaurant. They arrived in good spirits, and fifteen minutes later, they were seated and looking over the menus. Patience could eat tacos every day of the week if forced. And this particular restaurant made a special salsa that was out of this world.

"Tell me some of your hobbies," Sam asked as the waiter brought their waters.

"Hmm, let's see ... I love reading, especially romance and comedy. I'm also toying with the idea of writing a novel. Ever since I was little, I've enjoyed creating stories in my head, putting them on paper and reading them to anyone who would listen."

She told him the ups and downs of being a tenth grade English teacher, making him laugh with some of her stories about the kids. He also asked about her family, which made her smile.

"My parents and I are very close. I don't have any siblings, so that may be one of the reasons. They doted on me when I was a child and still do."

She grinned as she continued.

"People always tell me that I'm just like my dad, and it's true. We're outgoing, friendly, and a little crazy. We love people, mingling in big crowds and being in the public eye." She shrugged. "My mom is shy, well, except with me." She winked.

"Do you look like her?" Sam asked with interest.

She shook her head.

"I favor my father, actually. The only thing I inherited from my mother is her skin color."

Taking a sip of his water, he frowned.

"What do you mean?"

She brushed the stray curl from her forehead.

"Well, my mom is black, and my dad is white. She has dark skin, while he's as pale as a ghost. So even though mine is very light brown ..." Her voice trailed off.

" ... It's still closer to your mom's skin tone," he finished for her.

"Exactly."

Sam leaned forward slightly, his elbows resting on the table. He studied her face intently.

"Yes, I could tell you were biracial when I first saw you at the bookstore. What color are your eyes, by the way?"

"Green."

He squinted. Momentary silence descended upon them as he continued to look her over. Patience shifted in her seat uncomfortably, not used to someone she barely knew examining her so openly. He moved in even closer until his face was only inches from hers.

"You're gorgeous."

"Thank you," she murmured, for lack of anything better to say. She wondered if this was how lab rats felt while some new product or theory was being tested on them.

"I'm serious. You are the most beautiful person I've ever seen."

She took a sip of water, her mouth suddenly dry.

"Ah, I can see you're not accustomed to being showered with compliments," he observed.

She shrugged. "On the contrary, I'm approached daily by admirers. Sometimes I even need a bodyguard!"

The two laughed as the server returned to take their orders.

Although most of her female friends had trouble eating in front of men, Patience had never encountered that problem. She wasn't shy when it came to eating on dates. She and Sam laughed nonstop over their entres. He'd chosen steak, medium rare, with potatoes, while she had fajitas.

Each sampled the other's dish, and she contemplated dessert afterward. She was ravenous and didn't know if it was because of his nearness or the fact that she really was hungry.

"I should weigh three hundred pounds the way I eat!"

Leaning sideways in his chair to admire her body, he smiled.

"You probably *should,* but you definitely *don't.*"

She blushed, taking another sip of her water. Her eyes scanned the dining area for a distraction. She noticed an extremely tall man making his way to the restrooms. A giggle escaped her.

“I wonder if he has to duck as he enters each room.”

Sam nodded, wiping his mouth with a napkin.

“Ah, pretty clever of you, changing the subject like that. I’m impressed.”

Before they knew it, the waiter had come to set the check on the table. Sam suggested a movie, not wanting the night to end.

While standing in line at the theater, they talked about everything from pet peeves to phobias to world news. Sam was smart, very smart. After he paid for the tickets, they bought popcorn, ignoring the fact that they had just eaten.

Patience noticed an older woman staring at them with an obvious look of displeasure. She smiled at the woman, who quickly turned away with a smirk. While walking away, Patience couldn’t help herself, sneaking one last glance back at her. The older lady rolled her eyes and then looked away. Patience didn’t know why, but the stranger’s attitude bothered her.

On the way home, the two talked animatedly about the movie. Sam casually threw his arm around her as they walked to her porch. Rory was barking uncontrollably.

“Do you know how much obedience school is?” she asked as she fumbled for her keys.

Laughing, he answered, “You might get a discount for Rory. But at least he’s a good guard dog. I mean, a young, beautiful woman living by herself ... it’s good to have a protector.”

She blushed at the compliment, finally finding her keys.

“He’s the furthest thing from a guard dog as you can get. Sure, he barks all the time, but it’s from the *excitement* of having company. He loves people.”

Laughing again, he moved closer to her.

“I had fun tonight. Maybe we can do this again sometime.”

“I’d like that,” she said, suddenly feeling shy. He reached over to touch her cheek softly, gazing deeply into her green eyes.

Suddenly they both jumped as Rory seemed to ram his whole body against the door. She rolled her eyes and sighed.

“I guess my owner is hinting that it’s time to go in.”

Sam smiled, promising to call her. He turned on his heel and walked away.

CHAPTER 2

The phone woke Patience up at five that next morning. "Hello," she whispered, still half-asleep. She could not imagine who was calling her at that hour, especially on a Saturday.

"Why didn't you call me last night? I've been literally waiting by the phone. How was your date?" It was Jana.

With her eyes still closed, Patience told her a little about their evening. Rory was lying at the foot of the bed, totally relaxed for once.

"I want details! Why don't you call me back when you're more awake?"

After hanging up the phone, Patience showered and had some breakfast. She took Rory on a quick walk, thinking about Sam. She had had so much fun on their date the night before. Although he seemed shy, he was funny and even slightly flirtatious. And with his blond hair and sparkling blue eyes, he was attractive. When she returned home, she let Rory out in the backyard, and then called Jana back.

That afternoon, Patience went over to her parents' house. They lived in the same neighborhood as she. Her dad answered the door, immediately scooping her up in his arms. "Sweetheart, it's so good to see you."

He led her into the house, yelling into the spacious living room for her mom to come downstairs.

"Sharise, our baby's here!"

Her mom came running down the stairs, almost missing some steps along the way.

"Honey, come to Momma," she cried, her arms extended wide. They hugged for what seemed to be five minutes.

Patience giggled at her dramatic parents. She knew they loved her, but sometimes they acted as if they lived on different coasts.

"Hi, Mom. Thanks for inviting me over."

Sharise waved her hand in dismissal. "Nonsense; You can come over anytime. The only reason I invited you over is I never see you. I swear, no one would ever guess we all live in the same neighborhood."

As her dad grilled steaks for the occasion, Patience made a huge salad, and her mom prepared her favorite pasta salad. They had a great afternoon, eating and chatting.

She was helping herself to dessert when her cell rang.

"Hello?"

"Hey, it's Cole."

Cole was her best friend from childhood. They had met in second grade on the playground during recess. She remembered how he dumped a whole bucket of sand in her hair that first day. It had taken her mom hours to get it all out. Yet after the incident, the two were inseparable. They remained friends all through school and became even closer as they entered junior high. Even now, they were always going on outings or cooking dinner for one another.

"Hi. What's up?"

"Not much. Where are you?" He could hear laughter in the background.

"I'm at my parents'."

"Oh. Tell them I said 'hi.' Call me as soon as you get home. I need to talk to you about something."

"It sounds serious. Is everything okay?"

"Yes. I just need some advice about Kristen." Kristen was Cole's girlfriend. They'd been seeing each other for three months. Patience knew the girl was crazy about him, but he was a little more casual about her.

"Sure, no problem. I'll call you as soon as I get home."

They hung up, and she wondered what was going on between those two.

* * *

Patience arrived home around seven that evening. Her mom had let her go only after she'd promised to return the next day. The phone was ringing when she walked inside, so she ran to catch it. She tripped over Rory, who was nipping at her heels out of excitement.

"Hello?"

"Hi, it's Sam."

She had to catch her breath from running to the phone.

"Hi! How are you?" She smiled, happy to hear from him.

"I was just calling to tell you how much I enjoyed our date last night."

"Awww ... how sweet. I had a great time, too."

They talked until almost ten o'clock, and Patience was amazed at just how much there was to say. After all, the two had chatted nonstop on their date, as well. For an introvert, Sam sure could hold up his end of a conversation. Reluctantly, she knew she needed to let him go. She had to let Rory out and prepare for the next day. Then she heard him clear his throat.

"Um, I was just wondering if we could get together again soon."

"Of course! I'd like that very much."

They hung up, and the phone immediately started ringing again. It was Cole.

"I thought you were going to call me as soon as you got home."

"I am so sorry. Hold on, I have to let Rory out." She returned seconds later, giving Cole her full attention.

"Kristen is starting to complain that we don't spend enough time together," he began.

"Then spend more time with her." It seemed pretty simple to Patience.

He explained that he was already seeing her four to five times a week.

"I take her out constantly, catching a quick bite to eat, playing golf, or attending those poetry readings she likes so much." He paused to take a breath. "She's always on my back about not calling her enough! She even whines when I have my boys' night out every Tuesday."

She had to admit that Kristen was being unfair. Cole wasn't the type to need "space" or to leave the girl wondering why he called only once a week. She knew he was a good catch and a very attentive boyfriend.

"Can you talk to her for me? She likes you. Plus, she knows we're best friends, so she may take constructive criticism from you. Please?"

She hesitated before agreeing to do it.

* * *

For the next week, Sam called frequently. He asked Patience over to dinner that Friday, assuring her that he was an amazing cook. He was such a nice guy and fun to talk to. She thought about him quite a bit, even at work. He gave her directions to his house while she tried to think of something to take with her. She decided to make chocolate mousse, which was yummy but easy to prepare.

Patience arrived promptly at six. He lived across town, but it didn't take long for her to get there. The houses were huge, and she gasped as she pulled up to his home. From the outside, at least, it appeared to be much larger than her parents', which was also expansive.

He greeted her with a hug, exclaiming, "You didn't have to bring anything!" Leading her inside, he took the dessert.

"I wanted to," she responded gleefully. She was happy to be there, ignoring the butterflies in her stomach. "Besides, you had the hard part; actually preparing a whole dinner. What smells so good, by the way?"

"Filet mignon and rice pilaf," he said proudly. "Would you like a glass of wine?"

"That'd be great," she said, following him into the kitchen. "Your home is beautiful!" She admired the unique floor plan.

"Thanks. I designed it myself. Well, my dad helped some," he admitted. "He's an architect, as well."

"Wow! The only things I can draw are stick figures, and maybe a sun, moon, and stars."

He laughed, handing her the glass of wine. "That's a start," he joked playfully. His eyes lit up as he explained some new projects he was working on, including a school for children with special needs. Patience hadn't met many people who actually loved their jobs. She admired his passion for helping others, as well as for the fact that he could design buildings. There was definitely more than met the eye with him.

After dinner, they went out to sit on his deck, taking full advantage of the warm night air. He had a swing that seated two, as well as deck chairs, a patio table, and a barbecue grill. There were plants everywhere, which showed he took special care of his place.

Taking a sip of his wine, Sam sat beside her on the swing.

"Can I ask you something?" He admired her profile, thinking, as he had on their first date, that she was one of the most beautiful people he'd ever seen.

"Sure," she answered, turning slightly toward him.

"It's kind of personal," he stated with a look of bashfulness. He seemed younger than his twenty-two years, like a little schoolboy with a crush on her.

"You can ask me anything," she reassured him. Patience felt totally at ease with him.

"It's about being biracial," he began with slight hesitation.

"Okay."

"What's it like being mixed? I mean, your parents are different races. Did you have a difficult time when you were growing up, you know, in a society where some people are ignorant and closed-minded?" He was curious about her. She was such an interesting person. He wanted to find out as much as he could.

"I don't really know what to say. It was just ... normal, I guess. My dad is white and my mom is black. I love them and they love me. Growing up, I knew that some people didn't accept my family. My dad explained it to me at a young age. I was sad that we live in a world where we're judged by the color of our skin, but it is what it is. I'm blessed that my parents showered me with affection and attention, which is more than most children get."

Sam was absentmindedly playing with her hair while he listened.

She continued.

"Being biracial is definitely more accepted these days, but I do remember getting stared at while we were out to dinner, and overhearing my mom telling my dad about some racist comment she'd been subjected to. But actually, not all of the stories were bad."

Patience laughed, thinking back to when she was six years old.

"I remember when I had been invited to a pool party in the neighborhood. My mom had taken forever straightening my naturally curly hair for church that morning. The party was scheduled for that afternoon. Needless to say, as soon as I'd jumped in the water, it turned into a mixture of frizz and curls. My mom had to explain to the other moms why my hair was straight before I dove in the swimming pool and an Afro afterwards."

Sam laughed as he tried to picture it.

"And Heaven forbid if she had to go out of town! My dad would always wake me up extra early to tackle my hair."

She paused a moment, her eyes dancing as she remembered her childhood.

"My curls have calmed down some as I've gotten older, believe it or not. They're wild, yes, but not as frizzy."

Sam couldn't get enough of her stories, and when she stopped talking long enough to take a sip of wine, he touched her cheek lightly.

"Well, I just have to say that your parents made a beautiful person, inside *and* out."

She smiled shyly, setting her glass on the chair beside her. Leaning toward her, he cupped her chin in his hand before planting the softest kiss she'd ever had on her lips. It was so soft, she briefly wondered if she'd imagined it.

"I really like you, Patience."

"I like you too."

They sat a while longer in a comfortable silence, looking up at the stars and thinking about each other. He had his arm around her, and she felt the heat from his touch penetrate through her skin. Before they knew it, midnight had come and gone. Reluctantly, she told him she'd better go.

"Please don't," he said, looking deep into her eyes. He smiled, displaying the dimple she liked so much.

"I wish I didn't have to," she responded, true regret in her voice. "But it's getting late. Besides, Rory probably needs to be let out. I was so excited about seeing you that I forgot to take him on a walk earlier."

Sam walked Patience to her car, kissing her again before she left.

"Call me when you get home, okay?"

She thought about him the whole way back to her house. She called right when she got in, talking to him for two hours before drifting off to sleep.

* * *

"So, you and Jana have been friends for *ten years*," asked Sam. "That's incredible! The longest friendships I've had were with family members. I don't know. It seems as if I get on people's nerves or something. Hmm, maybe I'm just a loner at heart."

He shrugged then, appearing unconcerned. Normally Patience would have put on her most empathetic expression, held his hand in hers, and told him that it was okay, that there was nothing wrong with him, and that someday, somehow, he'd find a friend to connect with. But after sneaking a glimpse of his profile, it was all she could do not to laugh. He seemed so nonchalant about the whole thing, so content with his life, that she found it hard to feel sorry for him.

It was a flawless day as the two sat outside the café that Sunday afternoon. She had told him about the place one night over the phone when he'd casually mentioned his love for croissants and bagels.

"I'm absolutely addicted to any kind of bread ... pastries are my favorite," he'd told her.

"My dad is, too! He frequents a café downtown called Bagels & More. I've gone with him a couple of times. It's really good."

Sam had told her he wanted her to take him there sometime.

The place was busy that day as they sat eating croissants smothered in the owner's special homemade butter. The two were enjoying people watching and getting to know one another better.

Patience asked him about his family, wanting to know more about the people who'd raised him.

"I guess our childhoods were extremely different. It sounds like your parents are two healthy, normal adults who showered you with attention. Let's just say that my mom and dad adopted a stricter, more authoritarian style of parenting." He gazed at something across the street, but she could tell he wasn't really focused on anything.

"My dad never really talked to me. Usually he'd just throw money my way so I'd get out of the house. He wasn't mean or anything. He just didn't feel like being bothered. And my mom ..." His voice trailed off.

Patience glanced down at her plate, a small pang of sympathy shooting through her heart.

"My mother was the worst," he continued, his unseeing eyes glazed over. "She was, and still is, very overbearing."

Patience said a silent prayer thanking God for blessing her with wonderful parents. Sometimes she took it for granted *and* forgot that some people weren't as fortunate. She reached across the tiny table, giving Sam's hand a supportive squeeze.

He smiled weakly at her.

"You know," he continued, "sometimes I would lock myself in the bedroom and just read. Books were a great escape for me. And as a young teen, I'd engross myself in stories of any genre: science fiction, mystery, historical." He chuckled. "Don't tell anyone, but I even dabbled in romantic suspense once."

She pulled her hand away with wide eyes.

"Oh my! I can't believe my ears. I've been going on dates with a male who's read romance novels? What shall I do? Take me home now!"

They both laughed. She was delighted to see a smile replace his forlorn expression.

"Your sarcasm is enduring, but I'm serious," said Sam. "Don't tell a soul! Besides, women are more understanding about this sort of thing. But if my friends ever found out about it, I'd never live it down."

Patience finished her strawberry milkshake.

"Oh, so you *do* have friends?"

"Well, yeah, there are a few guys I hang out with, but I still consider myself to be more of a loner." His eyes rested on the remainder of her croissant, which she had been unraveling distractedly.

"What are you doing?"

She looked down at the mess she had created.

"Oh, I didn't even realize ..." Her voice faltered.

"Did you not like the bread?"

"Um, it was all right, but they smothered it with butter."

Sam stared at her with a puzzled expression.

"I don't like butter."

He furrowed his brow.

"Why didn't you just tell them not to put it on?"

She sighed.

"I did, but they put it on anyway. I guess they just forgot."

Shaking his head, he pulled out his wallet and told her to go get something else. But she held up her hands.

"Nah, that's okay. I'll just grab a sandwich later." They argued about it for a while, and then he finally relented.

"I give up. I'll let it go this time, but you should really speak up if someone gets your order wrong. People don't mind when you correct their mistakes or send a dish back." He chuckled, shaking his head.

"You're just *too* nice!"

* * *

The couple had a great afternoon revealing more about themselves, sightseeing and soaking up the sun's rays. They went window-shopping after the café, stopping in front of the pet store. Patience fished around in her purse for a miniature sized bottle of sun block and began applying a generous amount to her nose. She noticed Sam giving her an odd look.

"What?" she asked, the noise of puppies barking surrounding them.

"You use sunscreen," he answered. She wasn't sure if it was a question or statement.

"No I don't," she retorted sarcastically.

He touched her shoulder affectionately. "I'm not trying to sound like a hick, but why do you need it?"

She cooed at a cocker spaniel through the window.

"If I don't, I'll get burned."

He didn't say anything for a while, although she had the feeling he wanted to. She wondered how long he could wait before the questions burst out of him. She had been asked all sorts of things by friends, acquaintances, and even strangers she'd encountered on the street:

"Are you sure sunscreen will work on you?"

"Hmm, I've never seen Blacks wear sunblock before."

"If you get darker in the summer, does your skin
return to its original color in the fall?"

Once she overheard a girl telling her friend in college, "Look at her, thinking she's white. I can't stand seeing light skinned people trying not to get darker." Patience had to laugh at the absurdity of it all. She would have loved to be darker, but unfortunately, she just burned when skipping the sunscreen.

Sam surprised her, however, by not broaching the subject again. It was late evening as they headed back to her place. The windows were down on his truck, the warm breeze ruffled her curls, and the sweet fragrance of lilies from a nearby field surrounded them.

She stole a quick sideways glance at him, taken aback by his boyish good looks. He wasn't necessarily gorgeous, someone who made women stop in their tracks when passing by, but she definitely found him attractive, in an innocent farmhand kind of way. She bet he'd never uttered a curse word in his life.

Sam caught her staring. His face turned a shade of red.

"What're you lookin' at?"

"You," she answered assertively. "I think you're pretty cute."

Now his cheeks were crimson as they stopped at the intersection close to her home.

Only a handful of cars were around them, which surprised her. This particular street stayed busy all the time. A Jeep full of rowdy teenagers pulled up beside them, their music blasting as they laughed and shouted obscenities to one another. The driver didn't have his seatbelt on, the passenger in the front seat held an open container of beer, and the girls in the back stood dancing, holding on to the bar above them. Patience and Sam were in the middle lane. The left lane was empty. Although she tried not to gawk, she couldn't help it. They were right next to her, after all.

The driver winked at her. "Hey baby, wussup?"

Patience heard Sam instructing her to stop staring, so she faced forward again. A police car approached the intersection in the left lane, the officer's eyes focused on both vehicles. Sam smiled at him while the teens continued their wild behavior.

The stoplight finally turned green and the Jeep sped off ahead of the other cars. Either they hadn't noticed the policeman or the driver just didn't care. Patience knew those guys would be issued at least three tickets for all the laws being broken, but to her amazement, the policeman got behind Sam's vehicle instead. He looked in his rearview mirror, and then glanced over to make sure her seat belt was fastened. She checked her side mirror, unable to believe her eyes.

Although she had an obstructed view of Sam's speedometer, there was no doubt in her mind that he was going the speed limit, if not under. The kids in the Jeep were long gone. As fast as the driver had taken off, she was sure the vehicle had grown wings. Mr. Police Officer should have been ashamed of himself but more than likely wasn't. Turning a blind eye and deaf ear to the teens' reckless behavior, he'd chosen to follow them instead. And although she adored Sam, he did drive like her grandmother. This was even more proof that the officer was targeting them.

Sam drove on. There were two four way stops in her neighborhood. He came to a complete stop at the first, almost waiting *too* long before continuing on to the second. He slowed down slightly as a woman pushing a stroller crossed the street. He put on his signal to turn left. They were only three streets away from her house when the siren came on.

"What the ...?" he muttered under his breath, obediently pulling over in front of one of the houses.

"You have to be kidding me," she whispered, turning around in her seat to make sure her ears hadn't deceived her.

Sam began fumbling around his glove compartment, mumbling something about the registration.

Patience, on the other hand, was livid. What dumb excuse were they going to hear from this cop as to why he'd singled them out? He obviously had nothing better to do on a Sunday evening than mess with innocent citizens while the *real* criminals danced in the streets.

"I need your license and registration please," came the intimidating voice suddenly. Sam handed him the items quietly.

"Do you know how fast you were going, young man?"

"Excuse me?"

"I *said,* '**DO YOU KNOW HOW FAST YOU WERE GOING**?"'

"Um, I'm pretty sure I was going ten miles per hour, sir."

"You are correct. But the speed limit in this neighborhood is fifteen miles per hour. You were traveling *under* the limit, which can be just as dangerous as speeding."

Patience folded her arms over her chest in a huff. "Oh, you mean like those kids in the Jeep a few minutes ago?"

Sam rolled his eyes as the officer bent down to peer inside the vehicle.

"What was that?"

She leaned toward Sam's side.

"I *said,* '**YOU MEAN LIKE THOSE KIDS IN THE JEEP A FEW MINUTES AGO**?"'

The officer eyed her suspiciously.

"You'd better watch it, miss."

She sighed.

"Did you not see those teenagers in the Jeep? They were drinking, wearing no seat belts, and basically ignoring everything having to do with safety."

"You need to work on that attitude of yours," the officer suggested dryly.

"Is this your girlfriend?"

Sam nodded.

Shaking his head, the policeman muttered,

"Well, you know how *they* are. I see this all the time. They're all angry and carry chips on their shoulders. You might think about sticking to your own ..." His voice trailed off.

"My own what?" he asked tensely.

"Never mind. I'll be right back."

"No, I want you to finish your sentence. What were you about to say?"

"You two sit tight."

The officer had avoided his question again. He must have thought about it. He could get into a lot of trouble if he kept on talking nonsense. Forget freedom of speech.

Patience felt a little bit of fear as she watched Sam's reaction to the situation. Since she'd met him, he'd been pretty laid back.

She noticed him gripping the steering wheel with such force that his knuckles were turning even whiter than normal. Reaching over to touch his arm, she had to reign in her own anger. She couldn't believe the officer had come right out and said those things. Stereotyping her aloud was obviously no big deal to him. And she could tell Sam was livid.

There were many onlookers being nosy: the person who lived in the house they'd stopped in front of had opened the window blinds to peer out, and several men jogging had stopped to watch. A stray dog had even paused in the grass to stare. The scene would have been comedic had this been a television show and not something negative happening to her.

"This is unbelievable! He's abusing his authority, I can tell you that much. I ought to file a complaint. Better yet, we have grounds for a lawsuit."

Sam wiped a bead of sweat off his temple.

"You can't sue him. He has a right to say whatever he wants."

Patience whipped around to face him squarely, and then gagged as the seatbelt choked her. She'd forgotten to unfasten it when they'd pulled over.

"Oh, listen to you, Mr. Calm. It looked like you were about to reach up and smack that officer a minute ago. Now you're telling me about his rights as an American? Unbelievable."

Sam reached over to take her hand. "I'm sorry. It's just frustrating. Why is this even happening?"

"I'll tell you why. At that intersection back there, he saw something he didn't like or believe in: an interracial couple." She paused for a second, blushing slightly.

"Well, I mean, I'm not presuming we *are* a couple, since we just met, but Mr. People–Need–to–Date–Their–Own-Race didn't know that. He probably assumed I was your girlfriend before he stopped us. Now he wants to make us suffer for our wrong choices."

The two were silent a while. The onlookers had finally moved on; only the dog had decided to wait a little longer to find out what happened next. And as Patience sat staring Sam, a light bulb clicked on in her head.

"I'm your girlfriend?"

He chuckled. "I was wondering when those words would sink in!" He leaned in to kiss her tenderly on the cheek.

After what seemed an eternity, the policeman returned, writing Sam a ticket for failing to signal before turning. He then smiled and told them to have a great night.

The two sat for a while, trying to absorb what had just happened before continuing on their way. Her blood was still boiling, yet she knew anger didn't solve anything. She also felt for Sam, who hadn't experienced this type of treatment before. During one of their many conversations about race, he'd admitted that he had led a pretty sheltered existence. He had only seen the overt, obvious acts of racism one saw on the news, such as when a group of policemen were caught on video beating a Black man or coverage of a business owner hanging up a sign that read "No Mexicans Allowed." And, of course, his parents had introduced him to racist jokes and stereotypical comments. Yet it was she who had given him a crash course in the more subtle acts, such as racial profiling and not getting hired just because of your appearance.

Sam left Patience's house around ten that night. They'd rehashed the evening's events again and again, unable to wrap their minds around them. She usually prided herself on having street smarts and being on guard for anything that came up, but this honestly blew her away. Of course, she'd had some encounters with individuals (both Black and White) treating her differently because of how she looked, but for the most part, God's grace had allowed her to be spared any physical violence or things that could have scarred her. Jana, on the other hand, seemed to come in contact with discrimination once a week. Society's ignorance was a huge obstacle to her. In many ways, Jana, who had to fight for her rights on a regular basis, was so much stronger and wiser than her.

She stood on the porch with Sam, not wanting to say goodbye just yet. She wished it were morning again so they could revisit their day. Well, all of the events minus the *COPS* episode they'd starred in. He reached out to her, the moonlight shining softly around them. He kissed her good night, his arms tightly around her, his lips feathery soft and inviting.

"Can I call you tomorrow?" he asked politely.

She laughed.

"Yes, you may. I have summer school in the morning but might let the kids out early." She loved teaching from fall to spring, but the summers were difficult. If she hadn't needed the money, Patience would have taken the summers off. She did enjoy education, yet every year she fought laziness when school let out in May. She had something in common with her students, after all.

Sam stalled as long as he could and then reluctantly departed, pausing once to blow her a kiss. As soon as his truck rounded the corner, she hightailed it back inside to call Jana. She had so much to tell with limited time.

"Okay, so let me get this straight. He followed you guys about three blocks for no good reason, issued Sam a bogus ticket, and verbally abused the both of you? Yet all *you* did was comply, holding your tongue while he victimized two law-abiding citizens? I can't stomach any more of this horror story!"

Patience fed Rory his treat, catching her breath after relaying the whole experience to her friend.

Her friend continued.

"I mean, who does he think he is, harassing y'all as a group of rowdy teenagers speed past, drinking alcohol with no seatbelts and blasting music that produces noise pollution? Huh?"

Patience agreed wholeheartedly.

"I *know*! He had nothing on us but was determined to make a statement. He knew that *I* knew what was going down, which pleased him, I'm sure. He had to get his message across that we were wrong to even be riding in the car together. But what he *doesn't* know is that I'll probably marry Sam because of this incident just to spite him."

The two talked a long time that night, which made Patience feel better. Her friend made a great confidante at times like these. At least Jana empathized, having had similar experiences to draw from. It helped her get through it, knowing her pal was so supportive. The only time conflict did arise was when one of them insisted that she had been treated worse than the other. Being dark-skinned with full lips and "bad hair," as she called it, Jana swore up and down that she had a harder time being accepted. She joked that out of the two of them, skinheads would beat her up first, then move to Patience.

"That's ridiculous!" Patience had responded to her friend's absurd comment one day. "The KKK and skinheads of this world don't care what *shade* of black we are. They hate us equally, believe you me."

"You are wrong, so wrong." Jana always cut in, strong in her conviction that light skinned minorities had an easier time fitting in with American society than dark ones. "Our culture favors individuals who look similar to the Caucasian race. For instance, if you and I were window-shopping at the mall and a casting agent noticed us, he'd approach you before me."

"You're crazy!"

"It's true. Plus, you're gorgeous, with your green eyes and curly hair! He'd snatch you up in a minute!"

"You're the beautiful one. I'd do anything for a little more color."

Rory began scratching the patio door to be let out. Patience was glad to be brought back to the present. She needed to get to bed soon for class the next morning. After showering, she applied a facial mask to deep clean her pores. It usually took a while to dry, so she went to the bookshelf in search of the novel she'd started. The poor dog caught sight of her and ran to hide.

Minutes later, she crawled into bed, her body beginning to relax but her mind racing uncontrollably. What a day it had been! It had started out wonderfully, going to church and then hanging out with Sam. But it had ended pretty shaky with Sam on the verge of a nervous breakdown and Patience contemplating violence against a cop. She smiled, envisioning herself winning that battle. Turning on her side, her eyelids suddenly felt heavy. She did adore him, so no matter what opposition lay ahead, their blossoming friendship was worth it.

CHAPTER 3

The next three months were like a dream to Patience. Her relationship with Sam flourished. They could not get enough of each other. He loved taking Rory to the park with her, spending time outdoors in the warm summer air. They went bicycling and rollerblading on Saturday mornings. He had even taken her fishing, which she would have found extremely boring had it been with anyone else.

Jana was crazy about Sam. They double dated a couple of times with one of the new guys Jana was seeing. Cole even admitted that he seemed like a cool guy. A big group of them had all gone dancing one night at the spur of the moment. Kristen had clung to Cole like he was a life jacket during a storm, and he kept reminding Patience that she'd promised to talk to her. She never could find the perfect time to sit down with Kristen, however. That is, not until one night when they all went to a play downtown.

They had a great time, except for Cole, who yawned dramatically during the whole thing. Afterwards, Sam suggested they eat at Ching Shui, a Chinese restaurant nearby. The conversation was lively and animated at the table. Kristen hung onto Cole's every word, as usual, while Sam was very attentive to Patience. At one point, Kristen announced that she needed to go to the ladies' room, asking Patience to go with her. Once inside, Kristen turned to her with a look of exasperation.

"I'm going to ask you something, and I want you to be brutally honest with me."

Patience braced herself, having a good idea what the question would be.

"Yes?"

"Do you think Cole is into me? Lately, I've been feeling like he's losing interest."

She looked at Kristen with sympathy. She really was a nice girl, but insecurity was her downfall. With her friend's long blond hair, big brown eyes, and a killer figure, Patience found it hard to believe she had low self-esteem.

What a shame, she thought with pity.

Patience tried to soften the blow, but she knew that honesty was best for the poor girl. She chose her words very carefully.

"Cole likes you. He thinks you're an extremely caring, sweet person. Yet for as long as I've known him, he's been independent. He does like to maintain a slight amount of distance from the girls he dates. He doesn't want to lose his friends or his ... life when he meets someone. Please don't take it personally. He's never been close to *anyone*."

"Except you," Kristen interjected sadly.

"But our relationship doesn't count. We're just friends. I'm talking about girlfriends from his past," Patience clarified.

Kristen leaned in closer, whispering, "Just between you and me, I think he has feelings for you."

"That's ridiculous! Cole and I have been friends so long, it would be like incest."

"He talks about you *all* the time. And you should see how he looks at you," his girlfriend insisted.

"I think you're imagining things."

Patience could see now what Cole meant when he'd said that Kristen was emotionally draining.

"Maybe you can relax some. Try to take things slower with him. Cole will let you know when he wants to speed things up."

They hugged then, and Kristen's eyes welled up with tears. "You're right. I admit I do have a tendency to be overbearing. It's just that I like him so much. He's everything I've ever wanted in a guy. But I *will* take your advice and just follow his lead."

* * *

By the middle of September, Patience and Sam were crazy about each other. He'd met her parents a couple of weeks before, who absolutely adored him. Her mother went on and on about his charm and good manners. Even her overprotective dad admitted he liked him. Sam had also met most of her friends by then, who thought they made a cute couple. The weather was scorching, especially for September, but they took the opportunity to swim at her friend Amanda's house whenever possible.

One Saturday morning, Sam had made plans to take her to an art museum. She was less than thrilled, as she'd never been into those types of places. Reluctantly she agreed to go. She knew he loved museums, and she wanted to do something he liked. They arrived in the early afternoon, quietly walking around while he explained each sculpture and painting. She didn't want to tell him she was ready to leave after only an hour, stifling a yawn while they held hands.

He was telling her about one of his favorite artists when he stopped mid-sentence. She waited for him to continue, but he was silent.

"Is something wrong?" she asked. She noticed that his face had gone pale, and he began leading her to the elevators, still holding her hand.

"No, everything's fine. You know, we've been here a while, and I know this isn't your favorite place to be ... Are you ready to go?"

"It's okay. We can stay as long as you like. Sorry if I seem to be a little, um, bored."

She felt guilty because he'd always been willing to do things she liked, and he never complained.

Sam pushed the elevator button, reassuring her that it wouldn't upset him if they left.

"You know, I *am* getting hungry. How about we grab some lunch?"

She looked at him in amazement.

"We just ate breakfast! There is no possible way you're hungry. Quit joking around and tell me what's going on."

Just then a male voice shouted, "Sam! What's going on, man?"

They turned to see three guys approaching, looks of amusement on their faces. She heard Sam mutter something inaudibly under his breath.

"Hey guys, what's up?"

She could see the tension in his face and wondered what was going on.

"Man, nothing at all. I can't believe we got suckered into coming here. You know how much Melissa loves these kinds of outings," the first guy said.

"Yeah," the second one chimed in. "Avery tricked me into it, I swear! I thought we were all going to a sports bar. She told me it was a surprise. I should've expected it'd be a place like this."

Everybody laughed. The first one spoke up again.

"Oh yeah, I almost forgot that you like this kind of stuff," he said to Sam.

The third friend was eyeing Patience as the other two kept complaining about the museum. She kept waiting for Sam to introduce her, but he didn't.

As if reading her mind, the third guy held out his hand to greet her.

"Hi, my name is Eric. And you are ... ?"

She shook his hand with a grateful smile.

"I'm Patience."

Eric gestured to the others.

"These are my buddies, John and Cal. We're all friends of Sam's."

Everyone said hello to her as Patience looked over at Sam with a frown. She wondered why he was acting so oddly. She knew he was hiding something but could not imagine what it was. Eric turned to John and Cal, telling them they'd better go find their girlfriends or they'd be in hot water. Saying good-bye, the guys left.

She threw a sideways glance at her boyfriend and then slowly headed toward the exit. She pushed the elevator button without saying a word. Sam shifted uncomfortably from one foot to the other, cleared his throat, and ran a finger through his hair. One could hear a pin drop in the silent corridor. She focused her attention on a wasp that had landed on the wall near them.

"We need to talk."

The elevator doors opened and they stepped inside.

Her eyes met his.

"What is it?" asked Patience.

"I want to explain what just happened back there," he pressed.

She turned to him with wide eyes.

"Oh, do you mean when you acted embarrassed to be seen with me? Or that you were ashamed to introduce me to your friends? You would rather have snuck me out of the museum than let them meet me."

The two exited the elevator with Patience walking two steps ahead of him. He gently grabbed her arm, trying to get her to slow down.

"No, that's not it at all. I'm not ashamed of you!"

She wheeled around to face him.

"Oh, really? You could've fooled me. You didn't even mention to your friends that I'm your girlfriend. You weren't even planning on *introducing* us. Eric was nice enough to tell me who they were. What's up with you?"

She looked down for a second, trying to regain her composure. When she spoke again, her voice was soft.

"I wondered why I had never met anyone close to you. We've been together for three months, but you've never suggested an outing when everyone could get together, including your parents."

Sam was silent.

Patience began walking toward his truck but couldn't remember where they'd parked. She walked up the first row of cars she saw, not knowing what else to do. He followed her, speed walking to keep up with her fast pace.

"You don't know how many times I tried to tell my family about you. I could never find the right moment."

They found the truck, and she waited for him to unlock the doors. Once inside, she decided to go ahead and ask, just for the heck of it.

"What do you need to tell me about your parents?"

"Well, they aren't exactly ... open to the idea of interracial dating."

Her heart sank as he said the words.

"Actually, they would disown me if I even thought about bringing home a girl of another race."

"When were you planning on telling me?" Although it didn't matter, she asked the question anyway.

He sighed deeply, finally looking at her with sorrow in his eyes. "Honestly, I don't know."

She shook her head.

"Do your friends feel the same way? Well, you did a good job of hiding me, coming up with all of those clever excuses whenever I'd mention meeting them. How could I have been so blind?"

He quickly objected.

"My friends are some of the most open-minded, unbiased people you can meet. The reason you never met them is they all have big mouths. My parents would have found out about us the minute they met you."

Her stomach was in knots by the time he started the truck. She was hurt because he'd known what his parents were like before they'd started dating.

"Sam, you should have told me about them. I needed to know this information before our first date." Then she might have been able to control her feelings and not allow herself to fall for him so deeply.

On the highway back into town, Patience stared out her window, lost in her own thoughts. Sam kept apologizing, but she had tuned him out.

The drive was endless. She could barely wait to dive into a pint of ice cream when she got home. She knew Rory was waiting for her as well, full of the unconditional love he would lavish on her. He didn't care what color she was.

She jumped out of the truck before he had come to a complete stop in her driveway.

Sam yelled, "Are you crazy? You could've at least waited till I stopped." He ran after her, but she was already opening her front door.

"Will you at least look at me, please?" The tremble in his voice caught her attention.

"You have every right to be upset. Just know that I wanted to tell you about them the first time we went out. But what was I going to say? 'My hobbies are snowboarding, going out to eat, playing video games ... oh, and by the way, you'll never meet my parents?' I didn't want you to judge me based on how my family is. I know that I held some narrow-minded views when we first met, stereotyping different cultures, but you set me straight. I've learned so much from you.

Patience, every moment we've spent together, I've found more to like about you. I think about you *all the time.* In the back of my mind, I knew I had to tell you about my parents, but I didn't want to lose you. So I kept putting it off. Please believe me when I say that I never meant to hurt you."

He stopped, waiting for her response.

She knew she had to say something. It wasn't his fault. He could not control how others thought. She cared about him and knew he was a good guy. But she wanted a boyfriend with whom she could go to his house and not worry if his parents might show up. She wanted to be able to hang out with him and his friends. She told him that, adding,

"You're a great guy. I've really enjoyed our time together. But I need someone who's not afraid of what others think, who wants to show me off to the world. I deserve it. Goodbye, Sam," she said as she closed the door softly behind her.

CHAPTER 4

The next week dragged by for Patience. Each day seemed endless to her. It was absolute torture. Sam called at least twenty times during that week, but she didn't answer. She couldn't, for she knew her emotions would get the best of her if she heard his voice. He left her messages all throughout each day, pleading with her to call him back. He even suggested that they could still be friends. She had to laugh when she heard that one. The next day, he admitted on her voice mail that he refused to try to be just friends. He decided to go ahead and tell his parents about her. He said he didn't care what they thought anymore; he just didn't want to lose her.

Despite herself, Patience felt sorry for him. She knew it hadn't been an act when they had been dating. She truly believed he had deep feelings for her.

What a sad situation to be in, she thought, *always worrying that you might fall for someone of a different race and knowing it could never work out because of your family.* And besides, she was not the type to come between members of a family. It just wasn't worth it.

She went through the motions of her daily routine, but her heart wasn't in it. She would wake up, take Rory for a walk, go to work, come back home, and fix dinner. She felt as if she were in a hazy fog all the time. Jana called often to check on her, but she didn't answer her calls, either. Patience had phoned her the night of the breakup and told her the whole story. Her friend had been extremely sympathetic. But she was the only one who knew the details. When her mom called, Patience had acted as if everything were fine; she knew what a worrywart her mother could be.

On Saturday morning, Patience hung out at home to mourn the loss of her relationship with Sam. She felt as if she deserved to wallow in her sadness and self-pity. The kids at school distracted her, so she hadn't really been able to soak everything in at work, process it, and get over it. She made the decision, however, to snap out of it after that weekend. She didn't want to be depressed too long. She grabbed a book she had been meaning to read for a while and went out on her back porch to lounge around. Rory began running laps around the yard, enjoying the sunshine and chasing a bird that had landed in front of him.

Suddenly, Rory ran to the fence gate, barking wildly at a noise he'd heard. She looked up, wondering what it was. She saw Cole emerge from a distance with Rory jumping up on him. He immediately started laughing, roughhousing with the dog.

"Hey, boy!! What's goin' on, huh? Who's the best dog in the world? You are, that's who," he cooed.

Patience smiled, shaking her head. Cole loved her dog and turned into the biggest softie every time he was around him.

As if just realizing she was there, he suddenly looked over at her with a scowl.

"I thought you were dead. Why are you not answering your phone?" He walked over, sitting down on the grass beside her.

She shrugged, her eyes downcast.

"I haven't really been in the mood to talk."

He nodded his head in response.

"Yeah, Jana called. She told me everything. I've been trying to call, so I thought maybe I should come over and at least check on you."

Patience looked at him with unshed tears.

"I just don't get it. I was really beginning to like him. He waits three months to drop the bomb about his parents. And only then did he tell me because we ran into his friends. Who knows how much longer he would've kept it from me had we not accidentally bumped into them?"

"I don't know. I just don't know. When Jana told me what happened, I was shocked. He seemed to be really into you. At least that's what it looked like to me. I thought he was crazy about you."

She absentmindedly stroked Rory's fur while staring into space.

"Honestly, I don't know what I'm feeling. I go from being angry at him to missing him. Then the anger slowly creeps back in, and I really don't know how to get rid of it. I mean, he knew his parents felt this way when he met me. Why did he even ask for my phone number in the first place?"

Standing up, Cole held out his hand to her.

"Look, I don't have all the answers. Maybe he was attracted to you and decided to throw caution to the wind for a while. I'm willing to bet he didn't realize he was falling for you until it was too late."

She allowed him to help her up off the grass, smiling in spite of herself. He really was a good friend to her, especially in times like these.

"I'm really mad at myself," she said with conviction. "I mean, I know deep down that prejudice exists. Obviously everyone in the world isn't going to agree that races should mix. But still ... coming face to face with it feels as if someone has punched you in the stomach."

Cole nodded.

"I know what you mean. Being Cuban isn't easy, so I know where you're coming from."

"Oh, come on. You look white. You have no idea how it feels to be discriminated against."

"Yes, I do! I've had store employees watch me, making sure I didn't steal anything from their precious little stores. Once while standing in line at Brew, these knuckleheads behind me kept making racial slurs that I knew were meant for me. The funny thing is, they thought I was Mexican." He shook his head, rolling his eyes in irritation. "Like you, I can't stand ignorance."

She didn't have the strength to get involved in a Who's-Life-Is-More-Difficult discussion with him. She and Jana had had enough of those conversations to last a lifetime. In her gut, however, Patience knew it was harder to be her. Cole could easily pass for white, although he would never try or want to. He was extremely proud of his heritage. But at least he wasn't bombarded with questions and curious stares everywhere he went. He could blend in with the crowd.

Brushing the grass off her pants, she smiled. The two stood inches apart, each one studying the other. His eyes were his best feature: dark, almost black in color, with lashes that seemed to extend for miles. One could easily get lost in them. He ran a hand through his coal black hair.

"What are you thinking?" he asked.

Her smile deepened.

"I was just admiring your looks. I thought you could blend in with a crowd, but upon further inspection, there's absolutely no way that could happen. You're too gorgeous."

Pulling her against him, his arms went around her protectively. He held her for a long time, and she felt the love he had for her through body language alone. Their relationship was deep and special, almost unexplainable. Rory was lying in the grass underneath them, gnawing on his favorite chew toy. It was as if he knew the mood was somber and mellow.

"You're so wonderful," Cole whispered softly. "Sam's a fool. Any man would be lucky to have you."

Patience pulled away slightly, gazing into her best friend's eyes.

"Thanks, Coley. You always make me feel better."

Suddenly he let go of her, clearing his throat dramatically.

"I'm taking you out to lunch. And I won't take no for an answer. I have to get you out of this house."

Fifteen minutes later they were headed out the front door.

PART II: Jason

CHAPTER 5

The cold November air seemed to go right through her jacket when Patience stepped out of her car. She pulled the collar up higher as she walked up the front steps to Kylie's house. She and her roommate, Sasha, were throwing a party that night, and they'd invited her. She had met both girls during her freshman year in college, and they had hit it off immediately. The girls kept in touch over the years since then, always inviting her to their gatherings and social events.

She knew both Cole and Jana would be there, as well as his new girlfriend, Camryn. Kristen's insecurities had finally driven him away. Camryn definitely came across as more confident. He liked her spontaneity and carefree attitude. She was a far cry from his ex.

Kylie answered the door, squealing with delight at the sight of Patience. "It's freezing out there!"

She pulled her inside, yelling over the loud music that she was glad she could come.

"Me too! Thanks for inviting me!" Patience shouted back.

They headed to the kitchen, where Sasha was preparing hors d'oeuvres. When she saw Patience, she hugged her with a smile.

"You're late," Sasha teased. "Do you want something to drink?"

"Sure."

Patience noticed that, although it was only ten o'clock, the party was already in full swing. There seemed to be people everywhere. Some were dancing in the spacious living room, others were sitting around laughing and talking, while still others were shooting a game of pool in the den. They were a lively group, certainly, and she was glad she had decided to come after all. She had been down in the dumps after Sam, alternately feeling sorry for him and wanting to wring his neck.

Sasha handed her a soda, and she decided to walk around and people watch. She laughed when she entered the dining room and witnessed a couple making out on the table. After strolling around the house awhile, Patience spotted Jana out on the patio, talking to some friend of theirs. She went out to join them.

"You made it! You're late," Jana scolded her as they hugged.

"Why does everyone keep telling me that? Besides, who ever heard of being late to a party?" she defended herself.

Her best friend crossed her arms over her chest.

"Well, Miss Smarty Pants, we all arrived at eight. And if Cole asks me one more time if you're coming, I'm going to scream. So yes, you *are* late."

"He's here? I haven't seen him yet."

As if on cue, he and Camryn walked out onto the patio. Patience couldn't help but notice how attractive he looked that night. The white shirt he wore really contrasted nicely with his black hair and olive skin. He never had a difficult time getting girls. She always joked with him that she felt plain and ordinary when they went out. He was so strikingly handsome, and although she was pretty, Patience believed she faded into the background when she was around him.

She left the group after a while, heading to the kitchen to fetch some bottled water for them. Two men were talking as she walked to the cooler.

"I'm done with her, man. I am so sick of her games ..." the first guy was saying. They both turned to look at her, who suddenly felt self-conscious.

"Sorry, I didn't mean to interrupt."

She didn't see any bottled waters in the cooler, so she grabbed a soda instead.

The first one asked her, "Can I help you find something?"

"Um, I was just looking for water?" she replied. It sounded more like a question, and the second male laughed. They were both about six feet tall with broad shoulders. The first one was extremely handsome, with a big smile and dimples. His brown skin was flawless, and she had never before seen such an incredible body.

"Is that a question?" the first guy asked.

She blushed, walking to the refrigerator then, hoping there would be some in there, with no such luck. The first guy went to the garage and retrieved one out of the fridge there.

"By the way, my name is Jason. And you are ...?" His voice trailed off.

"Patience."

She shook his hand, and then she shook hands with his friend, Donovan. Jason gave his friend a get lost look, so he politely excused himself. After chatting a few minutes, he asked her to dance. She began to relax as she danced with him. He was very charming and sweet, making her feel totally at ease.

"You're a great dancer," she commented assertively.

"So are you," he replied. The two ended up hanging out together the remainder of the party.

Patience couldn't believe it when Cole told her it was three in the morning. The time had flown by. Jason was smart, funny, and very outgoing. He told her a little about his family and friends. They also discussed their hobbies. She noticed that people were beginning to leave, and Donovan approached them to tell Jason he was ready to go. They had come together, and Donovan was driving. Jason asked Patience for her phone number, which she supplied without a second thought.

"I'll call you," he promised her with a hug.

* * *

When Jason called the next night, they talked for hours. He asked her to dinner, and they agreed to go out the following weekend. That Friday evening, he arrived at five sharp, looking incredible. He took her to dinner and then they went to Brew, a popular coffee shop they both loved. She found out that he was twenty-three years old and had five siblings. He grew up in Texas and had had a great childhood. His mother was sad when he went to the University of California, but he moved back after graduating with a BA in accounting.

"Most of my family lives here, and I couldn't wait to move back and start working. We are all so close. Even my sisters and brothers admitted that they missed me when I moved to California."

Patience laughed, asking "What are their names?"

"Well, Josh is twenty years old and lives in New York. He's an aspiring actor. Then there are the twins, Jimmy and Jackson. They're seniors in high school."

"Are they identical or fraternal?" she interrupted.

"Identical. I have tons of funny stories about them switching places in school *and* at home. My mom still has a hard time telling them apart."

"My younger sister, Jaime, is in ninth grade. She's the sweetest girl you could ever meet. Last but not least, my baby sister, Jessica, is in kindergarten."

She exhaled dramatically.

"Wow! How exciting it must've been to grow up in your household. Sometimes I wish I had had a big family. I'm an only child, and there are definitely pros and cons to my situation." She took a sip of her vanilla latte. "I bet there was never a dull moment at your house."

He nodded in agreement.

"You're right about that. I was never bored or lonely. But when I lived at home, sometimes I longed for peace and quiet."

"Hmmm ... quiet can drive you up the wall, though," she revealed. "I guess it's true what they say. 'The grass is always greener on the other side"'.

"Absolutely," he agreed.

They didn't leave the coffee shop until after one, and Patience stifled a yawn as he drove her home.

"I have to warn you that I have a rowdy dog, so when you walk me to the door, please don't freak out."

He laughed and teased, "Who said I'm walking you to the door?"

She looked at him in mock dismay.

"Well, if I get kidnapped, it'll be on your conscience," she joked back.

Jason walked her to her door, and they could hear Rory barking inside. She unlocked the door and the dog pushed through the small opening before she could block him. He jumped up on Jason, and she apologized.

"That's okay. I love dogs," he reassured her as he stooped low to pat Rory. Suddenly she thought of Sam, who had said the same thing the first time he had come over. Patience wondered how he was doing, feeling a small tug at her heart. Quickly she brushed the thought aside. Surely it was bad manners to think of him while saying good night to her new friend.

He leaned forward to give her a peck on the cheek.

"I had fun tonight. Can I call you tomorrow?"

Looking directly into his eyes, she smiled shyly.

"Nothing would make me happier."

CHAPTER 6

Jason called the next morning, inviting her to go dancing with him and his friends that night. She was surprised he called as much as he did and wanted to see her so often.

"I don't know. Crashing your boys' night out is not a good first impression to make with your friends."

"But you wouldn't be. Everyone is bringing his girlfriend, which would make me a fifth wheel. So see? You'd actually be helping me!"

In the end, he convinced her to go. They picked her up that night, and she had a great time. His friends were fun, and each of them had a great personality. Their girlfriends were easy to get along with as well. And she could not believe how attentive Jason was to her, especially being in that type of environment.

By the time Donovan dropped Jason and Patience off at her house the next morning, it felt as if the temperature had dropped thirty degrees. She shivered as they entered her house. In Texas, one never knew how to dress each day, no matter what the season was. She made hot chocolate with marshmallows for the two of them. They snuggled close together on the couch, Rory lying content at their feet on the floor. Even he seemed to have mellowed some with the cold weather.

"Tonight was fun," she said. "Your friends are hilarious. And they made me feel totally comfortable. Thanks for inviting me."

"You're very welcome. I could tell they adored you."

He ran his fingers through her hair, studying her face intently.

"You know you're very beautiful, right?"

She smiled, feeling his hand begin to massage the back of her neck.

"So are you," she whispered back, leaning in toward him slowly, nervously anticipating their first kiss.

Jason's lips met hers, tentatively at first and then with more passion. He pulled back from her, a seductive look on his face. She wanted him to kiss her again but was too shy to initiate it. As if reading her mind, he pulled her close to him, softly kissing her left cheek, then her right, and finally her lips. As they parted, she could feel the electricity in the air.

"I'd better go," he started hesitantly.

She sighed, saying nothing.

"I don't *want* to leave, yet I *need* to in order to remain a gentleman." He looked at her with a boyish grin, trying his best to look innocent.

She nodded, standing up to walk him out.

"At a loss for words?" he asked as he stood up as well, bending over to pat Rory on the head.

She smiled at him with a sheepish look.

"I just don't trust myself to speak right now. If I do, I'll end up begging you to stay." She was completely honest about her attraction to him. They both laughed.

Jason reached for her hands and held them as they gazed into each other's eyes. He gave her one last kiss before leaving.

* * *

Patience arrived at Cole's house the next morning wearing sweatpants, an old worn T-shirt, and her hair in a messy ponytail. She had a less than amused look on her face when he let her in.

"I can't believe you tricked me into being your slave for the day," she greeted.

He wore a wounded expression as he turned to her. "*Slave* is such a harsh word. How about being thankful I felt close enough to you to ask for your help today?"

She rolled her eyes, following him into the kitchen. She could not believe the mess that surrounded her. There was a mountain of dishes in the sink, empty potato chip bags on the floor, and a broken chair in the dining room. The floor looked as if it hadn't seen a broom in the past year, and when she went into the living room, it didn't look any better. One could tell that Cole had had a party the previous evening. The small get-together he was throwing that night was only hours away. She couldn't imagine the place being presentable before the first guests arrived.

"I'm just being honest when I say this to you. There is positively no way we can have this place cleaned up by tonight." She was terrified to see what the bathrooms looked like.

"You're so dramatic. Where's your faith? We can do this. We *have* to do this!"

He walked over to her as she bent over to pick up some empty soda cans. "I really appreciate your coming over today. I realize you have better things to do on a Saturday. I knew I was unable to fix this place up by myself, but everyone I called for assistance fed me silly excuses. Steven said he had a wedding to attend that he just *could not* get out of."

Steven was his younger brother. They both knew he abhorred weddings, anniversaries, baby showers, or anything else one might have to dress up for or bring gifts to. "And can you believe Jana had the nerve to tell me she was studying at the library ... On a Saturday ... Jana??"

Patience felt sorry for him.

"It's okay. I'll help you, but I am not doing the bathrooms!"

It was after five when they finished cleaning. Cole promised to thank her appropriately with dinner and a movie for all she had done. She hurried home to shower and change, not knowing what she was going to wear. Jason was picking her up at seven, so she knew she had no time to waste.

* * *

Patience snuggled closer to Jason on the couch, breathing in his spicy cologne. He draped his arm across her shoulders, kissing her on the cheek. She glanced over at Cole, who was slow dancing with Camryn.

"Have I told you how much I, I mean, my friends, like you?" Jason asked Patience quietly.

"Your friends?" she repeated.

"Um, yeah, they were just telling me the other day how beautiful you are."

She smiled.

"Oh, really? What else did *they* say?"

He shrugged, trying to seem nonchalant.

"Oh, I don't know. I think I remember them saying that you are smart, funny, and one of the sweetest girls they know. Not a day goes by when they don't think about you."

She sat up then, teasing him mercilessly. "Wow! I think your friends have a crush on me. You'd better do something about that."

He leaned toward her until they were just an inch apart. "Good idea."

CHAPTER 7

It was the first week of December, and their relationship had grown tremendously. Jason opened up to Patience one night, telling her that she was the only girl he was dating. And he wanted her to meet his family. He had told them about her, bragging that she was everything he'd ever dreamed of. She was extremely excited that he wanted her to meet his folks. She got along great with his friends and couldn't wait to see what his parents and siblings were like. He invited her to his parents' house for dinner one Thursday night, and she was ecstatic.

Thursday evening approached rapidly. Patience felt unbelievably nervous while baking a chocolate cake to take with her. She wanted to make a good first impression and knew that almost everyone loved chocolate.

What will they think of me? she wondered. After all, she knew from all of her talks with Jason that he was a mama's boy. She had no idea if his mother would approve of her, not to mention all of his brothers and sisters.

Jason rang her doorbell as she was frosting the cake. Rory left her side where he had been shamelessly waiting for her to drop some crumbs, barking all the way to the door.

By six-thirty, they were pulling up to his family's house. The door was unlocked, so Jason let them in, and they were immediately greeted by his five-year-old sister, Jessica. She squealed with delight, jumping up into her brother's arms. As they hugged, she glanced over at Patience with a smile. She politely extended her hand to Patience, introducing herself.

"Your girlfriend is really pretty," Jessica informed Jason in a hushed tone.

"You're absolutely right," he agreed as he set her back down.

They walked into the living room, the aroma of grilled steaks welcoming them in. Jason's parents entered the room, and his mother immediately pulled her into her arms.

"It is so nice to finally meet you! Jason talks about you *constantly.* I couldn't wait to meet the girl who has occupied so much of his time."

Patience detected a hint of sarcasm in the woman's voice.

"Thank you, Mrs. Peterson. It's so good to meet you, too. Thank you for inviting me over for dinner."

Handing her the cake, she added,

"I hope everyone likes chocolate." She was extremely nervous, the butterflies doing somersaults inside her.

"Please, call me Carolyn. And this is my husband James."

"Thank you for baking a dessert. That was extremely thoughtful of you," Jason's father said. "Dinner should be ready shortly."

The five of them sat talking for a while, with Jessica interrupting every ten seconds to tell them something important. They were just sitting down to dinner when Jimmy, Jackson, and Jaime burst in through the back door, coming from the mall with friends.

"You're late," their mother reprimanded. "What kind of an impression do you think that makes on Jason's new friend?"

"Sorry mom, we got caught up. What's for dinner?" Jimmy asked with no remorse.

They all said hi, and halfway through dinner, she could see what an open, friendly family they were. The twins were a riot, typical seventeen year olds, and Jessica wanted to be the life of the party. She could also see where Jason got his personality from. His father cracked jokes and told entertaining stories all through the meal. He also tried to include Patience in the conversation, making her feel more at ease.

His mom was a different story, however. Carolyn drilled her on everything from her family to her occupation, asking her questions about where she went to college, where she saw herself in five years, and what her hobbies were. Patience couldn't help but sit up straight with her shoulders squared, feeling as if she were on an interview instead of at dinner.

"Carolyn, *please* ..." Jason's father let his voice trail off, giving his wife a stern look. "Let the poor girl relax, for heaven's sake. We're not on that show, *The Bachelor*."

Everyone laughed, dissipating the tension in the air. The remainder of dinner went smoothly. Jason's mother fell silent after her husband's warning.

Patience found out a lot about his family that night. She easily felt the warmth and sincerity that filled the house. Jackson sat staring at her while she played Trivial Pursuit with his siblings, a goofy expression on his face. His twin, Jimmy, quickly picked up on that fact, teasing him mercilessly about his obvious crush on her. She also had a new best friend; Jessica showed off her room to Patience, proudly explaining all of her soccer trophies and medals.

At one point later in the evening, Jason's father sent the children upstairs to shower and prepare for school the next morning. The procrastinator of the family, Jimmy, confessed he still had homework to finish, while Jessica began crying because she didn't want to go to bed.

"I want to stay up with Patience," the child stated matter-of-factly.

Carolyn instructed Jaime to take her upstairs for a bath.

"I WANT TO STAY HERE!" Jessica repeated loudly, planting herself on the carpet in the middle of the room.

"Now, sweetheart ..." James began, but his voice was drowned out by the full-blown temper tantrum that ensued. It took five minutes for Jaime to transport the wailing child to her room. Patience tried to hide a smile as the family appeared embarrassed.

Jason shook his head, sitting beside her on the love seat.

"I am so sorry you had to see that."

"Don't worry about it. I work with teens, remember? I encounter tizzies on a regular basis."

Everyone laughed as James and Carolyn sat down across from the couple on the couch.

The four made small talk for a while. The atmosphere was quiet and calm, despite the occasional arguing they heard coming from upstairs. It was clear Jess wasn't going down without a fight. She had been so charming earlier but had quickly flipped the switch to defiance. His parents ignored the chaos, their focus solely on Patience. She smiled, tucking her hair behind her ear.

"Your hair is gorgeous," Jason's mother observed, taking a sip of tea.

"Thank you."

"If you don't mind my asking, how did you get that amazing color? Highlights?"

"Um, no, Mrs. Peterson, this is my natural hair color."

Carolyn's eyebrows immediately shot up as she leaned in closer.

"Really? Hmm, I don't know many African-Americans with your hair color. I must say, you are blessed."

Although the woman was complimenting her, Patience felt scrutinized, as if she were under a microscope being examined.

"My dad is white, so I imagine that's the reason my hair is light brown."

James shifted uncomfortably in his seat while Carolyn's eyes narrowed.

"And your mother?"

"Black."

Jason jumped in immediately.

"She's mixed. Isn't my baby beautiful?" He took her hand in his, squeezing it gently.

His father sat quietly, his eyes focused on something across the room. Carolyn set her tea on the end table, her eyes never leaving Patience.

"Ah, so that explains your light complexion and those green eyes. I see. So do you consider yourself African-American?"

"Carolyn!"

Patience let go of Jason's hand, sitting up straighter in her seat. She held her head high as she answered.

"I'm biracial."

Jason sat motionless beside her. His father had stood abruptly, attempting to grab his wife's arm to pull her aside. However, Carolyn was too quick for him, moving out of his reach.

"Well, my dear, I hate to tell you, but the white community considers you one hundred percent black."

Patience bristled. She had two choices: she could change the subject or challenge this aggressive woman. She chose the latter.

"What about the black community, Mrs. Peterson?"

Jason coughed. Clearly it made him uncomfortable to have his mother and girlfriend discuss race on their first meeting, especially when the undercurrent was somewhat hostile. Patience knew Sam had tried to avoid this scene as well. The only difference would have been that *both* of his parents were supposedly prejudiced. But so far, Carolyn seemed to be the only one finding a problem with her. She briefly wondered why Jason wasn't jumping in to defend her or at least redirect the conversation.

"Honey, why don't we leave these two lovebirds alone for a minute? Let's go into the den for a while."

Carolyn ignored her husband completely.

"The black community, as you call us, believes we should stick to our own race."

"Well, *I* think love is color blind. When two people meet and sparks fly, it doesn't matter if one person is green and the other yellow."

Carolyn rolled her eyes.

"Oh, please. That is such a naïve concept. Bless your heart."

Both Jason and his father reacted immediately.

Patience stood up as well. She'd had enough. How dare this woman, this *stranger*, insult her parents this way? It was none of her business if her mom hadn't stayed within her race when choosing a mate. Carolyn knew nothing about her family and had no right to judge. Who knew whether Jason's parents had a healthy marriage? The fact that they were both African-American didn't guarantee a happy union. Personally, she couldn't see how James put up with the arrogance this woman possessed.

She gathered her purse and strode purposefully to the front door.

"Thank you for an interesting evening," she yelled over her shoulder.

"What a witch," she added under her breath.

Jason held the door open as she burst through it with a vengeance. She could have beaten anyone down at that moment. She knew the amount of anger soaring through her body had given her superhuman strength. She could have jumped off a ten story building and survived. She wanted to punch something, or someone, right then and there. Jason, on the other hand, appeared to wither in the face of a storm. His shoulders were slumped over as he practically fell into his car.

It was after eleven when they turned onto the highway. Patience twirled one of her curls nervously, staring out the window. After ten minutes of silence, Jason finally broke the silence. He cleared his throat loudly.

"They *loved* you. I am so serious. And did you see how Jackson gawked at you the whole time? I mean, *how cute is that?* And Jessica thought you were her new friend. She may actually invite you over for a slumber party ..." He went on and on as they pulled up to her house. Obviously he was trying to take the focus off his mother.

"What about your mom?" she asked directly.

Pulling up to a red light, his hands gripped the steering wheel tightly. He turned slightly to face her.

"Believe it or not, she's a wonderful person. I don't know why she drilled you on your heritage tonight. I'm definitely asking her about it next time I see her."

She heard no conviction or emotion in his voice, which worried her. She wondered where his passion was. After all, Carolyn had insulted her upbringing. According to his mother, her parents had broken the rules by dating outside their race. Worse, the two had married. Carolyn did not hold her tongue when it came to important matters such as this. Her parents had made a huge mistake in Jason's mother's eyes. Patience was a mistake.

At her place, she sighed wearily, letting them both inside. On the one hand, she couldn't believe how different this experience was from Sam. She liked the fact that Jason wanted to share her with his family. Yet on the other hand, she hadn't expected Carolyn, a black woman, to be closed-minded. Worse yet, she was so confrontational about it.

Jason stayed over long enough to watch a little television. They avoided the subject of his mother the remainder of the evening. She had a mouthful to say but knew he didn't want to talk about it. Besides, they were both tired, and the subject matter was too delicate to discuss that late. She would definitely bring it up, however, and soon. If he planned on having her around his family, they needed to deal with this situation right away. She would not tolerate ignorance. Life was too short.

Walking hand in hand to the door, Patience had to admit silently how much she liked him. Being near him was intoxicating, which made it harder to believe Carolyn was his mother. It escaped her how someone so opinionated and hateful could raise a wonderful man. His father must have played a significant role in his upbringing.

Suddenly Jason pulled her close to him, so close it felt as if they had become one. He laid his head on her shoulder, inhaling her sweet-smelling shampoo. He kissed her neck, searching for the willpower he always bragged about to her. The last month had been a test of strength, for both of them. The few times things had almost gotten out of hand, he had had the restraint of a priest, insisting he wanted to take things slowly.

He kissed her longingly on the lips as she wrapped her arms around his neck. He was a great guy, and the two had fun together. It almost made her want to call Carolyn to convince her that she was a good person. The fact that she was biracial didn't make her an alien. Jason and the rest of the family adored her. She wondered why his mother's mind was already made up about her.

"Jason ... " she began.

He put a finger to her lips.

"Sweetheart, I know what you're thinking. Please don't worry about my mom. I'll handle her. I promise we'll have a long talk about you first thing in the morning."

Patience opened her mouth to say something else, but Jason quickly kissed her cheek, said good-bye to Rory, and left.

* * *

The couple talked for an hour on the phone the next morning. She was grading the last few test papers at the last minute when he called.

"What in the world are you doing calling me at this hour?" she asked with a big smile. He was supposed to be getting ready for work. She glanced at the clock to see that it was six a.m. She actually *did* have a few minutes to spare.

"I had to hear your voice before I started my day."

“Awww,” she purred, temporarily forgetting about the tests on the table. She got up to fix a bowl of cereal.

“That is so sweet. I’m glad you called, to tell the truth. I wanted to tell you again how much I enjoyed your family,” she said sincerely. It was true. His entire family, minus Carolyn, was delightful.

“Me, too. I had such a good time that I want to take you out tonight, too.”

He suddenly started laughing.

“What’s so funny?”

“Well, when I got home last night, there was a message from my sister Jaime. She went on and on about how cool you were and commanded me to bring you over again. Soon. But then Donovan called to ask how our night went, and I told him it was awesome, that I planned on taking you out again tonight. But he said there was some law about how guys aren’t supposed to call so soon after a date ... something about a three-day rule and if you break it, you’ll seem desperate.”

She laughed.

“Hmm, you definitely broke that rule! But I think I’m going to have to side with Jaime; I’m thrilled you called.”

“Really? I’m not being too pushy or aggressive?”

“Maybe a little desperate,” she joked. “But I think I can handle it.”

* * *

The weekend went by way too fast for both of them. Friday night, they went Rollerblading in Jason’s neighborhood, which was conveniently located near a basketball court and huge pond surrounded by a trail of concrete. There was plenty of room for biking, jogging, and other activities. They were the only two outside, as the weather was extremely cold. However, Texans rarely saw snow, so the ground was dry for skating. Both Patience and Jason had a high tolerance for forty degree temperatures, so they were fine.

Afterward, he cooked her dinner, which was awful. He’d attempted to grill steaks, steam some vegetables, and bake strawberry shortcake for dessert. But as she sat across the table from him, Patience wondered how she could magically make the food disappear without actually eating it. He was excited, so proud of his culinary skills, and he watched with anticipation as she took a hesitant bite of the rice. Clearly, cooking was not his forte, but he didn’t seem to know that.

As she slowly chewed her food, she closed her eyes for a moment.

“Mmmmm,” she hummed, hoping she looked and sounded convincing.

Opening her eyes, she tried to smile as the rice finally slid down her throat like sharp tacks.

Jason was grinning from ear to ear.

"It's good, huh?" He began eating after making sure she liked it.

It took her at least two minutes to cut the steak.

Maybe it's just tough. Surely it tastes good, she thought. *But what is that smell?*

She put the piece in her mouth and realized it not only looked and felt bad, but tasted bad as well.

"Excellent," she lied. He didn't have a dog she could sneak it to, and she was afraid to spit it out in a napkin, for fear of hurting his feelings.

By the grace of God, the phone rang. As soon as Jason rose to answer it, she spat the meat out and hurriedly gathered most of the food to put in a napkin.

"Hey, Jaime! What's up? As a matter of fact, she's sitting right here ... Okay ... Yeah, that's a great idea ..."

He talked to his sister a little longer before returning to the table.

"Wow, you ate fast!" he exclaimed with wide eyes.

"I know! It was just so good! I tried to wait for you but ..."

He waved his hands.

"No, no, that's all right. I'm glad you liked it. I'll have to cook for you more often."

She almost gagged and took a long drink of milk.

"My sister wants to know if we'd like to join her, Jimmy, and Jackson tomorrow. They're catching a matinee and maybe going shopping."

Patience smiled. "I'd love to."

* * *

Sunday night, Patience was on the phone with Jana, giving her a play-by-play of the entire weekend.

"He is wonderful, absolutely amazing! We had such a good time *all weekend long*! You know how when you spend so much time with someone too many days in a row, he has a tendency to get on your nerves? Well, not Jason! I miss him already. He's all the things I want in a guy, all rolled into one. He is smart, sexy, close to his family, and charming."

A sigh escaped her.

Jana giggled on her end.

"Yeah, everything except an award-winning chef!" The two girls laughed again. "I'm so happy for you. It's great that his family loves you as well. I know it makes things a lot easier for you."

They both thought of Sam.

"It does," said Patience. "I don't have to worry about being hidden and sneaking around all the time. It's great."

She hesitated a moment.

"Well, actually, I'm not sure his mother is too fond of me. On Thursday, she drilled me with questions during dinner, as if trying to find something wrong with me. When she couldn't, she waited until the kids had gone upstairs to drill me about my ethnicity. To make a long story short, she doesn't approve of interracial dating."

"I don't understand. Jason is black."

"I know. By interrogating me, Carolyn found out *I'm* biracial. She made it known that my parents should not have dated. She doesn't think blacks should date outside their race."

"You're kidding!"

Patience sighed. "I wish I was. When Jason and I went to pick up his siblings yesterday, she didn't acknowledge me until he'd called her on it. He was like, 'Mom, do you not see Patience standing here?' And his mother rolled her eyes and said, 'Of course, dear!' But she never really looked at me."

"What a drag!"

"Part of me wants to prove how wonderful a biracial person can be. I need to show her how wrong she is. But isn't that ridiculous? I mean, who has that kind of time? Part of me is furious with Jason for not standing up to her. Why do I have to fight this battle alone?"

Her best friend exhaled deeply.

"I think you should stick to your guns. Spend time with the family and just *be yourself.* Mrs. Peterson won't have a choice but to see how kind and perfect you are. She'll fall in love with you in no time, especially when she sees how happy you make her son. I'm sure she'll warm up to you."

But the following week, things had gotten worse. They tried having dinner again with Jason's parents on Tuesday, and it was disastrous. Patience had taken special time that evening to prepare a dessert from one of her new cookbooks. It was a triple chocolate cake with pieces of Oreo cookies sprinkled on top. There were white, milk, and dark chocolate swirls inside. Her mouth actually watered as she covered it with vanilla frosting. However, after the family had finished dinner and was preparing to cut the cake, Carolyn stated, "I already made a dessert for tonight."

Silence fell upon the room, and then Jason's father cleared his throat.

"Good! Then we can have *two* treats tonight. I hope no one's on a diet!"

His brothers and sisters laughed awkwardly, and Carolyn's eyes narrowed.

"To be honest, I'm not a huge chocolate fan."

Patience wiped her mouth with a napkin and pretended she didn't hear her.

"Mother! Why are you being so rude?" It was clear Jason was beginning to get irritated by his mother's rudeness. "Just try the damn cake!"

Jessica giggled and then covered her ears.

"Jason used a naughty word," she sang.

Patience placed her hand on his.

"It's okay."

She made eye contact with his mother.

"I didn't know what to make. I won't be offended if you don't try it." She tried to smile at the woman who loathed her.

Jason squeezed her hand. "No, it's not. I think my mom needs to sign up for Manners 101."

He made a point of cutting two slices of the cake.

"This is delicious! Next time, I want you to make me one with chocolate frosting!"

James agreed. "This is really good, especially the white chocolate."

For the next few minutes the family talked about other things as they enjoyed the dessert. Only Jimmy, the peacemaker, ate a piece of his mother's cheesecake. Carolyn sat at the table fuming but said nothing.

On Friday, Jason's family took Jessica to see *Disney on Ice*, and Jaime suggested they invite Patience. Everything was fine until halfway through the show. She and Jaime went to the restroom, and as Patience was washing her hands, Carolyn entered.

"Thanks again for inviting me, Mrs. Peterson. It's a lot of fun watching Jessica's face light up during the show."

Carolyn didn't respond as she closed the stall door. Jaime came out and was reapplying her lip gloss when her mother finished. Apparently Patience was blocking her path to the paper towels; Carolyn bumped into her pretty hard but didn't say anything. Jaime noticed.

"Mom!" She put her hands on her hips and glared at the woman who'd raised her.

"What is your problem? I'm sick of this! You've been nasty to Patience from the beginning, and I want it to stop!"

Her mother shrugged her shoulders, an insincere smile tugging at her lips.

"I apologize. You're right. I've just been in a bad mood lately, and your brother's, um, *friend,* has been the unlucky victim of my mood swings. I'm sorry, dear."

She then turned and exited the restroom.

"Thanks," said Patience. "I know why I rub your mom the wrong way, but there's nothing I can do about it."

The young girl still had her hands on her hips, looking unsatisfied with the results of her confrontation.

"You're welcome, but I didn't believe a word she said. She's not sorry for treating you like a dog. She just wanted to get out of here safely!"

Jaime reapplied her lipstick, her face suddenly serious.

"What do you mean, you know why my mother can't stand you?"

Patience decided to brush it off for now. There was no need of ruining the young girl's night. She'd find out soon enough.

"We'll talk about it later. Let's get out of here before restroom germs kill us!"

The two laughed. Jaime hugged her tightly.

"Well, at least the rest of the family likes you."

CHAPTER 8

Jason's sister Jessica called the next morning. It was Saturday, yet the phone rang at six o'clock.

"Hello?" she answered sleepily, trying to focus on her alarm clock.

Who in the world is calling at this hour? she thought.

"Um, hello, Miss Patience. Uh, this is Jessica."

"Who?"

"Jessica." It took Patience a moment to realize it was Jason's younger sister. She sat up as Rory looked at her from the foot of her bed.

She smiled into the phone.

"Well, hello, Miss Jessica. How are you this morning?" Rory jumped off the bed to bark at some birds chirping outside her window.

"What's that noise?"

"Oh, it's just my dog. He's trying to scare some birds away. They're not even doing anything to him."

They both laughed.

"What kind of dog is he?" Jason had told Patience what a big animal lover Jessica was.

"He's a lab. I adopted him from a shelter three years ago. He's pretty awesome."

"Does he like five-year-olds?"

"He *loves* kids of all ages," Patience assured her. "He is the friendliest, most lovable dog I know. Well, except to birds!"

"Awww," Jess sighed dramatically. "I wish my mom would let me have a dog ... or a cat ... or a horse ..." Her voice trailed off.

"Well, they're a lot of work. And horses are even more work." She got up to raise the blinds Rory was trying to destroy. He then followed her out to the kitchen. She could hear Jason's voice in the background then.

"Oh yeah!" the child said. "The reason I called is to inbite you to the carnival today. It's at our church."

"Invite," she heard Jason say.

"That's what I said," his sister told him a little too loudly. Patience held the phone away from her ear.

Jessica explained that there would be games, prizes, and candy.

"We're gonna have soooooo much fun! You just *gotta* come!"

She couldn't resist. The child was cute as a button. "What time does it start?"

Not that it mattered.

"Um ..." (pause) "Thirteen o'clock, I think."

Patience laughed.

"Perfect! I just happen to be free at that time."

"Yay!"

She could hear Jason telling Jess to give him the phone.

"But we're not finished yet," his sister informed him.

He mumbled something, and Jessica told her that they would pick her up at one o'clock.

* * *

As promised, Jason and Jessica knocked on her door at one. And when Jess saw Rory, she immediately let herself in and began playing with him. The dog began licking her face and hands, excited to see that a child had come to visit. He loved kids. They always allowed him to be wild and untamed without nagging and telling him to sit, roll over, shake, and get off the table.

"He's so cute!" Jessica squealed. She looked up at her brother. "Isn't he cute, Jay?"

Jason agreed and, stepping over the two new best friends, pulled Patience into his arms with a sigh.

"Are you sure you don't want a sister? You told me yourself that being an only child was lonely sometimes."

She smiled down at Jessica.

"I distinctly remember saying that *sometimes* it's boring. I don't think I have the energy for a five-year-old all the time. I'll just borrow yours," she whispered.

They kissed then, and she nuzzled his neck, breathing in his scent. He didn't have cologne on this time, but she loved the way he smelled. And looked.

They both jumped as his sister screamed again with delight. Rory was jumping up on her and trying to pull off her bracelet.

"Rory, stop that!" She pulled him off of the child. The last thing she needed was to rush her dog to the vet on a Saturday with a bracelet in his tummy. He tried to eat everything that was not tied down.

"It's okay," Jessica assured her. She looked up at her brother. "Please, can you ask Mommy to buy me a dog?"

"No way! Mom would shoot the messenger, believe me," he said with wide eyes.

Jessica looked terrified.

"Mommy has a gun?" She stood and held her arms out for him to pick her up.

"No, I didn't mean that she would really shoot me," he chuckled. "That's just a figure of speech," he said as he carried her in his arms.

Patience went to make sure all the lights were turned off as Jason continued to explain what he meant.

Ten minutes later, as they headed toward the highway, Jessica was still concerned.

"If you ask Mommy for a hamster, will she still shoot you dead? Hamsters are small. And we can get a friendly one that doesn't bite." She went on and on, so Jason finally turned the radio's volume up to drown her out. Patience laughed so hard her stomach hurt. She silently thanked her parents for not having more children.

They arrived at the church in good spirits, and she could already see tons of people walking around outside. It seemed to be a huge turnout. They had to park on the grass across the street.

Patience carried Jessica as they entered the building. She couldn't believe how elaborate the carnival was. There were different booths set up for games, snacks, and contests. At the far end of the building, she spotted Jason's parents working the concession stand. Popcorn, cotton candy, and hot dogs combined to make a mouthwatering smell in the room. Children were running, around carrying stuffed animals and balloons. A teen sat soaking wet in a dunking booth while people threw balls at the target. The church had gone all-out for this event, and it was nice.

"I'm hungry," Jessica stated. She was the boss, so they all headed toward the food area. On the way, they were stopped by Jason and Jessica's brother Jackson.

"Patience!" he yelled over the crowd as if she were the only one he saw. He broke away from his group of friends to hug her.

"Hi, Jackson." She smiled. He blushed and told her he was happy to see her.

"I'm hungry," Jessica broke into their reunion.

"Where's Jimmy?" Jason asked, ignoring Jess.

The twin waved a hand in dismissal.

"He snuck outside to talk to some girl he likes. She's in one of our classes. But if you ask me, the girls in our school are too immature." He looked adoringly at Patience. "I like older women."

Jason rolled his eyes.

"How embarrassing," he muttered, setting Jess down and grabbing her hand. "Let's go get you something to eat."

"Finally," his little sister said.

Patience and Jackson followed them through the crowd. He made small talk with her, asking what she thought of the cool weather and how long she was going to hang out with them. As walked up to the concession stand, Patience saw their dad handing out popcorn and chips while their mother refilled a container of straws. James spotted the group first.

"Patience! It's so good to see you!"

He walked from behind the counter to hug her.

"We didn't know you were coming. What a great surprise," he said, welcoming them. Carolyn hadn't looked up.

"Daddy, I'm so, so, so very hungry!" Jessica whined.

"All right, sweet pea, Daddy will take good care of you," he assured her as he went to fetch a hot dog. He handed Patience a bag of peanuts and a drink while Jason held up a hand signaling he didn't want anything.

Jason faced Carolyn.

"Mom, did you notice that my girlfriend is here?"

"Oh yes. Hello, dear," she said in a flat tone.

"Hi Mrs. Peterson. How are you?"

Carolyn busied herself by wiping off the counter top.

"She must not have heard me," Patience mumbled.

"She heard you," he said as he squeezed her hand lightly. "C'mon, let's go."

Jason's eyes were two slits as he glared at his mother.

James spoke up.

"Carolyn, what is the matter with you? Is this how we treat Jason's friends?" He crossed his arms over his chest. "You're being unbelievably rude."

Jessica and Jackson watched with interest as Carolyn threw the towel on the counter in a huff.

"I don't know what your problem is." She spat the words at her son. "What do you want me to do? I've been nice to your little friend. I don't know where this new attitude of yours is coming from, but I want it to be gone. Now."

"CAROLYN!" His father walked closer to her, but Jason spoke up.

"It's okay, Dad. Don't worry about it. We're leaving." Carolyn came around the counter, digging in her apron pocket for something.

Suddenly Jessica screamed.

"She's got a gun!"

There was a momentary pause, and then people around them suddenly started screaming, diving behind tables and chairs. Carolyn's mouth flew open in shock and disbelief. Patience was knocked over by a middle-aged man running past her. Everyone was out of control, and complete chaos took over the church. Jason reached down to help Patience up while James immediately grabbed Jess. They overheard a teenage girl on her cell with 911, giving them the address of the church in a panicky voice.

Jessica tightly squeezed her father's neck with tears in her eyes.

"Mommy's gonna shoot Jason! He told me so," she sobbed. "It's in her pocket!!"

"What are you talking about?" Carolyn's eyes blazed with fury. She was enraged at the scene unfolding, and the child shrank back from her into James' arms. Carolyn lowered her voice slightly as people scurried around them. Jason tried to calm everyone down but to no avail.

His mother was an inch from his face in three seconds. "What's going on?" Her forehead was moist with sweat, and her hands were clenched into fists at her side.

Before Jason could answer, they were approached by one of the deacons of the church.

"Mr. and Mrs. Peterson," Brother Mason began cautiously. His eyes were focused on Carolyn's hands, which were still at her sides. "May I ask what's going on here? Clearly, you have no weapons." He smiled with trembling lips. He held up his hands toward the crowd, gesturing to those who were panicked that everything was okay.

Jessica was still crying, and Brother Mason touched her arm.

"It's all right, Miss Jessica. Everything's going to be just fine."

"Is it?" Carolyn looked as if she were ready to blow up the church. "Just what the hell is going on?"

In a shaky voice, Jessica recounted the story of how Jason told her that their mother was going to shoot him. James shook his head as he listened. They could hear the sirens getting closer as Jessica spoke.

" ... and Mommy doesn't like Patience ... She is so mad all the time ... Is Jason going to Heaven when he dies?" The five-year-old kept chattering as Patience decided to speak up.

"Jessica, your mommy would never shoot anyone. She's a wonderful person, and no matter how upset she gets, she would never hurt anyone. I promise nothing like that is ever going to happen."

Jason put his arm around her, and they all headed toward the front of the building.

Carolyn was still steaming about the whole incident, and she made certain everyone knew it. Patience tuned her out after hearing " ... and I have *never* been so humiliated in my whole life! Jason, we have a lot of talking to do when we get home!"

A couple of the ministers and the pastor were at one of the side doors explaining everything to the police. A bystander told them what he had overheard the Petersons saying.

Jessica jumped when a booming voice suddenly came on the loudspeaker overhead.

"May I have your attention please? This is Brother Barry, one of the youth ministers here at the church. We want to inform you that everything is okay, just a misunderstanding," he began.

* * *

The Petersons left shortly after the incident. The carnival had resumed when the police finally left, and the crowd was in good spirits. A couple of members of the church had even approached the family, joking about the whole scene that had unfolded. One of the deacons even said how much more exciting the carnival had been.

"All we needed was a camera crew. Why, we could've been on television or something!"

"Yeah," the church secretary piped in. "I've always wanted to meet Oprah."

But Carolyn and James were not amused, and Patience had a throbbing headache.

Jessica was getting cranky, as well. She had missed her afternoon nap, so she was physically and emotionally exhausted.

Jason and Patience sat in silence as he pulled out of the parking lot. Jess falling asleep in the backseat. The radio was the only sound in the vehicle, which was fine with Patience. She had had enough. It angered her to always have to be the nice one, the bigger person who let everyone run over her. She shouldn't have allowed Carolyn to mistreat her anytime, anyplace. Even if there was something about Patience that irked her, his mother didn't have to be so nasty about it.

She crossed her arms over her chest, sighing deeply as she looked out the window. She felt Jason's hand resting supportively on her arm. When they reached the Petersons' house, he leaned toward her. She reached over, and the two sat in the car for a while holding one another. Jess was snoring behind them.

Patience allowed the tears to fall. Jason reached up and gently brushed them away.

"Sweetheart, I am so sorry about all of this. My mom is a monster, and I'm letting her have it after I drop you off at your place."

She opened her mouth to respond, but before she knew it, he was scooping Jess up into his arms to carry her into the house.

Patience felt her cell vibrating as she waited for him to return.

"How's it going?" Jana whispered on her end. She was such a wonderful friend.

"Terrible. Why are you whispering?"

Jana laughed. "Oh, I just thought you were still with the family and couldn't talk, but I don't know why *I'm* whispering! Where are you?"

"I'm sitting outside their house, waiting for Jason to take me home. I'll call you tonight."

He soon returned, informing her that Jessica was asking where she was when he laid her on the couch.

"She really does love you," he reassured her.

"She wanted to come with me to take you home, but her eyes kept closing. She's so tired! Normally Jess would have whined and run back out here, but the poor child didn't have the strength."

"Did anyone say anything when you walked in?"

"My dad wanted you to come in so he could apologize for my mom, but I told him no. One, you've been through enough for one day, and two, *she* needs to apologize for her own behavior."

They chatted awhile, and Jason invited her to go ice-skating the next day.

"Haven't you seen enough of me already? We've been together almost every minute this past week," she teased.

He kissed her hard on the lips.

"I wish it could be every second."

* * *

Jason was late picking Patience up the next day, which was unlike him. She usually teased him about always needing to be on time everywhere, even to parties. She turned on the stereo, heading into the kitchen to feed Rory.

She decided to call her mother, whom she hadn't seen in a couple of days. Sharise was very excited to hear from her. While talking to her, Patience glanced at the clock, realizing that thirty minutes had gone by and still no sign of him. *Maybe I should call*, she thought, beginning to worry.

She hung up with her mom and went to look out the front window, just as he was pulling up.

She met him outside and opened his car door for him.

"What's up?" she greeted, trying to sound casual. He leaned against his car with his arms crossed.

"Hi. Sorry I'm so late. Something came up."

He looked a little distracted as he leaned forward to give her a peck on the cheek.

"That's fine. Did you try to call?"

She wondered if he had called her cell. Sometimes she didn't hear it in her purse.

"No. By the time I realized what time it was, I decided I'd better just hurry and get here."

He hesitated for a second, looking at something just over her shoulder. "So, are you ready?"

Patience ran in to gather her things and lock up the house. She couldn't put her finger on it, but Jason just wasn't acting like himself. The drive to the rink was awkward; every time she would ask a question, he would answer with just a quick yes or no. If she asked him something that required more words in the answer, he would still make it a short reply.

Finally, she couldn't take it anymore.

"Is there something bothering you?"

Stopping at a red light, he told her that he was fine.

"Look at me, Jason."

Rolling his eyes, he turned in his seat slightly toward her. He looked as if something was definitely on his mind, but she just couldn't read his face.

"I know we haven't been dating long, but I still know you well enough to see that you're not acting like yourself."

The car behind them honked, signaling that the light had turned green. Neither of them had noticed.

Reaching for her hand, he squeezed it affectionately.

"I guess I'm just a little tired, that's all."

"Well, do you want to take a rain check on the ice-skating? We don't have to go today," she offered.

But he insisted on keeping their plans. Patience decided to let it go. Whatever it was that was occupying his thoughts, he obviously didn't want to talk about it.

CHAPTER 9

The Christmas tree lights were all tangled up. Patience sighed with relief when she finally undid the last knot in the cord. She could not believe there was only one week left until Christmas. She had been so extremely busy with work, family, and friends that she was just putting her tree up.

She took a sip of eggnog, savoring the sweet taste. She loved this time of year: the coziness of her house, the nonstop hustle and bustle of the crowds shopping for loved ones, and of course the fresh baked cookies her mom made every year.

She listened as the wind howled outside, then stepped up on her footstool to hang the angel on the top of the tree. Rory was crunching on something. Hopping off the stool, she bent low to retrieve an ornament from his mouth. She was scolding him when the phone rang. It was Jana.

Her friend always became very stressed out during the holidays. Patience tried to make sure to spend a little more time with her, inviting her over to help with decorating or just to watch old movies. Jana's parents had been divorced for several years, and Patience knew she carried around a tremendous load of guilt. Jana had confided in her that she never spent enough time with either side of the family, especially during Thanksgiving and Christmas.

They were going to the mall that day to finish up their shopping. She also wanted to get some advice about Jason, who was still acting weird toward her.

The girls were prepared for the crowds at all the shops, knowing that there would be many people who waited until the last minute, just as they had. After getting bumped into for the hundredth time, Patience decided they should go get something to eat. Sitting down at the food court, they both sighed with relief.

"Whew, I wasn't sure we'd make it out alive!" Jana exclaimed. She took a bite of her hamburger, suddenly starving.

"I know! Did you see that lady almost knock me over and then give *me* a dirty look? Some people are so rude."

They talked and ate, watching as kids ran wild while their parents tried to catch up with them.

Jana suddenly looked over at her with concern in her eyes.

"So what's going on with Jason?"

"For the last week or two, he just hasn't been himself. When we are on the phone, I seem to do all the talking. If we go out, he's usually late picking me up with a real attitude. And he always seems so distant. I just don't understand what's up with him."

"Have you talked to him about it?"

Patience took a sip of water, her mouth dry.

"I'm not sure how many times I've asked him if something is wrong. He brushes me off most of the time, or feeds me some silly excuse like he's tired or that I'm imagining things."

Jana looked at her friend with sympathy.

"I am so sorry. I know he cares about you. Maybe he's going through something at work. You know how guys are; they usually don't want to talk about their feelings. He probably thinks he should work it out himself. Give him time. He'll come around."

"You're probably right. But I can't help wondering if his mom has something to do with this. We brushed that problem aside, temporarily putting a Band-Aid on it. So we never dealt with it." She shrugged.

Jana exhaled slowly.

"Right, I totally forgot about that. But Jason's a big boy. He likes you, so he's not going to let Carolyn ruin a good thing."

"I don't know. They're pretty close."

The two sat in silence for a while, eating their lunches and people watching.

"I don't know which situation is worse: being hidden by my boyfriend because his parents are prejudiced or dealing with an overprotective, obnoxious mother who doesn't like me because I'm mixed."

Jana smiled sympathetically.

"If I were in your shoes, I'd pick the first one. For me, it's much easier to deal with something I can't see. I would never have to meet Sam's parents. We could date, get engaged, marry, and have five children without them ever knowing!" She laughed.

"You're crazy!" Patience never knew what would come out of her friend's mouth.

"I'm serious. I am *way* too aggressive myself to deal with Carolyn on a daily or even weekly basis. We'd butt heads constantly, and I swear one of us would end up in the hospital after she called me a zebra."

"That is hilarious. You're absolutely right. My stomach is always in knots when I'm around her."

* * *

Patience let herself into her parents' house, dropping a couple of the packages she balanced in her arms. Her mother ran to help her, shaking her head.

"What have I told you about trying to carry everything from the car in one trip? For one thing, it's dangerous. A predator could just come and snatch you away from all of us!"

Patience laughed and went to place the presents under her parents' tree. She decided to just agree with her mother this time.

"Sorry Mom. That was an incredibly naïve thing to do. It definitely won't happen again." They went into the kitchen to start baking desserts for her father's company party.

Patience's cell phone rang, and it was Jason. She hadn't heard from him in two days. When she answered, he didn't greet her. He got right to the point.

"We need to talk."

Her heart skipped a beat as she walked into her mother's sunroom for privacy.

"Well, hello, stranger! It's nice to hear from you today."

He exhaled loudly, beginning again.

"Hi, how are you? Busy?"

"No, not at all. I'm just bonding with my mom right now." She smiled and continued, trying to prolong the inevitable. "My mother is so crazy in love with me! She always complains that we don't spend enough time together, even when I spend a whole weekend with her ..." Her voice trailed off.

"That's nice. Listen, I was wondering if we could meet somewhere and talk. There are some things I want to explain to you. I know I've been acting weird lately, and you deserve an answer to the questions you've been asking."

Twenty minutes later, Patience was sitting across from Jason at Brew, staring intently into his brown eyes. Taking a sip of his latte, he began.

"Patience, you know how much I adore you ..."

She felt her palms start to sweat and wiped them on a napkin. With absolute certainty, she knew he was breaking up with her.

" ... You are the most caring, giving, thoughtful girl I have ever dated. Please believe me when I tell you that this past month has been wonderful."

Just get to the point, she thought impatiently.

He reached for her hand across the table and held it while looking into her eyes.

"I'm not ... we can't ... I can't see you anymore."

He squeezed her hand lightly, and when she looked into his eyes, she saw regret.

She waited for him to continue, feeling a lump in her throat forming. She couldn't understand why she was so upset. The signs of a breakup had been written on the wall for the past two weeks, so this conversation was no surprise.

Why in the world is it affecting me like this? she wondered.

"My family thinks you're a great girl, especially my brothers and sisters. You know that they think you hung the moon. We had so much fun that night you met them. And my dad told me that he couldn't imagine a better girlfriend for me."

"But your mother doesn't think I'm good enough for you," she finished for him.

"She says you're not black enough."

When Patience heard this, everyone in the coffee shop seemed to disappear, leaving only the two of them sitting there. For a second, she seemed to forget there were others around them.

"Carolyn is a racist!" she stated, her voice raised a few octaves. The older couple sitting at the table next to theirs turned to look.

Jason leaned forward in his seat, clearly embarrassed by her reaction.

"Would you mind lowering your voice?" he almost whispered.

"Why, am I embarrassing you? I don't care what these people in here think! I've had it!"

The man making coffee stopped to listen with interest.

Jason squirmed in his seat, contemplating whether to leave or try to reason with her.

Narrowing his eyes, he glared at her.

"She most certainly is *not* racist! How dare you say that?! Just because she believes races shouldn't mix doesn't mean she's prejudiced. She has white friends, ya know. Even her best friend in high school was white. So don't sit here and judge her ..."

"*What?* You're telling *me* not to judge? What about *her*? From the moment I set foot in that house, she made it clear I was a horrible person because I'm biracial. She has been nothing but rude, damning my parents for being together. You were supposed to talk to her about it, but I guess it wasn't a priority, huh?"

He sat silently.

"I thought you liked me enough to fight for this relationship," Patience continued. "I can't take on this battle alone. I refuse to spend time with someone who cuts me down all the time, not because I'm a thief or a lunatic, but because I have a black mother and white father."

"I am so sorry. I know this hurts, but I have to be honest with you. My mom likes you and says that you seem like a nice girl. She's just always wanted me to be with someone who is more in touch with her African heritage."

"I don't believe this! *You're* not even in touch with your roots. We listen to alternative music, and you've got more white friends than black ones."

"Patience, you're being unfair. She is just set in her ways, that's all."

His voice shook with emotion while trying to get her to understand.

"I'm caught between a rock and a hard place. Please try to see my side, sweetie."

He sighed, his eyes filling with fresh tears.

"It's been really difficult trying to prevent my mom from killing you. Don't get me wrong, I love our relationship, which is why I've been willing to fight in this war. But, well, I'm starting to think there will never be peace."

Patience nodded in agreement.

"I've always known that. And I swear, I'm so surprised I haven't developed a stomach ulcer from trying to please your mother. I just wish we'd had this conversation a little earlier before I got so attached to your brothers and sisters."

She stood up to leave, grabbing her purse and keys.

"Can you at least come by tomorrow to pick up the gifts I bought for all of you? I really do want y'all to have them." She forced a smile.

Jason was staring down at the table.

"Sure. That was very nice of you."

Before Patience left, she asked another question.

"Can I just give you my opinion on something?"

She saw the tears slowly falling as he nodded yes.

"You have a wonderful family. I really admire the way all of you are so close to and open with each other. Yet it's a shame you allow your mother to control your life. I mean, what about your wants and desires? We were pretty happy, or at least I thought we were. Now you're willing to throw me away because of what your mother says. How are you going to be happy when you can't choose your own mate? Well, at least when you meet the next girl, maybe your mom can go with the two of you on your first date. Then you can find out sooner if she has potential."

Everyone in the coffee shop started clapping after her speech. One girl who was standing in line yelled, "He doesn't deserve you!"

Patience wiped her sweaty palms on her jeans, trying to regain her composure. She wasn't accustomed to making scenes in public. At that point, however, she didn't care. She was sick to death of these situations where the men in her life only cared what *others* thought.

Not waiting around for a reaction from Jason, she grabbed her purse, turned on her heels, and stormed out.

* * *

"You have got to be kidding me. Please tell me you're making this up," Jana said in her usual hyper way. "And the people started clapping afterwards? I don't believe you. Why do you make these stories up?"

Jana was shaking her head in disbelief. Sitting in her friend's apartment, Patience had relaxed somewhat after such a long day. She sought refuge at Jana's place after the scene at Brew with Jason. Luckily, her friend had been home to comfort her. Her cat seemed to feel the sadness in the air, jumping up on Patience's lap swiftly. She could feel the cat purring, and she pulled her closer to snuggle.

"Yes, it's all true, word for word. Can you believe this crap? First Sam tries to keep me hidden from his family, and then Jason breaks up with me because of his mom. How crazy can it get?"

She burst into tears, and Jana hugged her.

"It's going to be okay. One day you'll meet someone who wants to be with you, showing you off to the whole world with pride. You are such a wonderful person, and someone is out there looking for you. I know it's easy for me to say, but try to be patient. Your time will come; you just have to believe."

"But what have I ever done to deserve this? All my life I've tried to treat people the way I want to be treated. It didn't matter whether they were black, white, or green. My parents taught me that everyone is the same on the inside. We all bleed, we all have organs and veins and muscles, and ..." Her voice trailed off as the tears fell. Jana's cat scurried away after feeling the tears land on her fur.

Patience got up to grab some Kleenex, stopping for a moment to look at the photo of Jana and her boyfriend, Scott. They looked perfect together, with his arm draped casually around her shoulders. He was a very attractive guy, and his dark brown complexion was flawless. Jana's skin tone was slightly lighter than his, and for a moment, Patience envied their relationship. She knew they had disagreements every now and then, but at least they didn't encounter any strife for being interracial. When the two of them went out in public, they didn't have to worry about getting glared at or snubbed. And if Scott wanted to take Jana to his parents' house, he could.

"Are you okay?"

Patience returned to the present.

"No, I am definitely not okay. But I do feel better, thanks to you." She smiled through her tears at her best friend as the phone rang. Jana answered it as Patience sat back down on the couch.

"Oh, hey, Cole! What are you up to?" She paused. "Yes, she's over here."

Jana looked at Patience, who was waving her arms and shaking her head that she wasn't there. She didn't feel like talking to Cole or anyone else, for that matter.

"Um, I mean no, she's actually not. She *was* here a minute ago, but she just left."

Jana and Cole chatted a little longer, and then she let him go, a questioning look in her eyes.

"I know what you're going to say," Patience told her before she could hound her with questions, "and I promise I'll call him later. I just need a little time to myself."

The tears threatened to fall again, but she fought them with all her might.

The next day, Patience waited for Jason to drop by to pick up the gifts, but he was a no-show. She tried calling several times and kept getting his voice mail. Placing her phone back on the receiver, she walked over to the pile of presents in her foyer, wondering what to do with them. She'd spent quite a bit of money on his family. There were gift cards for the twins and Jaime, and a Barbie doll that happened to be a veterinarian for Jessica. It came with tiny dogs and cats. It was cute, and she knew Jess would love it. Then there was a nice shirt for Jason, plus a gift card to their favorite movie theater.

She had no choice but to return it all. Something inside let her know she wasn't ever going to see him again.

CHAPTER 10

On Christmas Eve, Patience went to Jason's favorite department store to return the shirt she had bought him. At the last minute, she'd decided to save the others' gifts. They'd done absolutely nothing wrong, so it wasn't fair to punish them. Maybe she could just have the packages delivered to them.

The past three days had been torture for her. She felt as if this were a cruel joke being played, and she just knew there were no tears left to be shed. Jason hadn't called at all; he'd made a clean break with her because of his mother. She briefly wondered what the rest of his family had thought about the decision to dump her. She had a feeling his siblings were disappointed, but there was nothing she could do about it. In a weird way, this was a much more difficult situation than with Sam. He had really liked her, fallen for her even, but his parents were prejudiced. They had not even met her, so it wasn't a rejection of her as a person. He couldn't bring *any* other girl home that wasn't white, so in a way, she didn't take it personally.

But Jason's family *had* met her. His mother had rejected Patience's whole being, her personality, her looks, *everything* about her, concluding she wasn't a good enough person for her son. She snubbed her because she wasn't African-American. Patience's parents had raised her to have a healthy sense of self, making sure she knew she was capable of achieving anything in life. However, she wasn't Superwoman. This event had blown her self-esteem.

To the saleslady's dismay, Patience began bawling after getting her money back on Jason's shirt. The clerk sympathetically handed her a tissue from behind the counter. Utterly embarrassed, she found the nearest restroom to regain her composure. She hastily brushed the tears away, pausing to stare at her reflection. She wasn't used to crying in public.

"How could I have been so blind?" Patience said aloud.

Her mind raced as she stood alone in the department store's restroom. Dabbing her eyes again, she found it difficult to grasp the concept of prejudice. She wondered why it was so hard to fit in with both blacks and whites. In movies, television and real life, she witnessed white people's intolerance and black people's reverse racism. However, it was hard for her to fathom Carolyn's prejudice against *her*.

Patience grabbed a brush from her purse and began tackling her curly hair with a vengeance. Brush after brush, stroke after stroke, she tried straightening the brown curls she loved and hated. Fresh tears began to fall as her scalp became red with irritation. She didn't care. She was sick to death of being judged because of her looks. Her skin was too light. Her lips were too thin. She wasn't hip enough. She was a white girl trapped in a black girl's body. She was a black girl trapped in a white girl's body. Turning quickly on her heel, she threw the brush against the wall with such force it broke in half.

"Ugh!"

With a huge sigh, Patience finally had had enough. Her eyes burned tremendously, but she felt better. There was something therapeutic about pulling one's hair out in the restroom while crying like a baby. She'd had a slight temper tantrum, allowing her thoughts to run wild and illogically. She knew her behavior was childish, yet she smiled as she exited the store.

Fifteen minutes later, Patience was in her car heading to her parents' house. She was not looking forward to her mom's concerned questions. This was the first time her mother would be seeing her after the breakup. She was tempted to call and cancel, feigning a headache or some illness. But she knew Sharise would end up rushing over to her house to nurse her.

When she arrived, her mother took one look at her and drew in a sharp breath.

"What on earth?" she began.

Patience tried unsuccessfully to distract her mother and asked, "Where's Dad?"

"He ran to the grocery to pick up some things. Honey, you look like crap! What in the world happened?"

Patience followed her mom into the kitchen to make some hot cocoa. Sharise knew that whatever it was, they would need something warm and soothing to drink. Sitting down at the breakfast table, she watched her mom flutter around the kitchen, throwing some Christmas cookies on a small plate. When the cocoa was ready, her mom dumped what seemed like a hundred marshmallows into her cup.

Sharise sat across from her, eyeing her daughter carefully. There were dark circles under Patience's eyes, and a pimple had made itself at home on her chin. She looked like she had been crying for days, and her hair was thrown haphazardly in a ponytail. Her mom instinctively rose and engulfed her in a much needed hug, feeling the tears fall on her shoulder as she held her.

"Baby, what is it? Can you talk about it?"

Patience told her the whole story, starting with the incident at the museum with Sam and ending with Jason's break-up at Brew. She saw tears in her mom's eyes as she finished talking. For a long moment, neither of them said a word. Patience just knew she would end up dehydrated from all of the crying she'd done, but she didn't know how to stop. She felt hopeless, insecure, and lonely.

Her mother looked at her with all the love she had for her.

"You know, I have been so blessed in my life to not have encountered this particular problem. All my life, I dated within my race. Your father was the first white man I met whom I wanted to have a relationship with. And it just so happened that we fell in love and got married. When we met, he courted me openly, always taking me to plays, museums, the park, out to dinner ... He was always showing me off. And after one month of dating, I met your grandparents. So I can't sit here pretending to know what you're going through or how you feel. I can only sympathize and feel your pain because I love you."

"I know, Mom, and I appreciate everything you do for me. You are always there to pick up the pieces when I'm hurt." She thought about something then and looked at her mom with pleading eyes.

"Please don't tell Dad about this. He would freak out. You know how protective he is of me. I may tell him one day but not right now. It's still too fresh, and I don't want to have to worry about seeing on the news how he killed one of them."

They both laughed, her mother reassuring her that it would be their secret for now. Finishing up the cocoa and cookies, they went into the living room to watch some old movies.

Sharise picked out *Casablanca* to enjoy first, and by then her father had returned with at least ten bags of groceries. When the movie ended, her mom handed her a couple of presents from under the tree to open early. She told Patience she deserved it, winking at her privately as she gave her the first gift.

* * *

On Christmas Day, Patience was feeling somewhat better about the situation. She had slept a little more the night before, and she put some makeup on to hide the dark circles. She spent most of the day at her parents', bringing Rory along against her father's wishes. They had gifts for him, but John wanted her to just take them to him. Her dad always gave her a hard time about being too easy on the dog, letting him tear up everything in sight. But she just ignored him, laughing at his expression as Rory tagged along behind her into the house.

Patience spent the latter half of the day with Cole and his family, which she loved. His parents were so open and loving, and she got along great with his brother. Although she was stuffed from her mother's cooking, Patience decided to go ahead and have more turkey at Cole's. His mom would not take no for an answer, piling dressing, mashed potatoes, and pasta salad onto her plate. After dinner and the gift exchange, Cole and Steven took her to a movie.

She asked about Camryn, but they had broken up recently.

"Any particular reason why?" she asked him in the car.

Cole shrugged noncommittally.

"Nah, I just got bored with her."

"Cole! Are you serious?" Her jaw dropped in disbelief. He laughed and shook his head.

"Of course I'm not serious, Patience! What kind of guy do you think I am? Camryn met someone else, and she was seeing him behind my back."

"I am so sorry! How did you find out?" She tried to search his face, but since he was driving, she could see only his profile.

"I dropped by her house unannounced to surprise her with a birthday gift. He answered the door, and the rest is history."

Patience didn't know what to say. Steven was in the backseat texting his girlfriend, but he looked up when he heard what they were talking about.

"I didn't like her anyway," he chimed in. "Man, you were too good for her. Camryn was too sure of herself, always acting like people were supposed to bow down to her."

Cole laughed at his brother.

"You didn't even see her very often! She only came to our parents' two times when you were over there!"

Steven was nineteen and had his own apartment. He bragged that he was independent, yet their parents still paid for everything. Cate, his mother, complained constantly that he came over only to raid the refrigerator or do laundry. Steven didn't deny the accusations, either.

"Well, twice is enough to get to know somebody. And she was all wrong for you, trust me."

"I am very sorry, Cole. She seemed nice to me," Patience interjected.

"It's okay. I'm fine. It's her loss."

Patience envied the way guys seemed to just move on after things ended with a girl. Cole definitely wasn't acting; he really *was* in a good mood and happy.

On the other hand, she knew that she would be down in the dumps the next day. The only reason she was feeling better temporarily was the distractions the holidays provided. It was good to be surrounded by friends at times like these. If nothing else, they took her mind off her problems.

* * *

After the movie, they all went back to Cole's parents' house in good spirits. Patience was a little jumpy, however, considering the boys had convinced her to see the latest horror film, *Someone's Watching.* She knew without a doubt there would be no sleep for her in the near future. Steven showed no sympathy. He kept tickling her neck from the back seat, making her scream.

"Stop it, Steven! Cole, please get your brother to leave me alone."

Cole turned in his seat towards her, exasperated.

"Will you *please* stop screaming every five minutes? You're gonna make me hit a car or a tree."

When he stopped the car at an intersection, Patience jumped out, insisting she and Steven trade places.

"You've got to be kidding me. Patience, you know it's me back here. Come on, get a grip, would you?"

She yanked open his door as the light turned green and several cars behind them began honking. Steven went ahead and cooperated, and ten minutes later they were back at their parents'. The smell of freshly baked pumpkin bread met them as soon as they opened the door. Cole's father was already on his second piece, and Patience sat across from him, waiting for someone to cut her a slice of the delicious dessert.

The night passed way too quickly for her. She thoroughly enjoyed Cole's family. She felt particularly close to his mother, Cate. Ever since elementary school, there had been a special bond between them. Cate had admitted to Patience that she was the daughter she had never had. While pregnant with Steven, the doctors told them he was a girl. Tom and Cate were very excited, purchasing a nursery that consisted of everything pink. All of their friends brought cute little dresses, bows, and baby dolls to the baby showers. They'd even picked out a name: Cassidy.

In the delivery room five months later, Steven entered the world among amazed parents and doctors. They had to rethink everything from a name to a nursery, yet once they'd overcome the initial shock, unconditional love for him sank in.

When Cate discovered years later what Cole had done to Patience that first day of school, she was horrified. Full of remorse, she'd taken him over to their house to apologize. Patience remembered how his mom had tried to help Sharise scrub the sand out of her hair. Almost instantly, Cate became a second mother to her while also developing a friendship with Sharise.

Patience finished up her second slice of pumpkin bread as the two women laughed while revisiting those memories.

Later that night, Cole drove Patience and Rory home. She asked him if he could stay for a while. She didn't want to enter the dark house alone after seeing that horrible movie. He felt sorry for her, so he ended up staying an hour or so, distracting her with funny stories about his kids at school. They both loved teaching and had always been able to call one another after a hectic day. Sometimes if a parent was hard to deal with, she could count on him to make her laugh and forget about the situation. Or if he needed advice about how to handle a tough student, he would ask Patience how he should handle him or her.

Being the empathetic friend, Cole advised her to sleep with the light on that night, knowing she was pretty scared. After he left, Patience went through the house, turning on every light. She'd never been a big fan of horror movies or television shows about unsolved mysteries. She was such a visual person, and it was difficult to erase images in her head that she'd seen. Climbing into her warm bed, she kissed Rory on the top of his furry head as he lay beside her.

PART III: TRIPP

CHAPTER 11

The class was silent as Patience waited for someone, anyone, to answer her question. They were reading The Epic of *Gilgamesh*, which was one of her favorite literary works. Once could hear a pin drop in the quiet classroom. One of her students, Claire, finally raised her hand. Pointing to her with a smile, Patience felt relief that at least one of her students was listening.

"Um, one of the differences between *Gilgamesh* and the Bible would be that in *Gilgamesh*, there are many gods and goddesses. Yet in the beginning of the Bible, there is only one God, right?"

"Very good, Claire! I can see that *someone* has been keeping up with the required reading."

The class moaned in unison, and Patience rolled her eyes. It had been like this ever since they had returned from the Christmas break. She was sure her students were sick of hearing her drone on and on about different literary devices. She felt sorry for them because even *she* didn't particularly want to be there. Sometimes she felt the urge to let everyone out of class early, more for her benefit than theirs. This was especially true during the holidays.

"Now, can anyone tell me how these two works are alike?" Again, Claire raised her hand. Patience pretended not to see her, trying to give someone else a chance. One of the students was staring out the window, obviously a thousand miles away from the discussion. Patience decided to bring him back to the lecture.

"Zach, can you compare *Gilgamesh* and the Bible for me, please?"

"Hmmm ... well, they're both in our textbook," he answered as the class laughed.

Patience motioned for them to calm down and then tried a different tactic.

"Okay, Zach, if you get this question right, I will let all of you leave early today. How does that sound?"

His posture straightened immediately, his brow furrowing while he thought.

"Well, Miss McKlendon, both stories have a boat in them. God gives Noah measurements to build a boat, and Utnapishtim does the same for Gilgamesh."

"I knew it! You are very intelligent and just needed a little prompting! Class is officially dismissed!"

She had to hurry to the front of the room for her safety. The kids seemed to grow wings, flying out of the classroom so fast.

Patience decided to run a few errands on her way home that day. It was beautiful outside. Although the weather required a jacket, the sun shined brightly, and the wind wasn't too strong. She bought just enough groceries to tide her over until the weekend, and after that, she ran to the post office to buy a book of stamps. She went to the pet store afterwards because Rory was completely out of treats.

Smiling to herself, she wasn't sure if he deserved them or not. On the way home, she found herself craving pound cake, so she stopped by Brew to indulge herself a little.

The place was nearly deserted when she stepped inside. An elderly man sat at one of the tables reading the newspaper, and two women in workout clothes occupied another table, eating muffins. She suppressed a giggle, being reminded of the times she and Jana would work out at the gym and then bake cookies later on to reward themselves.

Patience pondered how many slices of pound cake she should get when the young man behind the counter asked what he could get for her.

"I'll have two pieces of the pound cake, please." She knew that she would eat ten if she could, so she'd better get just two.

Putting them in a bag, he asked how her day was going.

"I'm having a great day! How about you?"

Smiling, he answered, "It's gotten better. This place was packed earlier, and we were understaffed. But now I can breathe." He sighed dramatically with relief.

She decided to eat the slices there and sat at a table for two, staring out the window. She loved the atmosphere of the place, and was even familiar with some of the regular customers. She also knew what times to come in that matched her mood. If she wanted to relax in a mellow atmosphere, she would go at night. However, sometimes she liked to people watch and laugh at the kids. Saturdays were good for that. She went back up to the counter for a drink, and the clerk asked what her name was.

"Patience," she told him.

"That's an unusual name. I like it, though." He handed her bottled water, extra napkins and another fork "just in case you drop it," he told her.

Thanking him, she went back to her seat. He grabbed a rag and went to clean off the table beside her.

"So, what made your parents name you Patience?"

She smiled.

"When they were dating, they each knew the other wanted children. As soon as they married, my mom and dad started trying to conceive, with no luck. Years passed, and after the doctors kept insisting there was nothing wrong with either of them, they decided to just keep trying, never giving up. After five years, my mom found out that their prayers had been answered. She went to the Ob/Gyn and he told her the good news: she was pregnant. My dad decided to name me Patience because they'd waited so long for me to get here."

"That's cool. I like hearing stories like that," the young man said.

Patience took the last bite of her cake and watched as a mother helped her little boy pull the hood of his jacket back up on his head outside.

The two chatted a while longer. When she rose to leave, the clerk informed her that she never asked what his name was.

"What is your name?" she asked him, laughing out loud.

"Tripp."

"That's different, too. No wonder you paid so much attention to mine!"

He told her that he was born Michael Anthony Cunningham after his grandfather. He started walking at nine months, his parents so proud because he was obviously advanced. However, as he grew, his clumsiness became apparent to everyone. He bumped into walls, fell off of the furniture, and tripped over everything from toys to lint.

It continued all through elementary school, accident reports constantly being sent home by teachers. As a joke, his father gave him the nickname Trip. It stuck, and soon everyone began using it. He even got a kick out of it, so at the tender age of eleven, he unofficially changed his name, adding the extra *p* at the end for good measure.

"I like it," she approved. Just then, she remembered she had bought a couple of frozen food items at the grocery. She told Tripp good-bye as she hurried out the door, and all he could do was shake his head and get back to work.

* * *

The remainder of January proved to be busy for Patience. She filled out paperwork for one of her students to be tested for ADHD, which included consultations with the school counselor and her parents. She had parent/teacher conferences throughout the month as well. Her nights were filled with grading papers, attending obedience school with Rory (her dad had put his foot down), and trying to find time to eat and sleep.

She did squeeze in dinner with Cole and workouts with Jana, but that was about it. Her visits to Brew were predominantly on Sundays after church. She loved the atmosphere and the sweet smell of the coffee. Sometimes she took her students' tests and papers with her to grade at the coffee shop.

Tripp worked every Sunday afternoon, so they chatted sometimes. He told her he was attending the University of Texas at Arlington, majoring in theater. He said he liked working at Brew because, for one, the manager worked around his school schedule. He was a people person, so he loved talking to the customers who came in. When he had an opportunity, he would sit with Patience for a while at her table, asking her questions about teaching high school kids. She made him laugh when telling him about their attitudes and the way one student always whined like a three-year-old.

They shared stories about their families. Tripp was an only child like her. He said that his parents had definitely coddled him, asking him "how high?" when he told them to jump. Patience told him that he didn't seem spoiled or anything to her. Quite the contrary, she could tell he was a people person and that he never met a stranger.

"Ahh, that's just my unbelievably superb acting skills. The true me is very narcissistic and pompous."

He squared his shoulders and held his chin up for added effect, which made her laugh. He turned toward the window to eye his reflection, running a hand through his shoulder length black hair.

"You're just acting like that to put me off. I can tell you're really a nice guy." She shivered when the door behind her opened, a crowd of people piling in to warm themselves with coffee.

"No, I am so serious. People tell me all the time that I am the most arrogant person they know."

Patience rolled her eyes, wondering why he was stressing his flaws. She didn't care what he said; he was nice to her, so that was the Tripp she wanted to get to know.

She hung out at the shop a while longer, then reluctantly stood up to leave. She didn't want to admit it, but she had started looking forward to stopping by Brew to flirt with Tripp. He was amazingly attractive, and his smile could light up a dark room. His personality was fun as well. She liked the fact that he made her laugh and seemed to strike up a conversation with anyone. People gravitated toward him like magnets to metal.

“Well, I guess I’ll see you soon . . . ” she began.

“Let’s hope so, P.”

How cute! He had started calling her P a couple of weeks before, and she liked it. Actually, she was beginning to think everything he did was cute.

Buttoning up her jacket, Patience waved good-bye to one of the other employees as she left, her body becoming rigid in the cold air. Unable to resist, she turned one last time toward the shop, needing to see his face one more time. To her surprise, he’d been watching her through the window. Their eyes met and she shivered, but not from the cold weather.

CHAPTER 12

Rory had no trouble keeping up with Patience as they jogged along the trail. She smiled to herself, proud to be on her fourth mile. She felt a sense of pride as she realized how far she'd come. This time last year, she could run only a half mile. The weather surprised everyone that last day of January, with the temperature hovering just under seventy degrees. She was more than happy to get out of the house that Sunday afternoon after being cooped up all weekend. No doubt about it, she and Rory had a serious case of cabin fever.

She began to slow down to a power walk for the fifth mile, trying to catch her breath. She let her mind wander, thinking of Tripp. Rory still wanted to run, but she ignored him, collapsing onto a nearby bench with relief.

I wonder if he has a girlfriend, she thought to herself, picturing his face perfectly. Rory brought her back to the present, suddenly jumping up and barking excitedly. She looked up to find Tripp walking toward her with a huge smile on his face. He was walking a golden retriever, who was eyeing Rory cautiously.

"Well, well, what do we have here?"

Tripp appeared happy to see her.

Patience moved over so he could sit down.

"It's good to see you. What brings you to my favorite park?" She laughed as she watched Rory lick his dog on the face.

"Your favorite park, huh? Actually, I live across the street." He gestured to the rows of houses across from where they were sitting.

Her eyes followed his, and she could feel her jaw drop open in amazement. The neighborhood he was referring to had mansions that she gawked at every time she passed by. She wanted to ask him how he could afford them while working at Brew, but thought better of it and kept her mouth shut. She definitely did not want to be rude and hoped her curiosity didn't get the better of her.

"My house could fit inside yours, I bet!" was all she allowed herself to say.

He waved his hand dismissively.

"It's just a place to lay my head," he told her modestly. "Do you come here often?"

"I jog here three times a week with Rory. It definitely provides an outlet for his pent-up energy. I am so happy the weather is nice today."

Tripp agreed wholeheartedly. "It's funny. I've never seen you here before. And I bring CG to the trail all the time."

Patience rubbed Tripp's dog behind the ears. CG seemed to be a really sweet, calm dog.

"I usually come at five in the morning because I have to get to school so early. Plus, that's when I have the most energy. I could build a house before noon!"

He laughed.

"I can tell that you're a morning person. You seem like the type who bounces out of bed at four singing *It's A Beautiful Day*."

Rory started to get antsy, so they both stood and began walking along the trail.

Patience and Tripp hung out at the park for a long time, getting to know each other better and people watching. A family of four passed them by- a mother, father, and two children. The boy was riding his tricycle and kept yelling at his family to keep up with him. Three young girls ran quickly up to them, asking if they could pet the dogs. CG immediately shrank back behind Tripp's legs, but Rory ate up the attention. It seemed as if the whole community was at that particular park, taking advantage of the unseasonably warm weather.

Tripp walked Patience to her car. She wanted to give him her phone number, but she didn't quite dare ask him if he wanted it. Rory jumped into the backseat, and she slowly opened up the front door, stalling for time. Tripp was leaning against the car, just watching her intently. She felt suddenly shy but didn't know why. The more she had gotten to know him, the more comfortable she had become in his company.

He smiled down at her, shaking his head in amazement.

"You know, you're a pretty cool girl. I like hanging out with you."

She smiled.

"Thanks. I have fun spending time with you, too." She was at a loss for words, which was unlike her.

He took a step closer, suddenly tripping over CG's leash. It had gotten tangled between his legs while they were talking, unbeknownst to either of them. Embarrassed, he let out a chuckle.

"I'm falling for you!"

She liked the fact that he could turn even the most awkward moments around. He was so easy to be with.

They chatted a while longer, and Patience glanced in the car to check on Rory. He was getting rowdy, so she didn't have much longer to talk.

She was only half listening as Tripp described one of his acting classes. Gazing into his blue eyes, she saw that they actually sparkled when he talked about school. She could tell drama was his passion. She thought it was adorable. His face really came alive when describing the different characters he played, other actors, and favorite scenes in some popular movies.

"I hate to interrupt, but Rory probably needs to get home. He's getting a little jumpy back there."

"Oh! I am so sorry! I have a tendency to go on and on sometimes. Forgive me for rambling ..."

"No, that's okay! I like hearing about your life and things you enjoy." Shyness overcame Patience again, so she decided to just get in the car. As she started the engine, Tripp suddenly ran over to the passenger side and hopped in, letting CG into the back with Rory.

"Hey, how about you come to my house? We can order a pizza, let the dogs run around in the backyard, and maybe watch a movie." He was certainly spontaneous. She smiled as she put the car in reverse.

* * *

"Oh my goodness! Oh. My. Goodness." Patience could not believe her eyes. Tripp's house really *was* a mansion. They stood in the foyer, and she just stared at the winding staircase to her right. Ahead of them, a huge living room decorated all in white could have easily been on the cover of a magazine. They walked further, and she saw a kitchen with marble counters and brand-new appliances. The den had several bookcases and hardwood floors. There were also two guest bedrooms downstairs.

"I take back what I said earlier. My house could actually just fit inside your kitchen!"

Upstairs, she could not believe there were five bedrooms, an office, a game room with a pool table, and four bathrooms. The master bedroom had a balcony that overlooked a small pond. It was the biggest house she had ever been in.

"Who has the master suite?" she joked. "You or your parents?" She assumed he still lived with them.

He shrugged.

"CG and I are the only ones who live here. She's my roommate, I guess." He laughed and led Patience out onto the balcony. The dogs were inside, chasing each other through the hallways.

Her eyes were wide as saucers. She exclaimed, "This is *your* house?"

He nodded in response. She leaned forward, resting her arms on the rail of the balcony. She decided to go ahead and ask the inevitable question.

"Are you a drug dealer, Tripp? Just be honest with me. I can take it."

They both laughed and he sat down on one of the chairs, his long legs extended before him.

"Of course not! My grandfather left me a huge sum of money when he passed away two years ago. Let's just say that I was his favorite grandson."

"So your grandfather was a millionaire, huh? That's interesting ..." Her voice trailed off as she watched some ducklings trailing their mother by the pond.

"Billionaire," he corrected her quietly. She glanced at him, surprised to see a sad look on his face.

"Are you okay?"

He smiled. "Yes, I'm fine. It's actually funny. I didn't want this huge house, as it only seems to mock the fact that I'm alone. My mom decorated it, which is why it's so elaborate."

They both jumped when they heard a loud crash inside the house. Racing down the stairs, they noticed both dogs hiding under the dining room table. A trail of broken glass began in the dining room and ended in the foyer. Patience gasped when she spotted what used to be a beautiful Persian vase splattered all over the tile. She'd seen it when they'd first entered the house.

"I bet Rory did this. I am so sorry! He gets so hyper and out of control sometimes. I should have kept him right beside me."

Tripp held up his hand to stop her.

"Will you please calm down? It's okay, really. And it doesn't matter which dog did it. Believe me, CG has broken plenty of things in this house, so don't worry about it." He went into the laundry room to get a broom and dustpan, and she grabbed the Dust Buster to help clean the mess.

Later that night, the two enjoyed a getting-to-know-you-better dinner, as he put it. They sat by the pool in his backyard, and she couldn't believe she had ended up spending the day with him. Time sped by quickly when she was with him. Looking up at the sky, there seemed to be a million stars above them. It added a romantic quality to the evening. The dogs were sleeping on the grass just beside the gazebo. She had honestly never seen a backyard the size of Tripp's. His whole house was amazing.

Shortly after midnight, Tripp walked Patience to the car. A yawn escaped her when she told him goodnight. He leaned his head in her car to give her a peck on the cheek.

"We had a great day, P. When can I see you again?"

She felt lightheaded being that close to him.

Whenever you would like is what she wanted to say but decided against it. She didn't want to seem too eager.

"I don't know. This week is pretty busy."

She was being honest with him. The next day she had two meetings after school, followed by a mandatory dinner with her parents. Her mother had called twenty times the day before claiming to need her Patience fix. In addition, she had to stay after school Tuesday through Friday with tons of paperwork. To top it all off, she had plans with Cole Wednesday night and a dentist appointment she'd been putting off early Friday morning. She yawned again while thinking about her hectic schedule.

Tripp rolled his eyes.

"I guess I have to wait for you to call me then, princess. Whenever you can find the time to pencil me in, do it. I would really, really like for you to grace me with your presence."

He covered his heart with both hands and closed his eyes, whispering, "I don't know how I'm going to make it this week without you."

On the way home, Patience thought about Tripp while listening to Rory snore in the backseat. She popped one of her favorite CDs in to drown him out.

She felt a slight tingle inside when remembering how much fun she had had with Tripp that day. He made her laugh and was so easygoing and spontaneous. She reveled in the fact that she could be herself with him and talk to him about anything. Over dinner, they had discussed their families, friends, and hobbies. He wasn't very close to his parents, although they adored him. She found out he had one very close friend, Damian, and a couple of acquaintances, but that was it. He explained to her that he didn't trust many people, hence his one best friend. She could understand that, even though she was a pretty open person.

Rory woke up when she pulled into the driveway, and she was amazed that he had gotten his second wind. She let him run around the yard a few times before they went to the front door, where she found a note taped to the doorbell. Curious, she went inside and opened it before putting her purse down.

> *Dear Patience,*
> *Hi. Remember me? I know it's been a long time, and you are surprised to find this letter on your door ... So many*

times I have picked up the phone to call you. So many times I have driven by your house, determined to knock on the door but didn't. I miss you so much! You are always on my mind. I miss the fun times we had, your smile, our long walks in the park with Rory ... Patience, please call me. I have so much to say to you, so much to explain. I understand if you don't want to have anything to do with me, but I'm hoping that by some miracle, you will at least respond to this letter. Hope you're doing well, and please know that I still care for you.
Love always,
Sam

CHAPTER 13

Picking up the phone the next evening, Patience hesitated for a second. She looked out her living room window at the children playing football in the street. The weather was perfect for February; it was cold enough to still be winter but warm enough to enjoy the outdoors. The kids weren't even wearing jackets, which was surprising.

Maybe it's because they're playing sports she thought to herself, stalling for time.

Deep down, she knew Sam's letter had touched her. He was such a sweet guy, which was one of the main reasons she had fallen for him so hard. And it had taken a lot of courage for him to contact her after so long. She noticed her hand shaking as she dialed his home number. It rang four times, and she hung up, partially relieved. She had no idea what to say.

She jumped when the phone rang.

"Hello?"

"Hi, it's Sam."

There was a pause as he waited for her reaction.

"Hi. I just called you," she said shyly.

"Um, yeah, I saw that. I was outside checking the mail. Sorry I missed your call."

"How are you?"

She smiled into the phone. She couldn't believe her heart was about to burst just from hearing his voice.

"I'm not doing too well, actually. I miss you, Patience."

She could hear the sincerity as Sam said it. Truth be told, she missed him, too. He was just braver than she was, posting a note on her door and driving by her house all the time. It was weird because he was so shy, yet he'd taken a risk by reaching out to her. She could have rejected him, but he cared for her enough to take that chance.

Sam cleared his throat and asked if they could meet somewhere to talk. She thought about it for a moment, then told him that they could. She agreed to meet him at a small café the following evening after school. She planned on staying late to grade papers.

"I'm not exactly sure what time I'll be finished," she told him. "Can I call and let you know when I'm about done?"

"Of course you can! I'll have my cell on me all day. Just let me know what's convenient for you."

After hanging up, Patience had to hurry to her parents'. She'd told her mom she'd be there by six. She knew Sharise would worry if she was late.

Thoughts of Sam occupied her mind as she dropped her keys on the way out. She ran toward her car, realized she'd forgotten her purse, and tripped over one of Rory's toys on the way back inside. What a mess she was! Talking to Sam had really knocked her off balance, yet she couldn't stop smiling as she finally hopped in the car.

* * *

Patience stood outside the café the next evening, waiting for Sam to arrive. She wondered if she was doing the right thing. Was she just opening up old wounds? After all, he had hidden her from his family and friends, which were a huge part of his life. On the other hand, this wasn't the 1920s. Many people dated without introducing their significant others to their families.

She checked her cell to see if Sam had called just as he was pulling into a parking space. She could see a huge grin on his face and found the smile contagious. Yes, she was meant to be there. He strode up to her quickly and pulled her into a hug. He held her so tightly it took her breath away. The two just held one another for a long time, oblivious to the people milling around them. She was the one who finally pulled away, but he still had his arms around her waist. She wanted to get a good look at him. He hadn't changed a bit. His boyish good looks made him look much younger than his age.

"Thank you for coming," said Sam. "I wasn't quite sure if you'd show up." He smiled sheepishly, motioning for them to head inside the café.

He ordered sandwiches and soup for the two of them. No sooner had the waitress walked away than he leaned forward and asked,

"Have you thought about me since we've been apart?"

Patience's eyes widened.

"Boy, you don't beat around the bush, do you?"

Her palms began to sweat, and she swallowed hard. Nervousness engulfed her. She wasn't sure what to say. After all, she didn't want to be a heartless wench and act as if she didn't care. Besides, he had gotten to know her well enough that he would have seen right through her. On the other hand, she was not about to pour out her heart and make herself vulnerable to him. No matter how nice he was, she didn't want to risk getting hurt again.

"It's not a trick question. Just answer me honestly."

Coming back to the present, she confessed,

"Of course I've thought about you. I cared deeply for you, and those feelings don't just go away overnight."

"*Cared* for, as in the past tense?"

She rolled her eyes.

"I *still* think about you. I remember going to the grocery a week after we'd ended things. This man passed by wearing your cologne. Against my better judgment, I followed him around the store for about ten minutes. When he noticed what I was doing, he quickened his pace and kept looking over his shoulder. I didn't want to scare him. After that, I decided to just go home. I kept wondering, 'When is it going to get easier?"'

Sam reached across the table to give her hand a gentle squeeze.

"I know exactly what you mean. I was convinced I would die of heartache. This may sound ridiculous, but I thought my heart would actually stop beating from losing you."

They shared a knowing smile as the waitress brought their drinks.

"Nothing sounds ridiculous to me when it comes to dating and emotions," said Patience. For some odd reason, she believed him. Although he had kept her from his family and friends, she knew he cared about her.

They were busy catching up when their food arrived. She giggled when she saw Sam immediately open his sandwich and take off the lettuce, tomatoes, and pickles. Laughing, she asked,

"Why in the world didn't you just order it plain?"

"I didn't want to seem high maintenance. And besides, the cooks have a hard enough time as it is," he answered only half joking.

"Yeah, I guess you're right. And who's to say they wouldn't have put those veggies on there anyway? Every time I ask BustaBurger for no pickles, they give me *extra* pickles!"

Sam's expression softened as he gazed into Patience's eyes.

"Please tell me you'll give me a second chance. I want you in my life again."

"Can we talk about this later?" She needed time to think, and she couldn't do that with him sitting across from her. His presence messed up her thought processes at times. "I promise we'll discuss it later."

"How much later?" he pressed.

“Um, I’m not sure. I can tell you this, though. You are such a great guy, and I miss you, too. I just don’t want to get hurt again, so I need to be cautious . . . ” Her voice trailed off.

“Okay, I’ll give you time to think. But I promise I won’t ever hurt you again.”

* * *

Sam had insisted on following Patience home “just to make sure you make it in safely.” She thought he was being a little over the top but realized he’d made up his mind. “You don’t know how many crazy lunatics are out there. And Rory does you no good if he’s *inside* the house,” he’d stated firmly.

She pulled into the driveway, immediately hopping out to run over to his truck.

“I want to thank you for being my own special bodyguard. I had a nice time at dinner, too. Thank you so much.”

She turned to head up the driveway and realized he had gotten out of his truck. She wasn’t sure how they ended up holding hands, but it felt so right. She leaned against the doorframe, and he moved closer to her.

“I will do whatever it takes to regain your trust,” Sam confessed, his voice a mere whisper. He softly kissed her on the cheek, then the tip of her nose, and finally her lips.

Pulling away slightly, Patience searched his face.

“Maybe this could work after all,” she dared to say. She wanted him back more than ever now. She’d missed everything about him . . . his smell, his touch, hearing his voice on the phone before turning in at night, and the look in his eyes after they kissed.

He ran his hands through her curls.

“I want you to meet my parents.”

CHAPTER 14

Patience returned Tripp's phone call the next evening. The poor guy had left four messages the night before, in addition to texting "Have a great day" that morning. Feelings of guilt swept over her as she dialed his number. He was such a fun, nice guy. She didn't want to hurt him.

"Well, it's about time, P! I thought maybe you had moved to another state."

She giggled.

"Nah, I just went gambling and won a million dollars," she joked.

"That's a lot of money. When do we go shopping?"

She paused, pretending to give it some serious thought. "Seeing as you're already loaded, I have to find someone else to spend it with."

"I don't have a yacht, though."

They talked for a long time that night, and he made her laugh with stories about the customers at Brew. She asked how CG was doing, and he said that she missed Rory.

"I'm glad you asked," said Tripp. "Just this morning, she told me to call and set something up with the two of you. Rory really livens up the house," he said only half-jokingly.

"Hmm, how weird is that? Rory told me today how much he misses CG!"

By the time they hung up, each couldn't wait till Saturday. They'd made plans to play golf that morning. And in the afternoon, they were taking the dogs to their favorite park. The idea of spending time with Tripp excited Patience. He was a dream, yet with Sam reentering the picture, she had a lot of thinking to do.

She went to the backyard to let Rory back in, telling him about their plans. He jumped up excitedly, and she knew dogs could really understand some things humans told them. However, she didn't broadcast that fact to the world. Some people didn't feel the same way about animals.

The phone rang as she was walking through the living room.

"Hello?"

"I am going to beat you down! Why haven't I heard from you?" It was Jana.

"I'm sorry I haven't called, but these past two weeks have been ... busy," Patience said with an air of mystery. Her friend took the bait.

"Who is he?" she asked immediately.

"You mean 'who are *they*?"' Patience corrected.

Jana informed her that she was coming over right then. Ten minutes later, they were sitting in front of the television, eating popcorn and chatting.

"I wouldn't give Sam the time of day. You're too good for him, and you know it. There's no excuse for keeping you a secret. Any guy should be proud to have you on his arm!" Jana didn't hold anything back. She wasn't a big fan of Sam, to put it mildly.

"Don't you think you're being a little too hard on him? After all, it took a lot of courage to get in touch with me after all these months. He said he thinks about me all the time and misses me."

"Bullshit. He just got lonely and hasn't found anyone else as good as you. You'd better believe he's been dating."

Patience disagreed.

"I don't think he has, Jana. He probably just buried himself in his work or something. He said I was all he thought about. And do you know what else? He told me that so many times he would drive by my house to see if I was home. Or that he'd pick up the phone to call me but chickened out."

Waving her hand in dismissively, Jana scoffed.

"You're so naïve. Of course he said that. He'll tell you anything to get you back."

"I believe him. Why would he take the time to write me that letter and risk rejection? If he was with other girls, he'd be too busy to pursue me."

Patience's best friend put the popcorn bowl on the coffee table and moved closer to her. Looking her directly in the eye, Jana said, "I didn't want to tell you this, but I think I'd better." She hesitated, not wanting to hurt her friend. "Scott and I saw Sam at the mall with some girl. And believe me, she wasn't his sister."

Patience sat back on the couch and looked up at the ceiling.

"When was this?"

"Two months ago. It was when we went shopping for Scott's mom."

Patience sat up suddenly and smiled at her.

"It doesn't matter. We weren't together then. Of course Sam had to fill in his free time doing *something*. His situation was the same as mine. Actually, I dated Jason during my time apart from him. So it's the same thing."

Jana grabbed her shoulders and spoke firmly.

"Listen to me good. Do not let him back into your heart. He will hurt you again. I know it. And next time it will be worse. Trust me."

She was glad when Jana left that night. Her best friend could be so annoying at times. Patience needed her to be more supportive during times like these. Jana should have been happy that she and Sam had made amends. Patience never said anything bad about the guys *she* had dated.

Jana called her when she got home, but Patience was short with her.

After a long pause, her friend said, "I hope I didn't step on your toes tonight. I care about you so much, that's all. And I will kill Sam if he does the same thing to you again."

"Whatever. I really thought you would be elated that he'd reached out to me. You know how much I like him."

In the end, the two agreed to disagree when it came to Sam. Patience knew that only time would show Jana he was crazy about her. Maybe he even loved her. She couldn't wait to meet his family. She knew he meant what he said. She saw the honesty in his eyes. And she felt it when they kissed. They had something pretty special. But she didn't explain all of that to Jana. Her friend would not have understood.

* * *

Sam called on Friday to see what she was doing that weekend. He wanted to take her out.

"I'm free tonight and Sunday," she told him happily.

He asked her about Saturday but she already had Tripp on her calendar.

"I have plans."

"You're busy *all day* tomorrow?"

"Yes."

"Ah, you and your mom must be doing something; I remember you saying how close the two of you are."

"No," she laughed. "I already spent time with her this week."

"So you're having a girls' day with Jana, huh?" he pressed.

"No."

There was an awkward silence while she waited for his next question.

"What are you doing, then? I mean, if your whole day and night is taken, it must be pretty big."

She wondered why Sam wanted to know so badly. When they'd dated before, he'd never asked where she was and with whom.

"I'm playing golf, if you must know."

"Oh, really? I didn't know you liked golf. Who are you playing with?"

"A friend. Would you like to do something tonight or Sunday?" She tried to redirect the conversation. "It's only six o'clock, so the night is young."

He sighed. "Tonight will be fine."

Sam took Patience to a comedy club they'd been to once before, which was fun. They both loved to laugh and wanted the date to be lighthearted and easy. Afterwards, they went to an ice cream shop to satisfy her sweet tooth. There were Valentine's Day decorations all over the windows in the mall. She liked the outdoor mall because they could get fresh air while shopping.

As they left Treats 'R' Us with their cones, Sam held her hand tightly in his. He took a big bite of his mint chocolate chip ice cream, and part of it fell to the ground. Patience laughed, almost choking on her rocky road.

He remarked on how cute the Cupids were.

"Which reminds me: what are we doing on Valentine's Day? It's only one week away," he reminded her.

"What if I already have plans? I mean, we *just* started hanging out again."

He looked hurt. "But sweetheart ... you're right. I'm sorry I assumed we would be together on the most romantic holiday of the year."

Her knees went weak. He had that effect on her. "Dinner and a movie?"

His face lit up immediately. Shaking his head, he answered, "Do you know how long we'll have to wait to be seated?"

She agreed and suggested ordering a pizza and staying in. But he didn't like that idea, either.

"You know I want it to be romantic, and pizza is not my idea of sweeping you off your feet." Tossing different ideas around, she finally decided to wait until the actual day to see what came up. Sam agreed.

On the way home, Sam implored her to tell him about her golf buddy again. He wouldn't let it rest. It was safe to say all his questioning was getting on her nerves. What she did in her spare time was *her* business. Besides, he didn't tell her everything *he* did when they were apart.

"Will you be playing golf with a male or female tomorrow?"

Patience turned abruptly in her seat to face him.

"You just don't give up, do you? Why are you so desperate to know?"

"Please don't answer my question with two questions." Sam reached over to touch her cheek softly.

"Male."

"You're going on a date tomorrow," he assumed incredulously.

She shrugged.

"I wouldn't call it an actual date. I told you he's a friend, and we're hanging out. It's very casual, Sam."

He turned onto her street, a look of disgust on his face. "I just don't think it's good for us if you're out golfing with another guy. I just got you back, and our relationship is a little shaky still."

She was at a loss for words.

He stopped the truck, looking at her with puppy dog eyes.

"Cancel the date, okay? *I'll* take you golfing."

"I can't cancel at the last minute. Don't worry. He's just a friend." Her tone meant the discussion was closed.

Sam was huffy when he left, giving Patience only a quick peck on the lips before leaving.

She called him after her shower that night and he apologized for his behavior.

"I know I can't tell you what to do. And I don't want to. You have a life outside of me, which is great. Guess I just got bitten by the jealousy bug tonight."

"Aww, that is really sweet. And it's okay. I promise that it's an innocent outing. Hey, a thought just occurred to me. Did you ever get a chance to talk to your parents about me?"

"Um, not yet, but I'm planning on calling tonight. I'll ask what night would be good for us to drop in."

* * *

Patience didn't want to admit how much fun she was having with Tripp. His energy and enthusiasm were contagious. He even managed to make golf exciting. He loved to play, but she had never been very fond of the sport. Her dad used to take her with him and his buddies when she was small, before she knew any better. Tripp told her he was going to take her back home and go pick up her dad instead. She obviously hadn't inherited her dad's skill or paid attention when with him. She was truly awful. One ball went into the lake, another hit a bystander on the back, and she tripped over the golf bag many times.

He was still giving her a hard time while they sat by the pond behind his house, talking quietly. The dogs were fast asleep beside them, spent after their evening at the park.

"I bet I could beat you at basketball, though. Or any other sport, come to think of it," she teased back. "The only reason I'm horrible at golf is because it makes my eyes glaze over so I can't see straight."

"You make me laugh, Patience. That may be one of the reasons I like you so much."

Tripp had moved closer to her on the grass while talking. His voice was husky. "You know, ever since I first saw you fighting with your boyfriend at Brew, I couldn't stop thinking about you."

"You were there that day?"

"Yep, and I must say how impressed I was with how you handled him. You've got a lot of self-respect."

Memories of Jason came rushing back like a tidal wave.

"I am so embarrassed! I didn't mean to cause a scene, but I was so offended and angry." She felt her face flush as she revisited those emotions.

"You don't have to apologize to me. We needed some excitement around there anyway," he joked.

He paused, sighing contentedly.

"What did he do to make you almost blow up Brew?"

Patience smiled at Tripp's exaggeration. "Let's just say that we got along great and were really starting to develop a good relationship. It was his mother that threw a wrench in the plans."

"She didn't like you?"

"I don't know if she liked me or not, but she thought I wasn't good enough for her son. In her words, I didn't have enough black in me."

He furrowed his brow.

"What does that mean?"

She sighed.

"Once Carolyn found out I'm biracial, she wrote me off. She didn't believe races should mix."

"Can't we all just get along? That's the craziest thing I've ever heard in my life! Patience, your social life sure is complicated."

She agreed.

"I'm pretty simple, though. If I meet a man I like, I just expect to date him and keep things light at first. And I would love it if he included me in his life. You know, we could cook out with his family and friends, or watch movies with my family ... and then we'd also have time to ourselves. Boy meets girl, boy asks girl out, boy marries girl. Who knew there were certain race requirements when dating? I had no idea the saying really goes like this: Black boy meets mixed girl who isn't black enough for the family. White boy meets mixed girl, but his parents don't like black people."

Tripp played with her hair as he considered what she was saying.

“I’m sorry that happened to you. You’re a neat person. You don’t deserve to be judged that way.”

“I actually had no problem with Jason or his family, but I didn’t want to jump through hoops while continuing to date him, either.”

Suddenly a giggle escaped her.

“What’s so funny?”

“I bet his mom had a fear that if we married and had kids, they would end up with blue eyes and fair skin.”

He pretended to be offended, crossing his arms with a scowl on his face.

“And that would’ve been a problem?”

Patience touched his shoulder.

“Not for me or my family. I think there is beauty in every race. And I’m lucky enough to have been raised to believe that. But not everyone feels the same way we do. My uncle Scott on my mom’s side of the family married a white woman two years ago. Her parents still don’t approve. They just had a baby boy, and the grandparents haven’t even gone to see him! He’s the cutest little thing. And I swear he looks totally white. Trace has straight blond hair, big blue eyes, and white skin. I honestly don’t know how that happened because my uncle has really dark skin and eyes.”

He was amazed.

“All of the interracial couples I’ve seen have children who look predominantly African-American. I guess you just never know which traits will be dominant.”

Later that night, Tripp drove Patience and Rory home. They sat in his car talking for a long time after he’d pulled up to her house.

“I can’t tell you how much I enjoyed your company today, P. You’re like a burst of sunshine in my otherwise dreary life.”

“That’s sweet.” He was so dramatic sometimes.

As if reading her mind, he said, “All kidding aside, you do brighten my day when I’m with you. You’re so down-to-earth, P. I like the fact that you’re low maintenance, in a good way. Most girls I meet are either preoccupied with their hair, makeup, and clothes or have bad attitudes. You’re very refreshing.”

Patience couldn’t think of a response. Tripp was so open about everything. It felt good being with him. She loved his personality, and she had to admit that the attention he lavished on her felt wonderful, especially at this vulnerable time. But no matter how engaging Tripp was, Sam still occupied most of her thoughts, much to her dismay.

“I’ve wanted to kiss you all day. I can’t believe I haven’t tried to yet,” he said with a shy smile.

She knew he had to be told about Sam. She didn't want to lead him on.

"Tripp ..."

She took a deep breath before continuing.

"I have a boyfriend."

"You have a *what*?" He looked at her incredulously.

Her eyes were downcast. She couldn't look at him.

"I know I should have told you earlier, but we just got back together this past week." She laughed nervously.

"You're kidding me, right? P, tell me you're joking."

She felt terrible. She should have been up front with him the whole time. But in her defense, Sam had resurfaced only recently. And she had no idea the buried feelings for him would be resurrected. She really liked Tripp, and had Sam not reappeared, she was sure they would have begun dating.

He stared out his window.

"All this time I thought we were interested in each other. Boy, do I feel stupid."

He turned the ignition, preparing to leave.

"Tripp, it's a long story. My ex left a note on my door the other night ..."

"Save it. Honestly, I was beginning to fall for you pretty fast. I thought we had chemistry. And I swear you seemed to like me in return. Maybe you should be the one taking acting classes."

She sat in the car, stunned by his reaction. Maybe he was right, because when she thought back to their first encounter at Brew, even a fool could have seen the attraction between the two. Each time they hung out, it got better and better. There was always more to say, more laughter, and an undeniable chemistry. He had every right to be upset. It did appear that she'd led him on. But Sam ...

She opened the car door, hesitating for a moment. Turning to him, she apologized.

"I am so very sorry! You're absolutely right. The least I could've done was tell you when my ex started contacting me again."

"Bye, Patience," he said with a tone of dismissal. He was having none of it. He seemed done with her.

She let Rory out and watched as Tripp sped away.

CHAPTER 15

On Valentine's Day, Sam showed up on her doorstep at seven a.m. with a dozen roses and chocolates. She was still in her pjs and had just let Rory out.

"Rise and shine, sweetie pie," he sang cheerfully. He tried to kiss her, but she held up her hands.

"Please let me brush my teeth first."

Sam laughed, walking into the kitchen for orange juice.

Patience ran into the restroom where she washed her face and brushed her hair quickly. When she emerged, Sam was putting her flowers in a vase. She pulled him into a big hug, thanking him for being so thoughtful.

He told her to go get dressed.

"I have a surprise for you."

"What is it?" she asked excitedly. She knew Sam had something fun planned for their special day, but he refused to tell her what it was. She ran to her bedroom quickly, and he followed her.

"Oh, I forgot to tell you: make sure to cancel any plans you have for the remainder of this weekend. And pack a small bag, you know, with your toothbrush and a change of clothes. We're going on a little ... day trip."

She paused at her closet and looked at him with serious eyes.

"What are you hinting at, Sam? You have to tell me *something*," she demanded. But his lips were closed tight.

Patience didn't know how much longer she could stand the suspense. They were in his truck, chatting about this and that. She knew he wouldn't budge about letting her in on where they were going. He loved surprises, especially when *he* was the one providing them. So she gave up, deciding on humoring him with funny stories of her as a child.

Thirty minutes later, they pulled into the parking lot of The Spa at the Crescent, a luxury hotel and spa in Dallas. Her eyes wide as saucers, she looked over at him in confusion. He was wearing the biggest smile she'd ever seen, obviously satisfied with her reaction.

"Well?" he prodded after she didn't say anything.

But Patience was speechless, not sure what to think about the whole thing. It hadn't registered yet, so she just sat there staring at the attendant who opened her door and waited patiently for her to get out. Sam laughed and walked over to her side of the truck, pulled her out, and led her inside the tall building.

She silently took it all in: the hardwood floors, beautiful antique porcelains and original works of art strategically placed throughout the waiting area, and spiral staircases. Sam had gone to check them in, returning shortly with the key to their room.

Without a word, she embraced him, all the gratitude and love for him expressed in that single motion. This was the most thoughtful thing anyone besides her parents had done for her. Growing up, she was showered with spur of the moment trips with her father, surprise gifts from her mother, and so on. But this literally took her breath away. Previous boyfriends had been good to her, but she'd never received a gift like this.

Finally finding her voice, she pulled away from Sam, staring deeply into his eyes.

"I knew you wanted to make this Valentine's Day special, but ... I had no idea it would be this elaborate!"

"So you like it?"

She giggled at the ridiculous question.

"Of course I do! I love it, as a matter of fact," she insisted.

Patience followed him to the elevators, holding tightly to his hand. Words could not express all the emotions she felt simultaneously, but if she had to pick, it would be love. They had never spoken the L word, but his actions led her to believe that maybe he actually loved her. And she felt the same way.

Their suite was huge, with a large living area and bath. She was impressed by the flat screen television and plush love seat that she collapsed on. Looking around, she noticed French doors that led to the balcony. Sam went to the mini-bar to fix them drinks.

"You look like a person who just won the lottery! Let me mix you a margarita to calm you down." He was still laughing at her reaction.

"I *did* win the lottery! Do you realize how much this means to me? You obviously put a lot of thought into this, as well as money," she replied.

He handed her the small glass of the sweet drink, which she took only a sip of. Patience didn't want anything to fog her memory of this wonderful day. Getting up to go look at the bathroom, a thought occurred to her. They were spending the night, and there was one king-size bed. Nervousness slowly crept its way through her, but she pushed it aside. Nothing was going to ruin this day.

Night approached before she knew it. Patience and Sam had spent the whole day at the spa receiving facials, massages, hydrotherapy, and so on. Sam turned down the manicure and pedicure, despite Patience informing him that men could have them as well. In the middle of the afternoon, they went their separate ways. She attended a yoga class while he worked out. When she met him later on, he suggested a swim. Afterward, they returned to the suite to shower for dinner. She noticed him staring at her hair, which had literally expanded after swimming.

"Is there something you need to tell me?" he laughed as she tried to get the tangles out.

In the shower, she'd left the conditioner on an extra ten minutes, but it didn't help. Her hair looked like she'd been struck by lightning.

Rolling her eyes playfully, Patience went to grab her hair oil and blow dryer from her bag.

Sam watched in amazement as she miraculously got her hair under control.

"Wow, the things African-Americans go through," he exclaimed seriously.

She laughed. "You have no idea."

The seafood was wonderful at the restaurant that night. He had gone all out for her. She didn't want to think about how much money he'd dished out. She wondered if she should offer to help with the bill. He was the type of guy who could be easily offended, so she wrestled with the idea for a minute.

"Sam," she began. This was too much to ask for, and she wanted to at least pay for her share of the stay.

"Yes?"

"You don't know how much I've enjoyed the spa today, and this is such a wonderful surprise. However, I can't even imagine how expensive a place like this is ..."

He held up his hand for her to stop.

"Don't even worry your pretty little head about the cost. I know you're about to offer to help pay for it, because that's the kind of person you are."

He reached across the table to hold her hand. "It's very sweet of you, but I've got this under control. If I couldn't afford it, I would've just taken you to dinner and a movie," he said with a smile.

She sighed with relief. She didn't really have the money to cover her half of the spa. She felt the need to offer, however.

Back in the room later that night, the two were in the sitting area watching a movie. Patience had packed cute pajamas for the occasion: a sheer pink tank top with pink and white shorts. They were the perfect combination of sexy and respectable, not revealing too much. She didn't know what Sam was expecting after the extravagant gift he lavished on her, and she wasn't sure how it would turn out.

Nervousness crept in again as she took a sip of champagne. She wasn't a virgin but was very close to it. She'd only been intimate with one boyfriend, back in her freshman year of college. She considered herself very inexperienced in that area.

"Penny for your thoughts?" he asked curiously. She was lying on the carpet while he read the newspaper on the couch behind her. Picking up the remote, she hit the pause button and rolled over on her stomach, looking up at him.

"Are you even watching the movie?" she asked.

"No, I'm pretending to read this paper while secretly staring at you."

She laughed. "I knew it! I felt your eyes burning a hole into my backside, but I didn't want to make you uncomfortable by saying something."

He put the newspaper down, joining her on the carpet.

"I am not easily embarrassed, sweetheart."

They lay there for a while, staring at each other. Patience was extremely attracted to Sam, and the champagne he'd had sent to their suite only intensified the feeling.

She reached out to him, placing her hand behind his neck. Bringing him toward her, she began kissing him with a passion that surprised her. He responded, rolling onto his back and pulling her on top of him. They stopped kissing for a moment, and she saw all the love he had for her in his eyes.

He furrowed his brow suddenly, as if deep in thought. "Are you sure this isn't moving too fast? I want you to know I don't expect anything from you tonight."

Patience knew he was being sincere. And she didn't feel any pressure from him. It was her own longing that let her know something was going to happen that night.

* * *

Their Valentine's Day went by far too quickly for the both of them. It was Sunday afternoon, and they were snuggled close on the couch back at Patience's house.

"I had the most wonderful time. Thank you for making this holiday so special for me," said Patience. She kissed Sam for a long moment.

Pulling her even closer, he sighed.

"I wish this weekend would never end. All I want to do is be with you."

They sat in comfortable silence for a long moment. It was Patience who spoke first.

"Well, this relationship is better than ever. Now all I need to do is meet your parents."

He leaned forward to pick up the remote.

"Mind if I channel surf?"

She frowned, wondering if she should press the issue.

"Um, don't you think your parents are the missing link? Once I finally have their approval, we can move forward."

Turning the television on, he sighed.

"Don't be so dramatic. It's no big deal. Let's just enjoy the remainder of the weekend."

She didn't respond, and Sam gave her a curious look. Exhaling slowly, he promised to call his parents that afternoon. He must have sensed she wasn't going to let it rest. She could be headstrong when up against a wall. And the wall was his parents.

She wanted to get the meeting over with, and quickly. She would rather have a root canal than spend an evening with prejudiced people. However, they *were* his mother and father. She loved him, so they all needed to get along.

Sam left Patience's house shortly after their conversation and called her that evening.

"What do you think about tomorrow night? My mom said we can come over for tea."

She felt her hands begin to shake.

"That sounds good. Did you tell them I'm black?"

"Patience! I really wish you would call yourself African-American or something! Black sounds so ... *black*. Besides, the color of your skin is tan."

She rolled her eyes even though he couldn't see her over the phone.

"Whatever. Did you tell them I'm not pure white?"

"Nah, they'll see for themselves when they meet you." He sounded casual and very sure of himself.

Patience was persistent.

"But I really think you should tell your parents before we just show up on their doorstep. You need to prepare them, Sam." She could not believe he was going to casually throw her in his mother's face.

"I disagree, sweetheart. You don't know my mom. If I tell her you're African-American, she'll stubbornly resist meeting you. But once she sees how beautiful and intelligent you are, she'll buckle. I know what I'm doing. Trust me."

* * *

Patience went to Brew that evening for their scrumptious pound cake. Deep down, she felt uneasy but couldn't put her finger on why. Sam was a good guy and didn't mean any harm. However, one of his remarks had rubbed her the wrong way: "once she sees how beautiful and smart you are." Did that mean his mother thought African Americans were unattractive and dumb?

Well, she is prejudiced, she thought to herself. It really didn't matter if she was pretty or had three eyes on her face. Sam's mom would only focus on the color of her skin.

Walking into Brew, Patience spotted Tripp immediately. He didn't see her come in, so she approached cautiously. He was refilling the napkin holders. As if sensing someone behind him, he turned around to find her standing there. He rolled his eyes and continued working. She watched as he put some sugar packets in a container.

"Hi," she said somewhat nervously.

He didn't say anything.

"Hi Tripp," she said again, this time moving to the other side of the counter to face him. He put an extra stack of Styrofoam cups beside the coffee and went back to the register. It looked like a slow Sunday. He was the only employee working.

Looking at the menu above his head, Patience ordered a slice of cake and a small decaf.

"Will there be anything else, ma'am?" he asked as if she were a stranger.

"That will be all."

"Your total is $4.59. Will that be for here or to go?"

"Here."

Tripp rolled his eyes again, reaching for her money.

Patience couldn't suppress a giggle and informed him that he'd have a headache if he kept rolling his eyes.

"Isn't there another coffee shop you can start going to?"

She didn't flinch at his rudeness.

"I like Brew. And where is your manager? The service around here isn't very friendly," she added, raising her voice slightly. Some customers sitting near them glanced over with curiosity, so Tripp held up his hands in defeat.

"You win, P. What do you want?"

She clapped her hands gleefully.

"You called me P! I am the happiest girl on earth."

He smiled.

"I'm still mad at you, so don't try to butter me up with your endearing ways."

"At least you're speaking to me again. I want us to be friends. I've apologized, swallowing my pride to come in here, risking rejection ... I think I've earned your forgiveness."

A customer came in just then, so Patience gathered her things and sat at a table nearby. The shop got busy for a while, but she patiently waited. She missed Tripp and wasn't leaving until they talked.

When business slowed down, he went to stand by her table, pretending to wipe the dust off the windowsill.

"I'll get in trouble if I sit with you. How about I call you tonight? It won't be too late."

Unable to suppress a wide grin, Patience hopped up. "That sounds good to me."

* * *

"So I thought maybe it could work this time. We do have something special. But it's no excuse for how I treated you. The fact that Sam and I had reconnected was important information to disclose, and I'm sorry," Patience finished.

Tripp had called her right after work, just as he'd said he would. She told him the whole story of Sam, leaving out minor details such as their kisses, mushy words, and night together. He seemed to want to know everything, such as how they met, the seriousness of the relationship, and what it meant for him. The entire conversation was extremely awkward for her, but he hung on her every word.

He exhaled loudly. "Whew! I am absolutely exhausted after that story, P! What a roller coaster ride you two are on. I'm not just saying this because I have feelings for you, but ..."

"What?"

"As a friend, I want to tell you that he doesn't sound like a good guy for you. I mean, he didn't tell his friends or family about you because you're *black*? What kind of man is he, anyway?"

"A great one, that's what kind he is."

She sat up on her bed, gripping the phone tightly.

"Sam was scared the whole time that his parents wouldn't approve of me, which is understandable. Although they're not a close-knit family, they *are* his parents. Besides, it's not as if he were going to keep me a secret forever. He just needed to find the right time to introduce me."

"Yeah, right. Listen, I hate to be the bearer of bad news, but whatshisname had no intentions of letting you into his perfect white world. It's a good thing you ran into his buddies at that museum."

"His name is Sam. I don't think we need to focus on the past. What's important is that I'm meeting his parents tomorrow."

"Are you prepared emotionally for this, Patience? The loser told you flat-out that his mom and dad don't like blacks. And I'll just bet some of his friends feel the same way."

Instinctively Patience began biting her lower lip out of nervousness. Her stomach felt as if it were tied in knots. Sitting up straighter on her bed, she inhaled deeply, trying to relax. She didn't respond, hoping the subject would change soon. It didn't.

Tripp continued.

"It's weird how he supposedly has all these feelings for you but wants to keep you hidden."

She was more confused than ever when she hung up the phone. Neither Tripp nor Jana saw her side. She thought love conquered all, but maybe Jason's mother had been right. She could be naïve about certain things.

Climbing out of bed to turn out her light, she knew she wasn't getting any sleep that night. But no matter how nervous she was, a part of her was ready to get the introductions over with. And she knew without a doubt that with Sam by her side, everything would be fine.

CHAPTER 16

Patience left school with a ton of unfinished paperwork. She needed to go find something appropriate to wear for that evening. Shopping, especially for clothes, was a chore she loathed. It had to be done, though.

Taking a deep breath, she pulled into one of the parking spaces at the department store. She felt her purse vibrating when she picked it up. Reaching for her cell, she saw that it was Sam. He sounded terrible.

"Hi. I am so sick. I think it's something I ate for lunch, food poisoning maybe."

"Oh no! Are you going to be okay? Maybe I should come take care of you."

She knew how bad food poisoning was. One time she had eaten expired meat and ended up in the hospital.

But he insisted he just wanted to crawl into bed to escape his misery. He told her the worst part was over.

"Are you sure, babe?"

"Yes, but thanks for offering. I'll be fine."

Patience told him she would call that night to check on him. Putting her cell away, she left the store to go home and let Rory out.

He was feeling somewhat better when she called. They didn't talk long because he needed to rest. She made him promise to let her know if he needed anything. She knew he wouldn't, however. He never wanted to impose on anyone, especially her. She made dinner and settled in to watch her favorite show, *The Twilight Zone.*

The next day, Sam e-mailed her that he was one hundred percent better. She breathed a sigh of relief at the news. She replied how glad she was. She had slept fitfully the night before, worried about him. That fact only confirmed her feelings for him. She knew she was in love with him.

Can I see you tonight? he wrote minutes later.

Absolutely, she replied.

Patience cooked a special dinner for him that night, and afterward they took

Rory for a walk. Although it was only Tuesday, she asked about rescheduling tea with his mom. She was free that weekend. Now that he was feeling better, she wanted to remind him about meeting his parents.

"I'll talk to Mom about it tomorrow. I'm sure Friday will be fine."

Sam was right. When he called his mom, she agreed to Friday evening.

* * *

Patience left school early on Thursday afternoon, which was a rare occurrence. She had made up her mind to do absolutely nothing when she made it home. The only activity she was willing to do besides taking Rory for a walk was lie on her couch with a bag of chips. Smiling to herself, she pulled up to her house and checked the mail.

She noticed a small giftwrapped package on her doorstep as she approached. Curious, she picked it up and saw that it was addressed to Rory. She didn't recognize the handwriting. She let herself in, and Rory came bounding toward her. He always acted as if she had been gone for eighty days when she got home from work. It was one of the things she loved about him.

"Santa Claus came early!"

She began tearing the gift wrap off of the box. Inside there were dog treats with a note attached that read:

> *Dear Rory,*
> *I can't stop thinking about you. Enjoy your treats.*
> *Sincerely, CG*

"Aww, how sweet is that?" she said to herself. She hurried inside to call Tripp, but her phone began to ring.

"Hello?"

It was Sam.

"Hi, it's me. You're not going to believe this, but my parents have to go out of town this weekend."

"Is everything okay?" she asked, worried.

"Yes, everything's fine. They just have to go visit my grandparents in Houston. It came up unexpectedly, but it's no big deal."

"Oh, well, that's good. When will they be back?"

"I think they'll be here Sunday night."

Patience talked to Sam awhile longer. After hanging up with him, she called Tripp.

"That was the cutest, sweetest thing anyone has ever done! Thank you so much for the treats!" she gushed.

"You're very welcome. I stopped by on my way to school this morning. Does Rory like them?"

"You bet he does. I gave him four since they're from CG!" They both laughed.

"I can't believe you had time to drive all the way over here before school. What a sweet thing to do."

"Yeah, it was either that or visit one of my girlfriends. But all of them were asleep at that time, sooo ... I decided to do something nice for Rory instead."

"Just how many girlfriends do you have?" She decided to play along.

"Only three. I take one out on Mondays, Wednesdays, and Fridays. Then there's the Tuesday/Thursday girl. And last but certainly not least is my weekend girlfriend. She's at the top of the list."

They bantered back and forth for a while, each of them trying to outdo the other. He had such a fun sense of humor. She truly enjoyed talking to him.

"How did it go with Sam's parents? Weren't you supposed to finally meet them?"

"Yes, but he got sick and couldn't make it. We were supposed to go over there this weekend but something came up with the family, and they had to go out of town."

Tripp listened quietly. Patience could tell he wanted to say something. She asked what he was doing that weekend, and he said he had no plans.

"We ought to do something, P," he suggested. "I promise I'll behave myself."

"You'd better! That sounds great. I'll let you know what day is good for me."

"Okay, I'll talk to you later."

* * *

March brought beautiful sunny skies and allergies to Patience. Although spring was her favorite season, her doctor's office made a fortune off of her. She blew her nose for the twentieth time that morning, wincing from the pain that followed. Her students were being unusually sympathetic, which made her nervous. Whenever they were nice, it usually meant they hadn't done their homework or were planning to leave early.

"You're wiping too hard, Miss McKlendon. That's why your nose is so red."

This piece of advice came from Shannon, one of her favorites. It wasn't ethical to like some students more than others, but she couldn't help it. Although she treated everyone the same, she had a soft spot for this particular student. Squirting more sanitizer into her hands, she thanked Shannon for the advice.

Patience climbed into her car at the end of the day, trying to remember if she had medicine at home. She knew stopping at the pharmacy was not an option, as she had absolutely no energy to walk through a store. Her eyes and throat were itchy, a sinus headache was brewing, and breathing through her nose had stopped three hours ago. She decided to take a chance and drove straight home. Luckily, there were allergy pills left in her medicine cabinet. As she lay down on the couch, she told herself it would be a quick nap.

It was pitch black outside when she woke up. Glancing at the clock, she muttered,

"Ten o'clock? You've got to be kidding me."

She checked her voice mail as she made some soup. Her headache was gone, and she could breathe through her nose again. There was a message from Cole.

"Hey, stranger, call me back."

She smiled and dialed his number.

"I'm beating you down the next time I see you!" he said. "And I'm stronger than you, so it *can* be done."

Laughing, she answered, "You're a wimp! I could easily beat you with one hand tied behind my back and my eyes closed."

"Quit dreaming! Where have you been?"

Sipping her soup, Patience brought Cole up to date on everything.

"Sam sounds like an ass," said her friend. "You *still* haven't met his family?" He had always been protective of her.

She sighed.

"No, I haven't. He keeps giving me excuses. Every time I'm about to meet them, something comes up."

The light finally went on for her as she said that. Sam was a pro at making up stories that sounded logical at the time. He'd kept her at bay for a whole month. Suddenly she felt very naïve.

"That's just what they are: excuses," said Cole. "You need to end things with this guy yesterday. You're my best friend, and I love you. Don't let him hurt you *again*."

"Too late," she responded, a quiver in her voice. Deep down, she'd stopped believing him two weeks before.

"Sweetie, is there anything I can do for you? Do I need to come over?" His voice dripped with sympathy. She smiled through her tears and told him there was no way he could fix this. She just had to figure out her next move. Changing the subject, she asked how he was doing these days.

"It sounds like I'm doing better than you, unfortunately. I'd much rather be hurt than watch you suffer. Anyway, Mom's been asking about you, work is boring, and I'm single."

"Cole, stop kidding around! Who's the lucky girl this month?"

"I'm as serious as a heart attack! I haven't been on a date since Camryn."

Patience shook her head in disbelief.

"Did she scar you for life? If she did, there's no reason for it. There are actually some good girls out there."

"No, it's nothing like that. Gosh, you can be so dramatic at times. Let's just say I like being single right now. I need time to myself, to discover who I am and the kind of person I want to be with."

She mulled over what he said.

"There's nothing wrong with that, I guess. And I must say I'm proud of you. It takes a certain kind of strength to forgo relationships for a while. Sometimes people think they *have* to be part of a couple at all times or they'll be lonely. But you can be with someone and still feel empty inside."

He started laughing.

"You're pretty deep tonight. But it makes sense."

"Besides," she added with a grin, "there really isn't anyone good enough for you. I was just saying there are good girls out there, but not for you."

"If I could clone you, that'd be excellent."

"Yes, and hopefully she'd have a brother for me. Can clones have brothers? I don't think so," she said, answering her own question. "Well, I could clone you as well, and we'd have a double wedding!"

* * *

Sam came over on Friday with Chinese takeout and a DVD. She let him in, and he kissed her in the foyer. Patience hadn't gotten much rest the night before. All she'd thought about was their situation. Something had to be said tonight. She was determined to resolve this matter once and for all.

"I missed you this week. How's it going?" he asked, holding her close.

She tried to stay focused, which was difficult while in his presence.

"Good," she said.

She began walking to the kitchen, but Sam reached for her again. Setting the food and movie down on the floor, he pulled her to him.

"What's wrong, sweetheart? You seem preoccupied," he observed as he nuzzled her neck.

Disengaging herself from him, she leaned back against the wall. She cut to the chase.

"*We* are what's wrong. Do you realize you've successfully kept me hidden from your life? It's been a month of excuses, and I say it's time to be honest with me. You've kept me at bay long enough."

Her pulse quickened. Confrontation was not one of her strengths.

"You have no intention of ever letting me into your world."

He moved toward her.

"Of course I do, sweetheart. I can't be blamed for the weird coincidences that happen when we have plans with my parents. Something always comes up when you're supposed to meet them."

He tried to reach out to her, but she sidestepped him. She didn't need him cooing in her ear, distracting her even further.

"*Does* something come up? Or do you create little stories to pacify me so we don't ever have to cross that bridge?"

"What in the world are you talking about?" Sam looked totally flustered.

Patience took hold of his hand, leading him to the couch where they could sit.

She faced him squarely.

"I'm referring to meeting your family. You're avoiding it, and I just want to know how much longer I have to wait."

He stood up and started pacing.

"I think you're reading way too much into this. And frankly, I'm getting pretty tired of you nagging me about it. Why don't you just relax and let things unfold naturally?"

She jumped up and walked over to grab the cordless phone off of her desk. She handed it to him.

"Fine. For argument's sake, let's say that I'm overreacting. Call your mom right now. Tell her we're coming over for a surprise visit."

Sam threw up his hands in aggravation.

"This is ridiculous! Not that I have anything to prove to you, but my parents aren't home now, anyway. They go out on Fridays."

She narrowed her eyes and glared at him.

"Hmmm, that's strange. I remember when we first started dating, you told me your dad was a homebody and that they never went out. We laughed about it and I asked if your mom was okay with that. You said she really was because she didn't like waiting in long lines everywhere they went."

His face turned red.

"Are you calling me a liar?"

Patience shrugged her shoulders. "I'm just saying that it's hard to keep up with lies you tell people. It's easier to tell the truth."

The two stood in silence. Rory left the room. It was as if he could take no more of the hostility in the air.

She studied the carpet, unable to believe it had come to this. Sam was defensive, agitated, and unwilling to admit she was right. She didn't know which was worse, the fact that he considered her a fool who'd continue believing his lies or his keeping her a secret this whole time.

When she dared to look up again, there were tears in his eyes. She watched as he picked up his keys, not once glancing over at her. Without a word, he headed for the door. She tried to stay strong but her heart couldn't take it.

"Sam!" she called after him.

He paused with his hand on the knob. She went to him, and he turned to face her.

"I'm sorry," said Patience. "Please stay and we can talk about it. I don't want you to leave, not like this."

He took her in his arms, holding her so tightly she could hardly breathe.

"I don't want to lose you. It kills me to know you think I'm lying to you. I promise we'll go to my parents' tomorrow, no matter what. You're right. This has been put off too long." His voice was a mere whisper.

They stood there for a long moment. When he spoke again, she could not believe her ears.

"I love you, Patience."

CHAPTER 17

On Saturday morning, Sam called while Patience was in the shower. She had taken Rory on a long walk; he was worn out when they came home.

Still wrapped in a towel, she dialed his number after listening to his message. There was no answer, so she left a quick message and went to blow-dry her hair. This was a hassle because it was so thick, sometimes taking up to forty minutes to dry. She received many compliments when she left her hair curly, but today she wanted it straight.

Sam still hadn't returned her call, so she ate a quick breakfast and began cleaning the house. After mopping the floor, she dusted the furniture and organized her papers in the den. Rory started sneezing from the cleaning products she used, so she let him outside. He was scared of the vacuum anyway, which was her next project.

Two hours later, she still hadn't heard from him. She picked up the phone to call him again just as her cell began ringing. It was Sam.

"Hi, sweetheart," she answered cheerfully.

The butterflies returned to her stomach, which amazed her. She thought that once you were with someone awhile, the nervousness disappeared. But she considered it a positive response because it meant the relationship was still exciting and breathtaking. On the one hand, they were comfortable with one another. On the other hand, she felt as if her heart skipped a beat whenever she saw him.

"Hi yourself," he answered, sounding out of breath.

"Have you been exercising?"

"Sort of," he began sheepishly. There was a long pause. "My truck stopped on me today at the grocery store. I went in to buy a few things, and when I came out, it wouldn't start. My friend had to pick me up."

"Oh, no! That's awful. Where is your truck now?"

"I had to have it towed to my mechanic. It's a good thing he's open on Saturdays. I'm just sorry it puts a glitch in our plans."

Concern filled her.

"That's not a problem," she said. "I'm sorry you were stranded today. It's good it happened at the grocery and not on a busy highway or some deserted road."

"Thanks for understanding. I was so scared you'd be mad again. Listen, I've got to go, but I'll call you soon. I love you."

"I love you, too."

* * *

Patience was climbing the walls from boredom later that day. Checking her cell, she saw that Tripp had sent her a text. He asked if she'd like to meet him at the gym. That was an hour ago. Pausing a moment, she contemplated calling him. Working out was the last thing she wanted to do, but she was desperate for some socializing. She dialed his cell to see where he was.

"Hey, I just read your text," she said when he answered. "What are you doing?"

"I'm sitting by the phone, putting my day on hold for you," he replied.

She giggled.

"Are you free right now?" asked Tripp. "I need a workout buddy."

She was stir-crazy enough to accept the invitation. Why else would she agree to meet him at the stinky old gym on a Saturday? Knowing she was desperate for companionship, she found her gym bag in the closet and went to get two bottled waters from the fridge.

Heading out the door, Patience tried to remember the last time she'd gone to work out at this place. Jogging along the trail at the park was her idea of fun exercise. Running out in the fresh air with Rory at her side had become more of a hobby than a chore. However, she had nothing else to do, and Tripp was such a fun person to hang out with.

She found him lifting weights when she arrived. Throwing him a water bottle, she began stretching out.

"How did you know I'd forgotten to bring water, P?"

He sat beside her on the mats while she prepared for her workout.

She shrugged in answer.

He smiled sincerely. "Thanks for coming today. I actually missed you, if you can believe that!"

She tried not to laugh while stretching. He was so funny and direct. She liked that about him.

They ran four miles on the track, and he had a hard time keeping up with her. She thought he was going to faint when they stopped for a drink. He insisted on watching her run the fifth mile, and then they took turns spotting each other with the weights. He had time to catch his breath, and she didn't give him too hard a time about his performance on the track. As she discreetly admired his profile, Patience realized Tripp was probably the only person she knew who made exercising fun.

He told her funny stories on the way to their cars afterward. Her sides were hurting from laughing and working out simultaneously.

"Where's Prince Charming today?" he asked suddenly.

She wiped her neck with a towel.

"His truck broke down at the grocery. We had plans, but of course they had to be canceled."

"Of course," he repeated dryly.

She didn't feel like hearing him bash Sam anymore, so she changed the subject.

"Isn't the weather nice? We should have taken the dogs jogging."

"I know what you're trying to do, but I've got to speak up about this. This guy is awful. You could be treated so much better."

"Tripp, things happen all the time. I know his behavior's been shady before, but this time I actually believe him. His truck has needed some work done for a while, so this comes as no surprise. The poor guy thought I'd kill him when he told me today. I mean, really, what was he supposed to do? Pick me up on horseback?"

He wasn't convinced.

"Hmm, I don't know. But I bet it doesn't take all day to have your vehicle fixed."

"How would you know? We're not even sure what's wrong with it. And we don't know how many cars are ahead of his." There was no one on her side when it came to dating Sam. Defending him all the time was tiring.

They were standing in the parking lot and Tripp turned to face Patience.

"You don't want to hear this, but what's his name doesn't appreciate you. He *knows* he has a great girl. You're funny, smart, so beautiful, and horrible at golf. But since a leopard can't change its spots, he's decided to pacify you with lies and excuses. Sam's not stupid. He figures you'll leave him if he tells you the truth."

"Which is . . . ?"

"Your relationship with him will always be in the closet, in the dark. You will never, ever be incorporated into his perfect white world. It's time for you to swallow this bitter pill."

But he told me he loved me, she wanted to say. Instead she kept her mouth shut.

Tripp took a step closer to her. He tucked a stray curl that had fallen out of her ponytail behind her ear.

"If you were my girlfriend," he said, "I would have it skywritten so everyone could see it. My family and friends would know you, and we'd have our own reality show on television. You would have no doubt in your head that I was proud to be with you."

Patience studied the pavement to keep from doing anything foolish. She'd never cheated on anyone in her life and wasn't about to start now. However, he was standing so close to her that, had she moved just one millimeter forward, their noses would touch. But no matter how unsure she was of Sam's intentions, she remained faithful. Looking back up into Tripp's adoring eyes, listening to the charming words any woman would find hard to resist, she didn't know how much strength she had.

They both jumped when a man in the car in front of them honked his horn, almost running them over. It broke the spell she was under, and she was thankful.

"Are you going to help me find my car?" She pretended his closeness hadn't affected her.

"I will only if you agree to have dinner with me tonight."

* * *

Stopping at a red light, Patience dialed Sam's cell. Part of her felt guilty for the feelings developing toward Tripp, but the bigger part knew she hadn't done anything wrong. Sure, he was fun to hang out with and easy to talk to. And he made her laugh, which was a good quality to have in a friend. She couldn't help it if all those characteristics came in a good-looking package.

"Hello?"

"Hi, Sam! How's everything?" She heard music in the background.

"Not too good, as a matter of fact. Turns out there are three cars ahead of mine at the shop. My truck only needs a battery, but I won't be able to pick it up until this evening."

She whistled.

"Whoa, that is such a bummer. Do you need me to take you anywhere today?"

"You're a sweetheart, but no thanks. I'm just going to hang out at my place until it's ready. Jonathan's coming over later, so he said he'd take me to get it."

"I guess you're lucky to have a mechanic who stays open later on Saturdays. The shop I go to closes early on weekends."

After hanging up, Patience drove around awhile, trying to figure out what she wanted to eat. She needed something healthy yet filling. Exercise always made her ravenous. Deciding on a sandwich from her favorite sub shop, she ordered one for Sam as well. He loved their meatball subs. She loved doing spontaneous things, and surprising him would lift both of their moods. She felt as if he deserved a treat after the bad day he was having.

Turning onto his street, she immediately spotted Sam's truck parked in the driveway. There were two other cars parked out front as well.

"That's weird," she muttered under her breath. "His truck is supposed to be in the shop."

Slowly passing his house, she made a quick U-turn and pulled up to the curb. She gathered the sandwiches and got out of her car. What an incredible liar he was. Her heart pounded as she made her way up the sidewalk. Covering the peephole with her free hand, she rang the doorbell.

Sam opened the door. The two stared at each other for an eternity, it seemed. At that precise moment she knew everything had been a lie. His truck was in great condition, and he had never planned on introducing her to his parents. She read it on his face. He looked like a deer caught in the headlights. She dropped the sandwiches on his doorstep and prepared to leave.

"Patience," he began.

She heard voices coming from inside. The music was low but audible. The smell of barbecue hit her like a slap in the face, as if teasing her for not having been invited to the small gathering. Obviously some sort of party was going on. However, the guest list was small. A female voice suddenly broke into a fit of giggles, and Sam tried to squeeze through the small opening he had created between himself and the door. Patience narrowed her eyes.

"Patience," he started again. His face was beet red, and she wondered how many other colors it would turn by the time she was done with him.

"Yes?" she retorted, waiting to hear what brilliant excuse he would magically come up with this time.

A pretty blond female came to the door. She gently pushed her way through the space beside Sam. Patience briefly wondered if she was the same girl Jana had seen him with at the mall. The girl asked Sam what was taking him so long, her eyes fixed on Patience with interest.

Sam's natural color finally returned to his face.

"Oh, um, Michaela, I want you to meet Patience," he sputtered.

The girls shook hands.

"It's nice to meet you," Patience croaked, standing awkwardly on the porch. She couldn't help but notice how cute the two looked together, their shoulders touching as they gawked at her in the doorway. Both Sam and Michaela had blond hair and blue eyes. They both had that innocent look about them. And to Patience's dismay, Michaela had a dimple just like Sam's. They would have made the perfect couple. It was almost too much.

"The pleasure's all mine," said Michaela. "Come on in!"

She pulled Patience in as Sam stood there with his mouth hanging open.

Inside, a gentleman sat on the couch, yelling at the television set. He was watching a basketball game and was apparently really into it. He looked just like Sam, only older and more muscular. Patience knew he was his father. Looking at Sam, she noticed his face was beet red again, and she had to stifle a laugh. Although she was angry, it brought her great pleasure watching his reaction during this ordeal.

"Honey, the steaks are burning! Can you please go take them off the grill?" A middle-aged woman suddenly emerged from the kitchen, a frantic look on her face.

"They're not burning, Jocelyn. Will you calm down? Sam, please go take the steaks off the grill for your mother."

"Stay right where you are!" said Sam's mother. "I told your father to do it. After all, it was his idea to barbecue in the first place. Now he can't tear himself away from that game long enough to follow through."

Sam, Patience, and Michaela stood listening with amusement as his dad rose from the couch, muttering something under his breath.

"What was that?" Jocelyn challenged him to repeat what he'd said.

Suddenly he looked over at Patience with interest. "Well, hello there!"

She could tell he was relieved to have a distraction.

Michaela hurried outside to save their lunch from burning, while Sam's dad waited for the introductions to begin. His mother was still standing a few feet away from them, but Patience could feel her eyes burning a hole through her.

With a huge smile, Sam's father shook her hand.

"Hi, I'm Grant. And you are . . . ?" he asked pleasantly.

Before Sam could say anything, she quickly answered.

"Patience."

As the two shook hands, Sam jumped in.

"She's a *friend* I met at the gym."

Her heart sank as his words sunk in. It was obvious the two knew nothing about her dating their son. Nor did he want them to ever find out. She could feel her face burning yet could do nothing about it. The writing was on the wall. All of the sweet talk he showered her with in the past was just words. Sam had no intention of messing up his perfect, lily white family.

Her mind raced as she tried to think of something acceptable to say. She wasn't good at lying on the spot, but she finally found her voice.

"Uh, yeah, we ran into one another all the time, so I introduced myself. We loved complaining about how neither one of us liked working out, and it just quickly developed into a friendship."

Sam shrugged.

"Yep. And we liked to laugh at the people who didn't really want to sweat, the ones who would work out for only five minutes and then leave."

Grant laughed and motioned for his wife to come closer.

"Jocelyn, come meet Sam's friend!"

Michaela had returned to the room, announcing that the food was ready. Sam's mother came forward with a fake smile pasted on. Patience knew it wasn't a real smile because it hadn't reached the woman's eyes. Plus, she was pretty good at reading people.

"It is so nice to meet you!" said Jocelyn unconvincingly.

Patience extended her hand toward her, but Sam's mother acted as if she didn't notice.

Grant cleared his throat uncomfortably, turning his attention back to Sam.

"Did you introduce the girls?"

Michaela smiled warmly.

"Yes, we met at the door. You *are* staying for lunch, right? Any friend of Sam's is a friend of ours."

If anyone said the word *friend* one more time, Patience was going to scream. She could feel her eyes welling up with tears. Looking down at the carpet, she tried to think of a way to regain her composure. It devastated her that she was so emotional, but there was no stopping it.

Looking back up at the people who had absolutely no idea she was involved with Sam, she shuddered.

"Um, I'm sorry but I ... have an appointment I can't be late for." It horrified her to feel the tears sliding slowly down her cheeks.

Sam's father went to her, touching her shoulder out of concern.

"Are you all right? What's the matter?"

She laughed through her tears.

"Oh, nothing, I just have horrible allergies. Uh, I'd better go. It was great meeting all of you. And thanks for the invitation." She turned and walked toward the door. Sam followed her.

Once outside, she took a deep breath of the much needed fresh air. She heard Sam calling her name, but she only quickened her pace. There was no need to waste any more time. Her instincts had been correct from the start. He obviously felt ashamed of her. He didn't want anyone, not his friends or his family, to know they were involved. Her cheek burned as if someone had slapped her.

Finally reaching her car, she fished in her purse for the keys.

Sam caught up with Patience and grabbed her arm, turning her to face him.

"If you will just wait a second, I can explain everything!" His voice was shaky, and she could see tears in his eyes as well.

She shook her head vehemently.

"No, *I* will explain everything to you. Your parents never went out of town, you didn't get food poisoning, and your truck is fine. You had no intention of ever introducing me to your family or friends, and I've been a fool."

"Please listen to me," he pleaded.

She folded her arms over her chest with an expectant look. "I'll give you five more minutes of my time, and then I'm leaving."

He moved even closer to her, desperation evident in his blue eyes.

"You're right about some things. I have been lying to you about the different emergencies that have come up. I can't remember the last time my parents have gone out of town, I'm perfectly healthy, and my truck didn't break down."

Sighing heavily, he continued.

"It's just been so hard, being torn between loving you and being loyal to my family. Honestly, I thought if I just gave it more time, eventually a miracle would occur. My parents would wake up one morning with new attitudes, and I could bring you home to meet them. You don't know how many times I've tried to tell them about you. Once, my dad and I were working on his car, and I came really close to opening up to him. He's more open-minded about things ... but my mother? It's amazing I didn't become a member of the KKK after being raised by her."

"It's not entirely her fault. She grew up in a very racist household. She thinks whites are the superior race. I've made comments when watching television with them about a phenomenal black actor or how pretty a Hispanic music artist is, but she either ignores me or makes a rude remark. My dad is more liberal, but he tries to keep the peace most of the time."

"Babe, I don't know how to convince you that I really do love you, but I'm so torn. I mean, my family will always be there, but ..." His voice trailed off, and he turned away.

Patience remembered what Tripp had said about families sticking together, which was natural. She didn't blame Sam for honoring his parents' wishes. She was just so hurt that he'd been stringing her along, lying to her and providing false hope where there was none. She didn't blame him entirely, however. Her involvement in this romance going nowhere played a huge part. When she thought of all the signs she ignored, it made her want to throw up.

Reaching for his hand, she turned Sam to face her. He looked grief-stricken.

"I don't know what to say. I am so hurt, but I know you can't change your parents. I'm sure that one day you'll meet someone who was born the right color and fall in love."

They both laughed.

"Patience, the problem is that you can't control *who* you fall in love with. I don't want to be with anyone else! You're the one I want, and it's so unfair that I can't have you!"

They held each other close for a long moment, and she could see his mother standing on his front lawn, watching them. She didn't want to cause any more problems, so she pulled back and told him he'd better go inside.

"I don't want to," he whined like a small child. "I'm afraid that if I let you go, I'll never see you again."

"You will see me again, I promise. I won't disappear. We're friends, and as weird as this may sound, maybe we can hang out sometime."

They both knew she was lying, saying anything to make the break easier. Yet nothing could relieve the pain in their hearts, for they both knew this was good-bye.

Reluctantly, he released his hold on her and she climbed into her car. With one final wave, she drove slowly down his street and out of his life.

CHAPTER 18

Patience was surprisingly calm and serene during the weeks that followed the end of Sam. She'd made her peace with the outcome of their romance, chalking it up to a hard lesson learned and experience under her belt. She didn't want to cry every time an obstacle came up in her life. It was time for maturity and a sense of reality. Life was not meant to be easy all the time. The irony was that she didn't hate him. Actually, she knew he would always have a special place in her heart, as he was her first true love. She couldn't control what family he came from or the beliefs they held, but her heart had known no difference. She had fallen in love with *him*, not his mother and father.

She woke up later than usual, even for a Saturday, and gazed out her window. The weather was perfect, nice and warm, and birds were eating crumbs she'd thrown out the night before. She couldn't believe April was right around the corner. Rory was still lying on the bed, looking more comfortable than a newborn baby in his mother's arms. She called him to follow her outside, but he didn't move.

"Okay buddy, I'll give you five more minutes. But if you pee on my bed, we're going toe–to-toe!"

He wagged his tail in reply, and Patience went to the kitchen for breakfast. The doorbell rang as she was trying to decide on an omelet or cereal with toast. She wondered who could possibly be stopping by before noon that day. Jana was supposed to pick her up for a jog, but that wasn't until two.

"What in the world are you still doing in your pajamas?" Tripp asked as she opened the door. She just stood there with a surprised look. Rory bounded toward him excitedly, barking and running circles around him.

"Hey, buddy! What's going on this morning, huh? Why didn't you wake Sleeping Beauty earlier?"

Patience laughed, shaking her head as she let Tripp in.

She was thrilled he had stopped by and wondered what he wanted.

He seemed to read her mind, as usual.

"I figured I'd come check on you. You haven't called in a while," he said as they walked to the kitchen. She offered to make him breakfast, which he eagerly accepted.

He set the table while she made omelets and bacon.

It wasn't until they were sitting when he turned to her with tenderness in his eyes.

"How are you doing? Are you feeling okay?"

He knew all about what had happened with Sam. Patience had stopped by Brew a week after they had broken up and told him the details. She didn't feel uncomfortable discussing the breakup with him. He was such a good friend and sympathetic listener, which made it easy opening up to him. Plus, she knew he'd be happy that she'd finally let Sam go.

"I'm doing well, thank you."

"You *look* like you're doing great, actually. Even with messy hair, you're gorgeous!" He looked at her approvingly, which made her blush.

"Thank you." She took a spoonful of her mixed fruit, savoring the sweet taste.

"I have to admit, had I been in your shoes that day, someone would've ended up in the hospital! If I showed up unexpectedly at my girlfriend's house and her parents disrespected me, the only survivor in that house would've been me."

She laughed. "What about your girlfriend?"

Tripp was shaking his head.

"I'd have to punch *her* lights out as well."

"Why?"

"Because she allowed her parents to treat me that way, that's why."

He handed Rory a slice of his bacon under the table, which led the dog to continue begging.

"Don't feed him human food! Great, now I'll never get him to leave me alone when I'm eating."

Ten minutes later, Tripp was helping Patience load the dishwasher. They were both soaked afterwards. He kept flicking water at her when he rinsed the plates off, and of course she had to retaliate.

"You're so childish!"

"Quit your whining, P. You were going to change your clothes anyway. You can't wear pajamas to the movies."

"What are you talking about?"

"I'm taking you to a movie later, silly." He flashed his beautiful smile as he started the dishwasher.

"I have plans today. And besides, that's pretty presumptuous of you to think I would say yes to your invitation." She laughed.

"I'm sorry. Okay, would you like to go with me to the movies tonight? Or do your plans extend through the evening?" he asked with a smirk.

"Sure, we can go tonight."

* * *

Tripp took Patience to see a comedy that evening, which they both thought was hilarious. He was the first person she'd been out with since Sam. She didn't call this a date or anything, but she'd stayed home every night for the three weeks after the breakup. It felt good to get out among the living, and she was glad they'd chosen a funny movie instead of romance or suspense. Afterward, he mentioned that his friend was having a party that night. He wondered if she'd like to drop in for a while.

"Sure, it sounds like fun."

She hadn't been to a party in a while, and it would be neat to meet some of his friends. He had mentioned his best friend, Joey, a couple of times since they'd started hanging out. The picture he'd portrayed of his friend was that of a childish, immature playboy whose only interests in life were girls, sports, girls, and drinking. Patience was not one to judge, however. Every now and then, she loved to let her hair down, to go out and have fun.

The two listened to music and chatted lightheartedly on the way to Joey's place. One of Tripp's best qualities was his sense of humor, and her sides hurt from laughing so hard. Saying yes to his invitation to go out had been a smart choice. He was such a fun guy, and they were getting to know each other even better than before.

She hated to admit it even to herself, but it also made her feel good to have a male shower her with positive attention. Although she knew Sam loved her, it was such a blow to have been rejected by not one but two families. Jason had seemed to really like her as well. But in the end, it didn't matter. She had lost both of them to circumstances beyond her control.

* * *

Joey lived in a plush two-story apartment across town. By the time Patience and Tripp arrived, which was close to eleven, the party was in full swing. A girl who looked about twenty-five answered the door. Patience would find out later that her name was Laurel, and she was Joey's latest girlfriend. Letting them in with a friendly "hello," Laurel introduced herself and offered to show them around.

She was one of those breathtakingly beautiful girls whom one wanted to dislike and could if it weren't for the fact that she was so nice and charming. Her dark brown skin was blemish free, her thin frame hovered over them at probably five feet ten inches, and her black hair cascaded across her shoulders perfectly. Laurel definitely stood out in the crowd of wild, drunken young adults surrounding them. There were people everywhere, couples dancing and making out in the living room and about five guys playing cards in the den.

Patience and Tripp followed Laurel to the kitchen where she asked what they'd like to drink.

"We have beer, wine coolers, tequila ..." she informed them. Patience chose beer while Tripp opted for bottled water. He didn't drink alcohol if he was going to drive, which was very responsible in her eyes. Unfortunately, he was her only friend who held to that principle.

They found Joey on his back porch talking to three other guys. He was grilling hamburgers and cracking jokes. His face broke into a huge grin when he saw Tripp, and an even bigger one after noticing Patience.

"Hey, what's up my man?" he greeted, high-fiving Tripp while still eyeing Patience. "It's about time you showed up!"

Tripp laughed.

"I would say it's an honor to be on the guest list, but by the looks of things" -he motioned at the people behind them- "I'd say that everyone in town was invited!"

Patience had to agree, sure that there were people from other states who had flown in just for the event.

Joey flipped the burgers, asking, "Who *are* all these people?"

"Honey, I think some of them are from neighboring towns!" Laurel added.

Joey still hadn't taken his eyes off of Patience, asking Tripp whom he'd brought with him.

"Oh, this is Patience. She's a friend for now ... but who knows? Maybe she'll come to her senses and give me a chance soon."

She felt her face get hot, and they all laughed. Flashing his most dazzling smile, "Romeo" took her

hand in his and kissed it softly.

"It is a pleasure to meet you, my dear. Why is it that Tripp hasn't mentioned you before now?"

She could feel him undressing her with his eyes.

Tripp reached over, disengaging Joey's hand from hers with a tense smile.

"Because I knew you'd try to take her away from me the minute you laid eyes on her."

Joey laughed confidently while Patience brushed imaginary lint off her shoulder.

Laurel cleared her throat, waiting for Joey to formally tell them who she was, but he never did. She stuck out her hand.

"Hi, I'm Laurel, Joey's girlfriend."

Joey finally caught on, apologizing for being so rude. The doorbell rang, so Laurel excused herself, braving

her way through the crowd once again. When she was out of earshot, Joey leaned in with a devilishly wicked grin.

"Isn't she hot? We met in California three weeks ago while I was on a business trip. She's a model and has a house in San Diego that she shares with a roommate, who's also hot, by the way," he added with a wink. "She makes so much money modeling in New York, and she's flown in to see me five times already! Can you believe that?"

Tripp gave him a pat on the back, a little too hard.

"What happened to the three girls you were dating last month?"

His friend handed Patience a burger.

"I'm a changed man! I'm sick of bouncing from one woman to the next, void of any real intimacy and commitment. Besides" -he paused for dramatic effect- "Laurel might just be the one."

Tripp chuckled. "And you know this after only a month of seeing her?" His face revealed his skepticism.

"Hey, she's the best looking female I've ever been with. It's got to be love!" He nudged Tripp with his elbow. "She's gorgeous!"

Tripp locked eyes with Patience.

"I hadn't really noticed."

She blushed again, trying to balance the plate that held her burger and chips, the bottle of beer, and her purse without dropping anything. It wouldn't have been a big deal for anyone else, but she was pretty clumsy.

Tripp wound up being the one to drop his plate on the patio before they made it inside. It was easy to see he wanted to escape Joey's company, rolling his eyes as his friend laughed and handed him another plate.

Following Tripp around the apartment, Patience watched as a couple began arguing and the girl slapped her partner across the face. He grabbed her arm and started pulling her toward the front door, saying something about taking it outside. Patience was so busy watching the couple that she hadn't noticed Tripp stop at the foot of the stairs, so she bumped into him. Hard. The food on her paper plate flew everywhere, and the dip for her chips landed smack on Tripp's back. Dropping her beer in the process, she was horrified to see it all over Joey's nice white carpet. It relieved her only slightly that she wasn't carrying anything red or purple. The beer stain should be easy to remove.

"I am so sorry! Look at your shirt!"

He laughed and told her that he didn't have eyes in the back of his head. She ran to the kitchen to grab some paper towels. She also found some carpet cleaner under the sink and a wet rag for his shirt.

Unfortunately, he wore black that night, which didn't go well with the white dip.

"Don't worry about it, sweetheart. I'll go get you more food."

He set his plate down at the foot of the stairs and disappeared.

No one seemed to notice Patience kneeling on the carpet, trying to clean up her spill. Everyone continued dancing all around her, and someone stepped on her hand.

"Ouch!" she exclaimed. She looked up and saw Laurel walking toward her with a trash bag and a fresh bottle of beer. Together they managed to get the stain out and trash the chips before people stepped on them.

"Thank you so much!" Patience smiled at the Greek goddess who had helped her. She took a long sip of her beer, wondering if she needed something a little stronger that night. She was so embarrassed, longing to exude the confidence and elegance Laurel possessed.

"Don't even worry about it," Laurel said, echoing Tripp's words from before. "It's happened to me many times. And besides, no one even noticed."

They stood in the kitchen talking for a while, getting to know each other. It turned out the two had much in common. Patience knew Jana would have liked her as well. She missed her best friend and made a mental note to call her the next day.

"There you are!"

Tripp told her he'd found the perfect quiet spot for them to sit and eat. Waving to Laurel, she followed him up the stairs to the guest bedroom, which was surprisingly clean and unoccupied. He had set their food on the bed. He closed the door to muffle some of the noise.

"Finally, I have you all to myself," he said, sitting on the bed across from her. She popped a chip in her mouth, totally comfortable with him. She was suddenly ravenous, for both something to eat and time with him.

Reaching for his hand, Patience gazed into Tripp's eyes with a sincere smile.

"Thank you for bringing me here. It means a lot."

He squeezed her hand gently.

"It's my pleasure."

* * *

Laurel and Patience exchanged phone numbers at the end of the night. Joey asked if he could have her number as well. She thought Tripp was going to blow a fuse when he overheard him. Throwing up his hands, Joey insisted he was kidding. The two girls rolled their eyes, sighing in unison. He was definitely a character.

Tripp had to practically drag her out of the place ten minutes later, as she and Laurel were in a deep discussion about cars.

"Aren't you ready to go yet?" he asked playfully. It was close to four in the morning.

"Okay, sorry! What's the hurry, anyway?"

She fell into step beside him on the way to the car.

"I didn't want Joey to ask you out before we left," he answered.

They climbed into his car and sped off, as if running away from the scene of a crime. She told him to slow down, and he obeyed. He still sped but not as fast as before. She looked over at him and saw that his face was tense. He could be so dramatic at times, and very temperamental. Out of the two, she was more even-keeled and consistent with her mood.

"Joey pisses me off all the time! He is so damn cocky! I don't even know why we went to his party. I mean, he thinks he's God's gift to women, that every female is supposed to fall at his feet, which actually ends up happening. He's never been rejected by anyone, and it's only because he's so good-looking and has lots of money. What a bastard,"

He went on and on while she listened, totally amazed at the effect his friend had on him. She had never seen him this upset before except when he'd found out she was seeing Sam. Clearly, Joey had touched a nerve.

Tripp was agitated and irritable during the drive home.

"And did you see how he gawked at you the whole time? The guy practically bedded you right in front of my face! How rude can you get? He doesn't even *like* black people! He said so himself one night a couple of years ago. We were drinking at my house, and he specifically told me he thought all blacks were criminals."

He stopped then, a look of horror on his face. He searched for a place to park the car for a second. They pulled into a vacant grocery store parking lot.

"Babe, I am so sorry. I didn't mean for that to slip out! Joey's an ass, and just because I'm friends with him, it doesn't mean I share his views about people. We couldn't be any more different as far as that's concerned."

Patience shrugged her shoulders.

"It doesn't really matter to me how he feels about things. He could be a member of the KKK for all I care. He's *your* friend, not mine."

Sure, it angered her to hear what Joey had said, but she didn't even know the guy. There were a lot of racists in the world, and it was inevitable she would cross paths with many. And if Tripp wanted to associate with people like him, that was his business.

"I do have a question, though. Why is he dating a black girl?" She had to ask.

He rolled his eyes, distaste written all over his face.

"He has always been attracted to black women, ever since we were in high school. He's so weird. He says they're the best looking females out there, so he goes out with them. He's such a jerk."

Patience reached inside her purse, rustling through it for chewing gum. As she opened the new pack, she thought about what he had said. One never knew what went on in the minds of different people.

Tripp seemed lost in thought suddenly.

She offered him a piece of gum, which he declined.

"Why are you friends with him?"

It wasn't that she cared. She just wanted to see what he'd say.

"I don't know. We met in high school and hit it off. He was a loner, and although I was on the baseball team and in the drama club, with lots of friends, I started hanging out with him. Believe it or not, he was a good person back then. I don't know what happened."

He paused.

"I guess I don't want to just throw him away over some character flaw. Even though all of those people were at his party, he only has one friend . . . me."

He looked pitiful next to her.

"Well, I have to admit that I've had friends who used to make racial comments about others, but I just told them not to say it in front of me." She laughed. "And I'm sure I hang out with people who are closeted racists. Yet they know I accept everybody and won't tolerate any nonsense."

He restarted the car, suggesting they talk about something else. The conversation had been sobering, and it was definitely time to think happy thoughts.

"I know, you can tell me how wonderful I am," she offered, which lightened the mood.

By the time they arrived at Patience's house, the couple were playful and joking around like two teenagers. They walked to her door, Tripp's arm draped casually around her shoulders. It felt comfortable, normal even. When he wasn't throwing a tantrum or being too sensitive, he was a joy to be around. She smiled to herself at the thought.

"Thank you for everything," she said. "The party really ... entertained me. Sorry again about your shirt."

"I'm glad you had fun. And for the twentieth time, don't worry about the stain."

"Okay."

The two stood there quietly, neither one knowing quite what to do next. Taking a step forward, Tripp hugged Patience warmly. Her mind raced, wondering if she should kiss him. As if reading her thoughts, he put his hands on either side of her face and pulled her toward him. She drew in her breath sharply, surprised by the effect his presence had on her. Slowly, he leaned in and kissed the tip of her nose playfully.

"You're terrific P. I'll call you when I get in."

Disappointment and relief swept through her body simultaneously. Although she wasn't ready for a kiss, she wanted one, *longed* for it. Unlocking the door, she turned to watch him for a second. When he reached his car, he waved good-bye and was gone in five seconds.

Patience climbed into bed fifteen minutes later, her thoughts drifting to Tripp. She liked spending time with him. He was adorably playful, charming, and thoughtful. She wondered if he thought about her often. He joked around so much, saying things like "I can't live without you" and "you're the one I've waited my whole life for," yet he said it while slapping her on the back and pretending to clutch his heart. A girl could easily become confused by his actions.

The ringing phone brought her out of the trance she was in.

"Hey!"

"Are you just getting home?" she asked.

An hour had gone by since he'd left, but he lived only fifteen minutes away.

"Yeah, I stopped and had breakfast after leaving you. I was famished."

Patience heard the birds chirping outside her window.

"I had to eat a bowl of cereal myself." It was six o'clock, yet she wasn't tired. She knew it would catch up with her later that day, though.

Pulling the covers up higher, she snuggled into her bed, still holding onto the phone.

"Did I tell you I had fun tonight?"

"Why, yes, you did. But you can tell me again if you'd like." He chuckled.

She closed her eyes, picturing Tripp's face perfectly.

"Thank you for being such a good friend. You've really been there for me."

"You're welcome, P." He was quiet for a moment.

"You know, I wanted to kiss you tonight, but you didn't seem, well, interested."

She opened her eyes, staring up at the ceiling.

"It's not that I didn't *want* to. Sweetie, it's only been a month since Sam and I ..."

"I know, I know," he interrupted. "And believe me, I do understand. Jumping into something quickly is not a smart move. But ..." His voice trailed off.

"What?"

He sighed.

"Okay, I'm just going to be honest. The more time I spend with you, the harder it is keeping my hands to myself. And no, I don't mean that in a sexual way. It's just that you're so fantastic, and you do all these cutesy things that make me laugh. I know it mortified you when you spilled ranch dip on my shirt and when you forgot that Rory was in my car ..."

"Hey, you forgot, too!"

"That's not the point. Anyway, I'm falling for you, P. And I want to be able to express it."

Patience's breath caught. She sat up straight on her bed. "You're doing what??"

He laughed at the question.

"I'm falling for you. And if I remember correctly, I've told you this before."

"I know, but now you've gotten to know me better!"

He laughed again. "I think you have low self-esteem. Anyone would be crazy not to be enamored by you."

"Aww, you're so sweet," she cooed.

"It's the truth."

They were silent for a minute, each lost in thought about the other.

"Listen, Tripp. I think you're awesome. And I am definitely attracted to you. Plus, I enjoy the time we spend together."

Patience paused.

"But can we take it slow? I'll understand if you don't want to wait for me."

"I'm not going anywhere."

* * *

Staying true to his word, Tripp remained a close friend over the following weeks after the party. He took Patience to an art gallery one weekend and camping the next, and he called her every night "just to chat." He even brought her lunch from one of her favorite restaurants to work one afternoon. He'd called the school to find out what time her break was and had surprised her.

"You didn't have to do this," she'd insisted, touched by his thoughtfulness. But he seemed so into her, wanting to spend as much time with her as possible. He appeared to have made his peace with the friendship status. It was as if he'd rather be her buddy than nothing at all.

One Friday evening, he invited Patience over to watch movies. She brought popcorn and sodas. He took the drinks, informing her that he *did* have snacks.

"I don't like that sweet popcorn you have. And I brought the soda for you."

She'd remembered that his favorite drink was Mountain Dew, which he'd mentioned casually when they first met.

He pulled her into a big hug.

"What a sweet thing for you to do! Thanks so much!" They stood in his foyer for a long time, holding each other. He made no move to end the embrace, and she had to admit it felt right being in his arms.

"You smell good," she murmured, her face buried in his chest.

He pulled back slightly, cupping her chin in his hand. They looked into each other's eyes, searching, and he slowly brought his lips to hers.

"I'm sorry," he whispered. "I just couldn't help myself."

She shook her head.

"Don't apologize, please. I wanted to kiss you."

CG sat at their feet, fully interested in the romance going on in front of her, wagging her tail excitedly.

Patience leaned in for another kiss, wrapping her arms around his neck. She knew their friendship was turning into something more, and she felt gratitude that he'd been patient with her while mourning Sam.

"Mmm," Tripp sighed. "That was nice." He still had his arms around her waist, holding her close.

"Yes it was," she agreed truthfully. He was a very good kisser, sending tingles up her spine.

He led her to his recliner in the living room, sitting down and pulling her onto his lap. She faced him with a sparkle in her eyes.

"You've got some smooth moves. I'm on your lap, so what happens next?" she teased.

"Well ... we're going to kiss some more, and then we'll watch the movie."

There was no mistaking the lust in his eyes, but she sensed correctly that he didn't want to scare her off by moving too fast. Relief swept through her. Although she wanted to lock lips with him, she was glad he didn't ask for more. Not yet, anyway. She had to pat herself on the back for all the progress she'd made since Sam. However, she didn't want to jump straight into another relationship.

"What are you thinking about?" Tripp broke into her thoughts.

She ran her fingers through his hair.

"I was telling myself what a great guy you are." She rested her head on his shoulder. They sat rocking in the recliner for a long time, neither one of them ready to move.

CHAPTER 19

By the time June came, Patience and Tripp were inseparable. Their friends couldn't find one without the other. Cole had a nickname for the new couple: Pipp. Ever the comedian, he put the two names together as the public did for famous couples. Jana thought the whole name combining thing was corny. However, she did agree the two seemed joined at the hip. Patience and Rory spent every weekend at Tripp's place, and he could be found at her house weeknights.

Jana called her one day after work, surprised to find out Tripp wasn't there.

"Was he in a car accident?" she asked, only half joking.

Laughing at her friend, Patience replied,

"No, he's working late at Brew."

"I can't believe you haven't applied for a position there yet."

They both giggled at the thought.

"No, but he did fill out an application at my school to be a substitute."

"Are you kidding?"

"Yes."

They joked around awhile, with Jana giving her friend a hard time about practically being married to him.

"That's just not true!" Patience objected.

Sure, she was spending almost every waking hour with him, but she still had her own identity. Besides, she knew without a doubt it would be a long time before she became serious with *anyone*. Although he was pretty addicting with his good looks and wonderful personality, she was scared to be hurt again. She confided all of this to Jana.

"Sweetie, don't let Sam, or Jason, for that matter, turn you into a bitter woman. There are plenty of good guys out there, and Tripp seems to be one of them."

It was no secret how Jana felt about him. After double dating with the couple, she had given him her stamp of approval.

“I know Sam’s not the only fish in the sea,” said Patience. “And he wasn’t really a horrible person, just confused about what he wanted. Nonetheless, I’m not anxious to find another true love.”

“Gosh, sometimes I can really tell you’re an English teacher. ‘Nonetheless’? You get on my nerves when you don’t speak like the rest of us!”

Patience rolled her eyes.

The doorbell rang, so she let Jana go, promising to meet her for lunch soon. It was Tripp at the door, hidden behind a dozen roses.

“Is it Valentine’s Day *again*?” she asked with a huge smile.

He handed her the roses, stooping to pat Rory.

“Nah, I just happened to be passing by the floral shop, and it had your name written all over it.”

“The floral shop did?” She laughed, leaning in to give him a thank you kiss.

“Yep, and I just couldn’t pass them up without getting my baby something.”

The two walked into her kitchen to put the flowers in water.

“How was work?”

He exhaled loudly.

“Not good. I accidentally gave a customer too much money back. She didn’t say anything, and I realized my mistake too late. She had already left.”

Patience wrapped her arms around him, pulling him close.

“If it had been me, I would have been honest and returned the money,” she cooed in a sympathetic voice.

“I know, because you’re such a good person.” He laughed. “Oh well, they’ll just take it out of my paycheck. That’s fine, because I’m rich.”

“I still don’t understand why you work so hard when you don’t have to.”

She led him into the living room.

“I already told you. It’s because I don’t want to be a lazy bum. Besides, I love people. I would go crazy sitting at home, counting my money in isolation.”

Tripp stayed with Patience most of the night, watching movies and cuddling. Things had gotten a little heated at one point, but he didn’t pressure her into anything. Although they’d spent many nights together, he’d insisted they not move too fast. She agreed. However, there were many times their make out sessions came extremely close to crossing the line. The mutual attraction made it difficult to behave, but somehow they managed to keep things respectable. She trusted him immensely, and each day she felt closer to him emotionally.

Before he left that night, he invited her to a party his parents were having that weekend. They were young, having had him when they were nineteen, and according to him were big partiers. He told her how his mom tried to be his best friend while growing up, keeping discipline to the bare minimum. And his dad was no better, trying to be cool when Tripp brought friends home. Ironically, he didn't feel close to them at all. He admitted once how he envied the relationship she had with her parents, who were authoritative in their parenting style.

"When is the party?" she asked.

"Like it matters; you're going to be with me anyway!" he laughed.

"Oh yeah, that's right!"

She gave him a peck on the cheek. "Well, I guess I just have to worry about what I'm going to wear, then."

* * *

Tripp's parents lived thirty minutes away in a small town called Princeton. As they drove, Patience looked out her window at the cows grazing in and the horses galloping around the fields. She saw a little boy riding his bike along a dirt road, and each house seemed miles apart from its neighbor. She knew that it was towns like this one that people from other states pictured when thinking of Texas.

"Now I see why people think Texans ride their horses to check the mail every day!" She laughed at the stereotype.

"Yeah, they do think that about us!" he agreed. "But nothing could be further from the truth, especially when it comes to my parents. The only reason my dad bought this house is because my mom fell in love with it. Wait till you see it. The house is one of the biggest I've ever seen in my life. I didn't grow up in it, though. They found it after I'd already moved out."

"If it's bigger than yours, I'll faint."

"Well, I will definitely have to catch you, because my house is a shack in comparison."

As they neared their destination, Patience began to get a little nervous.

"What are your parents like? I mean, besides being youthful partygoers."

Glancing over at her, Tripp gave her shoulder a gentle squeeze.

"I can tell you're getting antsy. It's okay, sweetie. Don't worry about them. They're just crazy. My mom probably won't even notice I brought someone; she'll be too busy drinking."

When they entered his parents' subdivision, a gasp escaped her. He was right. The house was definitely a mansion.

She turned to him and laughed.

"You've got to be kidding me! I should've worn a ball gown because this is a castle. I am underdressed, that's for sure!"

He stopped the car five houses down from his parents'. The long line of cars parked on their street prevented him from getting any closer.

"You look stunning, as always," he replied. "Don't make a mountain out of an anthill."

She leaned over to kiss him with a smile.

"I'm pretty sure it's mole hill," she corrected.

"Whatever, P. Let's crash this party."

They could see from the sidewalk that the front door was wide open, rock 'n' roll music filling the otherwise quiet neighborhood. Tripp shook his head like a disapproving parent and held Patience's hand even tighter.

The two walked into the house and stood there for a second, taking it all in. Compared to this scene, Joey's party had been a small, quiet gathering. She guessed there were at least fifty people in the living room alone, and she hadn't even entered the house fully. Couples were dancing, a man in his late forties was playing air guitar by the fireplace, and a young looking woman was doing shots at the bar. Three women were in a deep discussion in a corner; Patience wondered how they could hear one another over the loud Rolling Stones song that had just come on.

"Watch out!" a skateboarder yelled as he almost ran into the both of them. Patience jumped out of the way just in time, narrowly escaping a head-on collision.

"This is ridiculous," Tripp said as he put a protective arm around her. A middle-aged woman was carrying around a tray with glasses of champagne, and he asked if she knew where his parents were.

"I think your mom is upstairs!" she yelled over the music.

"Thanks!"

Patience followed him to his parents' bedroom, feeling the thump thump thumping of the music in her chest. She couldn't believe how big the house was; it seemed as if it would never end.

After walking down the long stretch of hallway, a beautiful dark-haired woman emerged from one of the rooms. She stood five feet ten or eleven, and her hair was in an elegant French twist that showed off her high cheekbones. Tripp looked just like her, Patience realized as she studied the grand figure. He had the same sparkling blue eyes, slender figure ... they even carried themselves the same way.

"Sweetheart!" the woman exclaimed, extending her arms out to her son.

A high-pitched scream came from one of the bedrooms upstairs, but Tripp's mother ignored it. A woman ran into the hallway, and her boyfriend emerged seconds later, dangling a toy mouse at her.

"Mom, who are all these people?"

She shrugged her shoulders.

"People from the neighborhood, hon. Well, some of them invited friends and family ... Wow! It sure does seem like a lot of people," she observed, her eyes wide in amazement.

He shook his head. "That's the understatement of the year." Patience laughed, and Tripp's mother looked at her as if just realizing she was there.

"Hello," she said to her with a look of curiosity.

"Oh! Mom, I'd like you to meet someone."

His mother smiled, extending a hand to Patience.

"Hi! I'm Valerie, Tripp's mother."

Smiling in return, Patience shook her hand.

"It's nice to meet you, Mrs. Cunningham." She glanced over at Tripp, who was grinning from ear to ear.

"I'm so glad my son brought a friend. He never wants to come to our parties. As a matter of fact"- she paused to give him a pointed look- "you don't ever visit like you should."

Patience smiled, being reminded of her own mother at that moment.

"Mother," he began, "she's not just a 'friend"'.

"Tripp, my boy!" a male voice interrupted from behind them. A tall, slender man approached the three with a huge smile. It was Tripp's father. He grabbed his son, picking him up off the carpet and swinging him around like a four-year-old. "It's so good to see you! To what do we owe this pleasant surprise?" Setting him back down, he looked from Tripp to Patience with interest.

Valerie rolled her eyes.

"Victor, please ... " she said. She leaned toward Patience with a grin. "He's so dramatic. I swear that's where Tripp gets it from."

"Hey, Dad. We heard you were having a party and decided to drop in for a while, if that's okay."

"Of course it's okay! Actually, it's fantastic! When was the last time I saw you? I think it was Christmas or New Year's when you blessed us with your presence."

Victor stood about six feet tall with broad shoulders and a slender build. His blond hair was shoulder length like Tripp's, and he had it pulled back in a ponytail. His big brown eyes were full of life and laughter, and he had a dimple that only added to his youthful appearance. His worn jeans were ripped at the knee, and the Rolling Stones T-shirt he wore showed off his muscular arms. To Patience, Tripp looked like his mother but had his father's personality.

"Leave the boy, alone sweetheart," Valerie chided.

The music seemed to get louder by the minute, and Patience had to stifle a laugh. He wasn't exaggerating about his parents when he'd told her about them. Their lifestyle annoyed him, but Patience thought it was cute. Sometimes she wished her own parents put more effort into being "hip."

Victor moved toward her, extending his hand with a welcoming smile.

"And who is this lovely young lady?" he asked.

Tripp draped his arm around her shoulders, a look of pride on his face.

"Dad, this is Patience."

A loud crash came from outside, startling them all. The four ran down the stairs and out the open door. Patience stared wide-eyed at the BMW on the Cunninghams' front lawn. Someone had crashed into their mailbox, which was now on the hood of the car.

Victor ran to the driver's side, helping his inebriated friend out carefully. Patience recognized the woman who had been doing shots at the bar. A large gash across her forehead oozed blood, and she winced with pain when Victor touched her arm.

"Tripp, come help me!" he yelled, but his son was already on his way over to them. Valerie had gone in to get some wet towels. Patience followed her, ready to do all she could.

Tripp and his father wove through the crowd inside, taking the woman into the library and gently laying her on the couch. Only a few of the guests offered to help while the others continued dancing and drinking. Patience had run upstairs to get some pillows, and they propped the injured woman's head up and applied pressure to the wound.

"Should we call 911?" Valerie asked, drops of sweat trickling down her forehead.

"I think we should, Mom. Her eyes are dilated. She may have a concussion, or worse."

"Don't be ridiculous! Just keep applying the compresses, and don't let her fall asleep," his father advised.

"Dad! Do you see how much blood she's losing? I really don't think this is a good idea. We're not doctors." Tripp was pacing back and forth nervously.

Victor wiped the sweat from his brow.

"You're blowing this all out of proportion. She'll be fine."

Although Patience was applying direct pressure to the gash, blood continued to escape, soaking through every thick towel she used. Panic tried to overtake her, but she knew freaking out wouldn't be helpful to any of them.

Victor closed the library door to avoid an audience while Valerie assisted her with their friend. Patience had to agree with Tripp. The woman's eyes were dilated, and she kept ordering them to let her sleep. Valerie had begun asking her questions such as where she lived and what her name was. She wanted to keep her awake as well as make sure there was no memory loss.

"What is your name?"

Her friend smiled despite the blood oozing down her face. "You know my name, silly," she slurred. The amount of alcohol consumed benefitted her, as it acted as a pain reliever.

"Humor me," Valerie pressed.

"Leslie." She closed her eyes.

Valerie shook her, telling her to wake up. Patience told Tripp to go fetch more towels.

"How old are you?" Valerie continued.

Opening her eyes again, there was a smirk on Leslie's face. "Twenty-five."

Patience smiled. The woman lying in front of her was clearly in her late -forties.

"Okay, so far her memory and sense of humor are still intact," said Valerie, exchanging a look with Patience.

"I'm calling 911," Tripp insisted.

Ten minutes later, a police car pulled into the Cunningham's driveway, followed by two fire trucks and an ambulance. As they carried Leslie away on the stretcher, Victor spoke to the policeman, who had many questions for him. The crowd had dissipated, leaving only a few who'd offered to stay and help get things in order. Ten guests had been planning on driving home like Leslie, but quickly changed their minds when the cops showed up. A married couple decided to stay in one of the guest bedrooms, while others called cabs to pick them up. One of their friends rode with Leslie in the ambulance.

Patience collapsed on the couch in the living room, gratefully accepting the glass of water Tripp brought her. Her throat was dry, and she felt dehydrated. The cool water calmed her nerves as well. She tried gathering her thoughts as she watched Valerie unsuccessfully attempt to remove bloodstains off the carpet. There were two men walking around with a trash bag, picking up beer bottles and food, while Victor stood facing the police officer with his arms crossed. He was still being drilled with questions. The night had been filled with drama, suspense, and action.

An hour later, Patience climbed into Tripp's car with a slight headache. It was four a.m., but she felt as if she had been awake four days straight. Tripp yawned, taking a moment to lean his head back on his seat. It was quiet in the car, and her mind raced as she replayed the events of the night. Her heart rate had finally slowed down to its regular pace and her body felt relaxed, but she couldn't get her head to stop spinning. She noticed that Tripp's eyes had closed; however, he suddenly burst into uncontrollable laughter.

"What in the world is so funny?" she asked.

"I'm just picturing my dad's face when he discovered Leslie's car on his front lawn. And then the look on his face when I told him I was calling the cops! Man, I wish I'd had a camera. It was definitely a Kodak moment!"

Patience tried to laugh, but her head had begun to pound.

"I felt sorry for your parents. All they were doing was trying to have a little fun."

Tripp sat up straight in his seat, turning toward her. "You've got to be kidding, P! They deserved everything that happened tonight ... well, except for Leslie getting hurt. I wouldn't wish that on anyone. But did you see the broken coffee table and the mess in that house? It's a result of their immaturity and irresponsibility. If they choose to act like imbeciles at their age, they have to suffer the consequences." He laughed again.

"Tripp! What a mean thing to say!"

"It's the truth, sweetheart. I love them, but sometimes they have to learn lessons the hard way."

He started the car, still talking about his parents.

"You know, I thought *I* was a pretty entertaining guy, but I'm chopped liver next to my dad."

It was her turn to laugh.

"But you act just like him!"

He shrugged. "I guess you're right. Our personalities do match. But I'm way more responsible than he is. Sometimes my dad doesn't think things through. He acts in the moment quite a bit."

The two chatted the remainder of the drive to Patience's house. Pulling into her driveway, Tripp turned to her, worry suddenly clouding his blue eyes. His moods were so unpredictable. She never knew what to expect from one moment to the next.

"I'm sorry my parents didn't have a chance to get acquainted with you. That was the sole purpose of us going over there. Are you terribly disappointed?" He reached over to hold her hand.

"Not at all," she answered. "I didn't expect to find out everything about your parents at their *party*."

"Well, I did," he pouted. "My dad told me Wednesday that they were having a small get-together. I thought we could all sit down and mingle, you know? This night wasn't at all what I expected. I didn't even get to tell them you're my girlfriend. There was always an interruption."

Patience waved her hand dismissively.

"It's not a problem at all. There will be plenty of opportunities to hang out with your folks."

She leaned over to kiss him. He caressed her neck, kissing her long and hard on the mouth.

When they broke apart, he sighed.

"You're right, P. As a matter of fact, I'm calling mom tomorrow to check on her. I can casually mention going out to dinner or something. Maybe we can all go to the club!"

She giggled.

"Your parents would take you up on that, I know. But I need some time to recuperate from this fiasco."

* * *

I'll have the steak, medium rare, and a baked potato, please," Patience told the waiter.

"Mmmm, that sounds good, too," Valerie said. She had ordered the salmon, informing everyone at the table that she was on a diet. With her tall, slim figure, Patience thought Mrs. Cunningham hardly needed to watch her weight. Then again, people often said the same thing about her.

"I may change my order," she told the waiter, winking at Patience.

Victor rolled his eyes. "Don't even think about it! Every time we eat out, you change your mind five times." He smiled at Patience. "It drives the waiters mad."

Patience giggled, and everyone laughed, the mood light and fun.

Tripp's parents had agreed to meet the couple for dinner when Tripp had called that Sunday morning.

"Yeah, dad, I don't know why Mom's so indecisive. She always takes food off of our plates anyway, so it doesn't matter what she orders!"

Valerie squared her shoulders and lifted her chin.

"We women can do whatever we want, right?"

Patience nodded with a grin.

"Absolutely! If we decided right now to have pizza, the boys would have to take us to the parlor down the street. *And* they'd still be obligated to pay for my steak and your salmon so we could take it home and eat it tomorrow."

Victor chuckled. "Over my dead body!" he protested.

"That could be arranged," Valerie teased. They all laughed as the waiter brought their appetizer and drinks.

Patience smiled adoringly at Tripp, batting her eyelashes. "You'd do it for me, huh, sweetie?" she cooed.

He visibly melted in front of everyone's eyes.

"Of course I would, pumpkin. I'd take you to six restaurants after this one just to find the perfect meal for you."

He leaned across the table, giving her a quick peck on the lips. She gazed into his eyes, temporarily forgetting his parents were there. The last few months with him had been a dream. Each day she found herself feeling closer to him than ever. And she knew he felt the same. He'd made it perfectly clear. And Rory absolutely adored him.

Suddenly Patience heard a gasp from across the table, bringing her back to the present. Tripp's mother had her hand over her mouth, eyes wide as she stared at them. His father held his wine glass to his lips, frozen still, his attention on them.

Tripp cleared his throat dramatically, a twinkle in his blue eyes.

"Mom, Dad, I didn't get a chance to inform you Friday night that Patience and I are dating."

Patience watched in amazement as Victor's face went from pale to bright red within a matter of seconds. Valerie sat there, motionless for a while. She then picked up her wine glass and downed the last few remaining ounces. She beckoned for their waiter to refill her glass. Then, looking over at Tripp with a confused expression, she said, "What do you mean 'dating'?"

Tripp sighed, reaching for Patience's hand.

"Patience is my girlfriend. We've been an item for almost three months."

"I don't understand," Valerie whispered, holding her glass up so their server could pour the wine.

He glared at his mother through narrowed eyes.

"You're not funny, Mom. You know what a girlfriend is."

Patience sat there watching as his parents tried to process the news their son had been so eager to share. Valerie chugged her wine while Victor took a pack of cigarettes from his pocket.

"Dad! You can't smoke in restaurants anymore!"

Without a word, Victor shoved the package back into his pocket. For a long moment, the four sat silently. The tension in the air was very thick. One could hear the other guests conversing in the restaurant; not a word was spoken at their table.

Their entrées arrived a few moments later, but Patience had lost her appetite. Victor thanked the waiter through gritted teeth. Tripp's hands were clenched into fists, and she wiped her sweaty palms on her napkin.

It was Victor who finally broke the silence.

"Well, this comes as a ... surprise." He choked on the last word.

Patience looked down at her steak. What happened to the friendly, inviting couple Tripp had introduced her to just two nights ago? It was a whole Dr. Jekyll/Mr. Hyde experience. Before Tripp told them about their relationship, Valerie had exuded nothing but warmth, kindness and charm toward her, and Victor had been more than welcoming and friendly. Now they acted as if their son had delivered bad news, tragic even.

"So ..." his mom began. "How long have you two been dating?" She took another sip of wine.

Tripp threw his napkin onto the table.

"Mother! I told you it's been three months!"

His voice was elevated, and a family sitting in a booth next to them glanced over. "Why don't you just say what's on your mind instead of torturing us with this awkward small talk?"

Victor stood up, the pack of cigarettes back in his hand. "What did you think our reactions were going to be? You invite us to dinner and then spring this news on us, expecting everything to go smoothly? Are you nuts? You know how we feel about ..." He stopped himself, looking down at Patience. He left the table, mumbling something about needing some air. Valerie excused herself as well.

"Tripp, you need to explain what's going on here," Patience said. "I feel like I've traveled into the Twilight Zone. What's up with your parents?"

He stood up.

"I promise I'll talk to you about this later when we're alone."

"We *are* alone!"

"I'll be right back. Eat your steak. It's getting cold."

He turned on his heel, following Victor's trail.

Patience sat at the empty table, wondering what to do. Part of her wanted to walk home. It didn't matter that it was ten miles away. Another part wanted to eat the free dinner, acting as if nothing was wrong. The waiter came to ask if everything was okay. After reassuring him that they were fine, she decided to eavesdrop on Tripp and his father, who were still outside.

She quickly took a drink of Valerie's wine, prayed she wasn't turning into an alcoholic, and headed for the door. It was dark, and she stood behind the bushes near the two men. The hostess at the door shot her a weird look, which Patience ignored.

" ... and I can't believe you didn't tell us about this sooner!" Victor was saying. She had to strain her neck to hear, but it was worth it. "I thought you two were just friends."

Tripp threw up his hands. "Oh, and that would have been okay, huh, Dad? As long as I don't date one, you're fine with it!"

"One?" she thought, bewildered. *What did he mean by that?*

"Exactly! Your mother's going to drink herself into an early grave after this!"

"Ha! Don't try to make me feel guilty about her alcoholism. She's never needed an excuse to drink."

She peeked through the bushes, watching as Victor took a few steps closer to his son.

"Don't you dare talk about your mother that way!"

His son didn't budge. Apparently he wasn't intimidated by his father one bit.

"What exactly is it about Patience that you don't like? Would it be her winning personality, brains, undeniable beauty, or charm? Tell me, Dad. I'd really like to know."

He folded his arms across his chest.

"That's not fair," said his father. "It has nothing to do with her personally. I just don't believe races should mix. Your mother and I have always felt this way, and you know it."

She gasped, and one hand flew to her mouth. Luckily, the two men hadn't heard her.

Tripp shook his head.

"I think you two are from the Stone Age! You always pride yourselves on being hip, cool, and liberal, yet your ideas are primitive."

"May I help you?"

Patience jumped at the voice behind her. The hostess and manager were standing there, curiosity written all over their faces.

"Um, no, I ... I lost my contact lens ... but I don't think it can ever be found in these bushes. I give up! I'll just order another pair tomorrow."

Feeling sheepish, she accepted the manager's hand as he helped her climb out of the bushes. Tripp was still arguing with his father, which was an incredible relief. The two never noticed she'd been eavesdropping. She thanked God for that gift. All she needed to do was make it back inside the restaurant unnoticed.

Approaching their table, Patience discovered that Valerie had returned. His mother smiled at her, but one could easily see it was forced. Father and son were coming in as she sat down, but before she could get comfortable, Tripp grabbed her hand, pulling her back to her feet. He picked up her purse and told his parents they were leaving. Victor didn't say a word, but his expression spoke volumes. Clearly he was not happy with his only son. Valerie fidgeted with a napkin, staring down at her plate.

Tripp almost pulled Patience's arm out of its socket as he took hold of her wrist, practically dragging her out of the restaurant.

The drive home was unbearably quiet, each of them lost in thought. She glanced over at the guy who had stolen her heart, sadness engulfing her.

How did this happen? she wondered to herself. The day before, she had seen no obstacles ahead of them. And since she had been friends with him first, Patience had truly believed their relationship was solid, able to withstand time. Their romance had appeared to hold so much promise.

But now all of her dreams that involved him were out the window. Why hadn't he told her about his parents not believing in interracial dating?

Memories of Sam came flooding back like a tidal wave. However, Jocelyn and Grant didn't even *like* minorities. Tripp's parents had friends of different races, but that's where it ended. Patience thought back to their party; almost half of the guests had been African -American or Hispanic. There could have been one or two Chinese people sprinkled here and there, but she couldn't remember.

In addition, the huge welcome they'd extended when introduced to her had been nothing less than heartwarming. Only after finding out she was his girlfriend did they go ballistic.

When they arrived at her house, she turned to Tripp with grief-stricken eyes.

"I can't do this. A romantic relationship is out of the question. I'll be your friend, but that's it."

His eyes grew wide.

"Look, I know my parents were less than friendly tonight, but they'll warm up to you," he promised.

She swallowed hard. "I know why they reacted to us so strongly tonight."

"What do you mean?"

"Tripp! I *heard* your dad say they didn't approve of us." She wondered why he was pretending he didn't know what she was talking about.

"How did you hear him?" he asked through clenched teeth.

She blushed.

"I was eavesdropping in the bushes."

To her surprise, he chuckled. "You know what? I just can't be mad at you."

"Mad at *me*? I'm the one who should be livid! Why didn't you tell me how they felt? All of this could've been avoided if you'd told me earlier- like on our first date- that they didn't want you dating black girls! Do you know how uncomfortable I was tonight?"

"I'm sorry, P. I can explain everything."

Running a hand through his hair, he began, "My parents are hypocrites. That's the bottom line. I am so sick of watching them pretend to be so open-minded, making sure to hang out with different races of people, buying CDs and movies with African-American artists and actors in them, blah blah blah. But they're racist if they don't approve of us. Face it. If you have to publicly announce how many black people you had at your house the night before or call CNN to let them know you went to lunch with Hispanic friends, it's all an act. Those kinds of things should be natural and unspoken, not broadcast all over the United States."

Patience sighed, taking hold of Tripp's hand.

"They're not racist just because they don't believe in interracial dating."

"It *is* racist, P!"

"No, it's not." She paused for a moment, putting on her psychologist hat.

"Is that why you shoved me in their faces? Do you think one of the reasons you date outside your race is to spite your parents?" She held her breath as she waited for his reply.

One would have thought she had slapped him because of the expression on his face.

"Absolutely not! How can you even *ask* such an awful question? You obviously don't know me at all!"

She quickly took him in her arms.

"Baby, I'm sorry! I didn't mean to offend you! I know you wouldn't do a thing like that. I apologize for even bringing it up."

Patience knew in her heart that Tripp cared deeply for her and that he embraced every culture and race. The two had spent so much quality time together the last few months that in some ways she understood him better than Sam. They could even finish each other's sentences, which she hadn't been able to do with anyone else, even Jana. He was special, no doubt about it. And she didn't want to lose him.

"Hello?" He lightly tapped her head with his finger. "Are you there?"

"I'm sorry. What were you saying?" Slightly embarrassed, she tried to focus on the conversation.

He kissed her softly, pulling her close.

"I love you."

"What?" She blinked, not sure she'd heard him correctly. The night had been a total disaster, with disappointment and confusion in the air.

Great. Now I'm imagining things, she thought in frustration.

Tripp searched her face, sitting perfectly still in the car. His voice barely a whisper, he repeated, "I said, 'I love you."'

Patience felt her eyes moisten with tears.

"You do?"

He nodded his head, his eyes sparkling in the dark. They kissed for a long moment, and she finally pulled away slightly, looking deep into his eyes. She thought about all that had happened that night. It was bittersweet, really. The irony of it all was that Tripp had professed his love for her, proving he didn't care what the world thought of him, yet his parents had shown their true colors, rejecting the idea of the two of them being a couple.

"What about your family?"

"Who cares? What matters most is how *we* feel about each other."

She stepped out of the car, totally confused and torn. She really did like Tripp, and possibly even loved him, but she just wasn't sure she was up to the fight. She didn't want to cause a rift between him and his parents.

Following her to the front door, he laughed as Rory barked continuously on the other side.

"I'm surprised he hasn't lost his voice by now," he commented while she struggled to open the door.

Patience's vision was blurred by the tears that had started to fall down her cheeks. Why did this always happen to her? She'd meet an awesome guy with whom she got along perfectly, yet race always tore them apart. Even Jason's mother, who was black, disapproved of her. She just didn't know if she could survive more heartbreak.

CHAPTER 20

Patience entered the house first, trying not to step on Rory as she went to search for a Kleenex.

"Hey, boy, what's going on around here, huh?" Tripp was roughhousing with Rory in the foyer. "Did you keep the burglars away?"

Patience laughed through her tears at Tripp. The dog adored him, and the feeling was definitely mutual. He always talked to him as if he were human, just as she did. And Rory responded positively to him.

She emerged from the restroom with red, swollen eyes. Tripp was in the kitchen helping himself to some chips in the pantry.

"P! Have you been crying?" With two steps, he was standing in front of her. He pulled her close to him, rubbing her back affectionately.

"What is it, baby? Are you still upset about my parents? If you are, don't be. They're stupid, ignorant people. I love them, but this is my life. I make my own decisions, and I will not allow them to ruin the good thing we have going."

She looked up at him with mourning eyes.

"Maybe if you just talked to them again-" she began.

He cut her off.

"It's no use, sweetie. They've been like this since I can remember. A couple of conversations are not going to change how they feel. I'm sorry, but that's just the way it is."

He cupped her chin in his hand and whispered, "This doesn't change a thing between us. I love you, and I know you love me, even though you didn't say it back."

They both laughed.

"I can't be with someone when I know there's no chance for a future together," Patience whined, still being held tightly by him.

He gazed into her sad green eyes for a moment. She held her breath, wondering what he was thinking. He gently stroked her face, leading her into the living room to sit on the couch.

"How do you know there's not a future for us?"

"I don't want to be hurt again. If your parents don't approve of us, eventually the stress will wear us out, whether you choose to believe it or not. And we'll have to break up, because I refuse to come between a son and his family."

But Tripp was shaking his head in disagreement.

"Uh uh. I'm not buying it. We can be together as long as we want. It doesn't matter what others say! You mean the world to me, Patience. I refuse to let you be consumed with unnecessary worries."

His eyes clouded over as she watched him. It seemed as if he was trying to make her feel better but couldn't stop himself from getting worked up again. He exhaled loudly.

"I'm just so sick of my parents! I really can't stand them sometimes."

He shook his head, his face turning red. "Look, I don't want to offend you because I know you go to church and all, but I think I hate my parents. The Bible says I'm not supposed to, but how can I not? They're so ... so ... horrible!"

Running a hand through his hair, he began pacing the floor. His hands were clenched into fists, and his eyes blazed.

"Calm down," she told him. "You're going to give yourself an aneurysm."

He took a few deep breaths, and she could see the bright red color slowly leaving his face. She actually felt sorry for him because she could see the predicament he was in. Sure, it was hard for her, too, but they weren't her parents.

He approached her again, this time with a slight smile.

"Sorry P. I just get so mad sometimes. It would've been nice for them to welcome you with open arms. But, hey, that's *their* problem, not ours." He kissed her lightly on the forehead.

Patience nodded, closing her eyes as she snuggled closer to him in the kitchen. At least for the moment, she tried to release her worries. She ignored the nagging thoughts in her mind about Victor and Valerie, which were gnawing at her like tiny gnats fluttering around her. Yet as hard as she tried, she couldn't relax, silently wondering why she continued to face this predicament.

* * *

Tripp phoned Patience the next day with unexpected excitement in his voice. She was convinced more than ever that he was either bipolar or had short-term amnesia, if there was even such a thing. His mood swings were so *frequent*, moving from high to low in a matter of seconds.

"Guess what?!" he practically shouted into the phone with glee.

She waited for his big news as she stood in front of her mirror, examining a new pimple that had developed overnight.

"Guess what?" he repeated.

She opened the drawer in search of zit cream.

"Oh! I'm supposed to really guess! Um, let's see … You've been promoted to manager at Brew?"

He laughed. "Try again."

"You're going to have a little brother or sister."

"Patience, we're not even going to joke about that! Okay, I'll give you a hint: it's about you and my parents."

She thought a moment. Applying the acne cream to her chin, she wondered what his big news could be. At the rate they were going, though, she'd probably never know.

"Your mom wants to kill me?"

He whistled.

"You are horrible at guessing, I see. When I got home last night, my dad had called to talk about 'the incident.' I gave him a piece of my mind-"

"I'm sure you did," she interrupted.

They both laughed, and he continued.

"Anyway, to make a long story short, they have agreed to spend some time with you to get to know you better. Isn't that great? I mean, I was going to keep dating you regardless of whether they liked you or not, but it would be nice if they approved. It would sure make it easier to attend family reunions, you know?"

"Family reunions?" she repeated, gazing into the mirror with a frown.

"Oh, sure! Three or four years down the line, after we're married and have had our first child, we'll be expected to attend those horrid events. And if my parents object to our union, I'll have to beat them down at every family gathering, the cops will be called, and you'll be forced to raise our son alone …"

Patience shook her head as she walked toward the kitchen. Tripp was out of his mind, she was sure of it. She tripped over Rory, who yelped and ran down the hall toward the patio. After letting him out, she went to her bedroom to get dressed.

" … So are we on for tonight?" he finished.

She paused, her hand on the closet doorknob.

"On for what?" she asked distractedly.

"Gosh, P! Have you ever been tested for ADD? You have the attention span of a four-year-old!"

She rolled her eyes, selecting a simple white top from her wardrobe. "As a matter of fact, I was diagnosed with ADD as a teen. Why?"

Tripp paused.

"Geez, I'm sorry, baby! I didn't know. Is that a touchy subject for you? Did I hurt your feelings? Man, why didn't you ever tell me?"

"It's okay. Don't worry about it. Now, what were you saying before? What am I supposed to be 'on' for tonight?"

"Oh, yeah. My mom is going to make dinner tonight. She wants me to bring you over."

Patience froze. She could think of ten million other things she'd rather do on a Sunday night than mingle with those two. Getting a root canal, being locked in a room with mice (which she was deathly afraid of), and running down the street with no clothes on were at the top of that list. Tripp was crazy if he thought she was going over there. She didn't see how spending one night with those knuckleheads would make a difference. The night before, they'd made it clear that they didn't agree with interracial dating. She didn't want to beat a dead horse.

However, was it possible to actually change their minds? If the only experiences they'd ever had with other races were bad ones, maybe, just maybe, she could show them that not all black people were bad. Perhaps all they needed was a night of good conversation and laughter with her. She could be sort of a spokesperson for all minorities. And it was so important to Tripp. She was sure he was holding his breath while waiting for her response. Besides, the Cunninghams couldn't be all that bad; after all, they'd raised Tripp right.

Patience sighed into the phone.

"What time are you picking me up?"

* * *

"Mom, Dad, you two remember Patience," Tripp said as they entered his parents' home. Valerie smiled wanly as Victor pulled Patience toward him. His hug took her breath away, and she could smell the liquor on his breath.

Victor laughed heartily, still pressing his body into hers.

"It's so good to see you, my dear," he cooed.

Tripp grabbed her arm, rescuing her from his father.

"Dad, you're going to smother her to death."

Smiling good-naturedly, Patience smoothed the skirt of her summer dress. "It's okay, Tripp. Your dad's just being friendly."

Victor laughed.

"She's right, you know. Quit being so uptight. I swear, you're just like your mother."

Valerie didn't respond as the four of them stood in the foyer awkwardly. Finally, Victor suggested they move to the living room. The smell of barbecue filled the air, and Patience could see the grill on their patio with smoke all around it.

"Um, Dad, do you think you need to check on the meat?" Tripp had noticed as well.

"Oh, crap!" His father's eyes widened as he ran outside, leaving Valerie to entertain the young couple. Patience smiled at the woman she sought to impress, but Mrs. Cunningham looked away. She muttered something about drinks as she disappeared into the kitchen.

Tripp led Patience to the couch overlooking the backyard, a huge smile lighting his face. He was holding her hand tightly, and they both laughed as Victor shouted curse words that could be heard inside. She could see the burnt steaks on a platter he held, and Tripp shook his head in amusement.

"My dad is not the domestic type. I don't know why he decided to grill for us."

Patience shrugged. "Maybe he wanted to make a good impression."

Tripp squeezed her hand lovingly. "You're probably right. Thank you for being so open-minded about my parents. It does seem like he's going overboard with the whole 'life of the party' thing. I mean, he is a friendly guy, but today he's really ... loud and obnoxious," he finished with a grin.

Valerie emerged cradling a wine glass, her eyes already appearing to have a glazed look. She sat on the love seat across from them, her posture perfect like the night before. Taking a sip of the red drink, she gazed at her son, disappointment written on her face.

Tripp moved closer to Patience, his hand resting on her knee.

"So, how's it going, Mother?"

"Fine."

She clearly had other things she'd rather be doing as well. Maybe she felt the meeting was no use, that she'd made her mind up about Patience the previous night, and nothing could change it.

Tripp chuckled as Victor burst through the back door. Sweat was trickling down his face, but he still wore the same dazzling smile he'd had before. He was very handsome for an older man, and the more Patience examined him, the more Tripp *did* look like him. At their party, she had been convinced he resembled his mother, but it was just that their hair and eye color matched.

"Well, kids, I put more meat on the grill. Dinner should be ready shortly."

He took the wine glass from his wife, taking a big gulp as Valerie glared at him.

"Honey, did you offer our guests something to drink?"

Tripp's mother didn't answer but dutifully walked toward the kitchen.

"What would you like to drink?" she asked them over her shoulder.

Patience could feel Tripp's body stiffen beside her as he let go of her hand.

Uh-oh, she thought to herself. Valerie was clearly being rude, but Patience knew that Tripp wouldn't stand for it.

"I'll be right back," he told Patience, striding purposefully to the kitchen.

Patience made small talk with Victor, who ended up being a pretty interesting guy. They chatted about where they both went to school, sports, and politics. She was surprised to learn that he was a Democrat. He asked about her family, her job, and her hobbies while Tripp's voice drifted out of the kitchen toward them.

"I'm sick of your attitude," he was saying, and then he began mumbling again.

Victor looked uncomfortable as he went to check on the steaks. Patience could feel her face burning and contemplated joining Tripp's father on the deck. At least she wouldn't have to stay perched on the sofa like a sitting duck.

"Well, you know what *I'm* sick of? I am so tired of your little rebellious streak. Every time I turn around, you're doing something just to go against the grain! You know how this family feels about ..."

Patience tried not to breathe so she could hear the end of the sentence, but Valerie's voice slowly faded. It was as if she knew Patience was eavesdropping.

Patience thought about lending Victor a hand with dinner, as he obviously didn't know what he was doing, when Tripp burst through the doorway of the kitchen, fury blazing in his eyes. Valerie stayed put. Patience heard the refrigerator door being slammed shut. Seconds later, the unmistakable sound of a glass being thrown against something, maybe a wall, could be heard.

Victor returned moments later, announcing that this time, dinner really *was* ready. His blond hair was tousled from the wind and smoke, his face red with sunburn, yet he could have lit a room with that gorgeous smile of his. As crazy as he appeared, the poor guy did put forth effort to make Patience feel at home.

"What's the matter?" Victor asked his son, taking off his apron.

Valerie emerged with two glasses of iced tea and a forced smile on her lips. Patience silently prayed there was no poison in hers.

"Don't be silly," his mother practically shouted before Tripp had the chance to respond. "What could be wrong? It's a lovely day, we're barbecuing, I get to entertain my only son and his ... friend," she almost choked out. "I couldn't ask for a better Sunday!"

But Victor's eyes stayed on Tripp.

"What's going on?"

His son shrugged.

"Oh, just dealing with Mom's same old attitude," he answered dryly.

Victor eyed his wife with contempt.

"You promised you'd make a genuine effort to be nice," he told her. He approached his son, who was standing beside Patience, holding her hand tightly.

"Look," his dad began, "I really want this dinner to happen. Just ignore your mother. I want all of us to sit down, enjoy the steaks I've burned, and get to know Patience better. She seems like a lovely young lady," he finished with a sincere smile.

Tripp looked over at Patience, and Valerie downed the remaining wine in her glass.

"Well, what do you think?" he asked hesitantly.

Patience smiled.

"I'd love to stay."

* * *

Mr. Cunningham led the others through the patio door to the smoke-filled backyard, excitement dancing in his voice. Patience laughed as Tripp rolled his eyes at his father, clearly embarrassed about his parents' behavior. But if she'd had the choice, she would have chosen to be stuck in an elevator with Victor over Valerie any day. She'd much rather endure corny jokes than rude behavior.

They all walked toward the picnic table with Valerie lagging behind silently when Tripp suddenly froze. Not paying much attention, Patience bumped into him. Victor was still talking animatedly as he went to get the steaks.

Tripp stood motionless, and when Patience caught sight of his face, she saw fury blazing in his eyes. She followed his gaze, which was on the table in front of them. She felt her heart begin to race. Placed next to the burnt steaks was a huge platter of fried chicken, a bowl of sweet potatoes, and another of greens. A dish with cornbread, which she actually loved, sat next to the greens. Two big bottles of hot sauce and ketchup stood beside them, and she knew without a doubt that the pitcher on the other table was either cherry or strawberry Kool-

Aid. To top it all off, the tablecloth was decorated with Aunt Jemima-looking figurines all over it.

Patience felt sudden waves of disappointment and disgust washing over her. Tripp wheeled around so fast to confront his mother that Valerie jumped. Victor had finally stopped the joke-telling and dancing, appearing to join the others in the real world.

Patience knew she needed to just get out of there, that the whole thing was hopeless despite Tripp's and Victor's best efforts. Valerie stood next to the patio door, rigid and stiff, eyeing her son with fear.

"Tripp, don't even say anything," Patience ordered with a trembling voice. "It's not worth it. Let's just get out of here."

"What?" his father asked, looking as confused as ever. Putting the spatula down beside the grill, he walked back to the group.

"This is it!" Tripp shouted loud enough for the neighbors to hear. He held up a hand toward Patience, as if to tell her not to try talking sense into him. The straw had finally broken the camel's back.

"How *dare* you insult my girlfriend with this ..." He waved his arm over the food grandly. "You are despicable! I don't know what you were thinking when you planned today's menu, but let me tell you, we are *not* staying to eat this garbage!"

Patience tried to grab his hand, but he yanked it away. His parents just stood there, Valerie's eyes still wide as saucers.

Victor placed a firm hand on his son's shoulder, turning him around to face him.

"Look," he began, "I don't know what has set you off like this, but you need to calm down."

Tripp ran a hand through his spiked dark hair.

"You're kidding, right? For your information, Patience and I weren't in the mood for 'soul food' today. And we don't appreciate the tablecloth decorated in blackface either. What a cruel joke," he finished with contempt in his voice.

"We had no idea ..." Victor began, turning to his wife miserably. Sudden realization registered in his eyes then, his shoulders beginning to slump forward.

"Why did you tell me this was a good idea?" he asked his wife. "You said Patience would love this and we'd score points for appreciating her culture. I should've known it was a lie. You didn't even want to *try* getting acquainted."

Tripp gave his father a firm pat on the back.

"It's okay, Dad. I believe you were making an honest effort here. We're cool."

Valerie opened her mouth to say something, but Tripp had already put his arm around Patience and was heading back inside. Patience felt tears in her eyes but refused to allow them to fall. There was no way she'd give his mother the satisfaction of seeing her cry. Besides, Patience shouldn't have been surprised by any of the events that had happened. Next time, she'd trust her instincts about people.

She quickly fell into step with her seething boyfriend out the door. She was sure there'd be a burning cross on the front yard. Victor called after them, but they were on the road in a matter of seconds.

At the speed Tripp was going, she knew they'd either be killed in an accident or that he'd hold her hostage somewhere, threatening to shoot her and then himself. He was just that type of person, someone who risked everything to be with the woman he loved. And if that meant pushing her off of a tall building and then plunging to his own death, that was fine with him.

"Tripp, do you see that stop sign up ahead?" she yelled out over his music.

No answer.

To her relief, he slowed down a bit as they approached the two-way stop. She didn't know where they were going or what was on his mind, but that was understandable. His mother was a dingbat. He had every right to be angry. The nerve of people really surprised her sometimes. She didn't know why Valerie hadn't just refused to have them over. Why did she insist on being so spiteful? Could she even help it? She didn't know if Mrs. Cunningham had been raised that way or not. In all the time they'd been dating, Tripp never talked about his grandparents on either side of the family.

They were a couple of minutes away from Tripp's house when he spoke.

"You're spending the night with me tonight, P," he ordered.

She sat peacefully in her seat.

"Okay."

He glanced over at her in surprise.

"That's it? That's all you have to say?"

She shrugged.

"Sure."

"Well, that was easy!" He laughed.

Tripp parked in the garage skillfully as the sound of CG's barking came from inside. Hearing it caused Patience to panic a second, knowing Rory would be home alone overnight. She made a mental note to call her neighbor, who had a spare key to her house, and have him check on Rory.

Tripp shook his head, banging the steering wheel with his fist.

"You know what, P? I cannot *stand* those people who call themselves my parents. They make me sick, literally." He touched her arm gently. "I know what you must be thinking. 'What if Tripp turns out like them?' But rest assured, I will never, ever be like those idiots."

She touched his cheek gently.

"Sweetheart, I've been around you long enough to know what kind of person you are. That's why I love you so much. Don't even worry your pretty little head about it, okay?"

She giggled and he rolled his eyes.

"You've been watching too many Westerns! 'Pretty little head?' What an interesting choice of words."

She smiled. "I think you're pretty."

He reached for her.

"Hmm, I've been called handsome and gorgeous, but no one has ever told me that I'm pretty."

They kissed while CG continued to bark. Finally, they went inside.

* * *

It was four in the morning when Patience felt Tripp's arms tighten around her. She turned over in the bed to face him, his warm breath tickling her nose with every exhale. CG lay contentedly at the foot of the bed, opening one eye to watch her. The dog adored her, and Tripp got a kick out of their newfound friendship. She believed CG would have come home with her at any moment, never looking back at her owner. Sure, the golden retriever loved Tripp and had a beautiful, spacious home to live in, but CG obviously preferred Patience over him.

Reaching her hand up to stroke her boyfriend's cheek tenderly, she sighed happily. She loved spending the night with him. All they'd ever done was sleep, to her relief. He'd never pressured her to do anything else. It was as if being together was enough for both of them. They had an unspoken bond, a chemistry, that didn't need to be secured with sex. Sure, the attraction was undeniable, and she knew he had needs. But for the moment, everything they did, which was basically just kiss, fulfilled them.

* * *

For the next few weeks, Patience tried to have fun with Tripp and savor each moment with him. Each time a worry would pop up about his family, she'd dutifully push it to the back of her mind. And he seemed to be just fine with the way things were. He never mentioned his parents while continuing to love and dote on her. She could not have asked for a more attentive, loving boyfriend.

Whenever she brought the subject up with her friends, they assured her that she was making too much of it.

"Who *cares* what his parents think? Half of the guys I know are dating people their parents don't like!" Cole had said with a wave of his hand. "It doesn't matter."

He'd reached out to ruffle her hair playfully.

"You are so old-fashioned, Patience!"

She'd received a similar reaction from Jana. Thinking she'd descended into an episode of *The Twilight Zone*, Patience decided everyone else was right. Maybe she *was* putting too much emphasis on the Cunninghams' disapproval of their relationship.

One Saturday morning, Patience woke up early to take Rory on a long jog at their favorite park. She had a lot of errands to run and wanted to get a head start. The dog had a blast in the warm July weather. Although the park was nearly empty, there were plenty of birds and squirrels for him to chase. He was unusually playful that morning, full of energy and excitement. They spent an hour there, as Patience wanted to wear him out so he wouldn't whine when she left him at the house later. They stopped by the pet store on the way home, picking up some new toys and treats for him. She was praying not to run into anyone she knew. She was still sweating from the jog and looked a mess.

When Patience got home, she showered and ate a light breakfast before heading back out to the grocery store. She saw that her mother had called while she was out and decided to wait to call her back. Sharise had a habit of rambling on and on about things, and Patience wanted to finish her errands first. Tripp was taking her to a play that evening, which she was excited about.

The more time they spent together, the closer they became. Each day it seemed as if she learned something new about him. He was such a complex person, very deep and intuitive. She thought maybe she'd met her soul mate. She was relieved she hadn't listened to her instinct a couple of weeks before. She had wanted to end things with him to avoid the drama she thought would take place with his parents. She realized what a huge mistake it would have been, and was thankful that her friends had talked some sense into her.

Getting dressed that night for her date with Tripp, Patience was pleased with her appearance. She wore a new black dress that had been hanging in her closet a while. It had been too dressy to wear on their other outings. It was strapless and fit her perfectly; not too tight, but it definitely showed off her slim figure. Her hair had even behaved that night. She had decided to let it grow out the past months, and the curls cascaded past her shoulders nicely.

She was happy to see no traces of frizz or tangles, which was rare. Rory sat at her feet, barking at his reflection in the full-length mirror.

The doorbell rang as she was applying mascara, and her breath caught at the sight of Tripp. He looked immaculate with dark slacks and a starched white button-down shirt. She smiled at his reaction to her as well. She thought his eyes would pop out of his head, they were open so wide. His mouth dropped open as he looked her over.

He stepped inside, taking her into his arms.

"You look spectacular!" he exclaimed.

"Thanks! You clean up pretty good yourself."

The two stood holding each other in the foyer, gaping openly. It was rare for them to dress up; their activities usually called for comfortable attire, such as sweats and t-shirts. Even Rory seemed to understand the importance of Tripp's trousers staying clean, for he just sat there wagging his tail with the expectation of being patted soon. But Tripp only had eyes for Patience at the moment. She bent down to pat him for his good behavior.

"Good boy, Rory! I am so proud of you! You noticed how nice Tripp looks today, too, didn't you, boy?" At that moment, he jumped up, his paws resting on her dress, and he began barking excitedly. Very carefully, she lifted his paws up off of her, backing away slowly. The material of her dress was so thin that his sharp nails could have easily ripped a hole in it.

"Rory! No sir! You can't jump on me when I look like this!" She was thankful she had taken him to the groomer just days before. At least they wouldn't smell like dog at the play.

Tripp laughed, kneeling down to rub Rory behind his ears. "Take it easy, honey! He can't help it. Give the dog a break," he kidded.

"Fine. You can let him mess up your clothes if you want, but we're not driving back to your house so you can change. We'll be late." They both laughed.

They left her house shortly afterward, with Tripp talking animatedly about his drama class. He had landed the lead in their adaptation of *Gone with the Wind*, and he was pumped up about it.

"You have to come to the show, babe. I'll make sure you have a front row seat. You've just gotta be there!"

"Of course I will. When is it?"

"I don't know. We received our parts yesterday. I'll let you know."

She laughed.

"Please do. I can't wait to see you in action."

Tripp's passion for acting reminded her of Sam. They both had that same gleam in their eyes when talking about either acting or architecture. The only thing that seemed to excite Patience lately was making it through each day alive. Sure, she loved her work, but the depression she'd overcome recently had taken the joy out of it. The only thought that put the pep back in her step was writing children's books. She had started journaling in high school and still did frequently. Sometimes it would just be a synopsis of her day. Other times she poured her heart out onto those pages, every thought and emotion explored each night. It was very therapeutic for her to write down her problems and obstacles in life.

They had a great time on their date, although she began to get antsy after intermission. She seemed to have difficulty sitting still for long periods of time, except when she was reading a novel. Her mother had informed her that she'd been diagnosed with ADD at a very young age. It was her eighteenth birthday, and she had invited tons of friends over for her party. Everything was going great until her mother decided to bring out the home videos for everyone to enjoy. What followed was embarrassing stories from her childhood that her parents decided to tell. Her friends had been so sweet, tolerating the never-ending tales of how Sharise had cried when she dropped her off for her first day of kindergarten or how five-year-old Patience had gotten her hand stuck in a ride at the amusement park. A boy she'd had a crush on had asked her mother what Patience had been like in school, and that's when the whole attention deficit disorder topic came up.

"Patience was adored by her teachers, but she would have to be moved constantly to the front of the classroom because she got so distracted, always talking to whomever they sat her by," Sharise had said. "I spent more time at her elementary school than I did at my job back then! Our little sweet pea had a great personality, but she just didn't know when to shut up and be still." Everyone had roared with laughter at the stories, much to her horror.

"Hello, are you there?"

Tripp was waving his hand in front of her face with an amused look. "I asked if you wanted to spend the night with me."

Blushing, she focused on the present.

"Sure. I just need to check on Rory and get some clothes."

Later that night, Patience sat beside Tripp on the couch, reading the paper while he worked on a paper for school. CG lay sleeping at their feet contentedly. The phone rang, and he ignored it. She reached for the remote to turn the volume down on the television. She wondered if he had heard it.

"Aren't you going to answer the phone, sweetie?"

"Nah, I'll just let voice mail get it."

After about four or five rings, there was a pause, then ringing again. Tripp continued working, seemingly oblivious to any outside noises and distractions. But she just couldn't ignore the constant shrill, and after about twelve rings, asked if she could get it.

"Sure, babe."

CG followed her to the phone.

"Hello?"

"Hi, may I speak to Tripp, please?" the female voice said on the other end.

"Sure, hold on a second."

He waved his hands at her, mouthing that he wasn't there. He buried his face back into his laptop.

"Um, he's not here at the moment. Can I take a message?" There was silence on the other end.

"Hello?"

Patience thought the caller had hung up and was about to do the same when the voice spoke again.

"Who is this?" the woman asked.

"Patience. Can I help you?"

Another long silence followed.

Finally the woman responded.

"This is Tripp's mother. What are *you* doing at my son's house when he's not there?" she asked in a tight voice. Immediately, Patience's hands began to sweat, and she gripped the phone nervously. She tried to get Tripp's attention, but he wouldn't look up.

She searched for something, anything, to say.

"Um, he had to run some errands, so he called and asked if I could check on CG for him," she lied. "He forgot to feed her this morning."

Tripp looked up then, and Patience whispered that it was his mom.

"Hmmm," Valerie responded. "Then how did you get in? Please don't tell me he gave you a key."

She looked down at CG, who had started whimpering. It was as if she knew Patience needed help suddenly.

"No, ma'am. Sometimes he leaves the back door unlocked."

Patience was relieved to see Tripp walking toward her. She wanted to kill him for putting her in this position. Valerie was not happy to find out she was over there, and Patience correctly guessed that his parents didn't know they were still dating.

"Are you sure that's all there is to it?" his mother asked skeptically.

Patience nodded her head quickly, forgetting that Valerie couldn't see her.

"Yes ma'am. I'm sure. I was just walking out the door when you called."

"Hmmm," Valerie repeated.

Tripp yanked the phone out of her hand.

"What the hell is your problem? How dare you call over here, giving my guest the third degree! It's none of your business who's over here and what we're doing."

He was furious, pacing back and forth in the living room while CG huddled closer to Patience.

"I don't care what you say, Mom!" Pause. "Of course we're still together! You and Dad are not going to run my life. I have a right to be with whomever I want." Pause. "No! Okay, you're being ridiculous. I'm hanging up now." He slammed the phone down on the receiver, his face red with anger.

"I swear these aren't my real parents! I must've been switched at birth, seriously. My real parents are out there somewhere, and I'm going to find them."

Patience walked over to him.

"Calm down. You're going to give yourself a heart attack." She knew he had a temper, and she constantly worried one of the blood vessels in his neck would burst.

They both walked back to the couch, each lost in thought. Tripp took a long sip of water, trying to settle down. She rubbed CG under her neck distractedly. It was silent in the room, and she didn't know what to say. Obviously he was very upset about his mother, but that didn't stop Patience from being irritated with him.

"Your mom didn't know that I'm still your girlfriend."

It was a statement rather than a question.

"I never told them we broke up. I guess they just assumed I ended things with you after the big fight at their house."

She felt her pulse quicken, and anxiety crept back into her body. "This is not good. Your parents are going to hire a hit man to kill me!"

"Forget them! It's all about us. I don't care what they think, but I do care if my mom calls *my* home, disrespecting *my* girlfriend. I'm not going to stand for it, do you hear me?" She swore she saw smoke coming from his ears.

Patience stood up, walking toward him. Putting her arms around him, she smiled sadly into his blue eyes.

"Maybe we should take a break," she offered hesitantly. It took every fiber of her being to utter those words, but she knew it was for their own good.

Tripp looked as if she had punched him in the stomach.

"What did you just say?"

She inhaled sharply, turning around so he couldn't see the hurt in her own eyes. "I'm saying that we should cool things for a while and let your parents get used to the idea of us. This is just too difficult right now. Even though you say it doesn't matter, in your heart I think you know it does."

He turned her to face him again, his voice trembling in agony. "You don't know what you're talking about. We'll be fine! Just ignore my mom. We don't even have to see or talk to them again. It'll be the two, well, four of us: me, you, CG and Rory."

But she had made her mind up. She couldn't stand it if she tore their family apart, especially if it ended up being a fleeting romance. It was useless to try to fight this battle, knowing she would lose in the end. She loved Tripp, probably more than Sam, but there was absolutely no way she'd forgive herself for coming between him and his parents. Her own family was so important to her, and she knew she'd die if they ever disowned her, which was what his parents were about to do to him.

"Sweetie, I know this is hard to hear, but-"

"Then stop saying it! We can make this work if you would stop letting other people's reactions influence you."

He started pacing.

"I can't believe this. What a nightmare! I find the girl of my dreams, and she refuses to be happy because of what others think! Unbelievable!"

Patience didn't have the strength to keep talking in circles, for this conversation was going nowhere. Tripp was stubborn, but so was she. Walking toward the couch to pick up her keys, she suggested going home while he cooled down. They could talk more about it the next day.

Tripp crossed his arms over his chest, his chin held high. "There's nothing else to discuss. It seems as though you've already made up your mind. If I'm not important enough to fight for, then I guess you don't love me like you say you do. And you're not the girl I thought you were."

She felt as if he had her heart in his hand, squeezing as tightly as he could. He really thought she didn't love or care about him! That was not the case at all! It was *because* she loved him that she was doing this.

She opened her mouth to say something, but he cut her off.

"Just go."

CG whimpered, huddling close to her legs. Kneeling down to the dog's level, Patience said good-bye to her.

She waited to see if Tripp was going to walk her to the door, but instead he turned and walked silently up the stairs to his bedroom.

As Patience let herself out of his house, she took one last look inside, wondering if she was making the right decision. It hurt so badly, she wanted to run after him. But deep down inside, she knew this was best for *everyone.*

CHAPTER 21

Patience didn't hear from Tripp the rest of the night. She wasn't surprised. He was so angry with her and disappointed. She sat at the table in Brew the next day, hoping he had to work. She needed to tell him that she loved him, that she was doing this so he could make amends with his parents. After an hour, she realized he must not be coming in, and she left. She drove by his house and sat in the car awhile, debating whether or not to ring the doorbell. His car was in the driveway, but all the blinds were shut. She called his home phone but there wasn't an answer.

Walking up to Tripp's door, Patience rang the doorbell six times. Other than the sound of CG barking, all was quiet inside. Standing on the porch, she was thinking about leaving a note when suddenly the door flung open, making her jump a foot.

A gasp escaped her when she caught sight of him. He still had his pajamas on, and his hair was a disheveled mess. There were dark circles under his eyes, and they had lost the sparkle she had come to love. He stood there watching her, a frown slowly creeping up on his face. For once, she was speechless.

"Um, hi. Sorry to bother you. I was in the neighborhood ..."

"Cut the crap, Patience. What are you doing here?"

Ouch. He wasn't going to make this easy, not that she expected him to. Wiping her damp palms on her pants, she asked if she could come in and talk.

"I think we said everything last night."

He spat the words at her like darts.

"You made it pretty clear how you feel about me, and I'm not one to beg, so ..."

CG was sitting at his feet, gazing through the doorway at Patience with sad eyes. She felt tears welling up and didn't know what to do. Maybe she and Tripp could be friends. She hated to lose him altogether and felt she needed him in her life. It had been only one day, but it seemed like he'd been mad at her forever. She had had no sleep the night before, all thoughts of him occupying her mind.

"Please, can I at least explain why I think we need a break?"

She shifted her weight from one foot to the other. It was very awkward standing there, knowing she was the cause of this heartbreak.

He sighed.

"I already know why you feel the way you do. You don't think our relationship is special enough to fight for. Well, I've got news for you: *every* friendship and romance has its problems. Nothing's perfect in life. You think everything has to be smooth sailing or you run away. Well, I'm done trying to convince you that we can make it through this. Like I said before, I'm not a beggar."

He closed the door softly on her, leaving her with the sinking feeling that her life was over.

Patience felt sad, guilty, and depressed. Why were her romantic relationships always like this? She drove to Jana's for comfort and support, but she wasn't home. Next she called her mother, who was still at church for the preacher's anniversary celebration. She wanted to curl up in a corner and just lie there, escaping her misery. Instead, she drove home to check on Rory. There were no messages on her answering machine, but she noticed on her caller ID that Sam had called.

She sat at the kitchen table for an hour, just staring into space. She had no energy to move or think. Rory was asleep in the living room, and all was silent in the house. She heard the birds chirping outside her window, but the sound made her mood worse. It was beautiful for July, very sunny and warm with no humidity. But her mood didn't match the weather one bit. She felt gloomy and depressed to the very core of her being. Part of her wanted to just sleep all day. That way she could escape her feelings of sadness and loneliness.

Sure, she had many friends and a supportive family, but she was still needed the companionship Tripp had provided. He brought out the best in her, making her feel alive and energetic. He made her laugh and act silly. But most of all, he made her feel loved. She truly believed he loved her.

Walking to the kitchen window, Patience gazed out as her eyes welled up with fresh tears. Her heart ached for him. It felt as if it had been twenty years since their discussion. She already missed his smile, the feeling of his arms around her, and even his temper. She loved everything about him, good and bad.

The phone began to ring, which brought her back to the present. Checking the caller ID, she decided not to answer. It was Sam again.

She wondered why he wouldn't let her go. Their relationship had had the chance to go nowhere as well. Sam, Jason, and Tripp all had families that disapproved of her. She was too black for two and too white for one. Her self-esteem was at an all-time low, and she knew she needed to snap out of it but couldn't.

Patience was in a funk, almost like someone drowning in the sea with no one to rescue her. She closed her eyes, picturing herself in the treacherous water, sinking down slowly to the bottom. She saw her mother reaching out to her, pleading for Patience to grab her arm so she could pull her to safety. But she refused, allowing herself to be pulled away from the surface, totally giving up on life.

* * *

Sharise called her daughter the following week to check on her. Somehow Patience gathered enough strength to answer the phone, knowing her mom had a million questions for her.

"How are you feeling, sweetie?" her mother asked, her voice dripping with concern.

"A lot better," she lied.

She gazed up at the ceiling, a small headache starting to set in.

"Honestly, how are you doing?" her mother persisted.

Patience knew she wouldn't let her off that easily. "I really am feeling a whole lot better," she lied again. The last thing she needed was for her parents to be worried about her. There was no use in everyone around her being sad, as well. She sighed.

Sharise hesitated for a moment, and then chose her words carefully.

"Honey, have you thought about ..." she began.

"What?"

"Your dad and I have been talking, and we're concerned. Maybe you should think about ..." Her voice trailed off.

"What?" she repeated.

"I don't know. Have you ever thought about seeing a professional? You know, maybe going to talk to a therapist or psychiatrist would help you sort out your problems and begin to feel better."

Patience scoffed at the idea.

"No thanks. I am not lying on a couch while telling a stranger my innermost feelings."

"Sweetheart, people don't lie on a couch anymore. That's just a cliché."

Her mother laughed.

"Your father and I really think you need to see some sort of counselor. We're so worried. You're not eating, barely sleeping, alienating all of us, and ignoring phone calls. This isn't right. I know the past year hasn't been easy for you."

"You're absolutely right. It hasn't been easy," Patience interrupted. "I have lost three wonderful guys back to back. And do you know why? Because of my *race*, mother! Not because I'm mean, not because I'm so ugly people can barely look at me, not because I'm conceited and full of myself, but because I'm mixed. Do you know how that makes me feel?"

Her mother was silent, so Patience continued.

"I'll tell you how it feels. Horrible! But no one can empathize with me because everyone I know is either white or black or Hispanic. I don't have any friends who are biracial. *You* can't even help me because you just don't know what I'm going through. So I think I have every right to be down in the dumps right now. I'm sorry I'm not snapping out of this like you and Dad think I should."

"Honey, we didn't mean ..." Sharise began with a trembling voice.

Patience told herself to calm down. It wasn't her parents' fault she didn't have any luck with men. Her mom cared about her and was trying to help.

"Look, I'm sorry," said Patience. "I'm tired and stressed right now, but I shouldn't take it out on you."

She could tell her mother was crying on the other end.

"Mom, are you okay? I am so very sorry," she continued and began to cry softly herself. What was the matter with her? She envied the people she knew who took life's hardships in stride and kept going.

"Baby, please listen to me. I think a therapist could really help you. And it's confidential. No one but us has to know you're seeing someone. Will you at least keep an open mind about it? Just take a few days to think it over," her mother persisted.

A sigh escaped Patience. She knew her mother would keep on until she relented.

"Okay, I will *think* about thinking about seeing a therapist. Happy?"

Sharise laughed. "Honey, that's all I ask. Promise me you'll call if you need anything. I don't like it when you isolate yourself."

* * *

The days that followed were horrible for Patience. Time crept by each day, and all she wanted to do was sleep. But when nighttime would finally come, all she did was toss and turn, unable to turn off her mind. The few times sleep did appear, she would have nightmares and wake up sweating or crying. It was unbelievable how the loss of Tripp was affecting her.

She didn't think the weekend was ever going to come. Collapsing on her bed right after work early Friday evening, she fell into a deep sleep and didn't wake up until noon on Saturday. In normal circumstances, her behavior would have alarmed her, but she knew it was the depression. Plus, she just didn't have the energy to be alarmed by the things she did.

Her eyes half-open, Patience walked down the hall toward the kitchen, wondering why Rory hadn't woken her up. He'd probably thought she was in a coma and had tried to dial 911. She had rescued him from a shelter two years before, and the latest she'd ever slept was eight am. They were both so energetic in the mornings, at least before things had ended with Tripp.

"Rory, where are you?" she called out in the silence. She finally found him hiding behind the couch in the living room, eyes downcast.

"What is it, boy?" Patience asked, reaching out to get him. Picking him up, she hugged him for a long time, not sure what was wrong. Still carrying him like a baby, she stepped into the kitchen and slipped on what she thought was water. She saw that he had peed on the floor, which he never did. He jumped out of her arms and stood over his 'accident,' tucking his tail between his legs and whimpering.

"It's okay, sweetie," she cooed.

She grabbed the disinfectant wipes off the counter and began cleaning the mess.

"It's all my fault," she continued, apologizing to him as if he were her son. "I just haven't been myself these days. Sorry I've been neglecting you."

A tear escaped and slid slowly down her cheek. Rory scampered over to her and nudged her arm with his nose. She sat holding him for a while, making up her mind to shake herself out of the funk she'd been in. No guy was worth all this sadness!

After her shower, Patience took Rory to a dog park across town, determined to cheer both of them up. She'd actually read somewhere that if you *acted* happy, it would cheer you up. It was some sort of trick you played on your mind, and one of her psychology professors in college had sworn by it. Desperation made her try anything at least once.

They drove with the windows down, Rory's ears blown by the wind as he stuck his head out. He sneezed a couple of times, and she laughed. He had the cutest sneeze in the world. The vet had informed her of his allergies when she'd first brought him home.

"Why in the world do you stick your head out the window in the summer?"

Patience yelled over her shoulder. Still laughing at him, she shook her head and pulled into the dog park, excited that her mood really had lifted a bit.

* * *

Each day for the next two weeks, Patience was relieved to find her mood improving. It was true that time really did heal all wounds. She started taking Rory out more, hanging out with Jana, and more importantly, actually *wanting* to get out of bed each morning. It was such a huge relief. Emotions could make or break one's daily activities. Her mom had noticed her attitude change, so she finally quit mentioning the therapist to her. Patience gave all credit to God. No other explanation existed. He performed miracles in her life all the time. No number of self-help books would have helped her get over Tripp.

One Saturday morning, however, Patience woke up feeling sad again. It was raining softly, and Rory was at the foot of her bed. She gathered up the energy to take him outside, shower and get dressed, but that was it. The remainder of the morning was a total waste. She lay on her couch in the living room with one of the self-help books she'd purchased the month before: *Get Over Him in Three Weeks or Less.* Her mission was to defeat this sadness and move on with her life. The television was on to keep her company, and her head up was propped up with a pillow as she read.

The phone began ringing, but she didn't answer it. The cordless was right next to her on the end table, but she had no desire to talk to anyone. After a few minutes, she could hear her cell go off. And about ten minutes after that, her home phone rang again. This went on for forty-five minutes, so she got up to answer, thinking it was an emergency.

"Hello?"

"Gosh Patience! I knew you were home! Why didn't you pick up?"

Cole sounded irritated, which was rare.

"I did pick up."

"Don't get smart with me, young lady. Really, what's going on?"

"I'm just having some 'me- time,' that's all. What's the emergency?"

"I just wanted to invite you to dinner."

She rolled her eyes.

"That's it? You rang my phone two hundred times for that? Well, I can't go."

"Why not?"

"I'm busy tonight."

She pretended to start getting onto Rory for something so she could hang up.

"Get down from there! Uh, listen, I'm going to have to let you go. I'll call you back."

"Okay. *Be sure* to call me."

They hung up, and Patience plopped back on the couch.

It was six that evening when there was a knock on her door. It was Cole.

"Don't say a word," he started. He let himself inside and turned to her. "I woke up this morning with a weird feeling you weren't doing so great. And it looks like my sixth sense was right."

Her wrinkled clothes were two sizes too big and she hadn't bothered to put her contacts in, wearing eyeglasses that were out of style. And she wasn't smiling, which was totally out of character.

"I'm taking you to dinner, so go get dressed."

Patience opened her mouth to object, but Cole covered it with his hands.

"And I'm not taking 'no' for an answer."

* * *

As he held out a chair for Patience to sit down, Cole said she could order whatever she wanted, that price was no object. She shrugged, her eyes cast downward.

"I'm not very hungry ... Maybe I'll just have a salad."

But he wasn't hearing it.

"Absolutely not! It already looks like you've lost twenty pounds. We need to fatten you up!"

He smiled, but Patience could see the worry in his eyes.

"I didn't drive you all the way over here for an appetizer, goofball."

Cole opened his menu, indicating that the discussion was over. She pretended to study the menu, but her eyes glazed over.

"Earth to Patience, are you in there?"

Cole broke into her trance.

"I'm here."

She just couldn't shake her bummed-out mood.

"I was asking if you wanted to split some nachos to start. I'm starving."

"Whatever."

The waitress came to their table. Cole told her they'd have chips and salsa for starters, and then asked Patience what she wanted to drink.

"Poison," she retorted, not cracking a smile.

He sighed theatrically, and the waitress sarcastically said they were out.

"I guess I'll have water, then," Patience mumbled glumly, staring at a point just above Cole's head. He ordered a beer, running his fingers through his hair with a look of frustration.

Sitting in silence for a while, the two watched as busy servers and busboys scurried to and from the kitchen. The restaurant was packed that night.

Gazing across the room, Cole broke into the silence.

"What're you thinking about?"

She shrugged her shoulders.

"Nothing. It's just weird that I was doing so well getting my life back in order, and then I woke up feeling crummy again."

Her friend listened sympathetically.

"Don't be so hard on yourself, kid. You've lost three guys you cared about back –to -back, all for basically the same reason. It would be tough for anyone. Give yourself a break. I think you're doing pretty well, given the circumstances."

Patience smiled.

Cole's eyes widened.

"What?? I can't believe it! Is that a smile I see?"

She giggled.

"And do I hear laughter coming from your mouth? This is unbelievable. Someone pinch me. I think I must be dreaming!"

The people at the table next to them looked over with a smile.

"Shh! Coley, please keep your voice down!" Patience commanded in embarrassment.

Shrugging his shoulders, he confided, "I'm serious. I was beginning to think I'd never see that beautiful smile of yours again, and it scared the hell out of me."

She didn't know what to say. Feelings of shame washed over her as she remembered all of her self-centeredness, complaining, whining, and snappy attitudes toward the important people in her life- except Rory. For some reason, she could never be cranky with him. Patience was so thankful that her parents, Jana, and Cole had put up with her recently.

"I want to apologize for being such a brat these past ..."

" ... months," he finished for her.

She leaned across the table to playfully swat at him.

"I was going to say 'weeks."'

As she was stretched over their table, she accidentally knocked over her glass of water. Cole grabbed a stack of napkins to clean up her spill, and she reached over to pick up the glass that had rolled onto the carpet. When she did this, her arm brushed against the huge bowl of chips already teetering on the edge. Chips flew all over the carpet area between their table and their neighbors'. She never realized just how many chips they'd been given until that moment.

A small child who happened to be passing by with his mother shouted with glee, happily stomping on the chips.

"Wooo hooo!!!" he yelled, still holding onto his mother's hand.

"Johnny, stop that!" his mom commanded, tugging his hand a little too hard.

"Ouch!" the little boy shrieked.

He massaged his hand with the other, pain etched across his face.

"That didn't hurt," his mother informed him. "Just wait till we get home!"

Johnny started whimpering, and his father came over to see what the fuss was about.

"Ellen, don't be so hard on the boy."

He picked the child up and hugged him. "They're just chips."

"Bad Mommy!" Johnny pointed a finger at her.

"Don't say that," his father scolded.

"She squeezed my hand!"

He held it up for evidence.

"Mommy didn't mean to hurt you."

"Yes, he did." Johnny insisted.

"Yes, *she* did, you mean. Mommy is a girl."

"I know that," the child snapped.

His mother put a hand on her hips.

"I swear, Bill! You're always coming to his rescue! You don't see how he behaves all day while you're at work. He's terrible. He knows better than to stomp on chips in a restaurant! We need to be on the same page about disciplining *your* son, or he's going to become more out of control than he already is!"

They continued to argue as they headed back to their table, and Patience looked at Cole with wide eyes.

"Can you believe that?" he asked with wonder.

"That was crazy," she agreed, kneeling down to clean up the mess.

As Cole stood up to help, he bumped into a waiter carrying a whole tray of food. *Crash*! Patience had never seen so much food. Her cheeks burned with embarrassment, and Cole began apologizing profusely.

The manager appeared and held out a hand to help her up.

"Don't worry about this," he soothed. "My staff will have it cleaned up immediately. Now, let's seat you two at another table, shall we?"

Patience stole a quick glance at Cole as they followed the manager. Her friend seemed very comfortable in the spotlight. It was almost as if he enjoyed being the center of attention, negative as it was. She, on the other hand, was mortified. It felt as if they had been there for five hours already.

She almost missed one of the two steps leading to the section they were headed toward. Cole caught her arm before she tumbled forward.

"Are you drunk?" he joked.

"I haven't had time to drink," she hissed through gritted teeth. "I've been too busy trying to destroy this place."

"Or at least put someone in the hospital!"

* * *

The remainder of their evening passed by smoothly, much to Patience's surprise. And as Cole walked her to her door an hour later, she told him what a great time she'd had. Despite all of the chaos and embarrassment, their outing really lifted her spirits.

"I'm glad to hear that," he said as he patted her arm, which was tucked snug in his. "Like I said before, I was worried about you. I'm your best friend, and I'm not just going to leave you alone at a time like this. You needed me, even though you put up a tough front."

They heard Rory barking inside, so Patience quickly kissed Cole on the cheek and said good night, letting herself in. She watched from the doorway as Cole drove off with a wave, and she quietly thanked God for sending her a great friend like him.

CHAPTER 22

"Honey, are you almost ready?" Patience's father asked for the fifteenth time. Her parents had come over to take their daughter out. It was the end of August, and school was about to start again. She wished she had taken a break that summer, but ever since she could remember, she worked summer school. Every year she promised herself that the *next* year she would take a real vacation, but in the end she always seemed to need the extra money. The downside was that she got burned out by the time the fall semester rolled around.

Her parents needled her endlessly about working too hard, but she couldn't help it. They had offered to help her out financially in the summers, but Patience wouldn't hear of it. They were the best parents in the world, and she would feel guilty taking their money. Her dad lavished her with monetary "gifts" all year round, and her mother constantly bought her things just to show her she loved her. The past month they'd really come through for her, helping her through her mourning of her relationship with Tripp. All her life they'd been there through thick and thin, and her heart overflowed with appreciation for them.

"One more minute, guys!" she yelled from the restroom.

She was having a hard time deciding on whether she should wear her hair up or down. They were going to Six Flags amusement park, so she thought a ponytail would be appropriate. But her hair had decided to behave that day, which was rare, so she contemplated wearing it down.

"That's what you said fifteen minutes ago!" her father yelled back with a laugh. "We're leaving in one minute, and if you're not ready, you'll just be left behind!" he teased.

Sharise playfully swatted his arm.

"Leave our baby alone! She can take as much time as she needs."

"Well, I *do* have to be at work by seven tomorrow morning," he joked.

"I heard that," Patience retorted as she walked into the living room. Rory was lying on the couch asleep, and she gave him a quick pat on the head before they left.

* * *

It never failed. Every time Patience went to Six Flags, she ate too much and got sick after one of the rides. She loved roller coasters and any other scary device that threw her around like a rag doll. Against her parents' advice, she always ate first, then immediately rode something that turned her upside down.

This time was going to be different, however. She was determined to go on the Shock Wave first and then eat something. But shortly after they arrived, her mouth watered at the delightful smell of funnel cakes and popcorn. Patience immediately headed toward one of the ice cream stands strategically placed by the entrance. Her parents followed close behind, shaking their heads dramatically.

"Remember you always get sick and regret eating too much when we come here?" her mother warned.

Patience waved a dismissive hand.

"Ah, it'll be okay this time. One scoop won't hurt."

John laughed, throwing up his hands.

"I give up, Sharise. Every year she says the same things: 'It's only one hot dog,' or 'My body's adjusted to eating all this junk now; I can handle it.' She'll never learn," he said good-naturedly.

"One scoop of cookies 'n cream, please," she told the vendor, totally ignoring her parents. "Oh, and can you add whipped cream and nuts?"

John chuckled, casually draping his arm around his wife's shoulders.

"I'm just glad *you'll* be the one she throws up on!"

Ever since Patience could remember, her father had had a terrible phobia: the fear of heights. Sharise, on the other hand, shared her daughter's love for scary rides at amusement parks. John's role was to hold the girls' purses and wave at them from the safety of the ground.

"Oh, Dad, loosen up, will ya?"

She took a huge bite of her ice cream, eyeing the roller coaster a few feet from them. Her mother followed her gaze.

"Uh-oh! Let me guess. You want to finish the ice cream in two more bites and then head for the hellacious roller coaster, right?"

"You guessed it."

* * *

Six rides, two hot dogs, and one caramel apple later, Patience and her parents were resting on one of the benches. The weather was perfect. The temperature had risen only a few more degrees from when they had arrived that morning. Patience smiled at a bird that had landed at their feet. This day was just what the three of them needed. Her parents always relished the time spent with her, endlessly begging for their daughter to just "hang out" with them. And she needed the emotional uplift this outing provided. Her parents were tons of fun, with sunny personalities and endless energy. Yes, they did treat her like a baby at times, but the good definitely outweighed the bad in their close-knit family.

"Well, what next? I'm getting hungry after all the screaming I've done," Sharise joked.

John laughed.

"How can you be hungry? Your daughter has eaten enough for the both of us! To tell you the truth, I'm a little nauseous after watching her."

Sharise grabbed her husband's hand, pulled him to his feet, and led them to the area where food was served.

"I need real food before I faint. *Your* daughter forced me to have popcorn and a funnel cake. Now I want pizza or something that will last longer than five minutes."

Both Patience and her mother were blessed to have naturally thin bodies, so they could eat whatever they wanted. Her father was long and slim as well, although he worked out four times a week.

Patience ordered chicken strips and people-watched while waiting on her parents. A group of young teenagers were laughing and horsing around at a table in the back of the food court. She smiled as one of the boys playfully threw a napkin across the table at one of the girls. She was cute, with dark -brown skin and long, curly hair pulled up in a ponytail. The girl grabbed some ice from her drink, leaned over toward the boy, and put the ice down the front of his shirt. Patience squinted as she looked at her. The young teen looked familiar.

"I'll be right back," she told her parents as she moved closer to the group of teenagers. She was wondering if the girl went to the school she taught at. Maybe she'd seen her in the halls.

The teen must have felt Patience staring at her because she began looking around the area. Their eyes suddenly met. The girl immediately stood up, a big smile lighting up her face, and she walked toward Patience quickly. Obviously, Patience looked familiar to the teenager as well, but for the life of her, she could not remember where she'd met her. Finally, when 'mystery girl' was one inch away from her, it dawned on her. The familiar smile tugged at her heart. It was identical to Jason's.

"Jaime!"

"Patience!"

The two girls screamed each others' names in unison and embraced like family members at the airport. She couldn't believe it. Of all the places in Texas to bump into someone! Six Flags was so big and overcrowded, one was lucky just to keep up with the people she came with!

"I cannot believe this!" Jaime exclaimed with glee.

"Oh my gosh! Oh-my-gosh!"

John and Sharise had approached by then, curious smiles on their faces. John was skillfully balancing both his and Patience's trays of food while her mother carried her own plate of pizza, the drinks, and plastic-ware.

"There's nowhere to sit," her father informed them as Patience helped Sharise by taking the drinks from her. But she was too busy wondering if Jason and the rest of the Peterson family were there than to listen to her father.

"Mom, Dad, this is Jaime, Jason's sister."

"Whose sister?" John looked blank.

"Oh, honey, you know ... *Jason*," her mother offered, extending her only free hand to Jaime.

"It's very nice to meet you, Mrs. McKlendon," Jaime said politely.

"Please, call me Sharise."

A family of five had just finished eating at a nearby table. No sooner had they gathered their trash when John power-walked toward them, setting the trays on the table with a loud *thud*. The family shot him a dirty look as they walked away, but he was oblivious.

"Thank the Lord," he sighed dramatically, motioning for the others to join him.

Jaime turned to Patience.

"Would you like to sit with me and my friends? They're really nice."

In so many ways Jaime reminded her of Jason: her tall, thin frame, contagious smile, and outgoing, friendly nature. At fifteen, she already stood eye to eye with Patience.

"Sure, I have a minute or two to spare."

She motioned to her parents that she'd be back shortly. Her dad shrugged his shoulders and proceeded to scarf down his daughter's chicken strips. She narrowed her eyes at him playfully, making a mental note to buy more, although, truth be told, her appetite had dissipated after seeing Jaime. She had so many questions to ask.

* * *

"So, what *really* happened between you and my brother? Did you really break his heart? Was it another guy?" Jaime began the interrogation as soon as they sat down.

Laughing, Patience answered, "Well, which question do I answer first?"

Jaime smiled.

"Just start from the beginning. Or should I say the ending?"

"What did Jason tell you?" Her palms began to sweat, as usual.

"Nothing much, unfortunately. The day he met with you for the last time at Brew- which I know because I was eavesdropping when he called you- he came over in a terrible mood. He was very grouchy at first and then became sad. My dad had invited him over for dinner, but he was in no mood to talk. If you ask me, he should've just cancelled."

Patience laughed. Jaime was a typical teenager, not one to mince words or hold back her opinion.

She continued.

"Anyway, I tried talking to Jason, but he ignored me. He can be so rude at times. So at dinner, he didn't touch his food, which made me nervous. Oh, and he was so rude to Mom. When Dad would ask him something, he'd answer. But he acted as if Mom didn't exist. And that's *my* job!"

They both giggled.

Jaime looked pensive.

"What *really* happened with you guys?" she repeated.

Patience chose her words carefully.

"Let's just say, your brother and I are wrong for each other. Separately, we're both great people."

Jaime smiled.

"But together, we just didn't quite ... click."

But Jason'ss sister wasn't buying it.

"C'mon Patience! It's *me* you're talking to! I saw the way the two of you looked at each other. I took a quiz in my magazine, and it showed I have very high interpersonal- or was it *intra* personal?- skills. That means I read people and have almost a sixth sense about things."

Patience laughed. Jaime cracked her up! She was so immature on the one hand, yet she acted very serious and adult like on the other. Just talking to her was an experience in itself.

Yet no matter how much Jaime thought she wanted to know the details of their breakup, Patience kept in mind that she was Jason's sister. There was no way she needed to know the real reason for the split.

"It's true. Our personalities clashed. Jason and I were just too different to be in a relationship."

Jaime leaned in closer toward her.

"By the end of dinner that night, Jason had tears in his eyes. Can you believe it? Actual, real tears were brimming in his eyes. That's not like Mr. Tough Guy at all! He finally excused himself and went home. Patience, you have to tell me the truth. Maybe I can help, and the two of you can get back together," she suggested naively.

The two sat looking at each other for a while. There was chaos all around them as Jaime's friends continued to clown around. Patience glanced over at her parents throwing their trash away and saw her mother signaling for her to wrap it up. Jaime noticed as well and desperately took Patience's hand.

"Please call my brother," she pleaded. "He really does miss you. We all do! Little Jessie still asks about you, and she sleeps with that Barbie you gave her for Christmas! And Jackson has your name scribbled all over his science notebook. I saw it when I was snooping through his backpack."

Patience felt a tug at her heart. Jaime wasn't kidding around.

"I want the two of you back together immediately," his sister said. "I mean, he has a girlfriend and everything, but, like, I can break them up easily."

Patience held up her hands.

"Whoa! He's seeing someone? You should've told me that in the beginning. Obviously he's moved on."

"No, no, no, it's not like that," Jaime insisted. "Mahogany is just some girl my mother fixed him up with about a month ago. She's from Nigeria or somewhere."

That figures, Patience thought begrudgingly.

"I can totally tell he doesn't like her. He's just trying to keep the peace with Mom. They've been arguing more lately when he comes to visit."

Both girls' cell phones began ringing simultaneously.

"Hello?"

"Patience, honey, we're leaving. Would you like to come with us or spend the night here?"

She looked up and saw her parents heading out of the food court entrance. Her father blew her a kiss, pretending they were going to leave her there.

Closing her phone, she overheard Jaime say, "Just talk to her. Yes, she's right here."

Patience mouthed the words, "Is that Jason?"

When she nodded her head yes, Patience rose to leave.

"I have to go," she whispered.

"I'll call you back," Jaime said quickly and hung up.

She began walking with Patience toward her parents. The girls hugged again, and Jaime thanked her for the gift card, telling her that her brothers loved their presents as well. She then made Patience promise to visit sometime.

"Maybe we can go to the mall or something. And I know what you're thinking, but you won't run into Jason or anything. He rarely comes over these days."

But accidentally bumping into Jason was the least of Patience's worries. Carolyn Peterson would have her thrown in jail for trespassing if she showed up there. She didn't put anything past that woman.

"We'll see," was all she could say.

PART IV: ROMAN

CHAPTER 23

"Rory! What are you *into*?" Patience sat in her living room one Sunday afternoon, working on her computer. It was September, and the cool breeze gently blew her curtains. All of her windows were open, and she had looked up just in time to see her beloved pet destroying her garden in the backyard. Jumping up, she knocked over her glass of water as she ran outside.

"Shoot!"

She didn't know whether to go grab a towel from the kitchen first or try to salvage what few flowers the dog may have left. She decided on the latter.

Rory ran away as soon as he caught sight of his master. When she approached, Patience could see exactly how much damage had been done. The entire garden was ruined. She had put so much time and energy into planting her favorites- tulips, lilies, and daffodils- but they were all uprooted. On top of that, Rory had proceeded to dig a huge hole by the fence. Shaking her head in frustration, Patience turned on her heel to go find him. He was hiding inside, behind the couch again. That was his favorite place to go when he committed a crime of some sort.

"Why are you such a naughty boy?" she asked as she pulled him out. Scooping him up, the two headed back to the scene of the crime.

Sitting him down beside the torn-up garden, she put on her firmest, most no-nonsense tone of voice and proceeded to scold him. She spent five minutes alternating between pointing to the mess, shaking her head dramatically, and using the words "no" and "not for Rory." She knew he wasn't paying attention. At one point he even jumped up to try to lick her face as she knelt beside him. It was clearly no use and a total waste of her Sunday. Later, she recounted the scene to her mother.

"I just don't know what to do! Mom, his behavior is totally unacceptable. He's been with me long enough to know better."

"Honey, give him time," Sharise advised calmly. "You can't expect him to be perfect. Why, he *just* graduated from that school you enrolled him in

... What was it called again? 'How to train a dog in one week'? I swear, sweetheart, those classes are horrible! It's for owners who don't want to deal with anything but perfection. I mean, why even get a pet if you're not going to love him unconditionally?"

Patience rolled her eyes. Her mom had a soft spot for Rory, but to a fault. She let him get away with murder whenever they had to pet-sit for her. Her dad was another story. He expected the dog to act like he had good sense. At all times. No warnings, no second chances, nothing.

"Mom, pet owners enroll their dogs in the class *because* they love them. He needs to have boundaries. If I allow him to do whatever he wants, when he wants, it would show I didn't care about him. He could get hurt- or hurt someone- as a consequence of his bad behavior. He's just like a child, and children actually like discipline."

"Hmph," her well-meaning mother scoffed. "All Rory needs is some nurturing from his grandmother. Why don't you let him spend the night with us tonight, and you can pick him up tomorrow after school? It sounds like you need a break anyway."

Instead of arguing further, she agreed and promised to drop Rory off in an hour at the McKlendons'.

* * *

As it turned out, Rory stayed with her parents the full week. Her mother had texted her that Monday, insisting she wanted to keep him longer. She had the tendency to get lonely, and Rory was the perfect companion. And he loved Sharise and John to death. They took him on longer walks and gave him more treats than his owner. In addition, she knew how much her mother loved animals, so it was the perfect temporary solution for all of them.

But by Wednesday, Patience began to miss him. He really was like a son to her, so she had to make plans for that night to take her mind off of him. She called Cole and invited herself over to his place, where they ordered pizza and played video games. He updated her on recent activities happening in his life. He had joined a Bible study group that met every Saturday evening for an hour, was still single (which surprised her to the utmost) and had contacted one of the local universities to begin working on his masters.

"Wow, you've been busy! No wonder I haven't heard much from you lately."

Cole smiled.

"I know. Since my best friend in the whole world abandoned me to 'find herself,' I decided to be my own source of entertainment."

They both laughed.

"What do you mean 'abandoned you'?" chided Patience. "I've just been busy, that's all."

"Well, regardless of the reason, we haven't seen each other in a while, and I don't want to hang out with Jana, so I had to spread my wings, think outside the box."

Cole and Jana didn't always get along, Patience knew. To be honest, the two weren't even friends, just acquaintances who happened to be thrown into the same room whenever Patience was around. Cole didn't really have many friends, just a couple of guys he knew in his neighborhood whom he played basketball with sometimes. And his brother, Stephen, although close to his age, was the total opposite of him. It was no wonder the poor guy got lonely. He didn't even have any pets.

She hugged him tightly.

"Let's make a pact. As of today, let's promise to spend at least two days a week together, no matter how busy we get. You know, like we used to."

It was true. The two had been inseparable for most of their friendship. Many people had assumed they would eventually start dating; that's how close they were. But with the recent turn of events in her romantic life, Patience needed time to work on her emotional self, unknowingly shutting him out for a while. But as she sat next to her best friend, she realized just how much they needed each other.

Cole's face immediately lit up.

"You're on!"

Friday evening, Cole accompanied Patience to her parents' house to pick up Rory. The two of them wound up staying for dinner and playing board games till late that night. Rory was beyond happy to see her, and clearly the absence had benefited them both. Sharise didn't want him to go, and Patience made a mental note to bring him over more often.

Toward the end of the night, the men talked sports while Patience joined her mother on the patio for a gossip session. It was well into the a.m. when she and Rory dropped Cole off at his house. Before he went in, he invited her to join his Bible study group the following night. They were meeting at Chili's before their class. She knew it would be fun and agreed to go.

* * *

By the time October came, Patience, Jana, and Cole had been invited to four parties. Cole's Bible study group was having a small gathering at church and had been kind enough to invite her. In addition, his parents were throwing a change-of-the-seasons celebration. Kylie and Sasha were having a Halloween party one weekend and a small dinner party the next. Fall was her favorite time of the year with the promise of upcoming holidays, cooler weather, and fun activities. And as an added bonus, Rory's behavior was improving slightly. He still did naughty things, but they were minor incidents instead of full-blown catastrophes. Life was going well, and she appreciated every minute of it.

As a reward for his efforts to obey, Patience decided to take Rory on a picnic to his favorite park. She packed a sandwich and fruit for herself, bacon-flavored treats and a Frisbee for him. It was a perfect Saturday morning for an outing. Ten minutes later, they were on their way.

The park was packed. She'd never seen so many dogs, children, and adults in one place. As she spread a blanket down, she quickly thought of Tripp, who lived across the street. Her pulse quickened from the fear of possibly bumping into him. She briefly wondered how he was doing but pushed the thoughts aside. This was Rory's day. All of her focus needed to be on him.

They had been at the park for an hour when Rory's ears shot up. She followed his gaze to the busy street in the distance. She couldn't tell what had caught his attention, as she'd cancelled her eye -doctor appointment twice and her contacts needed to be updated.

The dog began running through the crowd, his eyes focused on something.

"Rory, come back!" Patience shouted.

She jumped up and chased him, trying to grab his leash, but he was too fast. As she got closer to the street, she immediately saw what he was after. A small child was playing ball on the grass near the street. Cars were obviously going above the speed limit of twenty-five. Ever since she had adopted him from the shelter, she'd noticed her dog's protective instinct, especially with children. No wonder he noticed the child before she had. Their picnic was a good distance away from the street, but she knew animals' senses were of a higher magnitude than humans'.

Patience could see the small boy getting closer to the speeding cars passing by, and, predictably, the ball rolled right into the street. Her heart almost stopped as Rory barked and positioned himself in between the child and the curb, preventing the little boy from chasing the ball. As if in slow motion, her precious dog leapt into the street just as a sports car rounded the corner. In an instant, Rory was hit, the bumper knocking his body to the grass on the opposite side of the street.

Both Patience and the child were at his side in seconds, high-pitched screams coming from them both. Her precious pet lay there, motionless, gazing up at his owner with wide eyes. He was panting heavily, but no other sound came from him. She could barely see through her tears as passersby stopped to help them. The child reached out to touch him, but Patience grabbed his hand, telling him not to. She tried to explain that something could be broken, and it was best not to move him.

Digging for her cell in her pocket, she called the local 24-hour animal hospital where he'd been a patient before. Not long after she'd adopted him, he'd swallowed a coin left on the floor. Luckily, a friend who'd been there had helped by performing the Heimlich on him. They'd called emergency afterward, just to be on the safe side.

"I'm sorry ... sorry ... It's all my fault!" the boy sobbed uncontrollably. Patience wondered where his parents were.

The driver of the car knelt down beside them, her hands shaking.

Patience was not a violent person, but the rage she felt inside toward this stranger made her want to choke her! What an irresponsible and utterly out-of-control thing to do, speeding in an area filled with children and animals. She felt a powerful urge to punch the woman's lights out but fought the impulse. The only concern was her dog and rushing him to emergency care.

It was unbelievable how many people had stopped to see if they needed help. Even those driving by pulled over to assist. But nothing really could be done. They were too scared to move him, so she sat helplessly waiting for the emergency vehicle to arrive.

"What can I do?" the driver of the sports car offered. "I'm so sorry ..."

But Patience tuned her out, focusing only on her dog. The good news was that she saw only a tiny amount of blood coming from his mouth, and he was conscious. That gave her a ray of hope. She didn't know much about animals being in accidents. There probably wasn't much of a difference from humans except for the obvious fact that dogs couldn't talk and tell others what hurt.

One of the bystanders suddenly pointed in the distance.

"I see the van!" he shouted.

Minutes later, two men were unloading a gurney and kneeling down beside the dog. Patience quickly told them what happened as they began examining him. The driver was shining a small light into his eyes while his partner carefully placed a muzzle on him. She knelt down beside the man and informed him that Rory wasn't at all dangerous. She didn't see the need for a muzzle.

The attendant turned to her briefly, explaining that even the nicest animals had a tendency to bite when in extreme pain. She nodded, but it didn't make it any easier to see Rory like that. It was difficult enough just knowing all he had been through that afternoon. He was like a baby to her.

After checking Rory's left leg, which was sticking straight out at a weird angle, the emergency technician retrieved a medium-sized board from the van to use as a splint. Meanwhile, the driver checked his pulse rate by touching the inside of his right thigh. Patience had learned most of these things from websites about pet care. He told her that her dog was in shock, with a pulse of 190 beats per minute.

"Is he going to be okay?" she asked, not recognizing her own voice. It was more of a high-pitched squeak than normal. Touching her arm with compassion, the driver assured her he would. The two men worked well together, and within seconds they had Rory safely inside the vehicle.

As she followed them at top speed to the hospital, she thought about calling her parents, but the last thing she needed was to get in an accident using her cell phone. The tears in her eyes prevented her from seeing clearly anyway. She turned her car into the parking lot, knocking over the cones lined up along a construction area. And moments later, she was at Rory's side as they rushed into the main entrance.

"How is he?" she asked the man who'd ridden in back with Rory.

"Amazingly well," he said with a sympathetic smile.

"He lay still the whole way here, which is good. Many times, the animals we bring in are so panicked, we have a difficult time keeping them still. My co-worker, David, usually has to sedate the animal . . . "

Patience gasped.

" . . . for the safety of the animal." The young man smiled. "Don't worry. No animal cruelty goes on around here. Let's say someone's pet has a broken leg. Well, even if it hurts like crazy, his adrenaline can prevent him from being still. And more damage may be done."

Patience decided not to keep them any longer, as they needed to get Rory to the back. Besides, she had phone calls to make. After speaking with the front desk and signing paperwork, she called her parents, who were at the animal hospital in no time. Her mother was a nervous wreck, and there were worry lines all over John's face. He immediately began asking to speak with the veterinarian. The receptionist patiently explained that he was examining Rory at the moment.

"Well, isn't there *someone* who can give me answers? We need to know what's going on," he said, gesturing toward his family.

"Sir, the driver of the van is the only one available at the moment. Both the vet and his assistant are working on him."

Her father walked away in a huff, sitting down in the waiting area. Patience watched as he then proceeded to stand up and pace back and forth across the room. Watching him fed her nervousness even more. She and her mother stood by the window, holding hands and silently praying.

An hour later, the vet finally came out to update them on Rory's condition.

"Mrs. McKlendon?" he approached with a warm smile. She didn't bother correcting her title. Her mouth felt as if it were full of cotton.

"I'm Dr. Li. Rory is going to be just fine."

Tears of relief filled her eyes, and her mother was openly sobbing.

"We examined the X-rays of his left leg, which is fractured. The good news is it's what we call a greenstick fracture, which means the bone is still intact but cracked. I did put a cast on him, but don't worry. It's not as bad as it looks. With plenty of rest and TLC, he will be up and running within four to six weeks."

John chuckled. "A cast? Really? I didn't know animals wore casts!"

Patience and Sharise joined in.

"I'll be the first to sign it!" her mother joked, wiping the tears from her eyes.

The vet laughed as well.

"I can't tell you how many times I get this reaction. But yes, dogs can have casts. Just as with people, it helps keep the leg still so it can heal properly. Would you like to come see him?"

The three followed him through the double doors quickly to visit their beloved pet.

CHAPTER 24

John and Sharise suggested that Patience and Rory spend the night with them. They wanted to help nurse the dog back to health. Patience accepted their offer gratefully, as she was exhausted emotionally and physically. The three of them carefully loaded Rory in her parents' Tahoe that same afternoon. He seemed to be in minimal pain, which was a relief. The doctor had administered pain medication earlier, and Patience had two prescriptions she needed to fill for him.

She hopped in her car, promising to meet them at their house as soon as she could. Her first stop was the pharmacy, then the grocery for a couple of items, and finally home to pick up some clothes for the next day. She also gathered Rory's food and doggie treats. He definitely deserved them after all he'd gone through. When she called her mom to check on him, he was asleep and doing well.

Patience and Rory both received special attention that Saturday night from her parents. Her mother baked her favorite homemade cookies, and John spent most of the evening catering to the dog. Patience had to wake up only once that night to administer his pain medication. Sharise took care of the remaining doses. And Rory was a real trouper, whimpering only a couple of times early Sunday morning from his wounds. All in all, the night went pretty smooth for the four of them. Despite her worry, Patience slept like a log and rose early to help her mother make breakfast.

"How did you sleep, dear?" Sharise asked with a yawn.

The news was on in the living room, and Rory was still snoozing. They had made a pallet for him beside the couch, which seemed comfortable enough.

"Like a baby, actually," she answered. "I did have a weird nightmare, though. I dreamt that Rory and I were in the house just lounging around, when suddenly he started choking. I tried to jump up and run over to him, but my legs wouldn't move. So he stood up on his two hind legs and threw himself over the back of a chair, proceeding to perform the Heimlich *on himself*!"

They both laughed.

"Well, did he make it?" Sharise joked.

"Yes, I saw something fly out of his mouth. He then said to me in a sarcastic voice, 'Thanks a lot for your help.' So I began to cry," she finished.

"Hey, what's going on in here?" John came in and kissed his wife. "You two are going to wake Rory."

Patience repeated the dream to her father as he grabbed some orange juice from the fridge. He shook his head with amazement.

"Sharise, she gets that weird stuff from *your* side of the family."

They all sat around the breakfast table, enjoying scrambled eggs, bacon, and fruit. Every now and again, John would peek around the corner to make sure Rory was okay. She knew her father liked to play the tough -guy role, but deep down he really did love that dog. She smiled, taking a sip of her milk and glancing through the newspaper. The phone started ringing as they were finishing up.

"Hello?" Sharise answered. Her parents were the only two she knew, besides herself of course, who still had a home phone. She didn't know why her family refused to come out of the Stone Age. In every other aspect of their lives, they were pretty hip.

"Oh, yes, Cole, how are you?"

Her mother chatted awhile with him and then handed Patience the phone.

"Hey, what's up?" she asked with interest.

Patience had called both him and Jana the night before, telling them the whole story about the accident.

"I wanted to see how my favorite dog is doing," he answered.

"He had a good night. The pain comes and goes, I guess. But the medicine helps him sleep, which is what he needs."

Cole let her know he'd stop by later that morning to see him. They hung up, and she went to check her cell. There were two missed calls. Cole had tried to get in touch with her very early, and Jana hadn't left a message.

* * *

John decided to grill steaks that afternoon for their company. Both Jana and Cole were there, in addition to a friend of Patience's mom, who lived down the street. Rory was awake and soaking up all the attention he was getting. Patience videotaped him trying to bite his cast off, which was hilarious. Cole had volunteered to run up to the store with John, who needed more charcoal and lighter fluid. Jana was sitting on the carpet petting Rory while her mother was showing off her new furniture to the neighbor.

Patience heard her cell in the other room and ran to get it.

"Hi, is this Patience?"

She didn't recognize the voice, although it sounded slightly familiar.

"Yes."

"This is Roman. I'm the vet technician who assisted with Rory's care yesterday."

"Yes, I remember. How are you?"

He had been so kind and caring, patiently answering the millions of questions she'd asked. He was the one who'd ridden in the back with Rory and made the splint for his leg.

"The question is, how are you and Rory doing?" He laughed. "But I'm fine, by the way."

"We're doing great, actually. From what I can tell, the pain hasn't been too overwhelming for him. And he loves being doted on!"

"Ah, something tells me that even before the accident, he wasn't exactly starving for attention," Roman laughed. "Your family seems very loving and affectionate."

"We are close."

She smiled into the phone. "And he *is* very spoiled, but only by my parents."

"Mmm hmm," was his only response. He didn't sound as if he believed her.

"I'm serious," she said. "He can do whatever he wants at my parents' house, and my friend Cole lets him eat a whole bag of treats at one time."

He chuckled.

"So what you're saying is, you're the strict one?"

She nodded, forgetting he couldn't see her on the phone. "Definitely."

"Okay, I guess I have to take your word for it."

He sounded unconvinced.

Jana came into the dining room where Patience was, motioning for her to get off the phone. But she ignored her.

"So," she stalled, not wanting to hang up just yet. "How long have you been a vet assistant?" Anyone who chose to work with animals was a-okay in her book. "You seem to really know what you're doing."

Roman laughed again.

"I hope so! Thanks for the compliment. I've been working with Dr. Li for two years. I'm studying to become a veterinarian, and working as an assistant is great training. I love everything about this job: the animals, of course; the people I work with; the experience I'm receiving ... this will help prepare me for the day when I have my own clinic."

Patience listened with interest.

"That's awesome. I've always admired those who dedicate their lives to saving animals. I used to think I wanted to be a doctor, but my stomach isn't strong enough. Plus, I wouldn't make any money because I'd probably work on a sliding scale or undercharge patients who couldn't afford it."

"Yes," he agreed. "That's going to be my downfall as well. When I become a vet and a child brings me his cat that has accidentally ingested poison, I'm not going to wonder if they can afford the treatment. My first impulse will be to immediately save the cat."

"Yes, I know exactly what you mean. In a way, that's how I feel about teaching. I love kids, and although I worked with the little ones all through college, I later decided that teens probably needed me more. So in my sophomore year, I changed my major to secondary education."

Roman whistled.

"Whoa, so you mean to tell me you teach high school kids? Like, those brats who sit at the back of the movie theater and make noise while I'm trying to concentrate on the movie?"

They both laughed.

"Yep, they're the ones!"

"What are their ages?"

He seemed hesitant to hang up with Patience, as well.

"They're actually in junior high, so most of them are thirteen."

"And you honestly *like* them?" he asked incredulously. "Don't they talk back and defy authority? Pardon me for saying so, but you seem too sweet to be trapped in a classroom full of juvenile delinquents."

"On the contrary, my students respect me, and most of them really do come to class and try to learn." She thought for a moment. "Hmm, maybe I catch them right before they hit that you-can't-tell-me-what-to-do stage."

At that moment, Cole burst into the room holding up a piece of paper with the words GET OFF OF THE PHONE scribbled in huge letters. Reluctantly, Patience thanked Roman for calling, hanging up with a scowl on her face. Her friends could be so needy at times. She picked up one of the shoes lying next to her and threw it at Cole.

* * *

Rory and Patience went home that night with a huge care package from her parents. Doggie treats and toys filled his side of the basket, while homemade cookies and lavender body wash were on her side. Her mother swore by the scents of lavender and chamomile, claiming they relaxed your whole body and mind. She appreciated everything her mom and dad did for her, including loving her dog as much as she did. Rory's spirits were high, as the pain medicine and R&R had taken effect. His cast had all of their signatures on it. Cole had made tiny colorful paw prints to liven it up, as well. She turned on the television and went into the kitchen to check her messages. No one had called.

It was after ten when Patience had finished bathing Rory. She had been so nervous, trying to avoid his left leg entirely, even though the cast was covered in plastic like the doctor had advised. After feeding him, they both turned in, for it had been an eventful weekend. She lay in bed staring at her dark ceiling. Roman came to mind then, and she thought about their long conversation.

She was still annoyed at Cole for rudely interrupting them. Sure, she knew it was wrong for her to ignore company while they entertained her dog, but he had been so nice to call and check on them. Plus, many times throughout the years, both Cole and Jana had gossiped on their phones when she was visiting. She smiled as she remembered some of the comments Roman had made. He had a pretty funny sense of humor. She had told him she needed to let him go, that her friends were nagging her about it.

"That's cool. I have to run some errands anyway. But listen, would it be okay if I call to, um, check on Rory again?" he'd asked.

Patience hadn't hesitated, telling him he could call any time. And she'd meant it.

Roman called and left her a message the following evening. She had run to the post office after work to mail her cousins' Halloween cards and was thrilled to see his name on her caller ID. He also left a cute message.

"Hey Rory, this is Roman! Happy Monday to you! I hope you're steadily improving, and I wanted to let you know you're in my thoughts and prayers. (laugh) If you could please give me a call at your earliest convenience, that would be great. Oh, and I have something for you, so be sure to get in touch with me soon. Okay? Thanks!"

She shook her head and laughed at the absurd message. Her heart raced as she picked up the phone. Rory was asleep on her bed. She'd immediately checked on him when she got home from work.

"Hello?" the deep male voice answered.

"Hi, this is Rory's answering service returning your call. Your highness is asleep right now, but I will make sure he gets your message upon awakening."

They both burst into laughter.

"Well, ma'am, I appreciate you getting back to me so soon. How are you?"

Patience stayed on the phone with Roman for two hours. She straightened up the living room, cooked and ate a quick meal, and graded papers with the receiver stuck to her ear. The phone was hot to the touch when she finally let him go. He was such a sweet guy, and they had talked about an abundance of subjects. She got the feeling he was trying to ask her out, but in the end he promised he'd call again.

"What are you doing Friday night?" he'd inquired halfway through the conversation.

"I don't know. What do you have planned?"

She had wiped her sweaty palms on the kitchen towel as she waited.

"Oh nothing," he'd answered noncommittally.

Patience pictured him shrugging his shoulders.

"Oh."

She rolled her eyes as he changed the subject, and dismissed the idea that he might have been interested in her. After all, he really did care about animals. And Rory was so endearing. He stole the hearts of almost everyone he came in contact with. Of course Roman had called to make sure he was doing okay. She reluctantly decided not to let her imagination spiral out of control ... again.

* * *

Cole took Patience bowling Thursday night after dinner. Since their pact to nurture their friendship weeks before, they had stuck with it. He adored her, and she thought it was worth the extra effort to stay connected to him. She missed the long talks they used to have, when neither one of them had a significant other to focus on. They had a blast. She had become more relaxed about leaving Rory at home by himself since the accident. Cole brought him a new toy when he arrived to pick her up. He really did spoil her dog, but she secretly loved it. And that was just the type of guy he was: thoughtful, giving and sweet.

It was around eleven when he dropped her off at home. She could hear the phone ringing as she searched for her keys. Cole waited patiently while she checked her purse, pockets and porch, thinking maybe she had dropped them.

"I swear, I think you need to wear your house key on a string around your neck!" he teased.

Patience ignored him as she went back to his car to see if they'd fallen in between the seats. He followed suit, and after ten minutes found them under her seat.

"What are they doing *there*?" he asked with a scowl.

She shrugged. "I don't know. Why don't you ask them?"

"Wise guy," he muttered, and they both laughed.

She let herself in, smiling at Rory, who was fast asleep on the couch.

Next, she checked her messages.

"Hey Patience, it's Roman. Give me a call when you get this. Thanks!"

Wondering if it was too late to call, she picked up the phone anyway and dialed his number. He answered on the first ring.

"How are you?" he asked cheerfully.

"Great! I hope I'm not calling too late."

"Nah, I was just about to put in a DVD. How's our patient?"

"He's doing really well. I found him asleep when I got home. Normally the sound of my keys wakes him up, but that medicine puts him in a deep sleep!" She laughed.

They chatted for a while, and then there was a short pause. She heard him clear his throat.

"Um, I forgot to ask you something when we talked last time. Well, actually, I didn't forget. I got nervous, but now I'm just going to ask. Okay, so here goes . . ."

Patience waited anxiously for him to continue. Silence descended upon them, and she thought for a moment they'd gotten disconnected.

"Hello?" she whispered.

"Oh, yeah, I'm here. Listen, the question I want to ask you is: do you want to maybe go out sometime? Together?"

She giggled. He was so cute! His noticeable anxiety over asking her out was adorable. Here he was, this smart, educated, handsome man who could probably get any girl in Texas to go out with him, yet he was stuttering and mumbling over her. She couldn't believe it.

"That sounds great! What did you have in mind?" she asked enthusiastically.

"You mean you're saying 'yes'?"

Laughing, she nodded her head.

"Of course I am!"

"Wow! Well, I haven't really put much thought into where I would take you. I didn't think you'd agree to hang out with me."

"Hmm, we're going to have to work on that self-esteem of yours," Patience joked.

They talked a while longer, making plans for the upcoming weekend. She told him about Kylie and Sasha's get-together Saturday night, as well as some other events going on.

"How about I take you to dinner Friday night, so we can get to know each other better, and then Saturday we'll party like its 1999."

She felt her heart flutter.

"Perfect."

* * *

The date with Roman could not have gone more smoothly. He picked her up at seven, wearing a black turtleneck sweater and jeans. Coincidentally, Patience had chosen a black sweater and jeans herself. The smell of his cologne wafted into her house as he stepped inside. Rory hobbled up to him, finally getting used to his cast. He seemed to remember him, as he didn't bark and act all crazy like he usually did with guests.

Roman knelt down to pat him gently.

"Hey boy, how are you?"

Rory licked his cheek, placing his paw on Roman's knee.

"I have something for you."

Roman pulled out a chew toy with a big bow taped on it. A tiny tag with the words 'get well soon' hung off the bone.

"Awww, that was so sweet of you!" exclaimed Patience.

Roman stood up and faced her. He smiled, and she hadn't noticed before the big dimple in his left cheek. She also didn't remember how perfect his dark brown complexion was. Or the way his eyes sparkled when he looked at her. He took hold of her hand and kissed it.

"It's good to see you tonight," he said softly. His eyes were so dark they appeared black. Yes, he was a very attractive man. He stood quite a few inches above her. She guessed his height to be five-ten.

They both looked down when they heard Rory gagging. He had tried to eat the bow instead of chew on the bone. Roman immediately stooped down, retrieving half of the bow from his mouth.

"I think he swallowed some of it," he said.

Patience bent down and pried his mouth open. It was empty.

"Will it hurt him?"

She was half embarrassed and half angry. She wanted to choke Rory herself. He knew he couldn't eat ribbons and bows! She wondered what kind of impression Roman had of them now. Sometimes her dog acted like he had no common sense at all.

"Nah, he should be fine," Roman replied.

They left shortly after the incident, Bob Marley's music filling the car. Roman was taking her to his favorite Vietnamese restaurant downtown. He loved all types of food, music and art. He was definitely a diverse person, his mind always open to trying new things. She had been honest with him, admitting that she pretty much stuck with tacos, turkey and macaroni and cheese.

"Have you tried Vietnamese food?" he asked with a smile.

"Well ... I did have some sweet and sour pork at my cousin's birthday party, but that's about it. I don't like all those different sauces and herbs they put in food. Just call me Plain Jane."

"We need to get you out of your rut, Plain Jane," he insisted. "You can't live on chicken sandwiches and pizza forever!"

As it turned out, Patience found the restaurant delightful: very homey and romantic. She ate her entrée, which was okay, and even tried a little of Roman's. The owner came up to their table to greet them, telling her that Roman was their favorite customer. Everyone was extremely nice and accommodating, making them feel welcome.

"So," he smiled at her as she took in their surroundings, "you're really a high-school teacher, huh?" He was shaking his head in wonder, and she laughed.

"Well, actually, I work undercover for the FBI, but please don't tell anyone. My parents don't even know." She looked over her shoulder suspiciously and then leaned across the table. She cupped her hands over her mouth.

"We're trying to bust an underground drug ring here in Texas. But these guys don't play. If they find out you know anything, we're both dead," she said in a hushed voice.

He burst into laughter.

Patience continued, holding on to the serious expression. "I'm not kidding. They've already threatened to get Rory, just in case he wakes up one day with the ability to communicate with humans. He knows all the details of the case, as well."

Roman took a sip of Chardonnay, his dark eyes glistening. "You have an unbelievable imagination, Plain Jane. And it's quite entertaining. Have you ever thought of writing suspense novels?"

The dimple in his cheek deepened as he smiled at her.

"Actually, I *do* want to dabble in writing children's books someday," she admitted.

"Someday?" he repeated.

Patience shrugged her shoulders. "I've always wanted to be an author. I guess that plan is on the back burner for now."

"Why?"

She hesitated.

"I don't know. Maybe I haven't found the time to sit down and write. What if I'm not good enough? What if writing isn't part of God's plan for me? Teaching has been such a rewarding career, and I'm pretty good at it ..." Her voice trailed off.

Roman reached across the table for her hand.

"Have you ever thought you could do both?" he offered. "From what I know about you so far, you have a gift for reaching out to people and creating stories that entertain with humor. It would be a shame if you let it go to waste."

She nodded her head. "Yeah, you're right. I'll start putting some ideas on paper next week."

She looked down at her food and realized she was starving. Half of her entrée was untouched. It just didn't look very appetizing. The meat appeared slimy, and the sauce smelled sweet and tangy. She couldn't remember what the entrée was supposed to be. She longed for pizza.

Satisfied with her response, Roman picked up the menu to glance at the desserts.

"That's more like it."

* * *

Roman pulled into Patience's driveway, letting go of her hand just long enough to turn off the ignition. Dinner had been wonderful. They stayed long after he'd had dessert, talking about their families and jobs. He had two older sisters, Rachel and Gabrielle. They had all chosen the medical field, which Patience found intriguing. Rachel was a pediatrician who lived in upstate New York, and Gabrielle practiced family medicine in Austin. His father owned an engineering company in town, and his mom was a nurse. They were pretty close, never going more than two days without talking. She had laughed until her stomach ached at stories he told her of his childhood.

"When the neighborhood boys were outside playing football, I was indoors with my sisters, who played with dolls. Gabrielle would take her rag doll to Rachel, who would nurse her back to health. Then the two of them would bring their stuffed animals to me, the 'pet doctor'."

She giggled.

"How cute is that?"

"Yeah, well, my parents didn't think so! Mom used to yell at me all the time, finding Band-Aids and gauze all over the house. She told me they didn't make enough money for me to waste the first aid supplies on dolls. And my dad ..." he paused dramatically.

"What did he say?"

"Let me put it this way. Dad threatened not to pay for my college if I continued 'down the wrong path'. He's very old-school when it comes to things like that." Roman shook his head.

The two chatted a while longer about other things, and then she invited him in. Part of her didn't want him to say 'yes' because she was truly starving. She planned on making a frozen pizza or something as soon as he left.

"Sure, I can come in for a second."

Patience smiled as he followed her in, Rory barking until he realized who it was. She led him into the living room, turning on the television while he played with Rory.

"Would you like something to drink?" she asked.

"Nah, I'm good."

She decided to go ahead and preheat the oven. Taking the pizza out of the freezer, she asked him if he could let Rory out for her.

After doing so, Roman came into the kitchen.

"*What* are you doing?" he asked in amusement.

Patience's cheeks burned with embarrassment.

"I'm so hungry," she confessed. "I didn't want to say anything at the restaurant, because you were so excited that I was trying new things ... I didn't want to hurt your feelings," she finished.

He was grinning from ear to ear.

"Sweetheart, it's okay that you didn't like the food. You should've told me, and I would have driven you to Chili's afterward. I've been craving Baby Back Ribs for a long time!"

She laughed as he took a step toward her. She breathed in his cologne, looking up into those dark brown eyes she liked so much.

"So you're saying you don't mind having two dinners?"

He smiled, wrapping his arms around her waist.

"I'd eat five dinners in order to spend more time with you."

They hugged, and he released her when they heard Rory scratching the patio door with his good paw. He went to let him back in, and the three of them settled in to watch a movie, while she and Roman shared a pepperoni pizza.

CHAPTER 25

Roman stayed with Patience long after the movie was over, telling her stories about his childhood and teen years. He'd definitely had his share of 'growing pains' early in life, from losing his grandparents to being bullied in junior high. Being a sympathetic person, she felt her heart ache as she listened intently to her new friend. What struck her was the fact that he was so open, so willing to reveal the negative things to her, whom he'd only known for two weeks.

"My parents have a healthy marriage and everything, but they've hit some rough patches along the way. As a matter of fact, the two fought constantly in my teen years. They seemed to disagree about everything. Money was their number one concern. Dad felt like Mom was being frivolous with the finances, but she didn't really care what he said. She did whatever she wanted, totally ignoring him. Then there was the issue of raising us. My parents had totally different parenting styles. Mom was more permissive, while Dad chose to be strict and authoritative. It was crazy! Yet nothing was worse than when my dad's parents moved across the street."

Roman chuckled as he remembered that time.

Patience hung on his every word. "Were they from here?"

"No, Nana and Papa lived in Washington, where my father grew up. He had a really close bond with them, I guess because he's an only child and they spoiled him. When he met my mother and they moved to Texas, it tore my grandmother to pieces. She blamed my mom for stealing her 'baby' away from her. My dad held a little resentment toward her as well, wondering why they couldn't just stay in Washington."

"So they moved immediately after marrying?" she interrupted.

"Uh huh. They set up camp here, and then they found great careers, Rachel came along, and so on ... Nana and Papa were soon forgotten." He paused to take a breath. "I mean, sure, my dad still flew them down here often, remaining close to them, but the issue of living close to one another was dropped."

"Wow! This is like a soap opera!"

Roman laughed at her. "It gets better. About six years later, our neighbors across the street put their house on the market. The next thing we knew, dad was calling Nana, and they were flying here to check out the house."

"Don't tell me," she said with wide eyes.

"Yep, my grandparents were our new neighbors. My mom nearly killed herself. She could not believe my dad had encouraged them to live so close, knowing how much my grandmother despised her. And the feeling was mutual, definitely. So that didn't help their marriage any more than all of the other problems in the house."

The phone rang and they both jumped. Rory didn't move, lying on the carpet next to them. He'd already eaten the crumbs of pizza Patience had dropped.

"Hello?"

"Hey, it's Cole. What's up?"

"Cole! What are you doing calling at this hour?"

"It's nice to hear your voice, too!" He laughed. "Listen, what are you doing tomorrow?"

Patience shrugged her shoulders.

"What time?" They had the Halloween party that night, but she didn't have plans during the day.

"Around noon," he answered. "I thought maybe we could catch a matinee or something."

"Sounds great," she said, peering around the doorway of the kitchen. She giggled when she saw Roman sneaking a piece of pepperoni to Rory. Cole asked her what she was laughing about.

"Well, Rory is destined to have heartburn in a couple of hours."

"Why?"

"Not only is he *not* supposed to be eating this late, but Roman just fed him spicy pizza, of all things," she chuckled.

"*Roman?* He's over there? At this hour?"

She shrugged her shoulders. "Yes, we're still on our date."

Silence.

"Hello? Are you still there?"

"Um, yeah, well, I guess I should let you go then," he said suddenly. His voice sounded strange all of a sudden.

Patience blew it off. "Okay, call me in the morning when you find out the time of the movie," she told him distractedly, anxious to get back to Roman.

"You sure you'll still be up to going after your late night?" he asked after a slight pause.

"Of course I will."

What a weird question for Cole to ask. She briefly wondered what was going on with him. But just as quickly, she brushed her worries away. Maybe she was reading far more into this than there was. She did have the tendency to blow tiny things out of proportion.

Cole sighed.

"Look, just text me if you want to go tomorrow. Who knows? You may be worn out after your, ahem, late night," he finished sarcastically.

Patience motioned to Roman that she'd be back to him shortly. She sat down at the dining room table. Her brows knit together in concern, she lowered her voice slightly.

"What's up, Cole?"

"Nothing is 'up'. I just don't want to barge in on your busy weekend, that's all. Let's just tentatively plan on getting together sometime soon, okay? You know, keeping it casual."

She didn't know what was going through his mind, or why his mood suddenly changed, but she didn't have time to figure it out.

He obviously didn't want to stay on the phone, either. "Call me tomorrow. And have fun with Ryan."

"Roman," she corrected, hanging up with a funny feeling in the pit of her stomach. However, Cole was quickly forgotten as Roman called out to her that Rory was getting sick from the pizza.

* * *

"So, finish telling me about your grandparents," Patience encouraged her new friend, but Roman shook his head.

"Not all in one night," he told her in a quiet voice, leaning over to give her a quick peck on the cheek. "We have plenty of time to get to know one another. Now, are you going to walk me to the door or sit there with your mouth hanging open?"

She laughed, blushing slightly as she followed him down the hall. She could have sat talking with him all night. He was so interesting and funny. But it was late, or early, depending on how one looked at it. She couldn't believe the sunshine that met them outside. She'd assumed it was still midnight because time always seemed to stand still when she was having fun.

She turned to face him on her porch. Gazing into his almost-black eyes adoringly, she thought, *Please kiss me.* He stood close enough for their noses to touch, yet he didn't move. He just smiled, holding both of her hands tightly in his.

"Thank you for a lovely time," Roman whispered.

"Thank you, too," Patience responded, for lack of anything better to say. She tried sending subliminal messages to him, willing him to stay a while longer. But with one last hug, he left.

* * *

"What time did he leave?" Jana asked through shallow breaths. She had called Patience from the gym at nine a.m., waking her up from a fitful sleep. She'd had a difficult time winding down after her date. She dreamt about Roman first, woke up to a bird chirping outside her window, and then fell back to sleep. Unfortunately, she'd proceeded to have a nightmare about Tripp.

"Six o'clock."

"What? Six o'clock *in the morning*? Did you sleep with him?" she practically shouted into the phone.

Patience sprang up in the bed.

"I hope the people working out next to you don't know who you're talking to!" She laughed. "And no, of course not! Are you crazy?"

"Why was he there so long then?" Jana panted.

"We watched a movie and *talked.* That's it."

She paused and then added,

"He's a dream, an absolute dream!"

"That's what you (pant) said about Sam, Jason, and Tripp! Man, I can't stand working out! It's not fair that you stay skinny no matter what you do!"

Getting up to open her blinds, Patience rolled her eyes. "In response to your first comment, I did not say that about the other guys. And second, I do have to work out, just like everyone else."

She heard her home phone ringing as she stepped into the hallway.

"Yes, you did, and no, you don't," Jana argued. "Anyway, I've gotta hang up now. My cell keeps slipping out of my hand from the sweat. I'll call you later," she finished grumpily, then hung up.

After letting Rory out, Patience checked her messages. Kylie had called to remind her about the Halloween party that night. It was actually engraved in her memory, as Roman had agreed to accompany her after all. He wasn't a fan of that particular holiday, so it was sweet of him to go.

"I'd attend a KKK rally if you were going to be there," he'd joked during one of their lengthy conversations.

He had such a funny sense of humor, which was one of the reasons she'd developed such a huge crush on him.

Patience showered quickly after breakfast, determined to get all of her errands done before noon. She assumed she and Cole were still going to the movies, although she hadn't heard from him that morning. His behavior was pretty weird, even for him, and she made a mental note to ask him about it.

After dropping her dresses off at the dry cleaners, she bought a few groceries and ran by the pet store. She lifted the heavy dog food into her trunk and then sat in her car, thinking about Cole again. She glanced at the clock. It was almost noon. Her cell showed no missed calls, so she quickly texted him,

"Can't wait 2 hang w u 2day! What time is the movie?"

She waited a while, just sitting in the car with the music blasting, but there was no response from him. She decided to make a few more stops before heading home.

As usual, Rory was excited to see her when she walked through the door. The vet had told her his cast could come off early, due to his rapid improvement and healing. She couldn't wait, as it was very difficult giving him a bath with that thing on. He didn't like the whole bathroom routine even with no cast on, but Patience didn't like it when he smelled like the outdoors, or like a dog, so she bathed him constantly. Her parents thought it was hilarious, a dog owner who wanted her pet to smell like a human.

"I don't care. He's an inside dog, and sometimes he sleeps with me, so ..." Her voice had trailed off, not sure how to defend herself.

"I haven't done any research on the subject, but I'm pretty sure it's not healthy for a dog to be so clean all the time," her father had laughed. In the end, John and Sharise had dropped the matter, certain their hardheaded daughter could not be swayed.

While putting the groceries away, Patience began thinking about Roman. Just as her daydream started to take off, he called.

"Hi! I was just thinking about you," she answered cheerfully.

"What a coincidence! You were on my mind, as well. What's going on over there?"

"Oh, I'm just getting home from some errand-running. And you?"

He sighed. "Well, like I said before, you were on my mind, so I decided to call."

"Were they good thoughts or bad?" she asked mischievously.

He pretended to think a minute.

"Hmm, let's just say 50/50."

They chit chatted a while and then confirmed their plans for the night.

"How about I come over around eight? That way we can have some alone-time before the party," Roman suggested.

"That sounds good to me. I can't wait for you to meet Jana and Cole."

Cole! With a frown on her lips, she rushed Roman off the phone so she could call her friend who had decided to go MIA for the day.

"Is anything wrong?" he asked.

"No, no, I just have some loose ends to tie up before this evening."

She checked her cell again, but only her mother had called.

"Great! I'll see you tonight, PJ."

Patience thought it was cute that he'd chosen that nickname for her.

"See you at eight!"

* * *

It was early evening when Cole returned her call. She was irritated but decided to give him the benefit of the doubt.

"Finally," Patience said when she heard his voice.

"I know, I know," he started, his voice sounding forlorn. "You're mad at me, right?"

"You better believe it! I don't appreciate being stood up by my best friend. What's going on with you?"

She had no intention of letting him off the hook. They were always honest with each other, which was one reason their friendship was so strong.

He hesitated a moment.

"Look Patience, I truly don't know why I'm acting weird, especially with you. I guess ..." He stopped.

"What?"

"I don't know. Maybe I'm afraid I'll be pushed to the back burner again, you know, since you and Roman are getting along so well. I mean, he practically spent the night with you, for Heaven's sake, which is moving pretty fast, if you ask me."

"That's none of your concern, Father," she interrupted with a frown.

"It *is* my concern! You've only known him for, like, a week?! And now y'all are having fifteen-hour dates? That's the craziest thing I've ever heard. I just don't want you getting hurt ... again."

Patience could feel her face burning from anger.

"Are you finished?" she asked through tight lips. She didn't want to say anything else at the moment.

"Yes."

"Okay, well, I have a lot of things to do before eight, so I guess I'll just see you at the party."

Cole sighed.

"Fine, I'll see you there," he said with resignation.

* * *

Roman and Patience spent some quality alone-time before the party, getting to know each other even better than before. He talked more about his family, which was hilarious, while she opened up about past relationships. Normally she didn't talk about other guys to someone she was seeing, but he specifically asked about it.

"Yeah, I've met some really great people in the past," she began with caution. For a moment, words escaped her. She didn't want to be ugly about how some of her relationships had ended, but praising them wasn't such a good idea, either.

"Let's just say I've gotten along well with them all, but due to outside forces, we had to break up."

He laughed, reclining on the couch while studying her.

"You sound like you're choosing your words carefully."

Taking a deep breath, she smiled.

"Yes, I guess I am."

"What is your 'type'? Do you usually go for the active health-nut or the sensitive, brooding man?"

He was trying to find out everything about her, delving deep into her psyche.

"I don't necessarily have a 'type'. If you lined up all the guys I've ever dated, you'd find various personalities, looks, and interests. I'm a well-rounded individual, if I do say so myself."

"I can tell that about you," he agreed.

After an hour or so, Patience went to get dressed up for the party, leaving Rory to entertain. She emerged fifteen minutes later, donning a cat suit. She'd decided to play it safe, choosing a costume that was inexpensive, easy and would not offend anyone. She had on a black leotard and tights, which made her appear even thinner than she already was, a black tail that attached to the back, a headband with ears on top, and black ballet slippers. For makeup, she had drawn whiskers and colored the tip of her nose black with her eyeliner pencil.

Roman's eyes nearly popped out of his head at the sight of her.

"Whoa!"

Rory started barking hysterically, hobbling toward her with his cast. They both laughed, and she knelt down to pet him.

"It's me, you silly dog."

Roman stood in front of her, pulling her close.

"Whoa," he exclaimed again.

Patience actually saw desire in his eyes, which made butterflies flutter in her stomach.

"You're a man of many words," she teased. She was actually flattered by his reaction. A girl couldn't help but feel attractive when someone looked at her the way he did.

"You're hot," he murmured, his arms still around her waist. She could feel his breath on her face, which made her slightly dizzy.

"So you're okay with Halloween now?" she smiled.

"Oh yeah."

When they arrived at Kylie and Sasha's house, the party was in full swing. Michael Jackson's *Thriller* could be heard down the street, and Roman had to park quite a distance away. The weather was unseasonably warm, which was both good and bad. They wouldn't freeze while walking so far, but Patience knew she'd be sweating in the cat suit.

"I should've chosen the Beach Barbie costume instead," she complained as he opened the door for her. "You're not going to ask me out again when I'm dripping with sweat in a few minutes."

He put his arm around her shoulders. "Oh yes I will! As a matter of fact, what are you doing tomorrow?"

She laughed. They walked slowly down the sidewalk, prolonging their quiet time before the chaos.

When she didn't answer, he asked her again. Her eyes widened.

"Oh, you're serious?"

"Of course I am! I want to take you somewhere, a place I know you'll love. Do you already have plans?"

"I was just going to think about you all day, that's all. I guess I can work in a date with you, too."

Sasha opened the door for them, squealing with delight.

"Patience!"

She threw her arms around her while Roman laughed. Sasha did a double take when she saw him.

"And who is *this*?" she asked her with wide eyes.

"*This* is my date, Roman."

The two shook hands as they heard someone scream in one of the other rooms. Sasha rolled her eyes.

"That's just Megan. She's been wild since she got here. Some guy keeps scaring her with fake spiders and things." She grabbed Patience by the arm and proceeded to drag her away. "We're going to get some drinks," she yelled over her shoulder to Roman. "What would you like?"

Looking like an abandoned puppy, he helplessly called out, "I'll have whatever Patience is having!"

Once inside the kitchen, Sasha had a million questions.

"Oh my gosh! He is a Greek god! Where did you find him? Are you two serious? Does he have a brother? A cousin?"

Kylie had entered the room by then, hugging her with enthusiasm.

"Did you guys see that gorgeous hunk of a man standing in the hallway? Who is he?"

Patience updated them on how Rory had had the accident and Roman had assisted with his care, that this was just their second date, and that they were not a couple. They hung on her every word, asking again if he had any friends or siblings he could hook them up with. Finally he wandered aimlessly toward the group, desperation written on his face.

She immediately ran to his side, suddenly feeling guilty for leaving him. She handed him a soda, looping her arm through his.

"I am so sorry! I'm glued to your side from now on," she reassured.

"Good. I actually met someone who knows you. I think she said her name was Joanna."

She knew he meant Jana, so they headed toward the living room, where the majority of the guests seemed to be. Kylie and Sasha had gone all out for this party, as usual. The decorations were excellent, very creepy and ghoulish, with scary-looking treats and snacks, and they had even transformed the upstairs into a Haunted House. They also had door prizes and contests, which was a good idea. They found Jana making out with some random guy in the den, so Patience changed her mind about introducing them at that moment.

After people-watching for a while, she spotted Cole shooting pool in the game room. It didn't look like he'd brought a date, but she recognized the guy he was playing against as an old schoolmate of theirs. She debated approaching him with Roman, because there was no telling what kind of mood he was in. Deciding to hold off on the introductions, they headed for the snack table instead. Kylie had made cute little chocolate spiders, popcorn balls, chocolate Chex Mix, and more. Choosing a caramel apple, she laughed as he knocked over some pre-poured drinks while reaching for M&Ms.

"Oh, you think that's funny, huh?" He cleaned up his mess, and then proceeded to run his finger over her caramel apple, strategically placing it on the tip of her nose.

"Ha ha, very funny," she laughed. "Two wrongs don't make a right."

He waved a hand in dismissal. "You're always quoting scriptures and wise sayings. Do you think you're smart or something?"

Patience excused herself, weaving through the crowd toward the restroom. There seemed to be a million people squeezed inside the house. Halloween was such a crazy holiday to her. Everyone donned a costume, which was sort of creepy. Someone pulled the tail of her cat suit, but when she turned to look, all she saw was a ghost, a vampire, and Frankenstein. She shuddered and quickened her pace.

As she rounded the corner, she bumped into Cole.

"Hello," she said in a formal voice. She was still a little peeved at him, and apparently the feeling was mutual.

"Hi," he responded, his tone flat.

The two friends stood facing one another, with him staring at something just above her head. Finally she muttered, "See ya around," leaving him standing there.

She didn't have time for any attitudes. Besides, she could feel the caramel drying on her nose. There was a long line to the first bathroom, so she headed to Kylie's room upstairs. By the time she'd made it back to Roman, the party was in full swing.

He was standing with Jana, laughing at something she was saying. Patience put her arm around his waist, pulling him close.

"Hi sweetheart," he welcomed. "Your friend is hilarious!"

Jana bowed as if to an audience.

"Thank you, thank you very much," she laughed, bumping into a passerby. In doing so, half of his drink spilled onto her new outfit.

"Shoot!" she exclaimed dramatically, but Patience just rolled her eyes. More than likely, she and Roman would have to take her home. Time and time again, her friend stated that, at the *next* party, she would not get drunk. Patience didn't think she was an alcoholic; just overdid it at parties, which wasn't too often.

"It was your fault, goofball."

"Oh, be quiet, Miss Goody-Two-Shoes!"

Roman laughed again as Jana stumbled away in search of paper towels.

* * *

It was well after three a.m. when Roman drove Patience home. The 'tail' and 'ears' to her cat suit had been thrown haphazardly in the backseat, and her 'whiskers' were smeared from sweating. A million people must've shown up at the party, making it impossible to remain sweat-free. She hoped he wasn't too turned off. Realistically speaking, any guy she dated would find out about her perspiration problem sooner or later. She'd always been very hot-natured, which embarrassed her. No woman wanted to sweat more than a man.

"The party was fun," Roman broke into her thoughts.

"It sure was. Remember when that guy fell down the stairs? It was funny after we realized he was okay!"

"Yeah, and what made it funnier was that he'd been acting so cool at first, so conceited."

The two rehashed the night's events all the way home.

Once on her doorstep, Patience stood just inches away from him, searching his face intently. This was it! Right then was the perfect moment for their first kiss. Sure, her make-up was smeared and the perfume she'd sprayed on earlier had vanished. And yes, the sound of Rory barking on the other side of the door wasn't exactly romantic, but she didn't care. Excluding those factors, this was the best time for it to happen.

She still found it hard to believe they'd only known each other a week. It felt more like six months: long enough to be comfortable with him and know some details about his life, but short enough for the butterflies to still exist in her tummy. He was amazing, and the two enjoyed each other's company. She wondered if he felt the same way. Something in his eyes told her he did.

"What are you thinking?" Roman suddenly asked. "You have a dreamy expression on your face."

Patience blushed.

"I'm thinking about, um, how great this weekend has been," she stammered nervously. "And you?"

"Quite a few things, actually," he began. "I know we just met, but it seems like we've been friends for years."

So he could read minds, too!

"I'm so lucky to have met you," he continued. "You're smart, funny and very beautiful. Oh, and it's easy to talk to you, about anything, really." His dimple deepened as he smiled. "I also think it's adorable the way you treat Rory like a child."

She laughed, nodding her head.

"He *acts* like one, believe me. I feel like the parent of a two-year old!"

A car passed by with music so loud she felt the bass in her chest. Roman sighed.

"Well, I guess I better go," he said with regret in his voice. He leaned forward, kissing her lightly on the tip of her nose.

"Mmm, you taste like caramel. 'Nite, kitty," he whispered.

"'Nite."

Closing the door softly behind her, she glared at Rory.

"Why did you have to ruin the moment?"

He cocked his head to one side, looking up at her with his big, innocent eyes. He really was a pitiful sight, his white cast a stark contrast to his jet black fur. She knew he couldn't wait to have it removed. He sat there, panting heavily with his tongue hanging out, and she laughed. It was difficult to stay mad at him for any significant length of time. She really did love him.

After showering, Patience tried getting hold of Jana to check on her. No answer. She was probably still with her new friend. She plopped down on her bed, exhaustion suddenly taking over her body. Events of the day spun around her head like a tornado. She smiled, picturing Roman's sweet face in her mind. He seemed like such a great guy. Each time she thought of him, her stomach did little flip flops. He made her laugh, acted like the perfect gentleman, treated her like she was the only one in the room when they were out ... she couldn't wait to see him again.

And then there was Cole. He was so ticked off at her. It made her so sad to know how angry he felt about whatever she had or hadn't done. He was her best friend. She didn't know if she could handle losing him. She made up her mind right then to call him the next day to try patching things up. Her alarm clock said four a.m. Patience fished around in the dark for her cell to try Jana one more time, but she still didn't pick up. And with Rory fast asleep at her feet, she fell into a deep, peaceful sleep.

CHAPTER 26

"Are you originally from Texas, dear?" Roman's mother smiled at her with warmth.

"Yes ma'am," Patience answered. "I was born right here in Dallas, and have only visited other places. My extended family is all over the map, which works out well for me. I never have to stay at hotels when traveling!"

Everyone laughed, and Roman winked at her from across the table.

They were at Three Forks, an upscale restaurant that Dallas was known for. Once they'd found out about her, his parents had insisted on taking them to dinner to get better acquainted. Although it was only the second weekend in November and the relationship was still fresh, he hadn't been able to help himself. He'd told his family all about her, and the excitement had spread like wildfire.

Patience wore a simple, yet very elegant black dress, which showed off her slim figure. She also went out on a limb and wore heels, a string of pearls that were her favorite aunt's, and makeup. Jana had come over earlier to work magic on her hair, manipulating the unruly mane into a French twist.

"Wow, you clean up well!" she'd commented as Patience stood in front of her. "I can't believe you have on more than your usual Chapstick!"

Patience continued talking about her family. "I have cousins in California, Tennessee, Georgia and Iowa. Two of my father's sisters live in Virginia. Then there's my favorite aunt. She's an attorney in Pittsburgh ..."

"My, my," Cynthia exclaimed in mock surprise, "I think I need a pen and paper to jot all this down!"

Erik and Cynthia Jenkins could not have been more friendly, welcoming and open. She and Roman had met them at the restaurant only an hour before, yet in that small amount of time, they felt like old friends. His mother had hugged her when they first arrived, which had caught her off guard and was a pleasant surprise. And Erik asked her questions about herself throughout dinner. He seemed genuinely interested in the answer, totally different from the interview

Jason's mother had given her. Eye contact was made, stories were shared, and respect was given with Roman's family.

"You know, she reminds me a lot of Rachel," Erik told his wife as he sat back in his seat, looking stuffed. They were done with the main course and preparing for dessert.

Roman whistled. "Wow, now *that's* a compliment," he assured Patience. "Everyone knows she's the favorite."

He winked again.

"That's just not true," his father objected, laughing in spite of himself. "Just because she's the smarter, sweeter, and more successful child doesn't mean I love her more." The four laughed, all in good spirits that night.

His mother studied her for a moment, nodding her head in agreement.

"Mmm hmm, you're right, sweetheart. They both chose careers helping children, and they are charming, lovely young women."

Patience blushed, taking a sip of ice water.

"We can certainly see why Roman likes you so much," Cynthia added. "He talks about you all, I mean, *all* the time! He couldn't wait for tonight to get here, so we could see for ourselves what a delightful young lady you are."

"Mom!" He looked horrified at his mother's choice to reveal his secrets, but she appeared unruffled.

The waitress came with their desserts, which gave Roman the perfect opportunity to change the subject.

* * *

"I love your parents!" Patience practically sang in the quiet car. Roman glanced over at her with a smile as he drove towards his house. They'd spent twenty minutes saying their goodbyes at the restaurant, his mother making her promise to come over soon for lunch. And once they'd made it through the cold, dark parking lot to his car, he'd stated seriously that he was kidnapping her.

"You're coming to my place tonight. I know it's late, and you usually go to the early morning service at church, but all I'm concerned about now is having you to myself for a while."

They'd stood beside his car shivering, and she giggled, holding up her hands playfully.

"I surrender!"

She couldn't wait to see where he lived. She knew his home wasn't too far from hers, "about fifteen minutes", he'd told her.

"They love you too, especially Mom. I could tell she approved. My dad thought you were wonderful, as well. I can say this with confidence because he compared you to Rachel."

"So she's the favorite, huh?"

"She really is. Maybe it's because she was the first-born, or the fact that she was so well-behaved and mature. I don't know." He pondered a moment. "I always thought sons were put on pedestals in families."

She watched his profile as they approached his neighborhood.

"Does that bother you?"

"No, not at all. Gabby and I were horrible as kids, always getting into mischief, lying to him and blaming each other for stuff we'd done." He shook his head. "It's a wonder he didn't put the two of us up for adoption!"

They pulled into the driveway of a very nice house in the middle of a cul-de-sac. It was huge, with dark red brick and a very expansive yard. A basketball hoop hung from the top of the garage, and she noticed various sports equipment lying all over the driveway. A bicycle was propped against one of the trees, and she noticed a couple of golf clubs by the front door.

"Now I see how you stay in such great shape!" Patience exclaimed. "You're a sports fanatic!"

Glancing at the bicycle again, she added, "And you're Lance Armstrong's brother?"

Roman opened her door with a smirk.

"Um, yeah, I guess you could say I'm active. I don't like going to the gym, even when it's cold outside. I'd much rather have fun while working out. It makes the time go faster."

"Makes sense to me."

As they headed up the driveway, she didn't see the tiny golf ball wedged between the grass and concrete. Stepping on it, her foot slipped, causing her to fall forward. Roman instinctively reached out to catch her, and she landed safely in his arms. She made no effort to move, nor did he seem in a hurry to let her go. The two stood there, gazing into each other's eyes, neither one making a sound.

Finally he spoke.

"Sorry about that, PJ. I have a terrible habit of leaving my things scattered all over the yard. You okay?"

His dark brown eyes searched her face.

"Better than okay," she whispered.

With his arms still around her, he slowly brought his lips to hers. He pulled back slightly after a moment, his breath warm on her face.

Patience smiled. "Now *you* have a dreamy look on your face."

"Of course I do. I'm with you."

* * *

The week before Thanksgiving was busy for Patience. Once again, the kids in her class were feisty, anxious for the upcoming holiday break. She seemed to be drowning in paperwork. Quizzes, homework and exams needed to be graded, as well as preparing for evaluations on a couple of the students. And one teen had begun giving her problems, talking back to her and not completing her homework. The previous Tuesday she'd even stormed out of class, claiming loudly that she didn't need an education to make it in the real world. Patience wondered if something was going on at home. Stacy had been one of her best students at the beginning of the year.

As for her personal life, Cole had started talking again but still seemed distant. She'd invited him to a movie the Sunday before, a comedy, yet he hadn't laughed at the funny parts. Afterwards, he'd been quiet during the drive home. Every question she'd asked was met with either "yes", "no", or "uh huh". It was emotionally draining just thinking about it.

The one-night stand Jana had on Halloween night was shaping into something more. His name was Brett, a thirty-two year old personal trainer, and her friend was thrilled. He had taken the initiative after their "magical night", calling to ask her out on a real date.

"He's amazing, Patience. He treats me like a queen! And have you seen him? He's the hottest guy on the planet!" she'd gushed over the phone.

But what about Scott? Patience had wondered. They were technically seeing other people, but she secretly hoped the two would reconcile. They were the perfect couple, or had been, as far as Patience was concerned.

"Yep, he is handsome," she agreed, trying to be supportive.

"Are you *blind*? He could be a model!"

"That's true." Patience had laughed. "Where is he from?"

Jana hesitated.

"I'm not sure. I think he's from here."

"Oh. Does he have any brothers or sisters?"

"Um, I don't know. I'll have to ask him."

After a few more questions about Mr. Irresistible, it turned out that Jana knew next to nothing about him.

On a happy note, Roman called her frequently, and they'd gone out a couple of times since she'd met the parents. Just as he'd said, his mom kept asking when he was bringing her over so they could "hang, as you young people say."

He'd laughed at her attempt to sound cool, promising to invite her to their house. His sister Gabrielle was coming down that weekend for Thanksgiving. Rachel couldn't get away until the following Wednesday.

"They'll be crazy about you, just like my parents."

It was Thursday night and he'd come over to spend a casual evening with her.

"I can't wait to meet them both," Patience gushed.

They were on her couch, ignoring the television as they talked about the upcoming holiday. He leaned forward to kiss her, running his hands through her curls.

"I like you a lot, PJ," he said softly.

"Me too." She could have stayed like that forever, just talking and kissing.

Later, when Roman was leaving, he confirmed that his mom was making a huge Thanksgiving feast, and he'd pick her up around four that evening. That worked out perfectly, as Sharise wanted her daughter at their place at noon. It was a tradition to eat early at the McKlendons. Cole's mother had invited her to their house as well, so she needed to fit that in to her day.

"What kind of dessert do you like? Mom told me to ask," Roman said as he stood in her doorway.

Patience waved a hand. "She doesn't have to ..."

"But she *wants* to. You better just tell me now, or she'll call you twenty times tomorrow herself."

They both laughed.

"Banana pudding."

* * *

Cole called the day before Thanksgiving. Patience was bent over a cookbook that afternoon, contemplating which potato salad to make. She had volunteered to contribute to the big dinner that year by preparing a couple of sides to take over. Her mother hounded her constantly, predicting that she'd never find a husband unless she learned how to cook. Sharise was pretty old-fashioned when it came to certain roles held by men and women. Patience had finally relented so she wouldn't have to hear her mother nag through the entire feast.

There were four different recipes in the first book, all of which looked the same. She just wasn't the homemaker type. If it were left up to her, she would live off of frozen dinners, grilled chicken and take-out. She did a lot of grilling in the summer and was ashamed to admit she made soup and salad four nights a week in the winter. However, she did love breakfast foods and went overboard sometimes making pancakes, bacon and eggs. Sharise swore the nurses had switched babies in the hospital nursery the day she was born.

"There is no way a child of mine has to follow a recipe for potato salad," she said.

The ringing phone was a welcome distraction. It only rang once before she picked it up.

"Hello?"

She hadn't bothered to check the caller I.D.

"Hi, it's Cole."

"Hi, how are you?" she asked cautiously.

"Doin' well," he started and then sighed heavily. "I'm miserable, actually. I miss you."

Patience leaned against the counter, gripping the phone a little too tightly.

"I miss you too, Coley," she said softly. She really did. Roman was terrific, but nothing, and no one, took the place of friends.

"I think about you all the time," she confessed. "I picked up the phone twenty-six times Monday to call but chickened out in the end."

"It's all my fault," he said.

"True."

She laughed.

"Gosh Patience, can't you ever be serious? I swear, a bus could hit you and you'd be lying in the street joking with the onlookers! 'Did you hear the one about . . . '?"

"I'd joke only if the bus damaged me from the waist down. If it messed up my face, I'd be ticked!"

She heard him snickering into the phone, which was a good sign.

"I cheered you up," she said smugly.

"You nauseated me," he corrected.

Patience sobered.

"Cole, I'm partly to blame for all this strife between us. You're right. Whenever I start dating, I *do* ignore you, although unintentionally. I get so wrapped up in romance, ya know? I can't stand that about myself."

"Don't say that! You're the sweetest, most down-to-earth person I know. And you always put others before yourself, to a fault sometimes. I'm just selfish. I want you all to myself."

She had to stop herself before replying, "That does sound selfish." She did joke a lot, which wasn't always appropriate.

"We're best friends, Cole. It's not the most horrible thing to want to be with me," she said instead.

The two stayed on the phone an hour more, patching things up. By the end of the conversation, they were buddies again.

"Mom says you're coming over tomorrow," Cole commented as they were about to hang up.

"Yes, but it'll be late. My day is pretty packed. Is that okay?"

She could almost see him shrugging his shoulders.

"Sure. My parents won't finish cooking until six or seven, anyway. What do you have going on during the day?"

"Well, I'm having Thanksgiving lunch with Mom and Dad, and Roman's family invited me over for dinner."

"That sounds like fun."

"Yeah, I'm looking forward to it. They're really nice."

"Oh, you've already met them?"

"We had dinner with them the other night."

"That's cool. Well, listen, I can't wait to see you tomorrow. Come hungry!"

She giggled.

"I always do!"

* * *

Thanksgiving was, without a doubt, Patience's favorite holiday. She loved spending time with family and friends and the warm, cozy feeling it brought. She made a conscious effort to show she cared all year round, but Thanksgiving reinforced it. Sharise shared her daughter's sentiment, yet John loved Christmas, claiming the gifts he received made it all worthwhile. But Patience knew better. Her parents held strong Christian beliefs and had always emphasized the true meaning of both holidays.

The sound of the doorbell brought her back to the present. After reapplying mascara for the fourth time, she decided to tear herself away from the mirror. It surprised her that she could still blink with all the makeup she'd put on. She was nervous about spending more time with Roman's family later on that day. Sure, she'd met his amazing parents, but today was even more special. His sisters would be there, and she'd probably be over there at least three or four hours. She worried she might trip over her own feet or spill dressing/dip/cranberry sauce all over someone. It wasn't unheard of.

"Happy Thanksgiving!"

Jana burst in, full of good spirits and holiday cheer. Rory barked excitedly, sniffing the aroma coming from the platter she skillfully balanced.

“Mmm, what in the world did you bake?” Patience tried lifting the shiny foil but Jana smacked her hand.

“These are pies *for your parents*,” she answered. Sharise loved pumpkin, while John favored sweet potato, which had always been funny to Jana. She joked that they went against the stereotypes some people held about race.

“Didn’t you hear that black people like sweet potato pie, while whites lean toward pumpkin?” she’d teased the couple years ago. They’d heard the same “breaking news” while growing up, which they thought was hilarious.

“I’m so sorry to go against my culture,” her father had laughed, cutting a huge slice of the dessert, “but that’s just how it is!”

The girls giggled as they remembered. Jana followed her into the bedroom to find a decent pair of shoes. She set the pies down on the bed, and then thought better of it.

“You must have lost your mind and then found it,” Patience laughed. “I was going to say that Rory would’ve snatched those right up.”

Jana moved closer to her friend.

“Just how much makeup did you put on?”

“Why?”

“It doesn’t look natural,” she critiqued. “You’re too pretty to even wear it in the first place.”

Looking in the mirror again, Patience groaned.

“But I want to look great for Roman’s family.”

Her friend began pushing her towards the bathroom.

“If good looks are what you’re after, go scrub that makeup off!”

CHAPTER 27

The girls had a wonderful time at her parents' house that afternoon. They ate, laughed, reminisced about old times, ate some more and enjoyed watching football on TV. They were all huge fans, especially Patience and her father. Even Rory joined in on the fun, barking every time they screamed over a touchdown. It was a great day so far, and Patience knew it could only get better. Roman was picking her up in half an hour.

"I know you're excited," her friend said as they scarfed down more dessert. Jana approved of him, which was important. It made things easier when friends liked the guy she was dating.

"Absolutely," Patience agreed. "He's so ... I don't know one word to describe him. He's caring, smart, and interesting. He always has these stories to tell about his family and life." She smiled.

"I really like him. I know it hasn't been very long since we met, but I don't care. It feels right to be with him."

"Yes, I know exactly what you mean. That's how I feel about Bret."

"Do you miss Scott at all?"

"Believe it or not, I do. I could tell he really loved me. And he was so good, so attentive. I really don't think I deserved such a nice, wholesome guy." Jana had a faraway look in her eyes.

"Jana! Of course you did! Don't say things like that. You're a wonderful person, and a fantastic friend. Any guy would be lucky to have you."

Her friend didn't say anything, so Patience continued,

"You know, maybe you two can get back together sometime. I think you just got scared. We *are* young, after all. Serious relationships can be overwhelming, and maybe Scott will realize he rushed things. He did put too much pressure on you. But be's so nice, Jana! I'm sure he understands."

She took a huge bite of pie, savoring the taste. The only flavor she liked was lemon, so her father baked her two every holiday.

"I know marriage is the last thing on *my* mind, so I empathize."

"I know that's right. I'll never get married, that's for sure." Jana's parents had divorced when she was only five. "I just want to have fun, and that's what appeals to me about Bret."

"Sure, for now. *However*," she laughed as Jana rolled her eyes, "I know you better than you know yourself. Partying and all is great, but what about when we hit our thirties? Well, for me, it's more like forties! It'll get old, and we'll probably want to settle down."

As she said the words, though, Patience shuttered. She didn't think marriage sounded appealing any more than her friend did. What a hypocrite she was, preaching to Jana about the 'M' word. Growing up, her parents had modeled the perfect relationship for her. The two always respected one another, worked hard at keeping the spark alive, and tried saving the huge fights for things like money, which couldn't be helped, especially with John's spending habits. Yet Sharise and John were the exception, at least in their daughter's tiny world. Besides, she didn't think she could financially and emotionally survive a divorce, which was inevitable in today's society.

* * *

Roman picked Patience up a little after three, looking handsome as ever. He held a single white rose in one hand and an envelope in the other. Upon further investigation, she could see the Hallmark symbol on the back, and she got excited. Sharise had answered the door, immediately pulling him into a big hug.

"Roman! Sweetheart! It's so good to see you! Come in, come in!"

Patience had forgotten that they'd already met at the vet.

"You too, Mrs. McKlendon."

He smiled at her over her mother's shoulder as John came out from the kitchen. He was holding a plate with turkey, dressing, and a slice of pecan pie.

"Please call me Sharise."

Jana was giggling at the sight of John.

"Dad! Didn't we just eat?" Patience exclaimed.

He stood in the foyer, resembling a child who'd gotten caught with his hand in the cookie jar.

Her mother wagged a finger at him.

"I'll deal with you later," she said sternly. Turning back to Roman, she said, "Thanks to you, our Rory is still with us." Her voice cracked.

Patience went to get some Kleenex, for she knew her mom tended to be more emotional this time of the year.

"I just don't know what we'd have done if he hadn't survived," Sharise went on. "He's our baby!"

After handing her mother the tissue, Patience hugged Roman.

"Happy Thanksgiving," she whispered in his ear. Jana shook his hand, and her father mumbled, "Good to see you again" through a mouthful of food.

How embarrassing, she thought, mortified beyond belief. Not only had her dog almost choked the first time he'd come over, but now her mother was crying and her father couldn't tear himself away from eating long enough to greet him.

"Would you like something to drink?" she asked, discreetly leading him away from the others.

Roman followed her to the formal dining room, where it was quiet. Rory was asleep in the guest bedroom. She couldn't believe the doorbell hadn't woken him.

"No thanks. I hope you don't mind my coming a little earlier than originally planned. I wanted to spend time with you before going to my parents." He kissed her on the cheek, then handed her the flower and envelope. "These are for you." He seemed almost shy as they sat down.

"Aww, you didn't have to do this! What's the occasion?"

Her eyes closed as she breathed in the smell of the rose.

"Thanksgiving," he answered with a huge grin.

"I know that, silly. I'm just surprised. My family doesn't exchange gifts until Christmas."

She opened the card, which had a turkey on the front, not knowing there was a man holding an ax behind it. On the inside he'd written:

> *Dear Patience,*
> *We haven't known each other long, but I can already tell what a special person you are! Happy Thanksgiving! I can't wait to spend this special occasion with you*
> *Roman*

There was also a gift card to her favorite pizza place, Pookie's Pizza. Patience told him about it one night a couple of weeks before. Her father had been taking her there twice a month since she was a child. It was a special treat to indulge in both the homemade Italian food and her father's undivided attention. Her uncle, one of her mother's brothers, actually owned it, so they always ate for free and received special treatment. But the gift card was still so sweet. Roman didn't know it was her uncle who owned it.

His real name was Clarence, which he loathed, so when his friends had nicknamed him Pookie back in high school, it stuck. He and Patience had always been close. He'd even named one of his specialty pizzas after her. It had a thin crust with pepperoni, cubes of grilled chicken, and extra cheese. Her mouth watered as she thought of it.

"Oh Roman, this is the sweetest thing you've ever done since we met almost three weeks ago!"

They laughed as she leaned forward in the chair, almost falling, and threw her arms around his neck. They kissed quickly, as both were aware of their surroundings. He was pleased with her reaction.

"Well, pizza's your favorite food, and I know how much you like flowers," he said with a sheepish grin.

She sighed. "I just wish I'd gotten *you* something."

He put a finger to her lips.

"Don't be silly. I don't want anything from you except *you*."

The two kissed again, slightly longer this time.

"Ahem."

They jumped at the sound of her father clearing his throat. "Am I interrupting something?"

Roman was on his feet in two seconds. Patience didn't think she'd ever seen him move so fast.

"Well actually ..." she started, but John threw up his hands.

"Please don't say anything. I don't want to know."

Roman turned to her with a desperate look.

"Guess we better head out. I bet my mom's looking out the window for us." He attempted a laugh that sounded more like a cough.

"Um, yes," Patience agreed. "I'm sure it's almost four, huh?"

* * *

Roman pulled into the Jenkins' driveway at exactly four-fifteen. They'd made perfect time, which would make Cynthia very happy. A BMW and a Lexus were already parked there, and Patience held her breath as he squeezed his Tahoe between the BMW and grass. She was sure he'd hit it, but luck was on his side that day. Four sports cars and an F150 were parked along his parents' curb. Obviously they had more company than just his sisters.

She couldn't believe the beautiful mansion that stood before her. It was more like a home built for a famous couple with ten kids. She briefly had a feeling of déjvu, the same emotions creeping up as when she'd met Tripp's parents at *their* mansion: excitement, a touch of fear, and the urge to turn around and run home. She always felt so poverty-stricken when thrown into situations such as these. It seemed like every guy she'd dated had rich parents.

Patience smiled as he lightly brushed her cheek with his finger.

"You look terrified, PJ."

He turned the car off so all was quiet. Taking a deep breath, she admitted how nervous she was.

"Don't get me wrong. I feel comfortable with your parents. It's like I've known them my whole life. I guess I'm afraid of meeting everyone else important in your life."

"Don't worry. My sisters are very inviting, especially Gabby. They'll make you feel right at home. You'll see."

She glanced over her shoulder as yet another car pulled up to the Jenkins' property.

"Who do all these vehicles belong to?" she asked, her brows knit together with worry.

"Oh, so that's what this is all about! Didn't I tell you? Some of my extended family is here, as well as my buddies that I couldn't wait for you to meet. I could've sworn I told you."

Patience shook her head.

"No, you left that small bit of information out during all of our conversations." She rolled her eyes, letting down the visor to check her hair in the mirror.

"Sorry." He had such an innocent looking face as he played with the keychain.

"*Sorry*," she mimicked in a low voice. Gathering her purse and the dish she'd made, she got out of the car. She'd decided on Potato Salad Number Three, which meant it was the recipe from the third cookbook the day before.

Roman fell into step beside her, taking the huge salad and her purse.

"I'll carry these, ma'am."

She didn't respond as she prayed silently for the evening to go well. Once they made it to the door, he turned serious for a moment.

"Look, I know you're nervous, and you don't know this, but your face is as pale as the front of this house. But you'll be great! I promise. You're so funny, and charismatic, and adorable. I know you're not shy, and my friends and family are going to flock to you like sheep. You'll see! Now smile. There are frown lines between your eyes. You don't want to wrinkle early, do you?"

She couldn't help but laugh at his choice of encouraging words.

Roman knocked on the door, winking at her.

"Everyone's going to love you."

CHAPTER 28

"Finally! What did you guys do, *walk* here?" Cynthia scolded them as she opened the door. "My goodness, we've been waiting for hours, it seems!" She hugged Patience, throwing her son a dirty look. "I almost picked her up myself."

"Whatever. We're here." Roman kissed her lovingly on the forehead, then handed her the dish covered with Saran Wrap.

"What is this?"

"Patience slaved over a potato salad for you guys. I told her you didn't deserve it, but she insisted," he teased.

"What a thoughtful thing to do! Thank you, dear."

Cynthia gave her a quick peck on the cheek before Roman took her hand, leading her deeper into the house.

Although they were in the front hallway, she could hear many different sounds blending together: the volume on their television must have been as high as it could go; female voices gossiping and giggling came from somewhere behind the staircase; and finally, there was the unmistakable sound of dominoes being slammed down and men talking animatedly. Her uncle had taught her the game in her teens, and she loved it. Her grandmother used to have to replace their glass tables quite often, as her uncle and grandfather foolishly played the games on them. Dominoes could be pretty intense.

"Come on in! I can't wait to introduce you to everyone," Roman yelled over the commotion.

Just then Erik appeared, full of smiles and good cheer. "Patience! Sweetheart! Come in, come in."

He took her hands and kissed her on each cheek. "I'm so glad you made it! Cynthia was about to drive me insane with all her questions: 'Didn't I tell that boy four-thirty? He couldn't be on time to save his life! Oh, wait, but what if they were in an accident? Did you check your cell, Erik? *Erik?*' By then I'd tuned her out!"

The three laughed, but his father soon straightened up as his wife passed by.

"These walls are not soundproof, honey," she said with a sugary sweet smile on her lips but eyes that read 'I'm gonna kill you later'.

They all went into the kitchen, where two women were getting everything prepared for dinner. Patience guessed correctly that they were Roman's sisters.

"Hi, you must be Patience," the taller of the two said. She looked just like their mother but was tall like Erik and Roman. Cynthia, on the other hand, appeared to be only five feet.

She extended a hand to Patience, smiling pleasantly.

"I'm Rachel, Roman's sister."

"It's nice to meet you," she responded, shaking her hand as some of the nervousness disappeared. She should have known his family would be nice and friendly.

All that anxiety for nothing, she thought as his other sister came forward.

"I'm Gabrielle, but please call me Gabby," sister number two supplied, hugging her like an old friend. "We've heard so much about you!"

Patience blushed as Gabby winked at her brother.

"She's just like you described." A huge dimple similar to his appeared. In fact, the two looked so much alike, it was uncanny.

"Let's spare her the details, please." He shot her a warning glance, but she was nonplussed.

Turning back to Patience, she confided, "He kept me on the phone almost two hours the other night, telling me how cute you were, how he felt a spark the moment he first laid eyes on you the day of your dog's accident ..."

"Gabby!"

Roman appeared mortified as Cynthia took the ham out of the oven. Erik had gone to check the score of the game. Loud shouts broke out as an interception was thrown.

"Man, I cannot *believe* this!" A male voice full of emotion could be heard over the others.

Rachel shook her head, filling empty glasses with ice. "What's the big deal about football, anyway?"

Roman motioned to Patience to follow him to the living room. Before they left the kitchen, he turned to Gabby.

"I'm not finished with you, Miss," he promised.

Gabrielle ignored him, joining them in the hallway.

They made their way to the huge living area, where four young men were watching the game. Patience could have sworn there would be thirty people instead of only four. She just knew their screams could be heard one block over. She stood with Roman and Gabby, slowly taking in the scene in front of her.

One of the four was sitting on the sofa, taking a bite out of a triple-decker sandwich. He was a bit on the heavy side, but part of his weight seemed to be muscle. He looked like he should've been one of the football players they were watching on TV. He had a bald head, dark complexion, and a friendly looking face. He resembled a teddy bear, actually, and also reminded her of one of her cousins, Pookie's son.

"Touchdown!"

The loudest of them all screamed at the top of his lungs, jumping up and down as if on a trampoline. He turned and pointed at the third guy, who was totally ignoring the game. He had his cell up to his ear, listening intently to the caller on the other end. He turned his back to his friend, using his finger to plug up his free ear.

"Yeah, that's what I thought! In your face, dude!" the loud one said as he took a sip of his beer.

She didn't see how Mr. Cell could hear anything over the racket in the house. The fourth friend yelled at the TV as well, but he wasn't quite as ear-piercing as the loud one.

"Hey guys, listen up! There's someone here I want y'all to meet!"

It took Roman three attempts, but he finally had their attention. He held her hand as they stood in the middle of the room, blocking the view of the game.

"This is Patience," he said as proudly as if he'd just won the Super Bowl. Sandwich Guy approached first, wiping his hands with a napkin. He smiled, introducing himself as Nate.

"I'm pleased to make your acquaintance," he said as everyone laughed.

Roman elbowed him in the ribs. "Wow, I've never heard you sound so formal before."

Nate shrugged.

"I save that for the ladies." He turned to Gabrielle with smitten eyes. "When did you get here?"

She smiled.

"Oh, I arrived about twelve hours ago. You didn't see me because your face has been buried in food all afternoon. How could you know?" she asked with a smirk.

He laughed good-naturedly.

"I see that Gabby is her usual charming self. Anyway, I'm Roman's best friend, so if there's anything you want to know about him, *I'm* the one to ask."

"Not so fast," a voice behind him interrupted.

It was Mr. Not So Loud. "We've been buddies since high school, so she needs to come to me with any inquiries. I'm Maverick."

"Dinner's ready!" Mr. Jenkins' announcement caught everyone's attention. "Come and get it ... or not! Then there'll be more for me!"

They had a difficult time prying Mr. Loud away from the television. Patience chatted with Gabby, noticing that more guests were surfacing from the back rooms. Cynthia was running back and forth through the main hallway, setting food on the tables and checking the sweet potatoes in the oven. Rachel put the finishing touches on one of the desserts, her mother almost knocking her over as she ran by.

"Whoa! Sorry sweetheart, but you need to move out of the way! Gabrielle Patrice Jenkins! What are you doing just standing there? I swear you're just like your father! Grab those extra cups and take them to the dining room. Hurry up!"

Cynthia's eyes darted to her son.

"Roman, set these two casseroles over by the rolls, and tell your Uncle Frank to come help with these drinks. I called him over ten minutes ago."

Mrs. Jenkins didn't play around when it came to entertaining. "Where's your father?"

"He's talking to Uncle Frank and Aunt Janice," Gabby answered, totally unfazed by her mother's earlier jabs.

Cynthia put her hands on her hips.

"Go tell those two to quit goofin' off and get in here."

"I thought you told me to take the cups to the dining room?"

Patience tried not to laugh but couldn't help it. She liked his sister already.

Her mother threw Gabby a warning look, so she dutifully followed directions.

Feeling sympathetic toward Cynthia, Patience offered her assistance. She spread a tablecloth on the kids' table. Apparently, there were children somewhere in the house that she hadn't seen or heard. After what seemed an hour, everyone finally occupied the same room. The formal dining area looked amazing. The Jenkins had really outdone themselves. There were beautiful, expensive looking table settings, fine China for the adults, and candles sporadically placed here and there, giving off different holiday scents. The room was done in soft colors, which had a calming effect on the guests.

Taking advantage of the momentary silence, Roman introduced her to the rest of his family and friends. There was Uncle Frank and his wife Janice, his other uncle J.J., and one of his grandfathers, Cal. She was ecstatic to find that everyone was so nice and friendly. They really seemed to be happy to meet her which, due to past experiences, she'd learned to appreciate and not take for granted. Cal gave her a warm hug, and she noticed immediately that both Roman and Gabby resembled him.

"Okay, who's missing?" Uncle Frank interrupted her thoughts as he studied the faces in the room and began counting heads.

"Where are the kids?" Aunt Janice asked with a worried frown.

Roman's dad offered to go get them, heading toward the spiral staircase. "Last time I saw them they were in Rachel's old room playing," he called over his shoulder.

He came down five minutes later, followed by two small children. Patience smiled. They were adorable. She guessed their ages to be about three or four years old. The boy appeared slightly younger than the girl. Both were on the chunky side, dressed in coordinating outfits. He had on jeans with a blue button-down shirt, while she wore a denim dress.

The guests were talking amongst themselves as Cynthia put her hands on her hips.

"What in the world have you two been up to? You both have guilt written on your foreheads."

As a matter of fact, they did. And Erik appeared displeased.

"Go ahead. Show your aunt what you did."

The boy obeyed him, turning around to show the crowd a huge area of missing hair from his Afro. Everyone gasped, and the children hung their heads in shame. Their parents, Frank and Janice, were outraged. They had been in the game room playing dominoes with the others.

"Hunter Aaron Jenkins! What on earth happened to you?" His mother knelt in front of him to inspect the damage.

"Haden did it!" the child accused, pointing to his sister's hand. It was clenched into a fist, and her eyes were cast downward.

"Young lady, open your hand please," their father commanded.

One could hear a pin drop as she showed them her brother's hair she'd been hiding behind her back.

"But the bubble gum was stuck! I *had* to cut it out." Patience could hear stifled laughter behind her.

Aunt Janice suddenly whipped around, her face inches away from Frank's.

"I thought I told you to keep an eye on them!"

"How could I? You know these kids are sneaky! I checked on 'em once and they were asleep."

His frustrated wife threw her head back, laughing sarcastically.

"Yeah, right! You're so gullible! You should've known they wouldn't really volunteer to take a nap."

Frank grabbed the boy's arm, almost pulling it out of the socket.

"Ouch! You hurt me, Daddy!" the child whined.

"Hush boy, or I'll give you something to cry about."

He glanced over his shoulder as he led the child upstairs.

"Give it a rest, Janice! Why couldn't *you* have helped keep tabs on them? They're half yours, after all."

Janice and Haden followed them, both parents still fussing as the children cried.

Cynthia raised her eyes heavenward.

"Lord, please help us all."

* * *

Patience felt as if she might burst any minute, she'd eaten so much. Sitting in Erik's comfortable recliner, totally entertained by the activity around her, she pondered taking an antacid for her full feeling. A different football game had just begun, so the yelling and jumping up and down by Roman's buddies had picked back up. Hunter and Haden, whom she had learned were in fact twins, sat on the carpet beside her playing board games. Their mood was subdued, as they'd both received spankings earlier. Roman kept popping in and out to check on her. He was helping his mother clear the table and clean the kitchen.

She was perfectly content but wished she'd made smarter choices on the amount of food she'd inhaled. Her stomach was way too full. Clearly, willpower was not one of her strengths. She should've had her main meal at her parents' and then eaten dessert at the Jenkins'. But no, that made too much sense. She hadn't turned down anything at either house. And she still had Cole's family to spend time with later on.

Gabrielle came in to join her, eating a bowl of ice cream with whipped cream on top. Patience inhaled and exhaled slowly, trying not to throw up. Gabby wore a huge smile, practically skipping over to the couch beside the recliner. She was very energetic and friendly.

"How's it going?" she asked, jumping a foot when Heath shouted at the television. He was the one who'd been on his cell phone.

Patience laughed.

"Great, except for the fact that I can't move. That ice cream looks good, but I'm not eating again until *next* Thanksgiving!"

"I know what you mean," Gabby agreed, scraping her ice cream bowl. She closed her eyes, sighing with bliss. "Mmm, there's nothing like mint chocolate chip to end the perfect meal."

Patience shook her head. Roman's sister was hilarious.

"You just said you couldn't eat anything else."

"No, *you* said that. I just meant I knew what you were talking about."

The girls giggled as Patience returned to an upright position. She needed to steal some quiet time with Roman before heading to Cole's parents'. He had to drive her back to get her car, but that wasn't the same. It would be dark in his Tahoe, and she wanted to be able to see his gorgeous face.

She found him in the kitchen loading the dishwasher. Miraculously, he was alone, so she approached him from behind, wrapping her arms around his waist. He turned to face her and she laughed. He wore an apron that read *Kiss the Cook.*

"What in the world?" she said, pressing her body into his. She smiled seductively. "I guess I have to obey your apron."

Their lips met in a tender kiss, allowing her to forget her tummy troubles.

Roman pulled back slightly, brushing stray curls off her forehead.

"Careful, I don't want to get caught again, this time by *my* family. Your dad probably can't stand me now."

"He'll be all right. I'm not a kid anymore."

He smiled. "Ooh, listen to you! Miss Goody Two Shoes has a little rebellion in her."

She started to lean in for another kiss but stopped short. The clock on the microwave read ten o'clock.

* * *

Patience apologized for the tenth time that night. Cole's mother refilled his cup of coffee as the three sat in the breakfast area of their kitchen.

"Don't be silly, sweetheart! We knew you had other commitments. Please stop saying how sorry you are!"

Cole nodded in agreement.

"Yeah, we're just happy you made it. You could've come over at midnight for all we care."

It relieved her to know he wasn't mad at her ... again. Their relationship had been rocky as of late. She could not have stood another disagreement.

"Well, just so you know, I'm spending the night Christmas Eve."

Cole and Cate laughed.

"That's fine with me. You're a part of the family anyway," Cate said as Cole's father came in. He'd been next door at the Robinsons'.

"It sounds like there's too much fun going on in here without me," he said as he gave Patience a hug. "Good to see you, dear."

He walked over to his wife, pulling her close for a warm embrace. The two began kissing passionately, as if they'd been apart for years.

"Gross," Cole commented, standing up with a sour look on his face. He gestured for Patience to join him. "That's our cue to get outta here!"

The two friends grabbed their jackets and headed outside into the cold air. The weather was bearable when one dressed appropriately. Plus, it felt good to move around after eating so much.

"This is nice," he said as he put an arm around her shoulders.

"It is," she agreed. "This is the perfect end to a wonderful day."

A stray cat scurried across the neighbor's front lawn. Soon after, they could hear dogs barking in the alley.

"Oh yeah, tell me about Ryan's family. How did it go when they met you today?"

They had reached the end of his street and she turned to face him, completely unaware of how beautiful she looked. She folded her arms over her chest in a huff.

"Cole!"

He began laughing. "I know, I know, his name is Roman. I'm just messin' with ya."

She rolled her eyes.

"Well, your humor leaves a lot to be desired. Besides, you know that this is a touchy subject for us. I don't know why you're even asking about him."

Crossing the street, the two walked in silence for a while. He dug his hands deeper into his jacket pockets as a cold breeze swept over them. His parents' neighborhood was quieter than usual that night, and a couple of street lights they'd passed were out. Patience could barely see in front of her.

It was Cole who finally broke the silence.

"If we come across any criminals out here, I'm running! You'll have to save yourself."

"Once the thief sees who I am, he'll offer to give *me* money! Everybody knows I'm broke," she responded.

They stayed out for about an hour, just happy to be together. She told him all about Roman and the crazy time they'd had at the Thanksgiving dinner with his family. She spoke very highly of his parents, going into detail about their first meeting at Three Forks the weekend before.

"I was so nervous at first, but after about five minutes, it felt like I'd known them forever. They were so loving and affectionate."

He seemed genuinely happy for her and apologized again for his behavior at the party.

"We all have to hang out sometime soon so I can redeem myself," he offered as they returned to his parents' house. They'd turned in, but Cate had left a note saying how great it was to see Patience.

"Aww, your mom is the best!"

She stayed a while longer, and the two reminisced about old times.

Cole walked her outside at three am. The stray cat from earlier was on top of her car. It didn't hiss or meow or even blink as they neared it.

"I guess I can give it a ride to wherever it wants to go, but it needs to cough up some gas money!"

He just shook his head with a smile, pulling her into a big bear hug.

"You're nuts."

"Thanks."

She gave him a kiss on the cheek, promising to call him the next day. The cat finally ran off.

"Aww man! I thought I had a new playmate for Rory."

Cole threw up his hands. "That's it! I'm calling David Letterman to let him know I've got a new comedian for his show."

They both laughed, and with one last wave, Patience headed home.

CHAPTER 29

Rory's cast came off the first week of December, which was the perfect Christmas gift to them both. His hind leg had healed one hundred percent. He was good as new. They were on their way home from the vet that Saturday afternoon, and Patience had the windows down and her music blasting. It was unseasonably warm for that time of year, even in Texas. She wore blue jeans with a white tank top and sandals. Her hair was in a messy ponytail from the wind, and she was happy she hadn't worn makeup, as her cheeks were moist with perspiration. She hadn't believed the weatherman that morning when he'd predicted eighty degrees.

Patience turned onto her street and noticed Roman pulling out of the driveway. Honking her horn, she stuck her hand out the window, waving excitedly. What a nice surprise! They'd chatted briefly on the phone the day before but he hadn't mentioned anything about coming over. He parked next to the curb and ran to her car.

"Hi sweetie!" she called out, almost forgetting to turn the car off. She jumped into his arms, leaving Rory inside to fend for himself. He barked nonstop as she and Roman kissed.

"I didn't know you were coming over," she said, holding him close.

"Me either," he responded with a shrug. "I was determined to go a whole day without talking to or seeing you, but I just couldn't do it. I missed you too much."

"I'm glad you did."

She wrapped her arms around his neck, her eyes glistening in the sunshine. "I miss you all the time. Even when we've spent a whole day together, after you drop me off at home, I can't wait to see you again."

She felt so comfortable telling him whatever was on her mind or in her heart. And she was sure he felt the same way.

The past month with him couldn't have gone any better if she'd been dreaming. He was so romantic and fun. They really clicked. The two shared many of the same interests, held similar values, and had formed an indescribable bond in the short time since they'd met. Sure, they had differences of opinion on some things, like all couples did. But even that fact made the relationship more interesting and exciting. They stood on her lawn holding each other, oblivious to the world around them, when one of the kids who lived down the street tapped her on the leg.

"Excuse me, Mrs. Patience," the small boy, Billy, said in a shy voice.

Winking at Roman, she whispered, "I didn't know I got married."

She knelt down to his level. They hadn't heard him approach.

Pointing to her car, Billy said, "I think Rory's throwing a temper tantrum."

The poor dog was still in the car, barking wildly and trying to jump out the window.

Patience and Roman ran quickly to set him free.

"I'm a horrible mother!" she exclaimed, her eyes wide as saucers. She couldn't believe she'd tuned him out as soon as Roman entered the picture. Rory jumped up to greet him as they released him, ignoring his owner momentarily.

"You are not!"

Roman began roughhousing with the dog and noticed his missing cast.

"Hey! No wonder he's so excited. His leg is free ... yea!"

The two started running all over the yard, chasing one another like children. Rory had really taken to Roman, and she couldn't blame him. Her boyfriend possessed many of the same great qualities both humans and animals liked. He was wonderful.

The kids playing down the street caught sight of them, as Rory's barking had gotten even louder. The four boys quickly ran over, Billy included, joining in on the fun. One brought a football, so after tag ended, a football game erupted. Now Patience knew how it felt to be forgotten. She smiled as she watched them play for a few minutes, and then walked back to the car to gather her things. Rory had obviously gotten hold of her purse. All of its contents were scattered on the back seat, and there was chewing gum stuck to the floor mat. Good thing her coins were *inside* her wallet this time. Otherwise, he'd have choked on them ... again.

She headed inside to check her messages and was back out ten minutes later. She'd prepared some snacks for the boys: sliced apples with cheese, crackers, grapes and cookies. There was also a huge jug of lemonade and a couple of bottled waters. The children's parents knew her well. They trusted her completely, which was why they hadn't asked first to come over. It was a great Saturday for them all. Eventually they'd allowed her to play with them, admitting that she was alright "for a girl."

The children reluctantly left after spending the entire afternoon with them. They adored Rory and now Roman as well. He promised to "hang" with them again real soon.

The two of them lured Rory inside and then went out to clean up all the napkins and paper cups the wind had tossed around. Once inside, they were in each other's arms, kissing more passionately than ever before. They ended up on the couch, unable to get enough of each another.

"Patience," Roman murmured, kissing first her mouth and then her neck, while she caressed his back, pulling him as close as possible to her. They were still on the couch, but things were heating up ... fast.

"Mmmhmm?" she finally responded, lost in the moment.

Her hands slowly found their way to his waist, but she made a conscious effort to leave them there.

He ran his fingers through her curls, sighing heavily.

"Wow."

She leaned back against the cushion, breathless.

"My sentiments exactly."

Her pulse hadn't slowed down and her face felt flushed, yet she was sure she could restrain herself if they took a break. Why did he have to be so darn attractive? It made situations like these even more difficult.

She watched him closely, running a finger up and down his arm softly. Deep in thought, they sat in the quiet living room. The only sound came from Rory. He'd fallen asleep and was snoring softly. Thank goodness he only snored when he was overly tired, or he wouldn't have been able to sleep with her.

"Are you okay?" she asked, cocking her head to one side.

"Hmm? Oh yeah, I'm fine."

He rose to go stand by the window. It was turning dark, and the fireflies were fluttering around her back porch light.

"Roman, I know things became a little heated a minute ago, but don't take it so seriously." She already knew him like a book. "Geez, you look so guilty, like you just stole a car or something."

He remained by the window so she went to him, turning his face toward her.

"You know what? It's only been three weeks since we first met. So what? We clicked, that's all. The length of time of our relationship doesn't matter. It's the *quality* that is most important. So let's just go with the flow, and not worry about how fast things are going," she soothed.

She placed her hands on either side of his face, leaving him no choice but to make eye contact with her.

He finally smiled.

"You're absolutely right. I need to lighten up. It's just that, well, I'd die if you thought I only wanted one thing from you, that I'm rushing into this just to get . . . "

"Sex?" She supplied the word for him finally, not wanting to wait all night for him to say it.

He laughed. "You're so blunt!"

"Ha! And everyone calls me Goody-Two-Shoes. You can't even say the word, but I'm supposedly the wholesome one."

He took her hand, leading her back to the couch.

"Sure, you can say anything you want, but you're still the number one candidate for a milk commercial."

He reached for the remote control, sobering up somewhat. "Seriously, though, let's hold off on the make out sessions for a while, okay? I gave myself too much credit, assuming I had willpower. I don't."

He shrugged, managing to look manly and vulnerable simultaneously.

Patience had no other choice but to agree. There was no middle ground if one wanted to make love and the other preferred abstinence. However, in her eyes, they could still make out. But compromise didn't exist for them, at least not that night. It was written all over his face. Had the two continued, neither one would've been able to stop.

"Sweetie?" He was on pins and needles, she could tell, waiting for her response with wide eyes.

With a casual wave of her hand she answered,

"Oh, sure, that sounds fine. I don't want you to ever be uncomfortable or feel pressured. Taking it slow will be good." She just needed a cold shower. Ice cold.

He gave her hands a gentle squeeze as he sat studying her face.

"You *sure* you're all right with this?"

I have to be, she thought.

"I'm sure."

Roman stayed with her until almost midnight. The initial disappointment Patience felt slowly dissipated after a while. They listened to music, played card games and talked. He cracked jokes and did great impersonations of comedians she loved. She in turn tried to make him laugh with some jokes she'd made up herself. She was not successful. Instead, she chose to open up more about her childhood and family life. More specifically, she talked about being biracial.

He asked tons of questions: Did she identify more with one race than the other? Had she ever experienced racism? What were her grandparents' reactions to her mother and father's relationship back then?

"My parents met in high school. Although my dad was a senior and my mom a junior, they were in some of the same classes. According to her, she was a genius who was a step above her class. Anyway, it was love at first sight. Dad asked her out at the beginning of the year, she said yes, and after a while, he took her home to meet the folks.

They were shocked, to put it mildly. He hadn't told them she was black. But they sort of had to get used to the idea, as my father is pretty stubborn. No one can tell him what to do. If he likes something or someone, he'll fight to get or keep what he wants. Luckily, though, my grandparents were liberal and open-minded. They *did* worry about the neighbors and some of their friends, because everyone wasn't as accepting as they were."

"What about your mom's family?"

He played with her curls as she talked, totally engrossed in her story.

"Nana was okay with it but Papa wasn't. It took him forever to accept the relationship. He always made comments like 'I just don't trust white people' and 'All white people are racist!' Talk about the pot calling the kettle black! Geez!"

She shook her head in disgust. "It's still hard to be around him for long periods of time because we're so different. At family reunions, or when there's a large crowd around, he really gets stirred up. He badmouths people of every race, color and creed."

Roman hugged her.

"I bet it *is* difficult. But you have to remember that he's from an entirely different era. We're so privileged compared to our grandparents and great-grandparents. I mean, they were slaves, Patience. Can you imagine? He probably went through some things he'd never tell you. *Then*, the next thing he knows, his daughter comes home with a Caucasian. I'm sure his protective instincts had kicked in."

Patience was shaking her head.

"But my dad was just a kid! He hadn't been the one to hurt or mistreat my papa. Why did he have to suffer the consequences of others' vicious acts?"

Even to herself, she sounded like a wounded child.

He sighed.

"I'm not excusing his behavior, just trying to understand it."

The two sat lost in thought for a moment. Rory had gone to the kitchen to sniff for food. Sometimes he found crumbs she'd unknowingly dropped. Roman kissed her hand tenderly.

"How does he treat you?"

She smiled.

"Oh, he spoils me. Mom said he'd been upset about the pregnancy. He couldn't see why they would purposely conceive a child of mixed race. He knew there'd be problems and didn't understand why they'd want to raise a child in this racist world. It conveniently slipped his mind that *he* was one of the closed-minded individuals he talked about. But once he laid eyes on me, he was smitten."

"Well that's good. At least he hadn't rejected you. Does he accept your dad now?"

"Accept is a strong word. I think he just tolerates him for the family's sake." She laughed. "Plus, I think Nana threatened him, so he has to be cordial, at least."

"What about your aunts and uncles? You said your extended family is huge."

Patience nodded.

"Correct; my mom has a brother here in Dallas, as well as two sisters in Atlanta. They're both married with kids. All of them love my dad to pieces. My dad has four brothers and one sister. Three of them are in Tennessee, one is in Oklahoma, and my aunt resides in Virginia. She is prejudiced but thinks my mother is okay. My uncles in Tennessee are great and adore my mom. Uncle Max has even dated outside his race. She was Asian."

"What about the one in Oklahoma?"

She shrugged. "He tolerates different races but thinks Caucasians are superior: smarter, faster and stronger. He believes white people are more beautiful, and definitely kinder, than all of the different groups in this world."

"Are you serious?" Roman's mouth was hanging open.

"Yep, and his wife is worse. She thinks segregation should still be enforced, that we are *not* all equal, and that anyone who associates with us is as bad as we are."

He chuckled.

"I bet your family reunions are interesting."

"We don't attend, thank goodness."

Patience felt closer than ever to Roman that night. There was something to be said about a couple really opening up to each other. He was so attentive. She could tell him anything without the fear of being judged or looked down on. Now they both knew a significant amount about each other's pasts. He was an absolute dream, and each day she uncovered more evidence supporting this fact.

As they stood in her foyer at the end of the night, trying to prolong their time together, she wondered if she should just hug him. After their strained conversation earlier about sex, she didn't want to take a chance of getting worked up again. There was a strong possibility, for the lust in his eyes was unmistakable.

"Well, thank you for yet *another* wonderful day, PJ." His dimple deepened as he took a step toward her. She expected Rory to jump in and interrupt, as usual, but this time he didn't bother.

"I think my dog is bored with us," she stated as Roman slowly made his way toward her. She felt his breath, his dark eyes piercing through her.

"I guess I should go."

It sounded more like a question, but Patience wouldn't have dared to ask him to stay. He was right. It was way too soon for anything more than this.

"I had fun," she said lightly, taking a step backward. Better safe than sorry. She didn't trust herself to behave, no matter what was said. Politely opening the door for him, she almost winced at the hurt written on his face.

"I don't get a goodbye kiss?"

Her heart raced as he placed his hands behind her neck, bringing his lips to hers in their most passionate kiss yet. Pressing his body into hers, his hands softly trailed her spine, finally resting on her lower back.

Mustering up all the strength she could, she pulled back with a smile.

"Thanks again for everything. I'll talk to you tomorrow?"

Roman mumbled something about this being harder than he thought, turned on his heel, and walked out the door.

CHAPTER 30

"Hmm, interesting, very interesting," Jana pondered aloud, failing to untangle the Christmas lights. She sat on the floor in Patience's living room the next day, drops of sweat beginning to trickle down her temple. The heat was on but not that high, as she had always been hot natured. Jana told her it had nothing to do with the temperature. She'd guessed she was premenopausal.

"Girl, you're only twenty-two!" Patience giggled.

She didn't know how her friend came up with some of her hypotheses.

Jana shooed Rory away for the tenth time, complaining about him in a whiny voice.

"Can't you put him outside?"

Patience shook her head.

"It's thirty degrees out there!"

She was thankful her Jana didn't have pets -or children- for that matter. If someone bothered her or proved to be a nuisance, she just got rid of him. She'd probably place her crying infant in the closet. In that sense, the two girls were as different as night and day.

"*Well*, he keeps getting in my way. And you said yourself that he tried eating the bulbs last year."

Patience rolled her eyes.

"Sure, but that doesn't mean I want him to freeze to death."

Jana stood up, stating that she was washing her hands of the tangled mess.

"All I know is this could go a lot quicker if he was out of our hair." She unwrapped one of the candy canes off the tree, scanning the room to see what needed to be done.

"Are *you* helping or hindering?" Patience asked. "You're just as bad as Rory. All you two want to do is eat and make more work for me." Patience climbed the short ladder, extending her arm out to her "assistant".

"Now can you *please* hand me the angel?"

It was the same black angel her mother had given her when she'd turned three. She was glad she hadn't broken it after all these years.

Jason had asked her the year before if her father ever felt bad when she put up the black Santa Claus or angel.

"No, not at all," she'd answered. "In our house we embraced both white and black figurines to decorate with."

He'd nodded.

"What about baby dolls and barbies? What colors were they?"

She had jazzed up her answer a bit.

"I didn't play with dolls, only trucks and racecars. But they were either black or white vehicles. Oh, I did have a Tonka truck, which was white with black stripes. It looked like a zebra ... perfect for me!"

They had burst into laughter, and as Patience stood on the ladder remembering Jason and his family, she suddenly missed those days.

"What are you thinking about?" Jana asked loudly, startling her out of the flashback.

She jumped, losing her balance and falling forward onto the carpet with a *thud.* Rory barked, running over in a dash, and Jana screamed.

Patience lay there, laughing uncontrollably. It hurt a little, but she was okay.

"Good thing it's a short ladder!"

* * *

Roman called that night after dinner. Jana was still there, playing fetch with Rory in the house. Patience wondered if guilt was the driving force behind her friend's actions. She'd been so anxious to kick him out earlier that perhaps she subconsciously wanted to make it up to him.

"Hi sweetie," she answered cheerfully. "What are you doing?" She tiptoed into the den for privacy.

"I'm just getting in from church. I went to the evening service this time. And you?"

"Jana's over here. We spent the day together. She and Rory helped me put up the tree."

Roman chuckled at her sarcastic tone.

"Did you make it to church this morning?"

She nodded.

"Yep, but I was late. I sure didn't want to waltz in after it had started, but

I definitely needed to go! When Pastor Johnson invited the congregation up for Alter Call, you know I was the *first* one up there!"

He sighed. "I hear you! I should've sat on the first row, that's for sure."

Laughing, she joked, "Did you repent?" She certainly had.

"Oh yeah," he answered quickly.

They chatted a few more minutes, and he invited her out with him and his friends that night. They were all going to shoot pool and then head over to Nate's for a small get-together. He had an apartment in Frisco his parents were paying for while he went to school. Nate had told her on Thanksgiving that he still hadn't made up his mind on a major but had narrowed it down to Computer Science and Business. Later that night, however, as Roman drove Patience to her parents', she'd asked how old his friend was.

"He's twenty-two like us," he'd answered with a wide grin. "I overheard you two talking about school. He's been enrolled for three years now; he took a year off after high school to find himself. Well, apparently he's still missing because he's made no move to decide on a major. I think he's scared to grow up."

"His parents don't mind paying his rent every month?" She'd been curious about him. Out of all of Roman's friends, she and Nate had really hit it off.

"No, his dad's loaded. I think its old money. They pay for his housing, and I think his mother keeps his cell phone and laptop on. *And* his uncle pays his car note every month."

That statement only confirmed her belief that everyone she knew had money. Well, all except for Jana and Cole. They were just comfortable like her.

'Man, I need new friends!' she'd joked.

Roman said he'd be by in an hour, which gave her barely enough time to kick Jana out, shower and do her hair. She was glad they'd already eaten, at least. But she had no idea what she would wear. The temperature was freezing, but she'd be okay with just a jacket. She wanted to be cute yet casual, since they were hanging out with his friends. After rummaging through her closet, she settled on a semi-dressy red top with black pants.

Her hair had tons of static from the cold weather, so she used both African-American and Caucasian styling products. Instead of straightening the wild mane with a flat iron, she curled it. The curling iron was on the highest possible setting. Smoke filled the bathroom as she performed a miracle. She looked pretty good and actually had five minutes to spare.

Roman arrived right on time, as usual. He kissed her hello, admiring her hair and outfit.

"Wow! You look amazing!"

He always played with her curls, twirling them around his fingers or gathering her hair into a ponytail only to release it again. He loved the way it cascaded over her shoulders and made a point of saying how much he liked long hair. She wanted to cut it in the summer, but he'd threatened to break up with her if she did. He said it was one of her best attributes.

He reached out to smooth one of her curls down but made a sour face. Rubbing his hands together, he asked,

"What did you put in your hair?"

He walked over to get a paper towel off the counter.

She shrugged.

"I used hair oil, a little mousse, and gel."

Self-consciously, she reached up to feel the curls she simultaneously loved and hated. They *were* pretty greasy.

"Eww," he exclaimed dramatically.

Putting her hands on her hips, she whined.

"Well, you don't know what Black women have to go through! My hair gets so dry in the winter. If I didn't put oil in it, I'd be bald, plain and simple."

But he was shaking his head.

"I know that, but did you have to put so much of every styling product in it?"

"Yes, I did."

Indignant, she decided to ignore his reaction, refilled Rory's water bowl, and headed towards the door.

"Come on, let's go," she called grumpily over her shoulder.

* * *

Roman's friends were impressed with how good Patience was at pool. She won many times that night. It could've been more, but she quit trying after a while. She didn't want them thinking of her as a show-off. After all, this was supposed to be a fun night. She was uncomfortable with winning too many times, as they didn't know her very well. Like Jason, Roman's friends were placed on pedestals. They were all extremely important to him. Tripp hadn't had friends, by choice, so he couldn't be counted.

By the time they headed to Nate's, she had learned more about their personalities. Nate was the only one she'd had conversations with. He was incredibly sweet and personable, always smiling and eating, and telling jokes. His personality fit his appearance: big and teddy bearish. He had dark skin and eyes that lit up when talking about either sports or women.

Heath, the one who'd been on the phone Thanksgiving Day, was tall and extremely thin. His blond hair was short and spiked at the top. He brought his girlfriend Ebony. She was, without a doubt, the most gorgeous girl on the planet. Standing at about five feet four inches, with a curvaceous figure and flawless skin, she could have easily modeled high fashion, even with her short stature. Her jet-black hair was cut in a simple bob, and her attire was casual. Patience felt very unattractive standing next to her. Ebony was also very nice, so she didn't have the luxury of thinking ugly thoughts about her. It was very unsettling.

Roman informed her that they'd been a couple for only eight months. However, when hanging out with them, they appeared to still be in that new-relationship phase, the "No-you-hang-up-first-okay-let's-hang-up-at-the-same-time", where people around them wanted to throw up. Heath talked to her in a baby voice and spoke to everyone else in his regular tone. Luckily, she and Roman had skipped that phase, but they did make goo-goo eyes at one another from across the room.

The guys gave Heath a hard time that night, claiming he was already whipped. He'd opted out of another game of pool because of Ebony, claiming that he missed her.

"She's right *there*, man!" James whined in disgust. He obviously did not tolerate the cute things couples did to stay attached at the hip.

Maverick, the friend who wasn't as loud as James, proved to be a sweetheart, much like Nate. He was working on his Masters in Psychology, wanting to be a therapist for low-income families one day.

"You know black people don't believe in therapy!" James had quipped when he'd overheard their conversation.

Maverick was telling her about some of his classes as the two went to the snack bar for drinks. She just rolled her eyes, already seeing that James was not her cup of tea.

Maverick's appearance was conservative and studious, with eye glasses and preppy attire. He loved talking politics, psychology, or business. The others ignored him when he brought up Wall Street or the economy, but there was one topic the four friends were passionate about: sports. Even James loosened up the minute football or basketball came up. She liked the fact that, although it was more of a boys' night out, all of Roman's buddies were very welcoming toward the girls. Well, *almost* all of them.

The last, but certainly not least, Mr. Loud seemed obnoxious, arrogant, and angry. He stood out among the group, much like Patience's hair on a rainy day.

Everything about him screamed, "Look at me! Notice me!"

James was five feet nine inches or so, yet he possessed the confidence of someone well over six feet. When she'd been introduced to him over the holiday, something about him had given her an uneasy feeling. That evening at the Jenkins', he'd been standoffish. A couple of times she'd felt him glaring at her, which was odd.

"We're almost there, sweet pea," Roman said as he trailed the others down the highway. She stole a glance at his profile, thinking again how weird life was sometimes. One of the worst days of her life, Rory's accident, had turned out to be one of the best. This was because she'd met him.

Patience had spent so much time with him these past four weeks, yet she still felt tingles all over like it was the first day. Every touch, smile and kiss sent her soaring, making her want even more hours to be added to each day so she could spend them with him. And one of the best things about it was that he felt the same way. It also didn't hurt that their families and friends approved of the relationship. Sure, she knew it was impossible to please *everyone*, but the most important people in their lives were okay with it.

"Great! I can't wait to see his place!"

He squeezed her hand as they drove along, Bob Marley music filling the Tahoe.

"So, what other types of music do you like?" she asked, needing to know every single detail about him. Surprisingly, the topic of singers and music groups hadn't come up.

"I like Reggae, R&B and Hip Hop."

Up ahead she noticed some apartment complexes to the right. From what she could see, they looked very nice. And expensive.

He continued. "Oh, and this may sound corny, but I *love* Anita Baker. Do you know her?"

Patience laughed. "Yes! My aunts listened to her constantly when I was little. Her voice is amazing."

He smiled. "I'm guessing you mean your mom's sisters." He chuckled.

She glanced over at him.

"Actually it was my dad's sister that listened to her."

"Really?"

Roman found a parking space easily, gazing at her with wide eyes.

She shook her head. "No, I'm kidding. My dad's family never owned soul music. I just wanted to see if you were paying attention."

He opened her door politely, shrugging as he put a protective arm around her. Darkness surrounded them as they followed a narrow sidewalk towards a cluster of apartments.

He tugged her curls playfully as they heard Heath calling out for them to wait up.

"Careful, you don't want your hands to get greasy again," she said dryly.

Patience caught sight of Nate struggling to carry drinks, snacks and paper products from his car. She ran to help him, as the others ignored his cry for help.

"Thanks, I appreciate you. Hey, if Roman ever leaves you, remember me, okay?"

The two laughed as they took their time joining the others. But Roman had overheard him.

"Very funny, man! I was going to pay for your last year of school, but now . . ."

Nate pretended to wipe a tear from his eye, laughing as he ran ahead of them.

Roman shook his head, taking one of the heavy bags from Patience. He took a step toward her, waiting until his friend was out of earshot before he whispered,

"I hope I didn't hurt your feelings about the whole hair product remark earlier. You know I love your hair, and I think you are the most beautiful woman I've ever known. Sometimes I put my foot in my mouth." His voice trailed off as he gazed into her eyes.

"I'm fine! I was just kidding around. The real question is: Are *you* okay? We joke all the time with each other. Don't be so serious."

The cold wind blew around them, but her hair stayed in place. She ran a hand through it with furrowed brows.

"It *is* oily, though."

They all headed inside as James was pulling his car into the parking lot. She followed the others, trying not to glance back at the last friend to make it inside. She didn't have a good feeling about him, which was odd. She was such a people-person that it was rare to meet someone who made her nervous in a negative way. He hadn't been outright *rude* to her, but still, she'd decided to keep her distance.

Patience couldn't believe how gorgeous Nate's place was. The high vaulted ceilings, spacious living room with den, and two huge bedrooms could have been in a magazine. The kitchen had stark white cabinets and marble countertops. She wondered if he had a maid to come in weekly, or daily, for that matter, as the place was immaculate. It resembled a model home, and she pondered taking her shoes off to keep the snow-white carpet clean, although it was really too late because everyone had trampled on it already.

The apartment also smelled of pine, which was pretty impressive in her mind. She giggled as a picture of big ol' Nate, donning cleaning gloves and a mop, popped into her mind.

She shared her vision with Roman, who burst into laughter.

Roman led her into the living room to join Ebony and Heath, who were playing cards. James had come in and was sitting on the arm of the couch, a bored expression on his face. Clearly there were other places he'd rather be. He reeked of arrogance, at least from her point of view. These people were his friends, yet he behaved as if he were better than them.

"Hey Nate, where's the booze?" he yelled toward the kitchen. Then, turning his attention to Patience, he stood up. She felt goose bumps begin to form on her arms. She wondered why he had such a negative effect on her. He definitely gave her the creeps.

"Well, well, well, if it isn't Ebony and Ivory Part 2," he joked. Glancing at Heath with a smirk he added,

"Or should I say Ebony and *Medium-Ivory*?"

No one laughed as Nate emerged from the kitchen with drinks for everyone. She noticed Ebony wince and felt Roman's body stiffen beside her.

"You're hilarious," he said, sarcasm dripping from his voice. He put an arm around her, pulling her closer to him.

James shrugged casually.

"No, don't get me wrong. I think it's cute. We have the white guy with his black girlfriend, and now there's the *black* man with his, um ..." he let his voice trail off as he snapped his fingers. He appeared lost in thought, as if trying to figure it all out. He walked toward Patience, studying her face intently.

"What *are* you, exactly? Because I can tell you're not white, per se." He crossed his arms, his eyes traveling over her hair and body. "But you're not black, either. Hmmm ..."

She opened her mouth to respond, and then thought better of it. But even if she had wanted to say something, Roman didn't give her a chance, as he jumped right in.

"Cut it out, man!" His body language confirmed that he meant what he said. "Do you have a problem? If you do, tell us now."

The others looked on, their mouths hanging open in disbelief and shock.

James took a beer from Nate, shaking his head in frustration.

"Whoa, take it easy buddy! I'm just asking a simple question. You don't have to get all huffy." He took a step backward, but kept his eyes on his friend.

Roman didn't budge.

"It's none of your business whether she's black, white, or green. So don't ask again." He let go of her, taking a step forward. "You're being disrespectful, and that won't be tolerated."

James friend threw up his hands.

"Man!" he exclaimed again. "What happened to my best friend? You used to have a sense of humor. I was just joking around."

"I do have a sense of humor, for things that are actually funny. Now, like I said before, if you have something to say, say it now."

"Nah, I'm cool," James responded as he turned abruptly on his heel and walked towards the bathroom.

* * *

The six of them had a good time the remainder of the night, despite James' attitude. He was cordial towards Patience, but an undeniable tension hung in the air. If she caught him staring at her, he'd quickly turn his head. Whenever their paths crossed, he'd make sure to avoid bumping into her. Roman hadn't uttered two words to him since their confrontation, either. Luckily, Nate's place was big enough for them to avoid one another.

Ebony turned out to be even sweeter than she'd thought. Tired of the boys' tasteless jokes and sports talk, the girls planted themselves in front of the television with chips and pretzels. They laughed as they exchanged stories about Heath and Roman, while the guys played dominos in the den. An old episode of Good Times was on, which made the laughter escalate. Both she and Ebony loved old sitcoms like The Jefferson's and I Love Lucy.

Ebony tilted her head to one side, a gleam in her eyes.

"Did you ever notice that Good Times was the only show where they started out poor and *never* made it out of the ghetto?"

Patience nodded, deep in thought as she munched on a pretzel. "That's so true! At least George built his dry cleaning business from the ground up, became successful, and was able to move to a deluxe apartment in the sky. Even Archie and Edith Bunker were able to live in a pretty nice neighborhood and keep food on the table."

Patience shook her head, watching as Florida threw the punch bowl down and start crying as the realization of James' death finally sunk in.

She continued.

"They never got ahead financially. Even after Thelma married Keith, the family stayed poor. Why couldn't they all put their money together and get a decent place?"

The girls silently made eye contact and then burst into a fit of giggles.

"We are sad, sitting here talking about these actors like we know them!" Ebony observed.

Patience jumped as one of the boys slammed a domino down hard on the table.

"It is pitiful. But what else is there to talk about?"

Just then, James passed by to go into the kitchen. Ebony rolled her eyes with a look of disgust. Leaning in closer, she whispered, "I can't get over the way he acted tonight."

Patience nodded.

"I felt like an actress on a soap opera! What is up with him?" she asked with wide eyes.

Her new friend glanced over her shoulder quickly. James was still in the kitchen.

"Honestly, *what* he said didn't surprise me as much as the fact that he said it to your face. When Heath and I first started dating, he was very nice when I was around. But Heath had let me in on what was said behind my back. James hounded him constantly for dating a black girl, saying things like 'Why you gotta take all our women?' and 'The white man just wanna keep a brother down.' Heath would get so mad!"

Patience felt her mouth open in disbelief.

Ebony laughed. "My baby was always in a bad mood, as a result. After a while, he and I started hanging out by ourselves. We just didn't feel like being bothered anymore."

Patience sighed. "Clearly James isn't a fan of interracial dating."

He reemerged then, smiling wanly at the two girls as he passed by. She felt the hair on her arms stand up trying unsuccessfully to return the smile. Ebony coughed and took a sip of water. Both sat in silence for a while, munching on the snacks in front of them. The boys had gotten even louder, if that was possible. Patience saw Roman pat Nate on the back with such force that it almost knocked his friend off the chair. She shook her head.

"What a goofball!" she said of her boyfriend.

"They're all nuts," Ebony agreed.

She touched Patience lightly on the shoulder.

"Don't let James get to you. It's his problem if he wants to judge the world and disapprove of everything people do. Don't worry about it. I don't." She smiled.

Patience nodded. She stood up to refill the bowl of chips.

"Well, I guess it's not affecting me as much as I thought, because my appetite is still going strong!"

CHAPTER 31

Patience leaned her head against the seat, staring out the window of Roman's truck. It had been a great Sunday. She'd gone to church, spent time with Jana doing Christmassy things, and also had the opportunity to hang out with Roman and his friends. She'd made a new pal out of Ebony, as well. Yes, life was good.

"Hey PJ, are you awake?" His husky voice broke into her thoughts.

She lazily turned her face toward his, a half smile tugging on her lips.

"Mmmhmm."

"Did you have as much fun as I had tonight?" The stoplight was red, so he was able to give her a quick kiss.

She nodded.

"I sure did. Your friends are hilarious, and Nate is a sweetheart. Don't tell them, but he's definitely my favorite out of all your friends." She laughed. "I wouldn't want James getting all jealous, so please keep that piece of information to yourself."

He frowned.

"Well, I'm not finished with him yet. I'm beating him down the next time we cross paths."

"Roman!"

"No, I'm serious! He can't treat you like that expecting to get away with it. No, we're having a long discussion when I see him."

Patience took off her seatbelt for a second, leaning over to give him a kiss.

"Thank you for allowing me to spend time with your friends tonight. It means so much that you're including me in your world, introducing me to the people you care so much about."

She put her seatbelt back on as he laughed aloud.

"You are truly hilarious, do you know that? One of my friends nearly curses you out, basically stating that we're not good for each other, yet here you sit with a smile lighting up your beautiful face. Unbelievable."

Roman pulled into her driveway, shaking his head in disbelief. Shutting off the ignition, he turned towards her with curious eyes.

"Has anyone ever told you that you're just *too* nice?"

She shrugged.

"As a matter of fact, I'm told at least once a day that if I were any sweeter, I'd melt."

He laughed, reaching for her hand in the dark truck.

"Well, they're not exaggerating. You can't let people walk all over you. James was so rude, and yet you were going to let him get away with it. You weren't even going to let me tell him off! Now I have to wait an extra day to really kick his ass. What's up with that?"

Patience didn't answer for a moment, looking straight ahead at her house. She wanted to invite him in but thought better of it. But she definitely wasn't ready for the night to end.

Finally she glanced over at him.

"I just wanted to let it go. Why should we give him all the power? I've learned that it's not good to fight every battle. It's not healthy. People who act like James just want attention. I know he's your best friend, but that's the impression he's given me so far. Why not ignore him? *He's* the one with the problem, not us. I mean, clearly he has issues."

Roman didn't budge.

"Have you lost your mind? He can't think there are no consequences for his actions. Plus, it's your responsibility to teach others how to treat you."

Patience sighed. Her eyes searched his as they sat in her quiet neighborhood. She studied his handsome face with interest, a seductive smile on her lips.

Crawling over the stick shift to him, which wasn't an easy task with her long legs, she sat on his lap facing him. He chuckled, wrapping his arms around her waist. The steering wheel dug into her lower back, but she didn't care. She loved being so close to him.

Her pulse quickened.

"Now," she whispered in his ear, "that's enough talk about James. Let's move on to something else."

Chapter 32

Patience invited Roman to spend Christmas Day with her family. He accepted the invitation enthusiastically, agreeing to come over in the afternoon. He planned on attending church services that morning with his parents and sisters, having a gift exchange and dinner with them afterwards. The Jenkins' Christmas mornings were always jam-packed with activities, leaving evenings free for each to do whatever he wanted.

“What time is your beau getting here?” her father asked with a chuckle. She glanced out the window for the tenth time.

“Beau? Dad, that is so old-fashioned!”

Sharise laughed. “Yeah honey, you need to get with the times. They’re just *seeing* each other.”

“Mom, that’s embarrassing! How about we not try to label our relationship?”

“Okay okay, what time is Roman arriving?” John asked, standing to join his daughter by the window.

“I’m not sure. He said he’d scarf down his food so he could get here at a decent time.”

Patience felt the butterflies return at the mere thought of seeing him. He was such a wonderful guy, and she couldn’t wait to give him his present. It was a video game for his Xbox and a gift card to his favorite sporting goods store.

As if on cue, they spotted Roman’s car pull up alongside the curb. She quickly opened the door as he practically sprinted up the walk, shivering from the cold. It was supposed to snow later that day, although no one believed the forecast. More than likely it would just rain and freeze over, making the roads hazardous. She’d left Rory home for that reason. He hadn’t put up a fight, either, as he wasn’t a big fan of the cold to begin with.

Ten minutes later, Roman happily finished his plate of desserts. Sharise had lovingly put together a sample platter of pies, rice pudding, and cobbler for him. He sat back in his seat with a contented sigh. He’d insisted upon arrival that he couldn’t eat another thing, but her mother had ignored him.

“My future son-in-law cannot leave this house without eating *something* on Christmas day! I don’t care if it’s a speck of chocolate from the cake!” she’d said.

Patience smiled as she sat watching him suffer in silence. She knew he was stuffed, having already eaten so much throughout the day. But he was just *so nice*, so she did feel sorry for him. Her mother had a tendency to be a little forceful, especially to the people she cared about, which was ironic. She adored him and probably just didn’t want him missing out on her delicious baking. She always thought people looked hungry.

Later that evening, Patience pulled Roman aside to give him his gifts. If she waited another minute, she might burst from excitement and anticipation. And of course he loved them, glancing around first before giving her a long thank you kiss. He pulled away slightly and she saw something different in his eyes. It was a look of longing like never before.

He smiled seductively, sneaking another quick peek over his shoulder.

"I want you," he whispered in her ear, his warm breath sending shivers down her spine.

"Mmmhmm," she answered, standing on her tip toes to wrap her arms around his neck. They kissed again, and she nuzzled his neck softly as he moaned.

"We better stop now," he murmured.

The two walked back to the living room and watched a movie with her parents, which thoroughly disappointed her. She'd wanted to make out with him more but knew he'd made the right decision for them both. She didn't want things getting out of control, especially in the McKlendon's house. Her father would've shot her first, then him.

At about three a.m. Patience walked Roman out to his truck, the cold air cutting through her like a knife. She didn't care how much the temperature dropped, however, as long as it prolonged the beginning of summer. She honestly believed she may be allergic to the sun, which made her so hot and uncomfortable, especially in Texas.

"I think my parents love you more than they love me," she joked as he opened the door.

He laughed.

"I hate to admit it, but you're right. Your mom wants to send you back and adopt me!"

They looked up as headlights turned onto her parents' street, then into the driveway. It was Cole. He waved at them as he put the car in reverse and parked alongside the curb. She glanced at Roman as her stomach did a little flip-flop. The two hadn't seen each other since the Halloween party, when Cole had made a complete fool of himself. Roman's face was tense, and she could feel his body stiffen slightly beside her.

"Hey guys! Merry Christmas!!"

His loud voice rang out in the otherwise quiet neighborhood as he balanced a bunch of giftwrapped boxes in his arms.

Patience met him halfway, taking some of the gifts before he dropped them. He planted a kiss on her cheek and approached Roman cautiously.

Cole held out his hand to him with a somber expression.

"Hey man," he began seriously as they shook hands. "I just want to formally apologize for my rude behavior. I'm ashamed and embarrassed for the way I acted. I've already told Patience how sorry I was, and believe me, she didn't let me off easy!"

Cole smiled, winking at her knowingly.

"I was such a jerk. I hope we can start over. You're very important to her, so now that I've moved past my selfish stage of wanting her all to myself, we can get to know each other."

She held her breath as she watched Roman's body language. His arms were folded across his chest and his lips drawn in a thin line. Finally he exhaled slowly and shrugged. A slight smile tugged at the corner of his mouth.

"That sounds good."

* * *

Patience's teeth chattered as she waited for Roman to say something. Cole had gone inside to visit with her parents while she said goodbye to her boyfriend. He leaned against his truck as he watched a dog search for food in the neighborhood. She wondered what he was thinking. He had that intent, don't-say-anything-until-I-get-my-thoughts-together aura about him.

Just when she was about to give up and go back inside, he reached out and grabbed her blouse, pulling her gently towards him. She giggled as he pressed his body into hers.

"Cole is an alright guy," he whispered, his breath warm against her cold cheek.

She blinked. "What did you say?"

Roman laughed. "I *said* that Cole is an all right guy. I think we're going to get along great."

She studied his face closely, for his words definitely surprised her.

"Really?"

He nodded.

"Yep. It takes a big man to apologize like that. And he obviously cares about you a lot. I think he was probably jealous because he saw that his best friend's time was about to be monopolized by someone else. And I can relate to that."

She sighed with relief, grateful that all was forgotten. It only confirmed once more what a great guy he was. She shivered against him.

"You should go inside," he said protectively.

He dug deep in his jacket pocket with a mischievous look. Pulling out a tiny box, he placed it in her hand.

"Now, don't open this until later, long after I'm gone." He chuckled. "I'm embarrassed enough as it is."

Patience's mouth dropped open.

"Roman! What on earth? You got me something?" She'd been wondering ever since she had presented him with his gift earlier.

He quickly opened the door to his truck and hopped in. Letting the window down, he motioned for her to move closer so he could kiss her goodbye. As they parted, he told her,

"I cringe to think of how mushy you're going to get when you open that, so I'll just take off now."

Patience shook her head, a wide grin on her face, and turned to head back inside. She caught a glimpse of the living room curtains closing as Cole's silhouette suddenly disappeared. She clutched the gift Roman had given her tighter and ran up her parents' front walk.

"Were you spying on me, nosy guy?" she accused, bursting through the door energetically.

His face turned crimson as he shrugged.

"I wanted to make sure you guys hadn't frozen to death," he stammered.

"Whatever," she said, amused by his behavior.

Following him into the den, she heard her mother's high-pitched laughter coming from the bedroom. She couldn't believe they were still awake. It was a little after midnight.

"Thanks for inviting me over," Cole said softly, reaching up to tuck one of her stray curls behind her ear.

"*Did* I?" she asked with a sly smile.

His eyes landed on the tiny box she had placed on the end table. She grabbed the remote control and began channel surfing, unaware that his facial expression had changed.

"What's that?" He reached over her to pick up Roman's gift. He examined it closely.

With a wave of her hand, she answered, "Actually I have no idea. Roman just thrust it in my hand as he was leaving."

"I wonder what it could be," he pondered aloud, twirling it around, and then holding it up to one ear, shaking it gently.

"Give it to me!" She tried to grab it but he jumped up. "You're going to break it!"

"Don't be ridiculous! It's not breakable," he laughed. "Calm down."

Patience began chasing him throughout the house, trying to retrieve the precious box. It was as if he held a million dollar check in his hand. He ran out of the den and down the hall, and then he headed toward the kitchen. He didn't see one of John's boots in the middle of the dining room floor, however. His head was turned toward her.

Suddenly he tripped, falling backward on the dining room's hard wood floor.

Roman's gift flew through the air, miraculously landing on one of Rory's soft pillows.

"Cole! Quit fooling around," she yelled.

She heard the bedroom door open.

"Is everything alright in there?" Sharise called out.

"Yes," Patience answered back.

She purposely strode over toward Cole. He sat massaging his shoulder, which he'd landed on when he'd fallen. Standing over her friend, she glared down at him with her arms folded. Sometimes he really annoyed her with all of his clowning around.

He held up a hand towards her, which she ignored.

"Aren't you going to help me up?" His dark eyes danced with laughter and she shook her head.

"No."

"Well, are you at least going to see if I'm okay?"

"Nuh-uh."

She wasn't giving him an inch.

He rolled his eyes and started to stand, but she placed her foot on his chest to keep him down.

"Ouch," he yelped, sounding pathetic.

Showing no mercy, she proceeded to pounce on him. They wrestled like two children for a while, and Patience could feel the tension slowly melt away. She hadn't been in the mood for her friend's immaturity at first, but she had never been able to stay mad at him for long. He had tears in his eyes when she finally had him pinned down.

Straddling him, she leaned forward to pin his arms above his head. He winced.

"Ouch!" he cried out a second time.

Against her better judgment, she released her grip on his wrists and stood up. Brushing the stray curl from her forehead, she strode quickly to retrieve the box lying on the pillow.

"You really *do* get on my nerves," she informed him seriously over her shoulder.

He followed her back to the living room, playfully tugging at a lock of her hair. She sat on the couch, intent on finally opening the gift before he destroyed it. Within seconds, she'd torn the pretty wrapping paper off of the tiny box with the word Gemvara written on it. Slowly, she removed the leather case and opened it.

Immediately, Patience understood why Roman hadn't wanted to be there for the big moment. She gasped, her eyes filling with fresh tears as Cole leaned in to catch a glimpse. The two gawked at the shiny ring before them. It was the most beautiful piece of jewelry she had ever seen. She carefully removed it from the case, her hands shaking slightly.

The band was a yellowish gold and had infinity signs engraved all the way around it. A blue diamond rested inside one of the signs, and the contrast was lovely. Silence descended upon them as they sat admiring the stone. Patience wasn't a jewelry expert, but she guessed it was 14K gold. She felt as if she were in shock, unable to process what the ring was a symbol of.

Her friend stood abruptly and began pacing the room.

"*What* is that?" he asked without looking at her.

She sat starting into space, a goofy grin pasted on her face. When Roman had handed her the small gift, she hadn't expected it to be a ring, although anyone could tell by the size and shape of the box that it was. No wonder he'd left so quickly. He probably knew she'd refuse to accept it.

Cole sat on the coffee table across from her, their knees touching.

"Patience ... Patience?" He tried jarring her out of the comatose state she was in.

"Hmm?" she finally responded, her eyes riveted to him but glazed over. A smile tugged at her lips as she thought about the wonderful gift Roman had surprised her with.

He waved a hand in front of her face, but to no avail.

"Can you hear me? Nod your head if you can," he directed.

She did as he said, so he continued.

"I don't know what Roman is thinking, but this is the most absurd thing I've ever seen. You've only been dating him for two months! You two barely know one another!"

His voice droned on while she focused on a spot above his head. Her mother had chosen earth tones when decorating the living room, much to her father's delight, which gave the room a cozy feeling. She stared at the brown curtain rod, although not really *seeing* it, as her friend continued his lecture.

" ... and I'll bet he doesn't even know your middle name, or your favorite food, or whether you plan on having children or not one day," he whined. "Has he seen how you react in emergency situations?"

Cole took her hand, giving it a gentle squeeze.

Finally out of her trance, Patience shrugged her shoulders.

"I have no idea why you're so upset, but it bothers me."

He sighed.

“I’m sorry my reaction is less than pleasant, but I just cannot hide my feelings. The fact that he would give you such an elaborate gift this early in your relationship boggles my mind. I mean, is it an engagement ring?”

Crossing her arms over her chest, she let out an exasperated sigh.

“I’m not really sure. Why don’t you ask *him*?” She’d had it with his bad attitude. “What if he *does* want to marry me? Would that be so terrible? What is your problem?”

He stood up, his eyes narrowing.

“My problem is your naiveté. Anytime a guy rushes a relationship, it’s usually just to, you know ...”

Patience knew exactly what he meant, but he was wrong about him. Roman had been nothing but a gentleman since they’d begun dating. Only her friend didn’t know that because he was always throwing temper tantrums, never bothering to stop and get to know him.

“I just don’t want to see you get hurt,” he finished, studying her face for a reaction.

Her eyes narrowed and she felt her face getting warmer by the minute out of anger. She stood to her full height, squaring her shoulders and lifting her chin a bit.

“That’s it! I am so sick of your negative attitude and childish behavior! Why can’t you be happy for me, just this once? You find fault with every single guy I date, Cole.”

He started shaking his head, opening his mouth to respond, but she quickly stopped him.

“Okay, maybe not all of them, but you really have been moody more days than not.”

She stormed toward her parents’ front door and opened it.

“If you can’t say something nice or encouraging to me this time, don’t say anything at all.”

Cole stomped to the coat rack, yanking his jacket off with such force that all the hats, coats and scarves came tumbling down.

Patience sighed loudly, bending over to pick them up. After helping her, he stood in the doorway glaring.

“Don’t mistake my concern for you as being negative. Obviously *someone* has to be realistic in this situation! You’re so busy with your head in the clouds, promoting all of this positive energy that you’re in danger of being hurt.”

She waved a hand in dismissal.

“Oh Cole, don’t be so dramatic.”

Rolling his eyes, her best friend turned quickly on his heel and exited the door. She stood watching, wondering why he had such strong reactions to every move Roman made. She wondered if it was because her boyfriend monopolized so much of her time. Maybe Cole was jealous because there was no one special in his own life.

Her mind raced with possibilities and questions about the situation. Perhaps he just couldn't handle the loneliness from not having *her* around twenty-four seven. The two used to be joined at the hip.

She waited as he started the car, his music loud enough for the people in neighboring cities to hear. Stepping onto the front porch, she shivered with her arms folded over her chest.

Part of her hoped he'd come back in, apologize for his rudeness, and watch a movie with her. Sure, it was around five a.m. However, a surge of renewed energy flowed through her since receiving Roman's engagement/friendship/dating ring. She felt as if she could leap tall buildings, swim across the Atlantic, or run fifty miles that morning. Even Cole's attitude couldn't bring her down from the euphoria she felt.

CHAPTER 32

"Have you lost your mind?" Patience lay on the couch, her eyes half-closed from exhaustion. Although the clock said two p.m., her living room was dark. She hadn't mustered enough energy to open the blinds since waking up an hour before. She tried to reach the remote, which had fallen off the coffee table, but she honestly could not summon enough strength to do so.

Yawning, she rolled over to her side with the cell balanced between the cushion and her ear. Her neck was beginning to hurt but she ignored the ache, intent on finding out what Roman had to say.

"What do you mean?" His voice sounded huskier than ever before.

Her eyes immediately went to the Gemvara box, which was sitting on the end table by her feet. She'd wanted to put the ring on after opening it but thought Roman wanted to do so. Besides, Cole had distracted her by acting like a two-year-old. His favorite words as of late were *mine* and *no* and *I don't want to.* He seemed to think Patience was his possession and that he didn't have to share her.

"I'm talking about the expensive looking gift you thrust in my hand last night before disappearing."

"Do you like it?"

Another yawn escaped her.

"I love it!"

"You sound tired," he commented. "What time did you get in?"

"Eleven o'clock."

Roman whistled. "You got home at eleven *this morning*? It's a wonder you answered the phone. Do you need me to let you go?"

Patience heard the concern in his voice.

Somehow she found the strength to stand, stretching her arms above her head and then bending at the waist to touch her toes. She tripped over Rory, who had somehow squeezed himself into the tiny space between the couch and coffee table.

"Rory! I'm so sorry!"

But her dog just lay there, apparently accustomed to getting stepped on and bumped into. After making sure he was okay, she stumbled into the kitchen, suddenly ravenous. Although she craved pancakes, she was too lazy to cook anything. After settling on a sandwich with fruit, she turned her attention back to the conversation.

"I need to see you," she whispered.

"When?"

Rinsing off a handful of strawberries, she answered with a laugh, "Now would be a good time for me!"

Roman promised to be there in fifteen minutes. She scarfed down her food, washed her face and changed clothes in record speed. There was even spare time to apply a touch of mascara. It miraculously erased the tired look in her eyes. However, nothing could hide the eerie paleness of her skin. It appeared she had the flu.

Pinching her cheeks to add some color to them, she wondered if Roman would even notice her appearance. Could he be as nervous as she? What would she say to him when he arrived? Oh well, it didn't matter. The most important thing was that she wanted to see him. She missed him. The sound of the doorbell brought a feeling of relief mixed with panic.

She exhaled slowly.

"Saved by the bell," she muttered to her reflection.

* * *

"*Cole?*"

The afternoon sunshine nearly blinded her when she opened the door. Shielding her eyes, Patience stepped carefully onto the porch. What in the world was *he* doing there? Once her eyes adjusted to the outdoor lighting, she gazed up at her friend, wondering what he wanted. Once upon a time, she'd have been thrilled to have him drop by unannounced like this. As a matter of fact, they used to frequently call one another spur-of-the-moment just to hang out. That had been yet another perk to their friendship. But those days were gone.

She felt her body stiffen in his presence.

"Patience."

He sighed theatrically, his hands clasped together behind his back. A chilly breeze ruffled his uncombed hair, and upon further inspection, she noticed dark circles under his eyes. He wore the same clothes as the night before and his skin was as pale as hers. Sympathy tugged at her heart, softening the stern expression she'd worn just seconds before.

Her body relaxed as she took a step toward him.

"Are you sick?" she asked, genuinely concerned for her friend.

"I was going to ask you the same thing."

Self-consciously, she ran a hand over her hair, knowing her curls were all over the place. She laughed despite herself.

"We probably both look like death!"

He smiled, his head tilting to one side.

"Can I come in?"

Her eyes instinctively went to the street, as she suddenly remembered Roman. As if on cue, he appeared, parking his truck expertly alongside the curb.

He quickly jumped out, sprinting up the walkway with a wide grin. She giggled as he scooped her into his arms, lifting her off the ground and then pulling her to him in a tight hug. Without a word, he pressed his lips to hers for what seemed an eternity. The scene came straight out of a romantic movie or greeting card advertisement, for sure.

Finally, Roman pulled back slightly, the grin slowly fading as he searched her face.

"Do you feel okay?" he asked, his eyebrows knit together with worry.

"Wow! I must be hideous!" Apparently she hadn't done a good job fixing herself up.

"You're gorgeous. It's just that you look a little, um, under the weather."

"Cole made the same observation."

They turned to acknowledge him and were startled to see that he'd left. She hadn't even heard him drive off. Either he was upset because Roman had interrupted them again, or he'd discreetly exited so they could have their moment. Her gut told her it was the former.

"Where did he go?" Roman broke into her thoughts.

She shrugged.

"Maybe he couldn't wait for our nauseating reunion to end."

* * *

"It's an engagement ring."

Patience sat with her mouth hanging open, stunned into silence. The pair faced each other at the kitchen table with Rory at their feet. She'd asked about the gift and its meaning as soon as they'd settled. She hadn't been able to wait another minute. With the box open between them on the table, she couldn't blink as she stared into his eyes.

Roman leaned forward expectantly, gently taking her hand in his. For the longest moment, the only sounds heard in the quiet room were the ticking of the clock and Rory's breathing.

"What does that mean, exactly?" She held her breath.

"I want to marry you."

She closed her eyes, allowing his words to sink in. He waited patiently for her to digest all that was happening.

"When?" she croaked inaudibly.

"Look at me."

She opened her tear-filled eyes, unable to focus for a second.

He smiled, his adorable dimples coming into focus again.

"Next week," he answered, his voice serious.

"Can we stop joking around for once, please?"

He placed his hands on either side of her face.

"Who said I was kidding?"

Patience reached over to gently stroke his cheek. The look on his face told her he meant what he said. She had no doubt that he loved her. Cole didn't understand anything about romance. The length of time couples spent together wasn't as important as the indescribable connection between them. She couldn't have explained their bond for a million dollars. But as he placed the ring on her finger tenderly, she realized that what others thought just didn't matter.

* * *

"And then what happened?"

Jana appeared to be holding her breath as Patience relayed every detail of that morning. As soon as she'd said goodbye to Roman, she hopped in the car and high tailed it to her friend's. Thankfully she'd been home. Patience knew she'd burst if there had been no one to tell the exciting news to.

Jana sat dumbfounded while Patience continued. The two were relaxing on the couch while sipping hot cocoa.

Classical music played softly in the background, which helped calm her nerves.

"Well," Patience paused dramatically, "I told him I'd think about it."

Jana shook her head.

"No, what did he say when you asked *when* he wanted to get married?"

"Oh, he never gave me a serious answer. But he did let me know he wanted to be engaged a while, since we haven't been dating very long."

"That sounds wise," her friend responded flatly.

Patience held up her hand to examine the ring for the fiftieth time. Although impossible, it seemed to become more beautiful each time she admired it. Roman had excellent taste.

She stole a glance at Jana, wondering what was going through her mind. She was usually so talkative and animated. She'd never been shy to voice her opinion, so it was surprising that silence had descended upon them.

"Can I ask what you're thinking?" Patience inquired finally.

Jana shrugged. "I'm trying to figure out how to say this without hurting your feelings. We both know how sensitive you can be."

Patience felt her heart sink.

"Just go ahead and tell me."

Jana stood and began rearranging the books on the shelf.

"I like Roman a lot. He seems like such a wonderful person, so attentive and sweet. I get nothing but great vibes when we all hang out. And your face absolutely glows when you talk about him." She bent down to pick up a book she'd dropped. Patience couldn't believe they were in alphabetical order.

"But ..."

"Don't you think it's a little too soon to be talking about marriage? Do you know how long you've been seeing him?"

Standing abruptly, Patience began pacing out of frustration.

"Of course I do! What a silly question to ask."

"Then why in the world did you even accept this gift? If you ask me, he probably hasn't thought this through either. You two are just caught up in a whirlwind of romance and infatuation. That's it. This can't be love because the relationship is too new."

"It *is* love. How would you know what Roman and I have? Can't you be more supportive and maybe the tiniest bit happy for me? This is a life changing event."

Jana crossed her arms over her chest.

"I'd be thrilled if you guys had at least one good year under your belt. Then I could feel more confident that you had a future."

"What about the couples who are together for ten years, get married, and then file for divorce soon after? There isn't a correct length of time to really know someone. Everyone is different."

Her eyes suddenly narrowing, Jana took a step toward her.

“Hey! You never even wanted to get married! What happened to your fear of commitment?”

Patience didn’t hesitate. “I fell in love.”

CHAPTER 33

Patience sat with a heavy heart as ducks chased Rory at their favorite park. He was terrified of them and they knew it. He ran to her for safety, trying to hide underneath the bench. She laughed, secretly rooting for the ducks. They were probably tired of him always barking at and threatening them, but never really doing anything about it. It was their turn.

She shivered slightly from the brisk air, amazed to see birds eating the scraps of bread she'd thrown. It seemed too cold for them to be out. It was the middle of January, and the only reason she'd brought Rory was because of cabin fever. He'd chewed through a piece of carpet in her bedroom, ruined a pair of new boots she'd bought, and had begun whining in the middle of the night. Freezing to death was the only answer.

Her cell vibrated in her jacket pocket. It was her mom.

She pressed *ignore* and continued gazing at the scenery. She definitely didn't feel up to chatting. She wanted to be alone with her thoughts. Rory ventured out to the pond again, his leash trailing behind him. She knew he wouldn't run off or attack anyone. He just wasn't that kind of dog. Plus, they were the only fools hanging out in the cold park.

Feeling her cell vibrate again, Patience decided to answer. Sharise had a tendency to worry when she disappeared.

"Hey Mom, what's up?"

"Where are you?"

Patience smiled into the phone at the sense of urgency in her mother's voice.

"I brought Rory to the park."

"Sweetheart, it's forty degrees out there."

"Yes," she agreed.

"Is there anyone else out?" Sharise practically yelled.

"No."

Patience winced, bracing herself for the inevitable speech headed her way.

"*Are you nuts*? I swear you're just like your father, always taking risks. It's enough to give me three heart attacks. I'll bet you're not wearing a coat or a sweater even. Why would you be hanging out in this weather? You *want* to get sick, don't you?"

Patience sighed.

"Mom, I needed to clear my head, which I couldn't do at home because Rory was constantly being naughty."

"You're begging to be kidnapped. If someone attacked you, he'd win because I know you quit that self-defense class."

"I'm sorry that my actions cause you such distress."

"Oh honey, I just worry about you, that's all."

And so the conversation went. After putting her mother's fears to rest, which took twenty minutes, Patience realized she had two choices. She could either continue sulking or do something productive. She realized how ridiculous it was to just sit there, feeling extremely sorry for herself and moping around.

Sometimes she fell into the trap of thinking everyone was against her. But that theory *did* seem true, as the people closest to her didn't share her joyful moment. Neither Cole nor Jana trusted her judgment. But it didn't really matter. Their opinions weren't so important. However, as she shivered for the third time, she realized what her friends and family thought *did* matter.

After loading Rory into the car, Patience dialed Roman's number. She'd made up her mind then and there to concentrate on him and actually enjoy their engagement. He didn't answer so she left a short message saying how much she missed him. It was Saturday. She thought about grabbing some Vanilla Coffee and curling up with a good book at home. Better yet, she could begin working on *her* children's book that had been on her mind for awhile. She had several ideas just waiting to be put on paper.

She stopped at a popular donut shop for the coffee, although Brew would've been her first choice. Theirs was the best in town. Yet she didn't want to risk running into Tripp. He probably didn't work there anymore, but one just never knew. Out of her three previous boyfriends, he was the one she dreaded bumping into the most. With his high-strung personality and childish antics, there was no telling *what* he'd say or do if he saw her. Plus, their relationship was the most recent, so her emotional wounds from him were raw.

Once home, she settled in to begin her project. With a pad of paper in her lap and the pencil behind her ear, she tried thinking of a catchy title for her work. When none came to mind, she tossed around different names for her characters. For some reason, her mind was a total blank, although she had tons of energy from the coffee. She began pacing the floor, her eyes focused on nothing in particular. Time was going by so slowly. The caffeine had definitely kicked in, for she felt jittery, the symptoms of her ADD in full swing.

I've gotta get out of this house, she thought as the walls appeared to cave in on her. She empathized with Rory for having had cabin fever earlier.

Patience called her dad to see if he was interested in catching a movie, but he'd gone hunting with a buddy from college.

"Did you give him a hard time about hanging out in these cold conditions, too?" she teased her mom.

"As a matter of fact I did. You two ought to be ashamed of yourselves."

They chatted a while. She tossed around the idea of inviting her mother to do something, partly out of desperation. But after spending too much time together, Sharise had the tendency to be suffocating. And since her mood swings were unpredictable as of late, she decided to try Jana or Cole instead.

Jana didn't pick up so she left a message. There was no answer with Cole, either. However, she received a text from him shortly after saying he was on a date.

For a fleeting moment, she felt a twinge of jealousy, which she thought was ridiculous. Never before had she been nothing but happy anytime he met someone new. She'd always wanted him to click with someone, fall in love, and get married. It was his lifelong dream.

After tossing around different options, Patience decided to work out at the gym. She hadn't been in months. It was the perfect solution to her boredom. This way, she'd be able to people watch, burn off the excessive energy threatening to burst out of her, and also brainstorm different ideas for her book.

* * *

The gym was packed with people of all sizes, shapes and colors. Patience guessed most of them were trying to lose the extra holiday pounds gained a month ago. It seemed like every January society as a whole made New Year's Resolutions to join a gym. Then, by March, life got in the way. Either they got too busy at work, had procrastination issues, or decided to exercise outdoors, weather permitting. She was the same way.

She spent a half-hour on the elliptical machine and fifteen minutes on the treadmill. The free weights were all taken, and the indoor track was crowded. She wiped her neck with the towel, guzzling the bottle of water she'd brought. Sadly, she was beginning to feel wiped out, a telltale sign that she hadn't worked out in a while.

She plopped down on one of the benches to wait for the weights, the different sounds from people's conversations and the televisions in front of the treadmills blending together. A little while later, two very attractive women sat down next to her, deep in conversation.

They appeared to be in their early twenties and obviously hadn't begun exercising. The two looked fresh, had tons of energy, and their hair was in place. Next to them, she felt like a wet puppy dog: stinky and unattractive. The women both had dark skin and medium length hair.

The girl sitting closest to her proceeded to pull hers into a ponytail while the other adjusted her sports bra.

"So then what happened?" one of them asked, her eyes wide with suspense.

"Well, I told him he needs to choose, of course. He can't be dating both of us. I am not sharing my man with *anyone*."

"I know that's right. You have to teach these men how to treat you. What did he say after that?"

The girl with the ponytail shrugged.

"There was nothing he could say. He stormed off. But he's been blowing up my phone ever since."

Patience listened intently. This was the best conversation she'd overheard in months.

"You know, I just wish I knew who the other girl was! I'd really give her a piece of my mind."

A ringing cell phone interrupted them.

Girl number one reached inside her duffle bag, mumbling something about how all men are dogs. She huffed as she looked at the caller I.D.

"Now he's putting his friends up to call. He thinks he is so slick, hiring everyone to find out where I am."

Her friend laughed.

"Which one is it this time?"

"Maverick."

Twisting her body around slightly on the bench, Patience dared to glance at the two women, trying to hear every word. Maverick? There weren't too many guys with that name around. It was pretty unusual. There was a brief pause as she held her breath, waiting anxiously for more dialogue.

Ponytail's friend nodded.

"That's weird. I ran into Heath at the grocery store the other day. He acted like he didn't see me. Maybe all of his friends are following us. You know, since we're always together."

The one with the ponytail rolled her eyes.

"Knowing Roman, they probably are. He thinks he can date as many women as he wants but keeps me under lock and key!"

"Are you going to call him?" her friend inquired.

"Who?"

"*Roman,*" she answered, sounding exasperated.

She sighed. "No way! Like I said before, he needs to realize I'm not taking this lying down. I refuse to be the other woman."

www.ingramcontent.com/pod-product-compliance
Lightning Source LLC
LaVergne TN
LVHW010604100826
845148LV00014B/2846

* 9 7 8 0 6 1 5 9 2 3 8 9 5 *